THE

CROGAN ADVENTURES

"CATFOOT'S VENGEANCE"

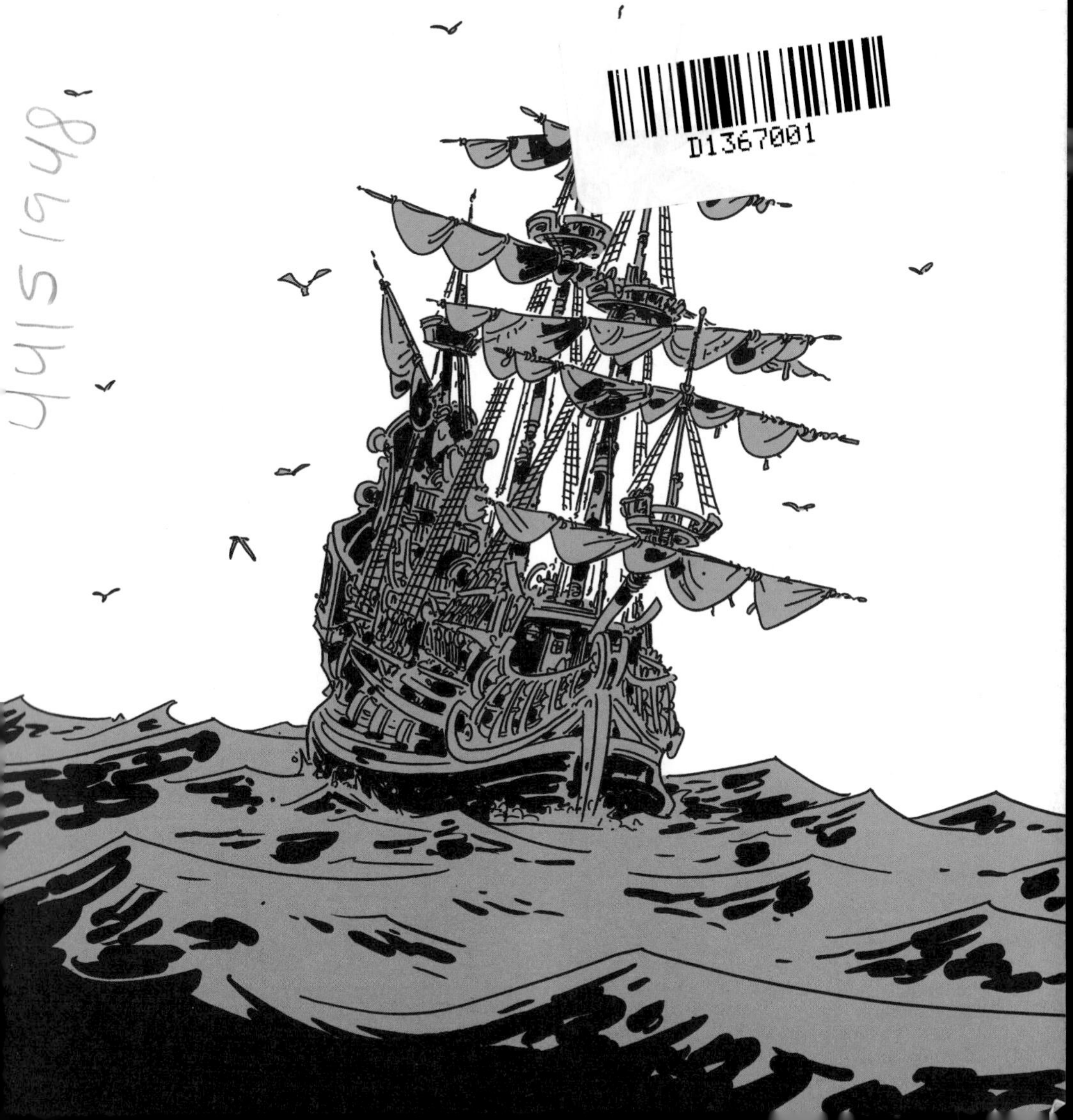

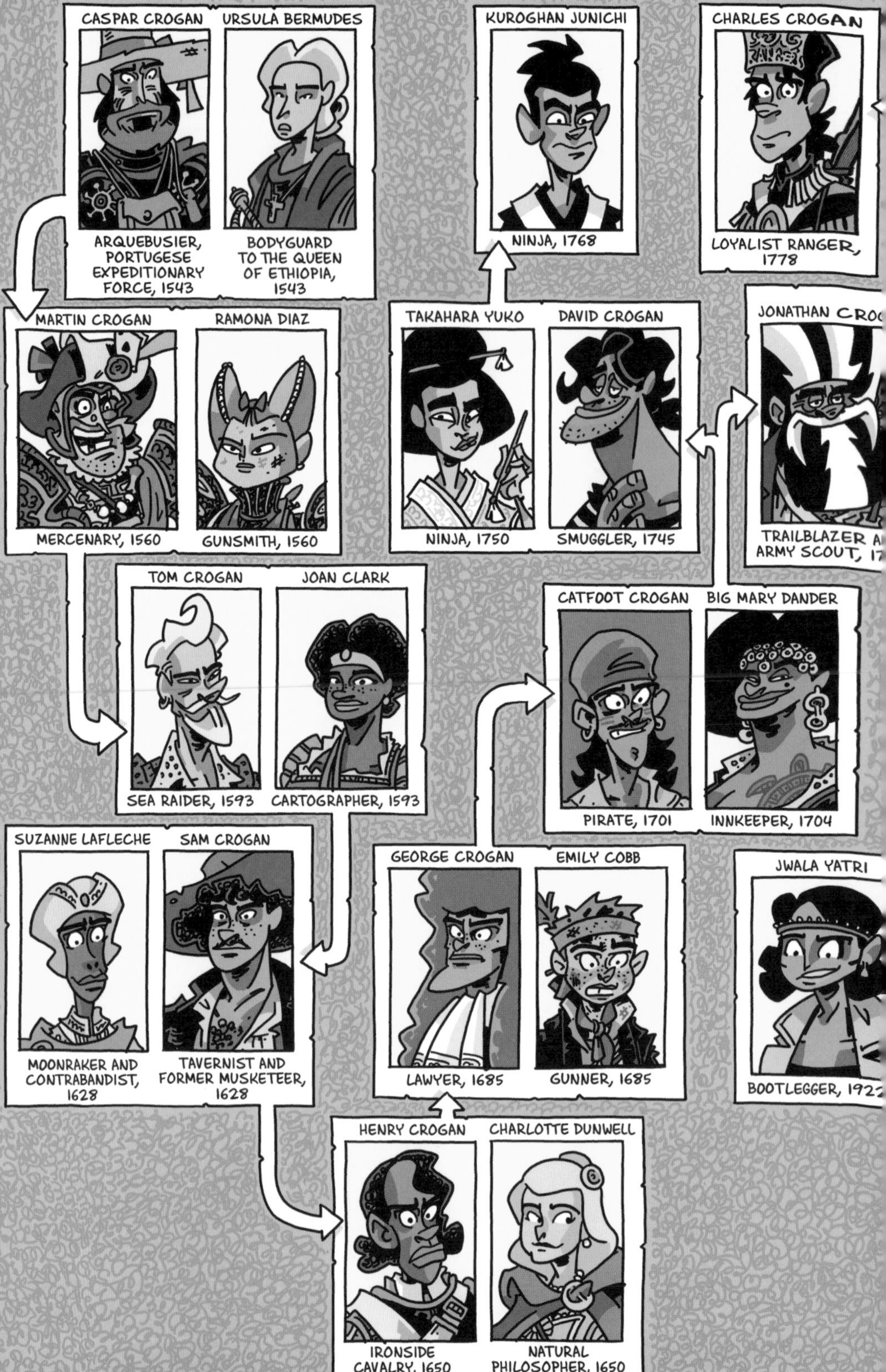
CASPAR CROGAN
ARQUEBUSIER, PORTUGESE EXPEDITIONARY FORCE, 1543
URSULA BERMUDES
BODYGUARD TO THE QUEEN OF ETHIOPIA, 1543
KUROGHAN JUNICHI
NINJA, 1768
CHARLES CROGAN
LOYALIST RANGER, 1778
MARTIN CROGAN
MERCENARY, 1560
RAMONA DIAZ
GUNSMITH, 1560
TAKAHARA YUKO
NINJA, 1750
DAVID CROGAN
SMUGGLER, 1745
JONATHAN CRO
TRAILBLAZER A
ARMY SCOUT, 1
TOM CROGAN
SEA RAIDER, 1593
JOAN CLARK
CARTOGRAPHER, 1593
CATFOOT CROGAN
PIRATE, 1701
BIG MARY DANDER
INNKEEPER, 1704
SUZANNE LAFLECHE
MOONRAKER AND CONTRABANDIST, 1628
SAM CROGAN
TAVERNIST AND FORMER MUSKETEER, 1628
GEORGE CROGAN
LAWYER, 1685
EMILY COBB
GUNNER, 1685
JWALA YATRI
BOOTLEGGER, 192
HENRY CROGAN
IRONSIDE CAVALRY, 1650
CHARLOTTE DUNWELL
NATURAL PHILOSOPHER, 1650

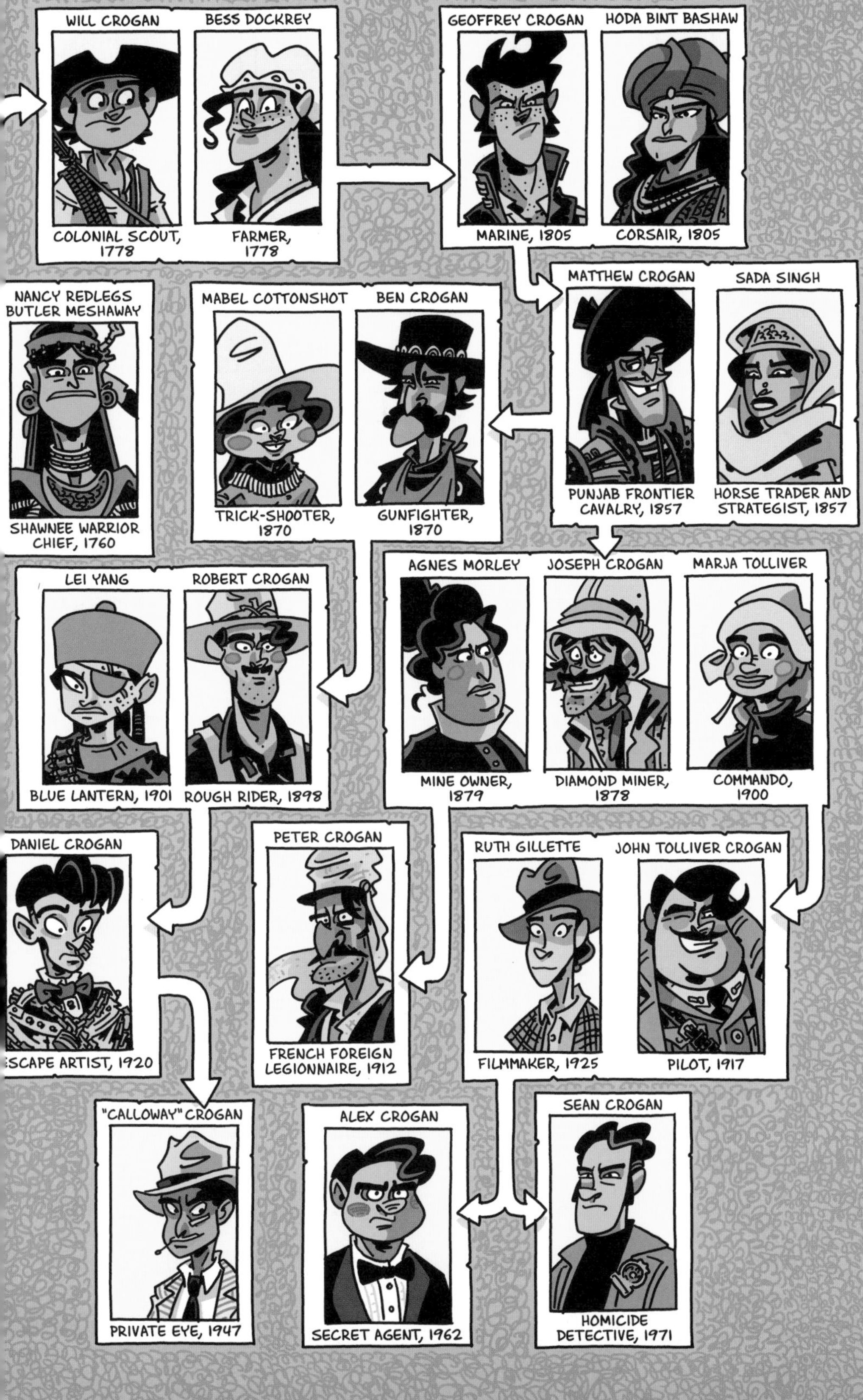
WILL CROGAN
COLONIAL SCOUT, 1778
BESS DOCKREY
FARMER, 1778
GEOFFREY CROGAN
MARINE, 1805
HODA BINT BASHAW
CORSAIR, 1805
NANCY REDLEGS BUTLER MESHAWAY
SHAWNEE WARRIOR CHIEF, 1760
MABEL COTTONSHOT
TRICK-SHOOTER, 1870
BEN CROGAN
GUNFIGHTER, 1870
MATTHEW CROGAN
PUNJAB FRONTIER CAVALRY, 1857
SADA SINGH
HORSE TRADER AND STRATEGIST, 1857
LEI YANG
BLUE LANTERN, 1901
ROBERT CROGAN
ROUGH RIDER, 1898
AGNES MORLEY
MINE OWNER, 1879
JOSEPH CROGAN
DIAMOND MINER, 1878
MARJA TOLLIVER
COMMANDO, 1900
DANIEL CROGAN
ESCAPE ARTIST, 1920
PETER CROGAN
FRENCH FOREIGN LEGIONNAIRE, 1912
RUTH GILLETTE
FILMMAKER, 1925
JOHN TOLLIVER CROGAN
PILOT, 1917
"CALLOWAY" CROGAN
PRIVATE EYE, 1947
ALEX CROGAN
SECRET AGENT, 1962
SEAN CROGAN
HOMICIDE DETECTIVE, 1971

THIS BOOK IS FOR MY FATHER, WHOSE
LOVE OF HISTORY, PIRATES, AND COMIC
STRIPS WAS CONTAGIOUS.

THE CROGAN ADVENTURES
"CATFOOT'S VENGEANCE"

BY
CHRIS SCHWEIZER

COLORED BY
JOEY WEISER & MICHELE CHIDESTER

BOOK DESIGN BY
CHRIS SCHWEIZER & KEITH WOOD

EDITED BY
JAMES LUCAS JONES

ONI PRESS

AN ONI PRESS PUBLICATION

Published by Oni Press, Inc.

Joe Nozemack, publisher · James Lucas Jones, editor in chief

Tim Wiesch, v.p. of business devleopment · Cheyenne Allott, director of sales

Troy Look, production manager · Charlie Chu, editor · Robin Herrera, associate editor

Hilary Thompson, graphic designer · Jared Jones, production assistant

Brad Rooks, inventory coordinator · Ari Yarwood, administrative assistant

Jung Lee, office assistant

Oni Press, Inc.
1305 SE Martin Luther King Jr. Blvd.
Suite A
Portland, OR 97214
USA

facebook.com/onipress · twitter.com/onipress · onipress.tumblr.com
onipress.com

croganadventures.blogspot.com · @schweizercomics
tragic-planet.com · @joeyweiser

First edition: April 2015

ISBN 978-1-62010-203-9
eISBN 978-1-62010-175-9

THE CROGAN ADVENTURES: CATFOOT'S VENGEANCE, April 2015. Published by Oni Press, Inc. 1305 SE Martin Luther King Jr. Blvd., Suite A, Portland, OR 97214.

Library of Congress Control Number: 2014949751

1 3 5 7 9 10 8 6 4 2

PRINTED IN CHINA.

SOME NOTES ON THE COLOR EDITION:

In the summer of 2012, I had the good fortune to watch two of my favorite cartoonists, Brian Hurtt and Matt Kindt, work on a series of watercolor commissions on which they were collaborating. I'd never had much luck with watercolor, but they walked me through their process and had me hooked. Soon everything I was drawing was in color, and it fundamentally changed the way that I drew. I knew that all future *Crogan Adventures* stories would be in color, and this raised the question about what to do with the existing books. Ought they be colored, too?

I had very mixed feelings about it. The pages had been approached with the intention that they be in black and white, and there are many things that I would have done differently had color been in my mind. But color is more accessible to a wider audience, and it would serve to unify the existing books with any new ones. It would also permit many opportunities to augment the storytelling and create a more visually immersive experience.

My editor, James Lucas Jones, thought going to color on the existing books a worthwhile endeavor, and I concurred. But my publishing schedule did not permit me to undertake the project of coloring the books on my own.

The role of coloring the books fell to Joey Weiser (the cartoonist behind *Mermin*, a favorite of my daughter's) and Michele Chidester, both of Athens, Georgia. I have known them since my time as a student regularly visiting my school's sister campus in Savannah, where they both studied (Joey earning his BFA in Sequential Art, Michelle her BFA in Illustration). They were part of the first group of cartoonist peers with which I had the good fortune to fall into, and I have treasured their friendship.

The pair was diligent and gracious; the *Crogan Adventures* books are ones in which I have an enormous personal investment and I do not for a moment believe that my notes and reference allowed for an easy undertaking on their part. They did an amazing job of bringing life to the pages, and I could not be more grateful for their involvement. I have made alterations to their colors to better suit my own notions for the series and the way that I want it to feel, and I hope that in doing so I have done no harm to the perception of their work. What successes are in the colors are theirs; any faults lie with me.

There have also been a few changes made to the book itself. The most drastic of these has been the lettering. The original publication had been lettered clumsily with a brush. There was no rhyme or reason to the size of the letters or their placement, and most every review of the book noted that the lettering overwhelmed the art.

I took this to heart and was much more satisfied with my lettering on the subsequent volumes, but *Vengeance* remained cumbersome. When we undertook this project, I decided that revisiting the lettering was a worthwhile endeavor, as it would make the books more legible.

As they are sometimes used in classrooms, I thought this an obligation to readers who might otherwise struggle with the clumsiness of the original.

I used a mix of hand-lettering and a font of my hand made by University of Central Missouri professor Eric Newsom, a man of much genius and many talents who volunteered to undertake this long and laborious task. Without his help this book would have been much more difficult to read.

My wife Liz typed up all of the dialogue passages over the balloons in which they would go so that I could skip that laborious stage and go straight to the word placement and what tweaks were needed to make it feel organic (there were many). The relettering would not have been possible on our schedule had she not carried this burden.

I have done my best to avoid redrawing the art. There are a few instances where a balloon size has changed due to the relettering and I have subsequently added to the backgrounds to accommodate this, but otherwise I have limited my alterations to fixing a mistake (giving the one-armed character Bill Toomy the wrong hand in two panels) and making the modern day character Cory match his design in the subsequent books. In both of these instances I did my best to mirror the original art as much as possible.

Lastly, the name of the book has been changed from *Crogan's Vengeance* to *Catfoot's Vengeance* to account for *The Crogan Adventures* being the new official title and *Vengeance* being the name of the volume.

CHRIS SCHWEIZER

Madisonville, Kentucky
November 2014

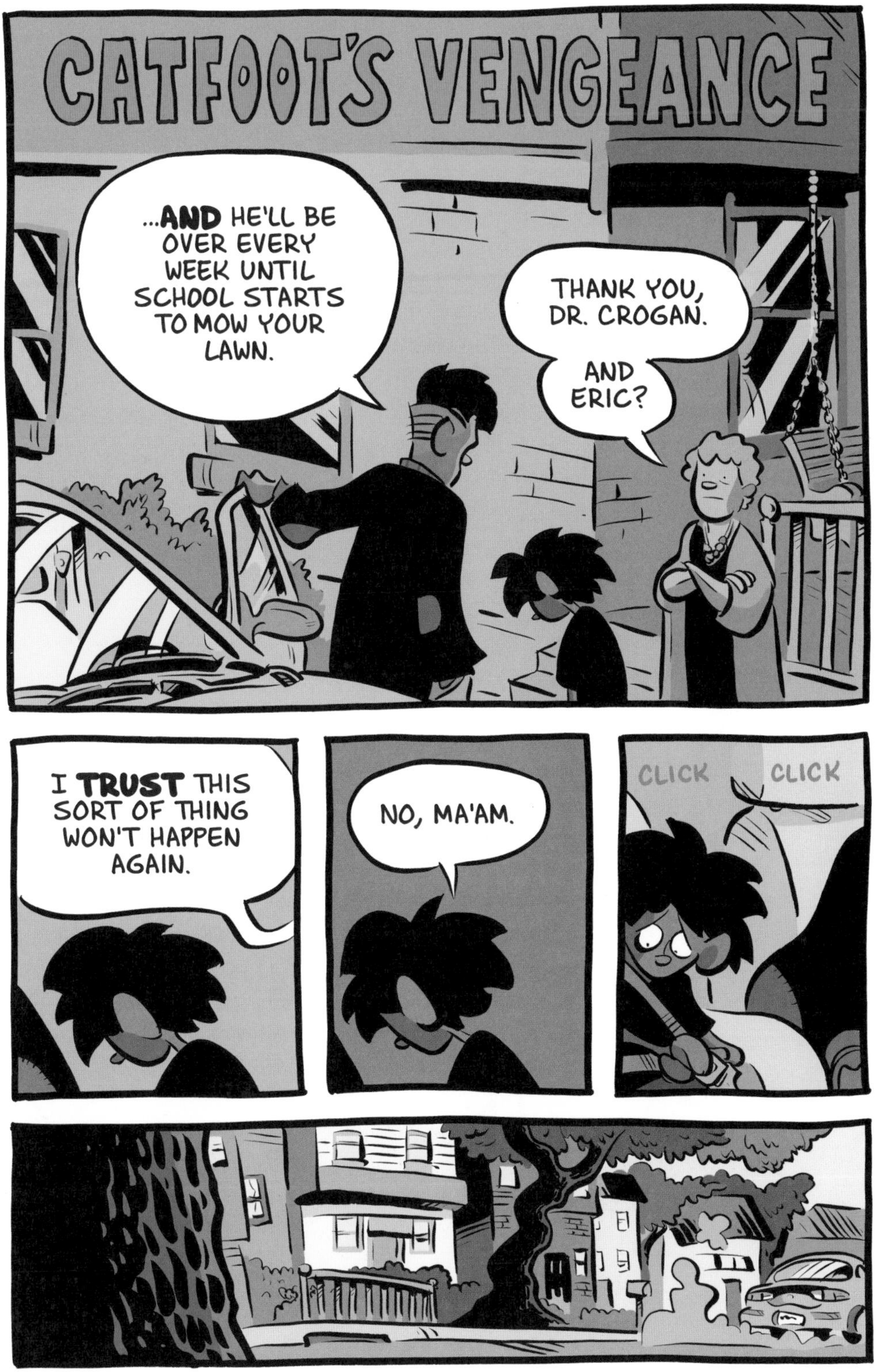
CATFOOT'S VENGEANCE
...AND HE'LL BE OVER EVERY WEEK UNTIL SCHOOL STARTS TO MOW YOUR LAWN.
THANK YOU, DR. CROGAN.
AND ERIC?
I TRUST THIS SORT OF THING WON'T HAPPEN AGAIN.
NO, MA'AM.
CLICK
CLICK

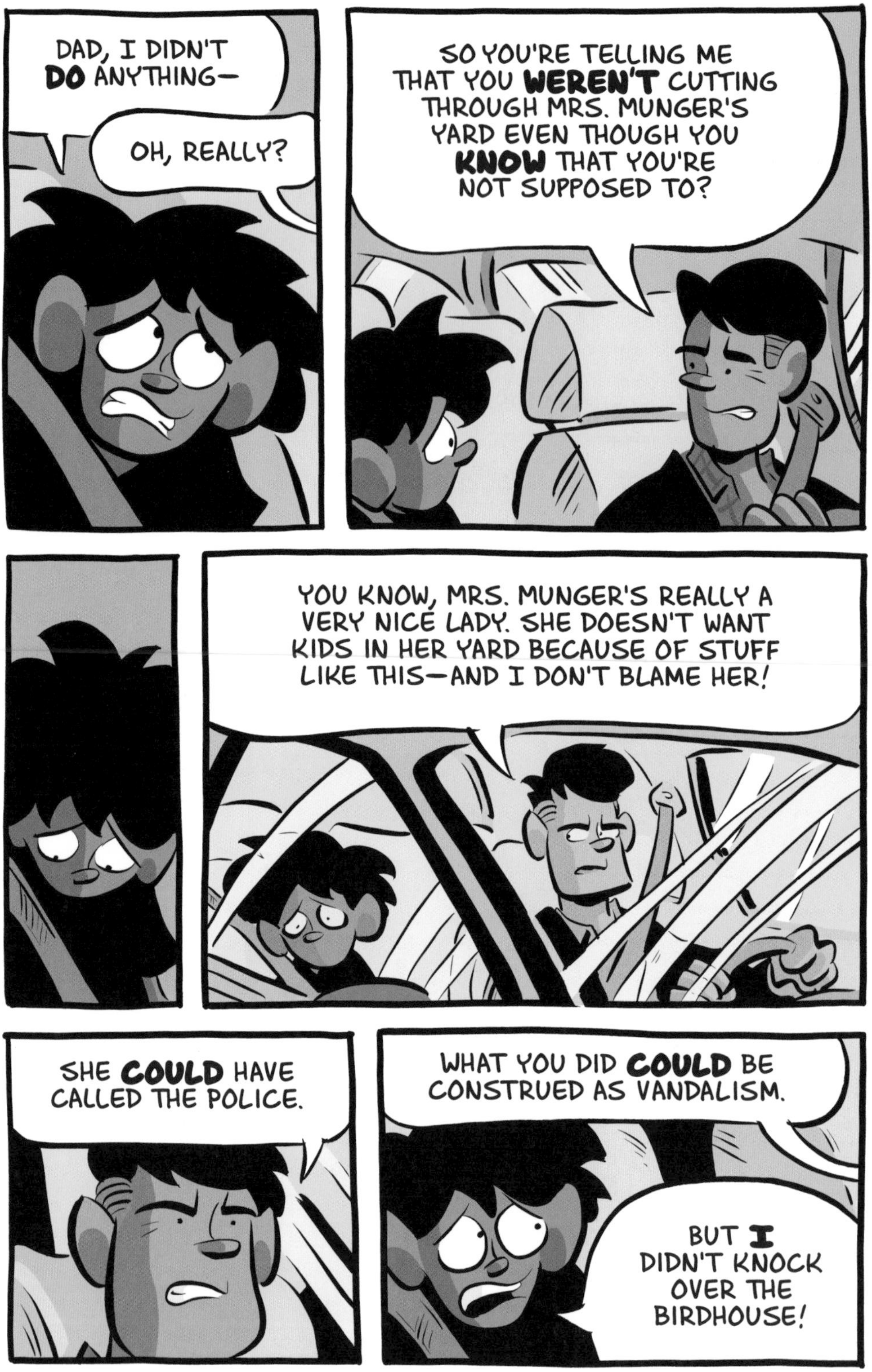
DAD, I DIDN'T **DO** ANYTHING—
OH, REALLY?
SO YOU'RE TELLING ME THAT YOU **WEREN'T** CUTTING THROUGH MRS. MUNGER'S YARD EVEN THOUGH YOU **KNOW** THAT YOU'RE NOT SUPPOSED TO?
YOU KNOW, MRS. MUNGER'S REALLY A VERY NICE LADY. SHE DOESN'T WANT KIDS IN HER YARD BECAUSE OF STUFF LIKE THIS—AND I DON'T BLAME HER!
SHE **COULD** HAVE CALLED THE POLICE.
WHAT YOU DID **COULD** BE CONSTRUED AS VANDALISM.
BUT **I** DIDN'T KNOCK OVER THE BIRDHOUSE!

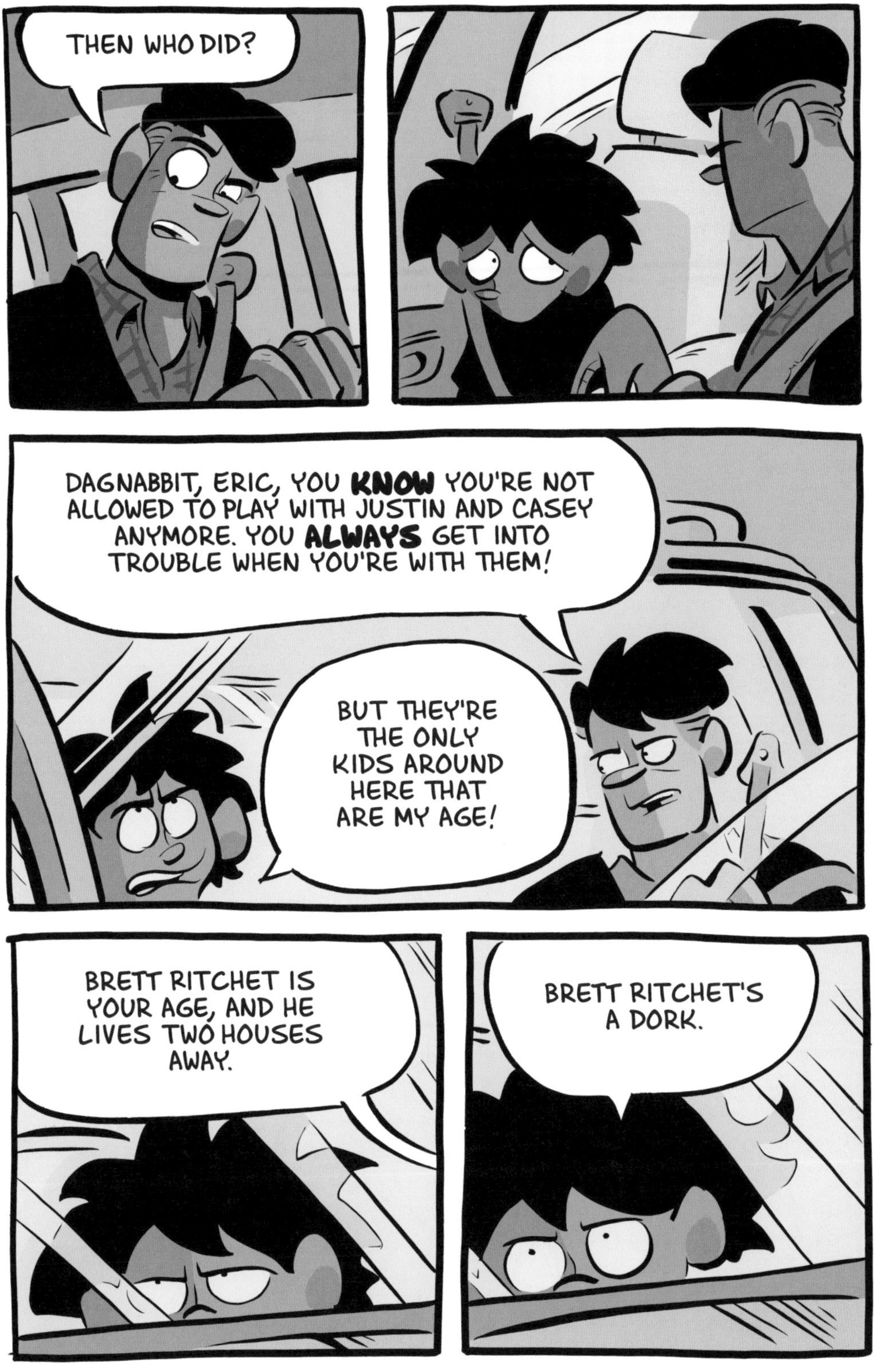
THEN WHO DID?
DAGNABBIT, ERIC, YOU KNOW YOU'RE NOT ALLOWED TO PLAY WITH JUSTIN AND CASEY ANYMORE. YOU ALWAYS GET INTO TROUBLE WHEN YOU'RE WITH THEM!
BUT THEY'RE THE ONLY KIDS AROUND HERE THAT ARE MY AGE!
BRETT RITCHET IS YOUR AGE, AND HE LIVES TWO HOUSES AWAY.
BRETT RITCHET'S A DORK.

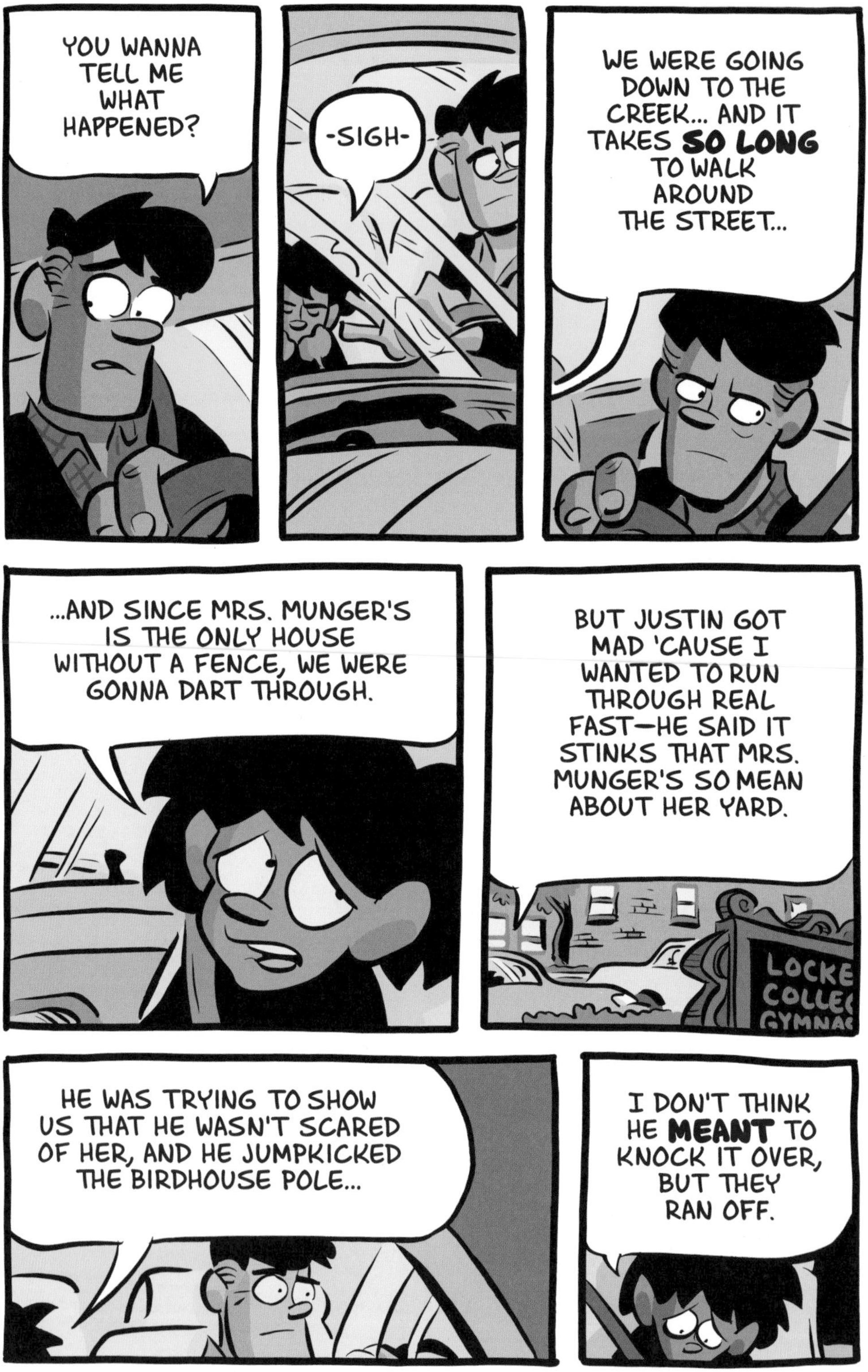
YOU WANNA TELL ME WHAT HAPPENED?
-SIGH-
WE WERE GOING DOWN TO THE CREEK... AND IT TAKES **SO LONG** TO WALK AROUND THE STREET...
...AND SINCE MRS. MUNGER'S IS THE ONLY HOUSE WITHOUT A FENCE, WE WERE GONNA DART THROUGH.
BUT JUSTIN GOT MAD 'CAUSE I WANTED TO RUN THROUGH REAL FAST—HE SAID IT STINKS THAT MRS. MUNGER'S SO MEAN ABOUT HER YARD.
HE WAS TRYING TO SHOW US THAT HE WASN'T SCARED OF HER, AND HE JUMPKICKED THE BIRDHOUSE POLE...
I DON'T THINK HE **MEANT** TO KNOCK IT OVER, BUT THEY RAN OFF.

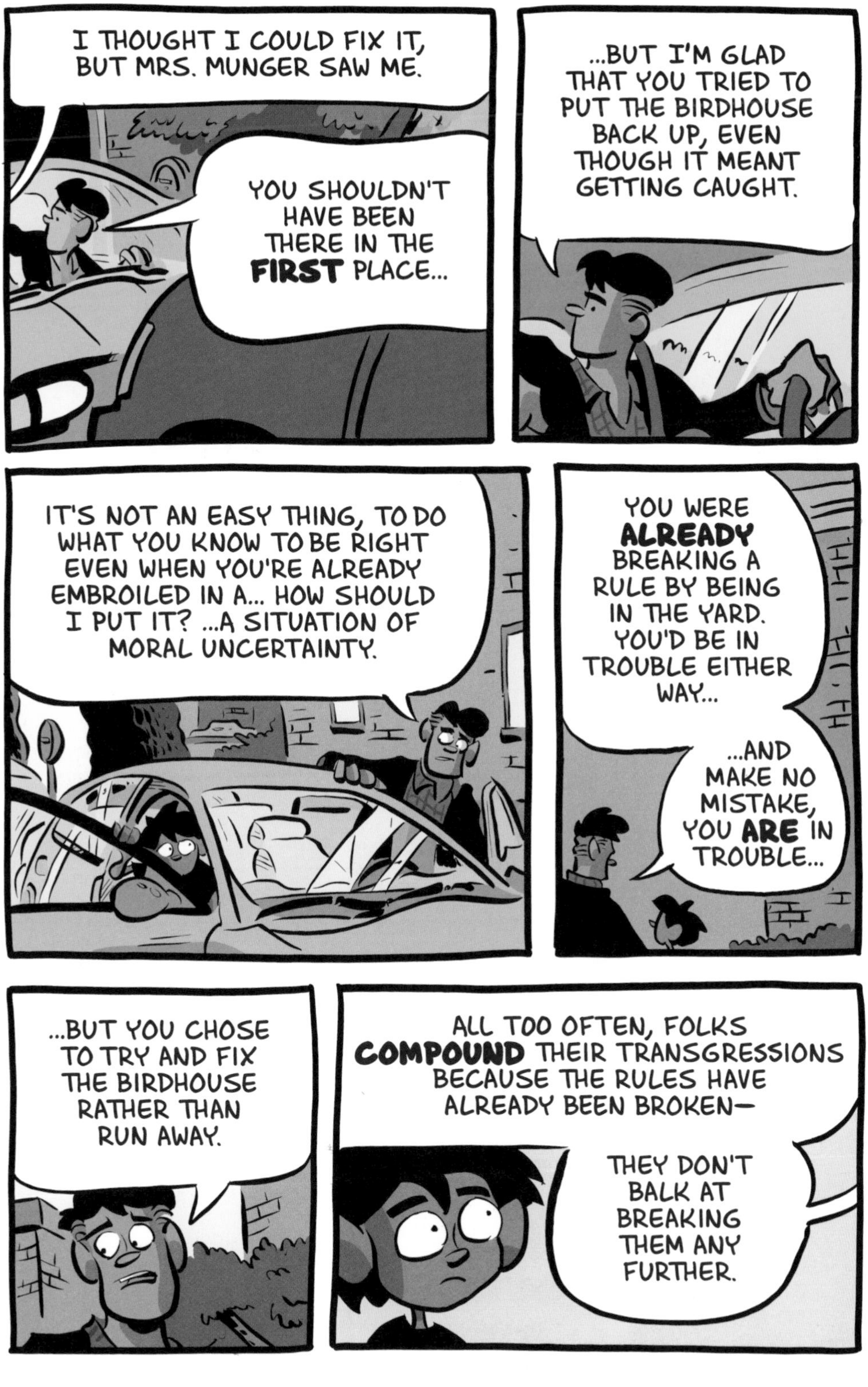
I THOUGHT I COULD FIX IT, BUT MRS. MUNGER SAW ME.
YOU SHOULDN'T HAVE BEEN THERE IN THE FIRST PLACE...
...BUT I'M GLAD THAT YOU TRIED TO PUT THE BIRDHOUSE BACK UP, EVEN THOUGH IT MEANT GETTING CAUGHT.
IT'S NOT AN EASY THING, TO DO WHAT YOU KNOW TO BE RIGHT EVEN WHEN YOU'RE ALREADY EMBROILED IN A... HOW SHOULD I PUT IT? ...A SITUATION OF MORAL UNCERTAINTY.
YOU WERE ALREADY BREAKING A RULE BY BEING IN THE YARD. YOU'D BE IN TROUBLE EITHER WAY...
...AND MAKE NO MISTAKE, YOU ARE IN TROUBLE...
...BUT YOU CHOSE TO TRY AND FIX THE BIRDHOUSE RATHER THAN RUN AWAY.
ALL TOO OFTEN, FOLKS COMPOUND THEIR TRANSGRESSIONS BECAUSE THE RULES HAVE ALREADY BEEN BROKEN—
THEY DON'T BALK AT BREAKING THEM ANY FURTHER.

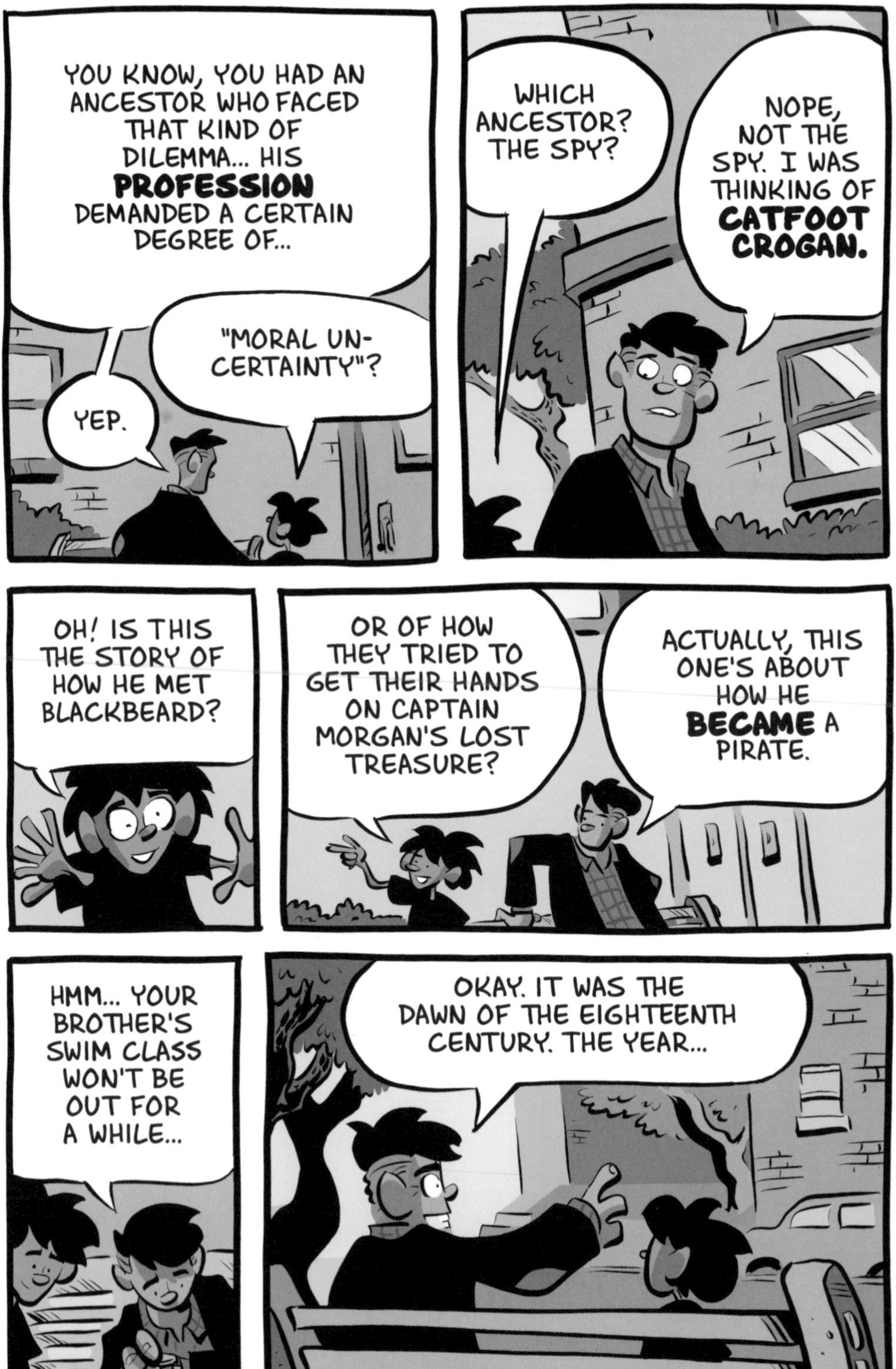

YOU KNOW, YOU HAD AN ANCESTOR WHO FACED THAT KIND OF DILEMMA... HIS **PROFESSION** DEMANDED A CERTAIN DEGREE OF...
"MORAL UN-CERTAINTY"?
YEP.
WHICH ANCESTOR? THE SPY?
NOPE, NOT THE SPY. I WAS THINKING OF **CATFOOT CROGAN.**
OH! IS THIS THE STORY OF HOW HE MET BLACKBEARD?
OR OF HOW THEY TRIED TO GET THEIR HANDS ON CAPTAIN MORGAN'S LOST TREASURE?
ACTUALLY, THIS ONE'S ABOUT HOW HE **BECAME** A PIRATE.
HMM... YOUR BROTHER'S SWIM CLASS WON'T BE OUT FOR A WHILE...
OKAY. IT WAS THE DAWN OF THE EIGHTEENTH CENTURY. THE YEAR...

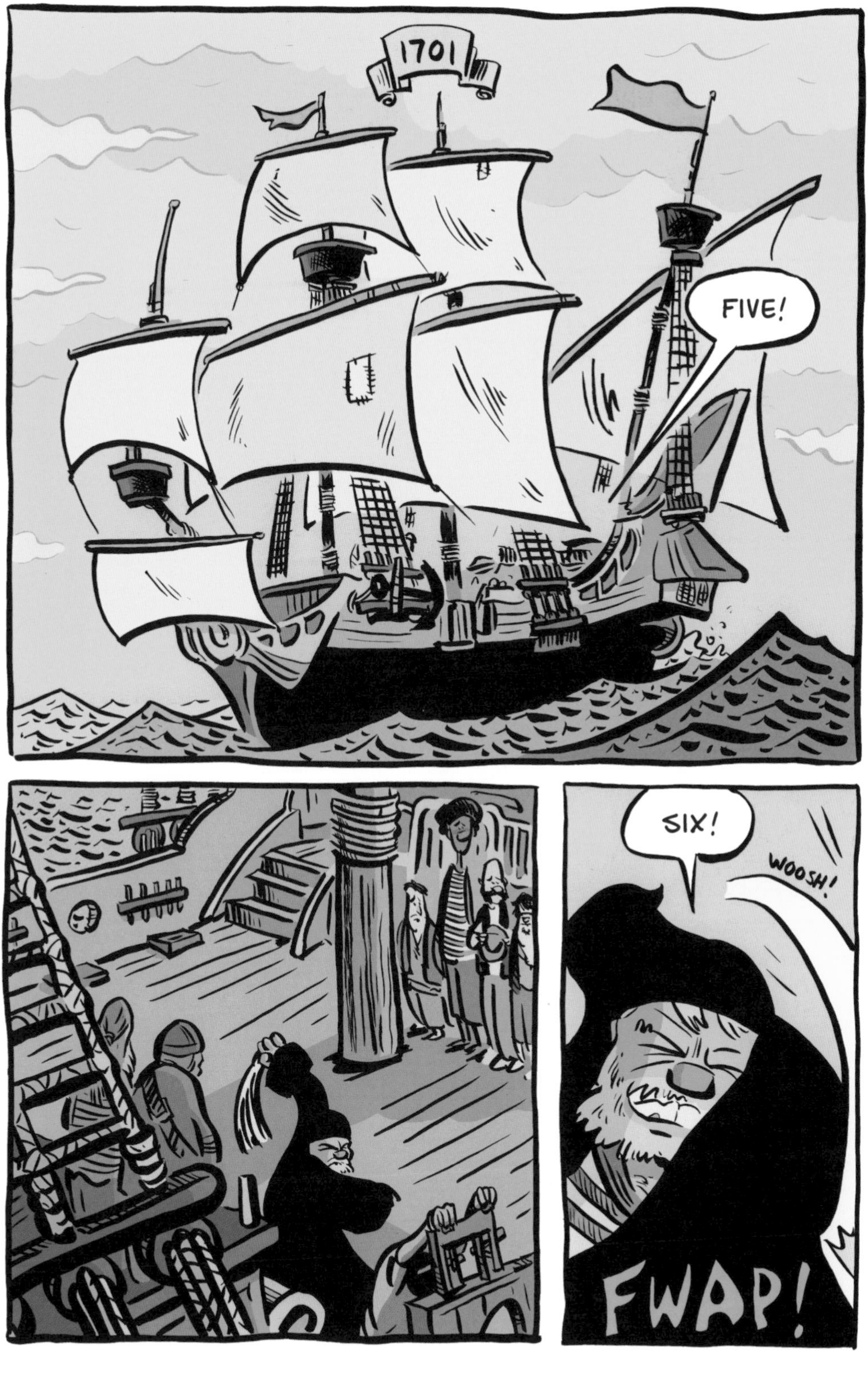
1701
FIVE!
SIX!
WOOSH!
FWAP!

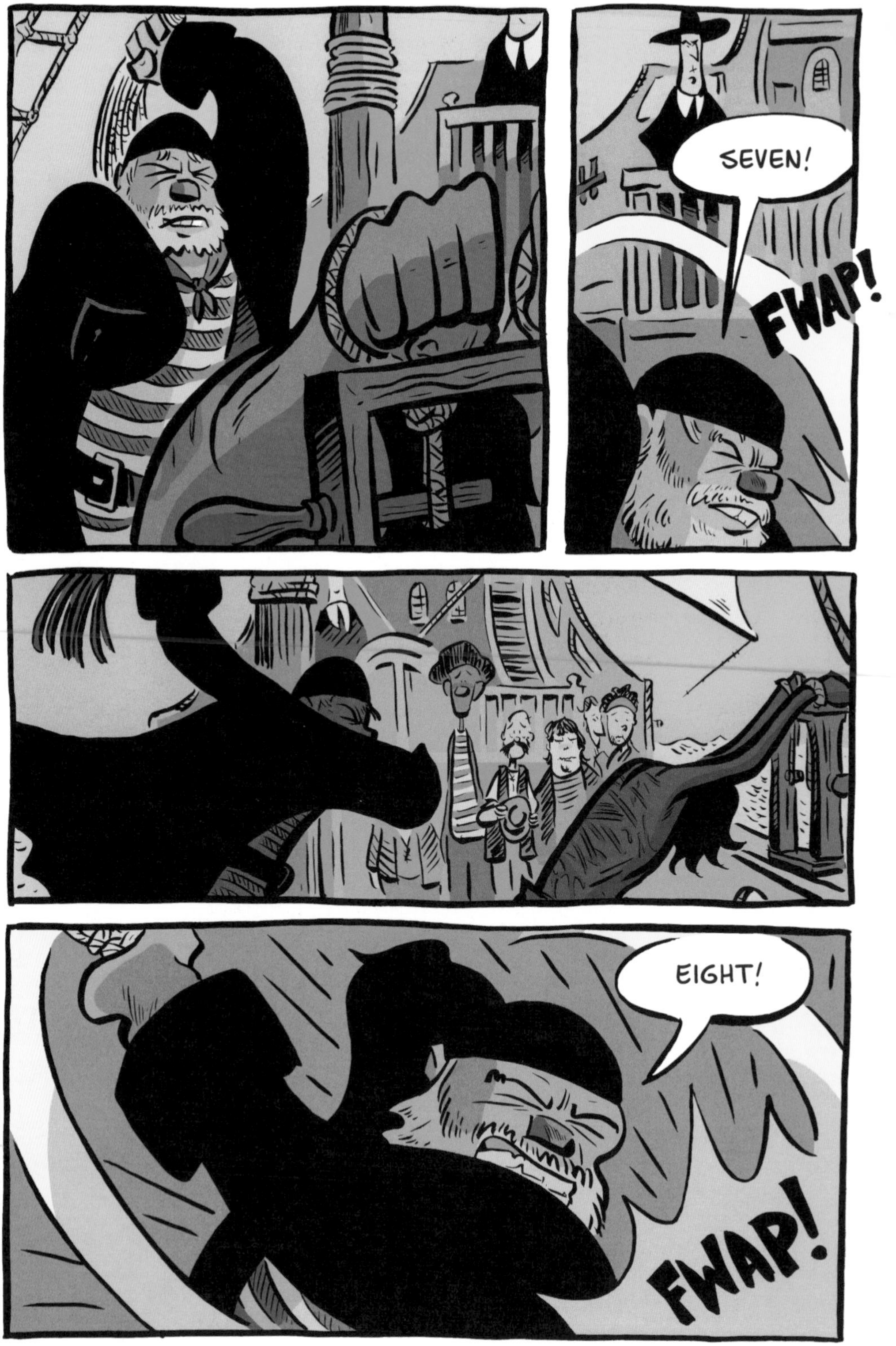
SEVEN!
FWAP!
EIGHT!
FWAP!

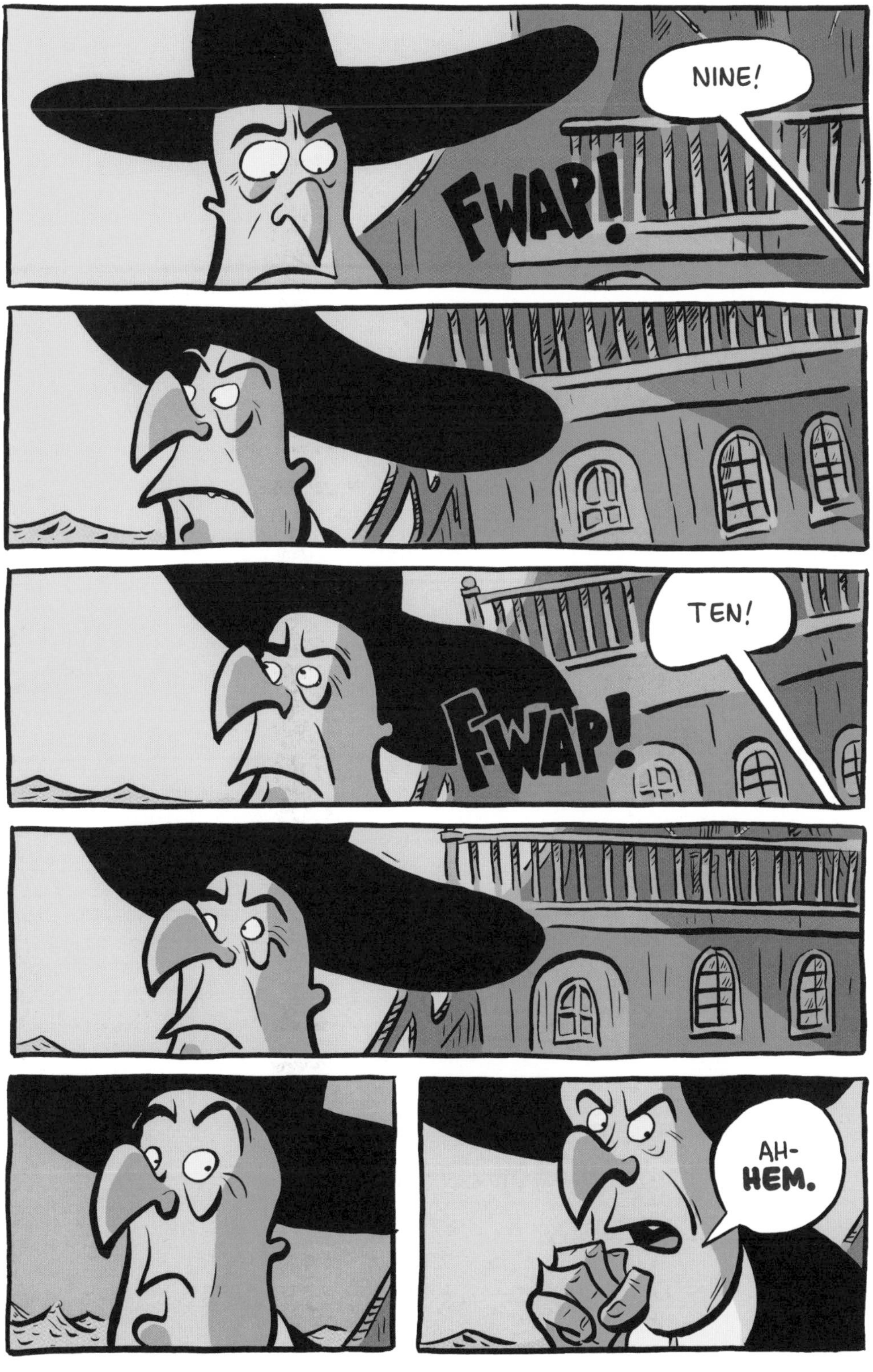
NINE!
FWAP!
TEN!
F-WAP!
AH-
HEM.

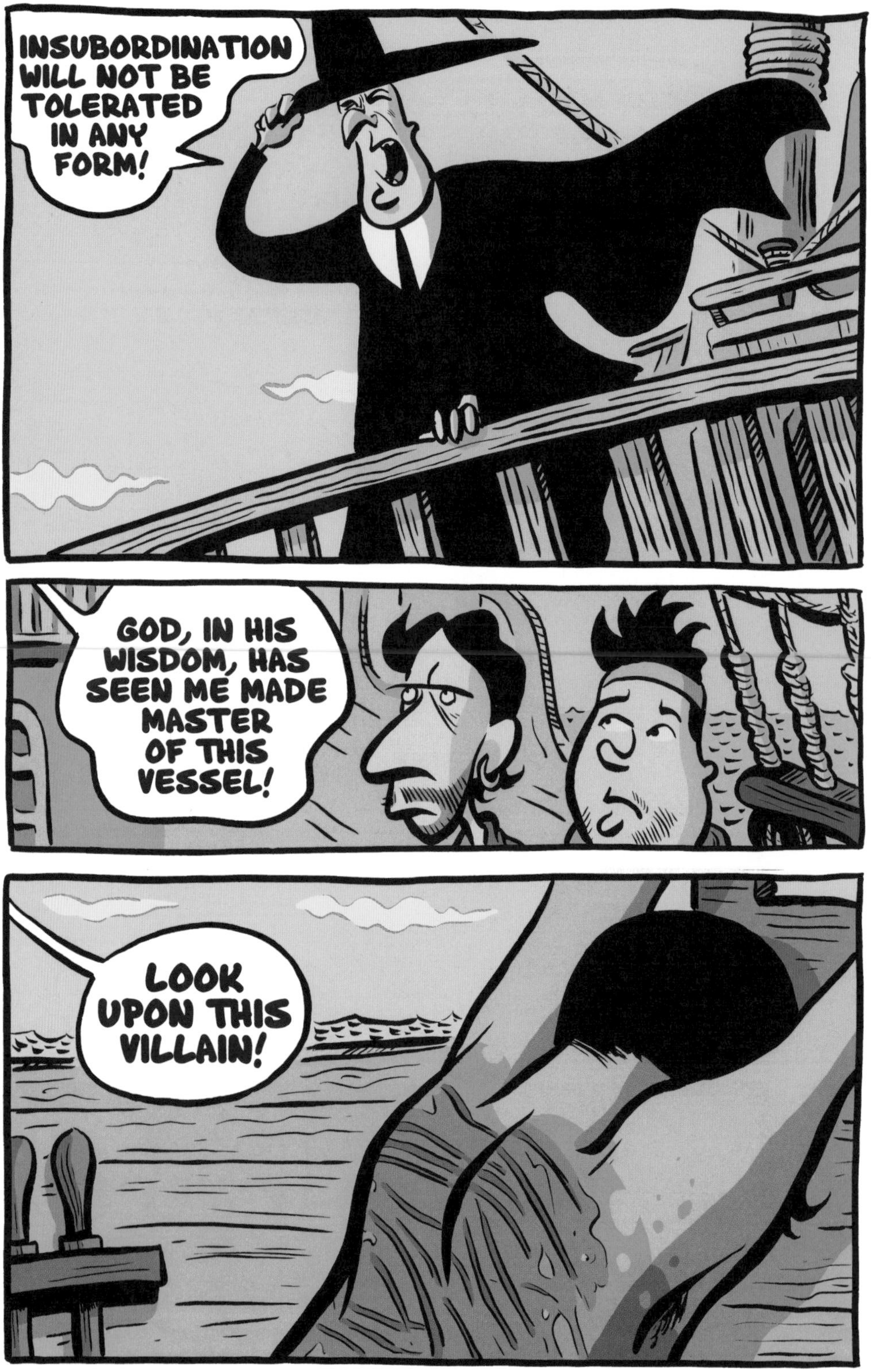
INSUBORDINATION WILL NOT BE TOLERATED IN ANY FORM!
GOD, IN HIS WISDOM, HAS SEEN ME MADE MASTER OF THIS VESSEL!
LOOK UPON THIS VILLAIN!

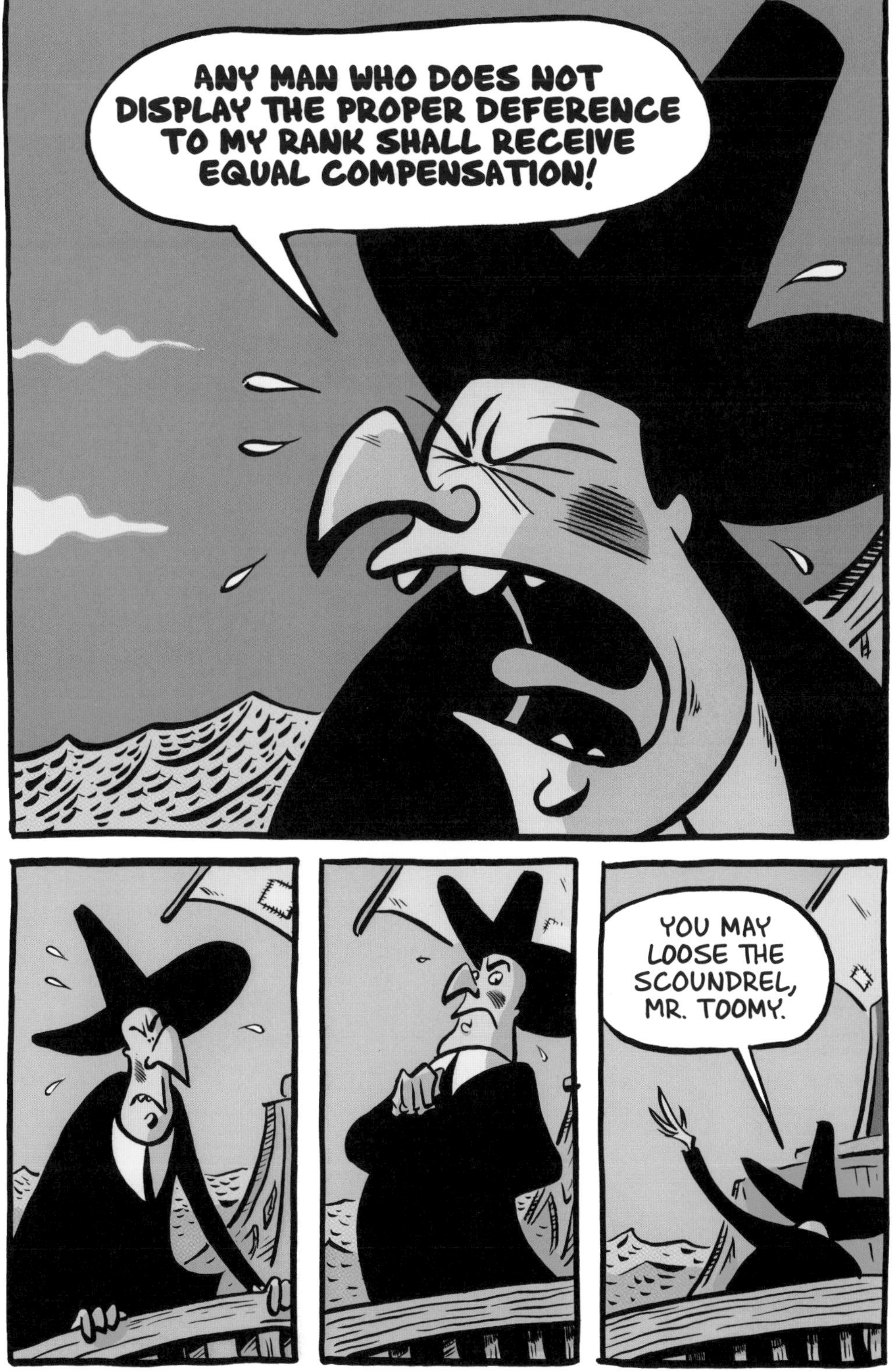
ANY MAN WHO DOES NOT DISPLAY THE PROPER DEFERENCE TO MY RANK SHALL RECEIVE EQUAL COMPENSATION!
YOU MAY LOOSE THE SCOUNDREL, MR. TOOMY.

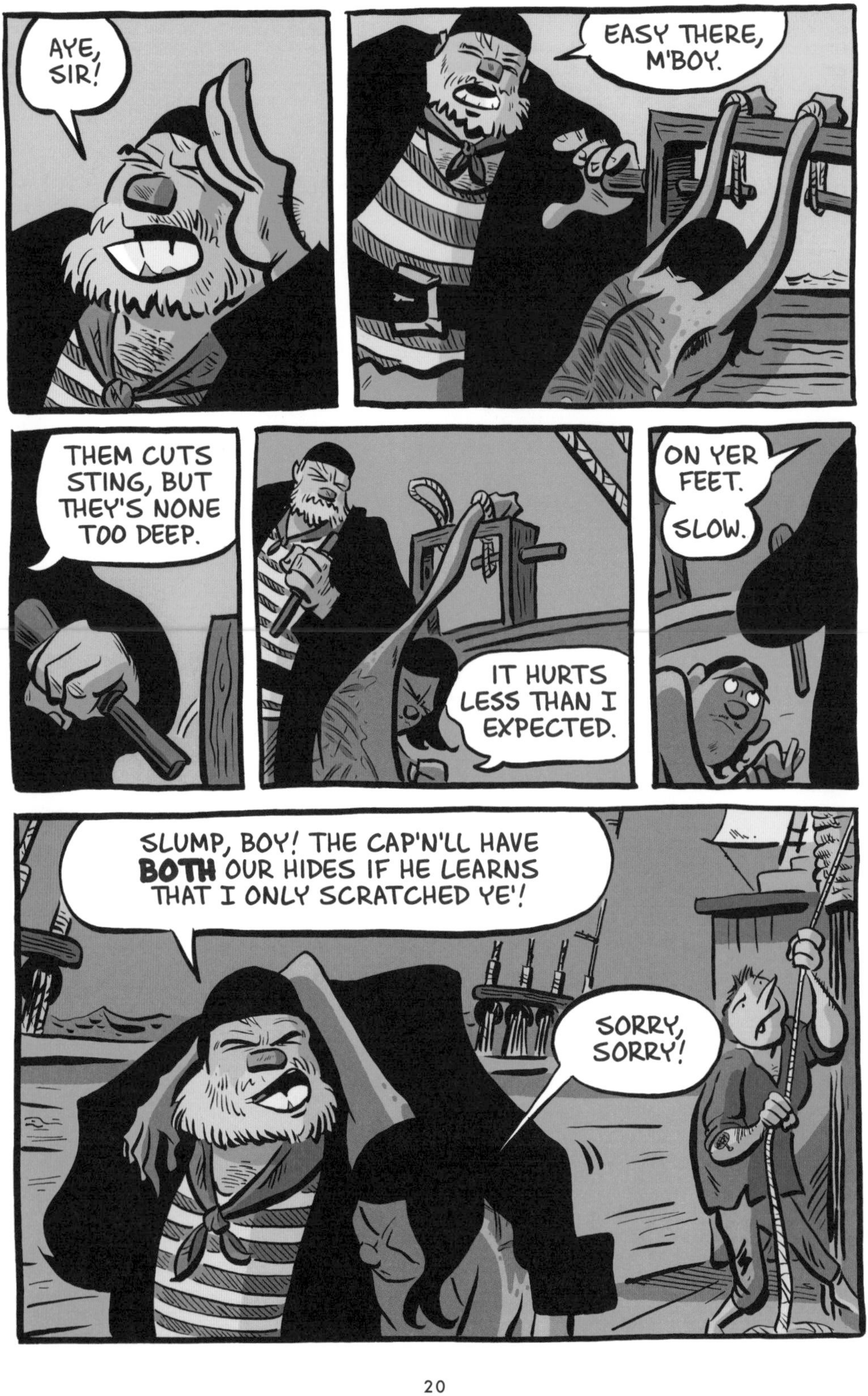
AYE, SIR!
EASY THERE, M'BOY.
THEM CUTS STING, BUT THEY'S NONE TOO DEEP.
IT HURTS LESS THAN I EXPECTED.
ON YER FEET.
SLOW.
SLUMP, BOY! THE CAP'N'LL HAVE **BOTH** OUR HIDES IF HE LEARNS THAT I ONLY SCRATCHED YE'!
SORRY, SORRY!

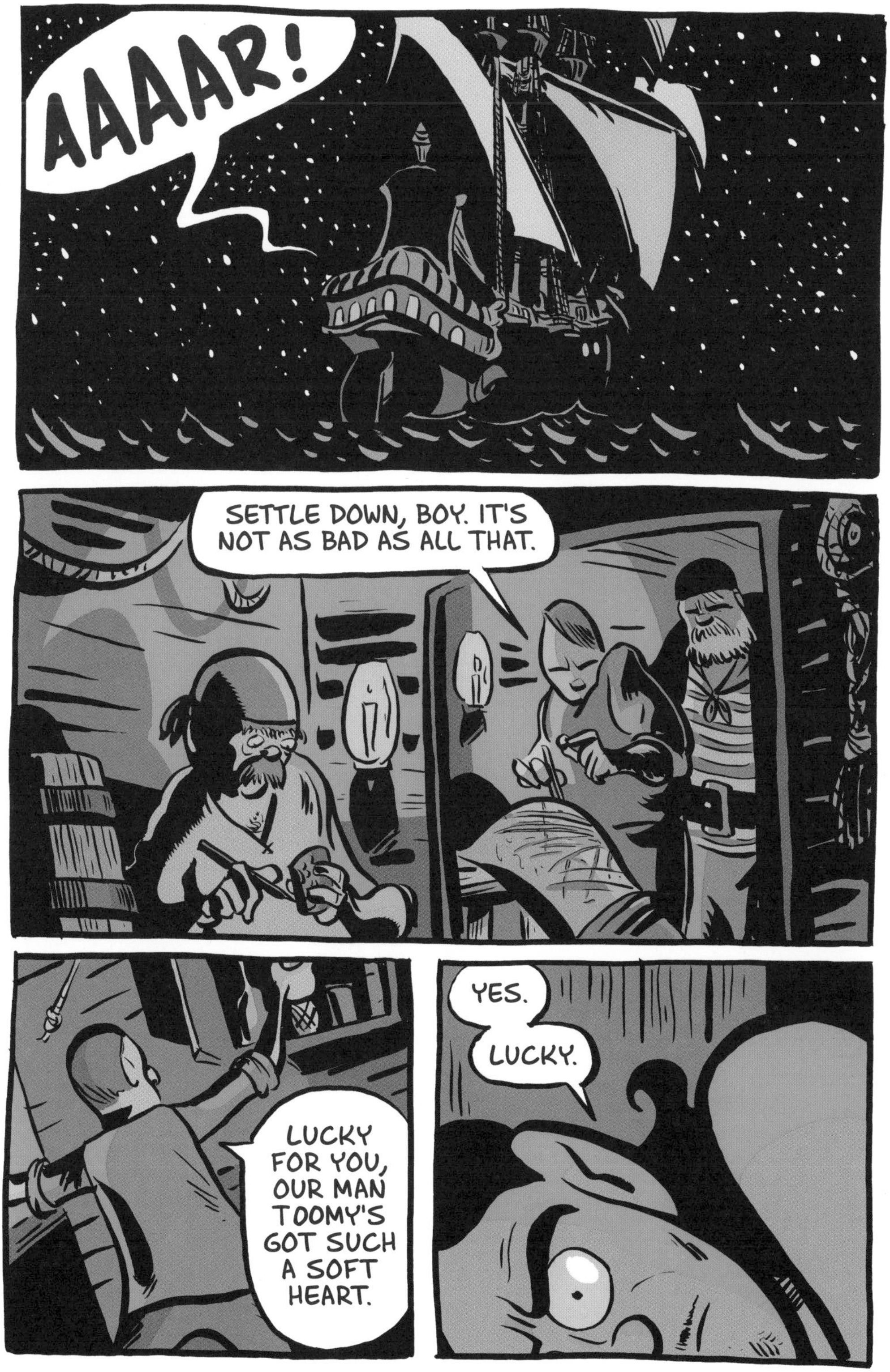
AAAAR!
SETTLE DOWN, BOY. IT'S NOT AS BAD AS ALL THAT.
LUCKY FOR YOU, OUR MAN TOOMY'S GOT SUCH A SOFT HEART.
YES.
LUCKY.

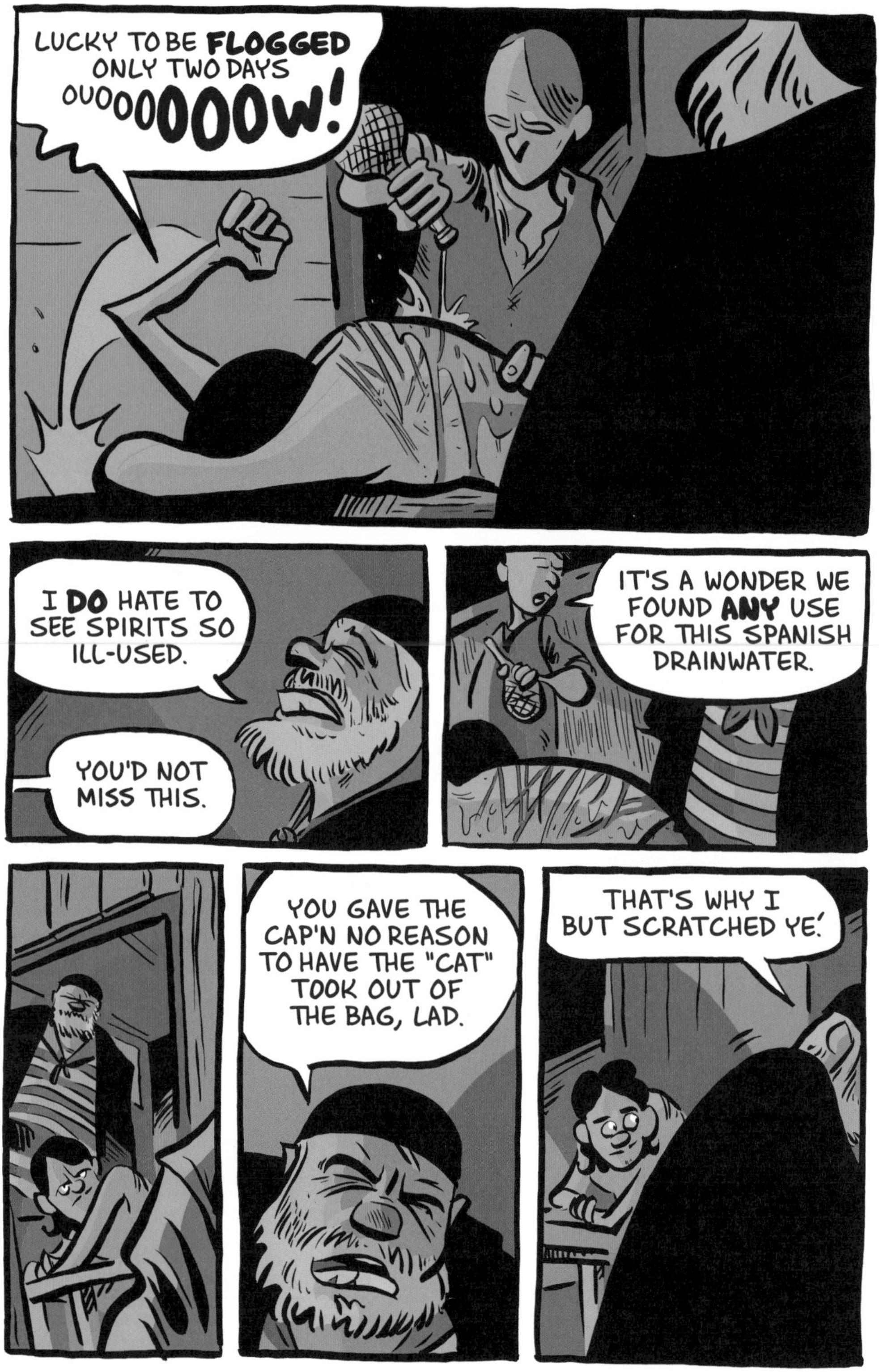
LUCKY TO BE FLOGGED ONLY TWO DAYS OUOOOOOOW!
I DO HATE TO SEE SPIRITS SO ILL-USED.
YOU'D NOT MISS THIS.
IT'S A WONDER WE FOUND ANY USE FOR THIS SPANISH DRAINWATER.
YOU GAVE THE CAP'N NO REASON TO HAVE THE "CAT" TOOK OUT OF THE BAG, LAD.
THAT'S WHY I BUT SCRATCHED YE!

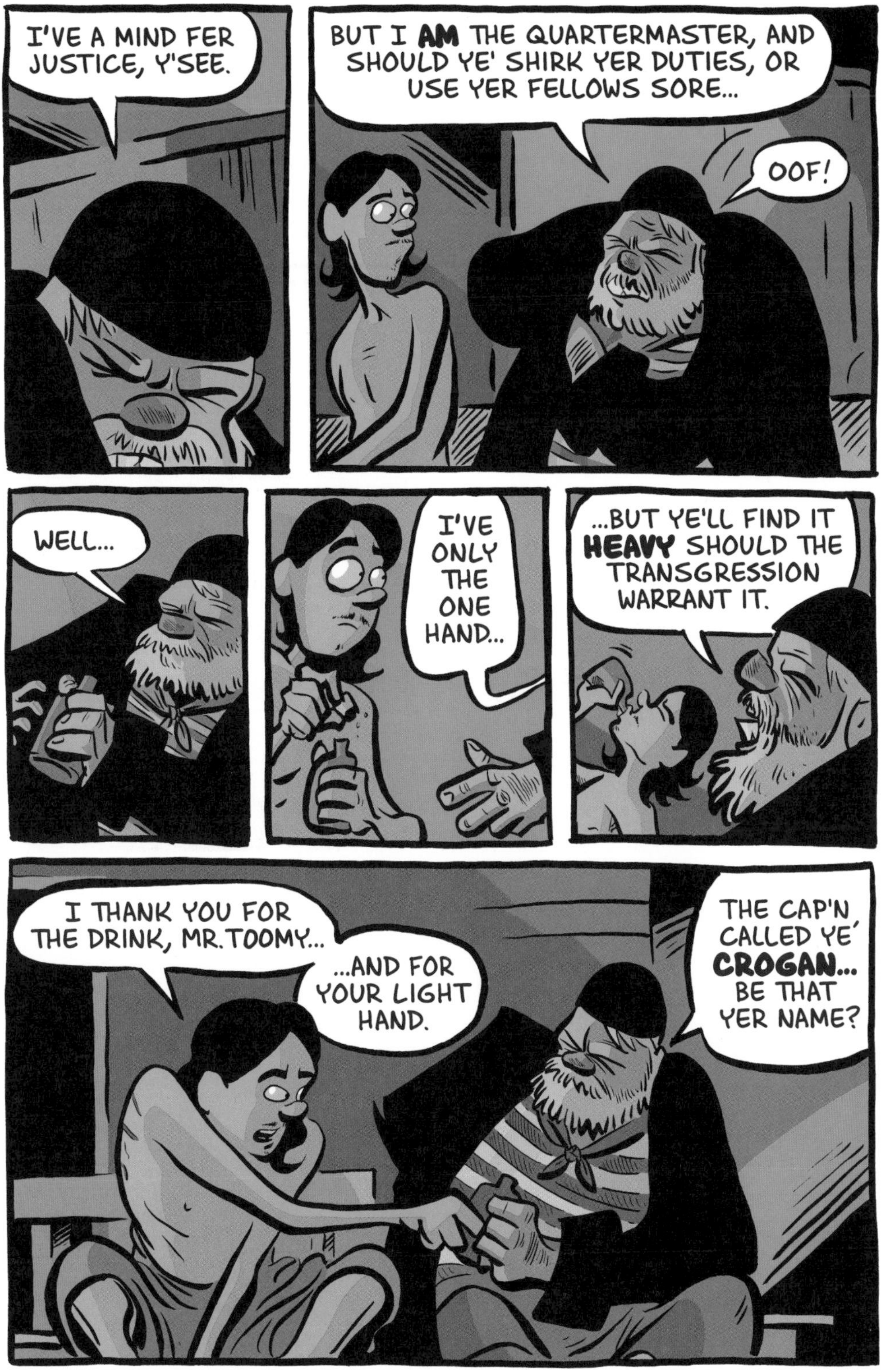
I'VE A MIND FER JUSTICE, Y'SEE.
BUT I AM THE QUARTERMASTER, AND SHOULD YE' SHIRK YER DUTIES, OR USE YER FELLOWS SORE...
OOF!
WELL...
I'VE ONLY THE ONE HAND...
...BUT YE'LL FIND IT HEAVY SHOULD THE TRANSGRESSION WARRANT IT.
I THANK YOU FOR THE DRINK, MR. TOOMY...
...AND FOR YOUR LIGHT HAND.
THE CAP'N CALLED YE' CROGAN... BE THAT YER NAME?

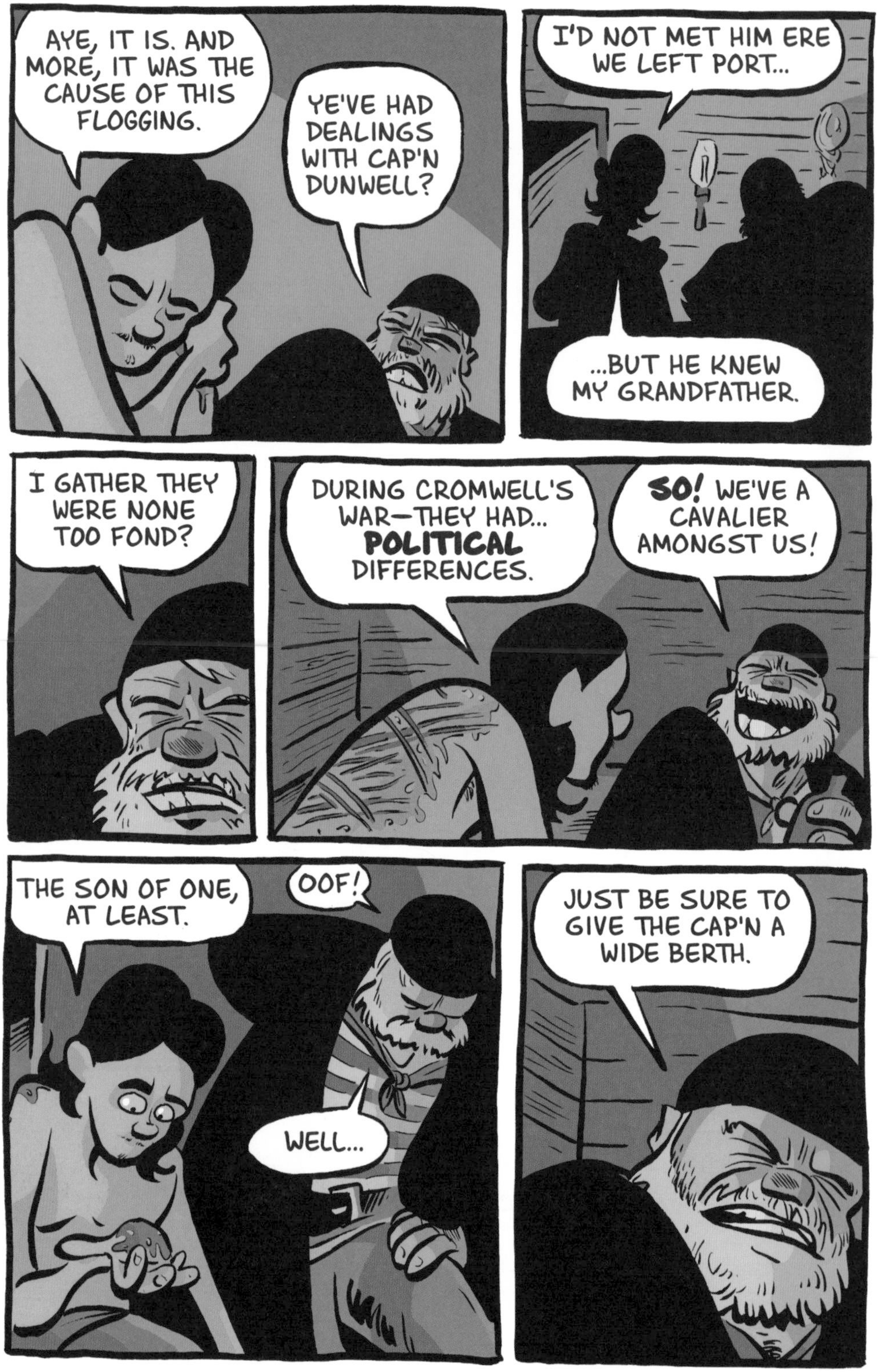
AYE, IT IS. AND MORE, IT WAS THE CAUSE OF THIS FLOGGING.
YE'VE HAD DEALINGS WITH CAP'N DUNWELL?
I'D NOT MET HIM ERE WE LEFT PORT...
...BUT HE KNEW MY GRANDFATHER.
I GATHER THEY WERE NONE TOO FOND?
DURING CROMWELL'S WAR—THEY HAD... POLITICAL DIFFERENCES.
SO! WE'VE A CAVALIER AMONGST US!
THE SON OF ONE, AT LEAST.
OOF!
WELL...
JUST BE SURE TO GIVE THE CAP'N A WIDE BERTH.

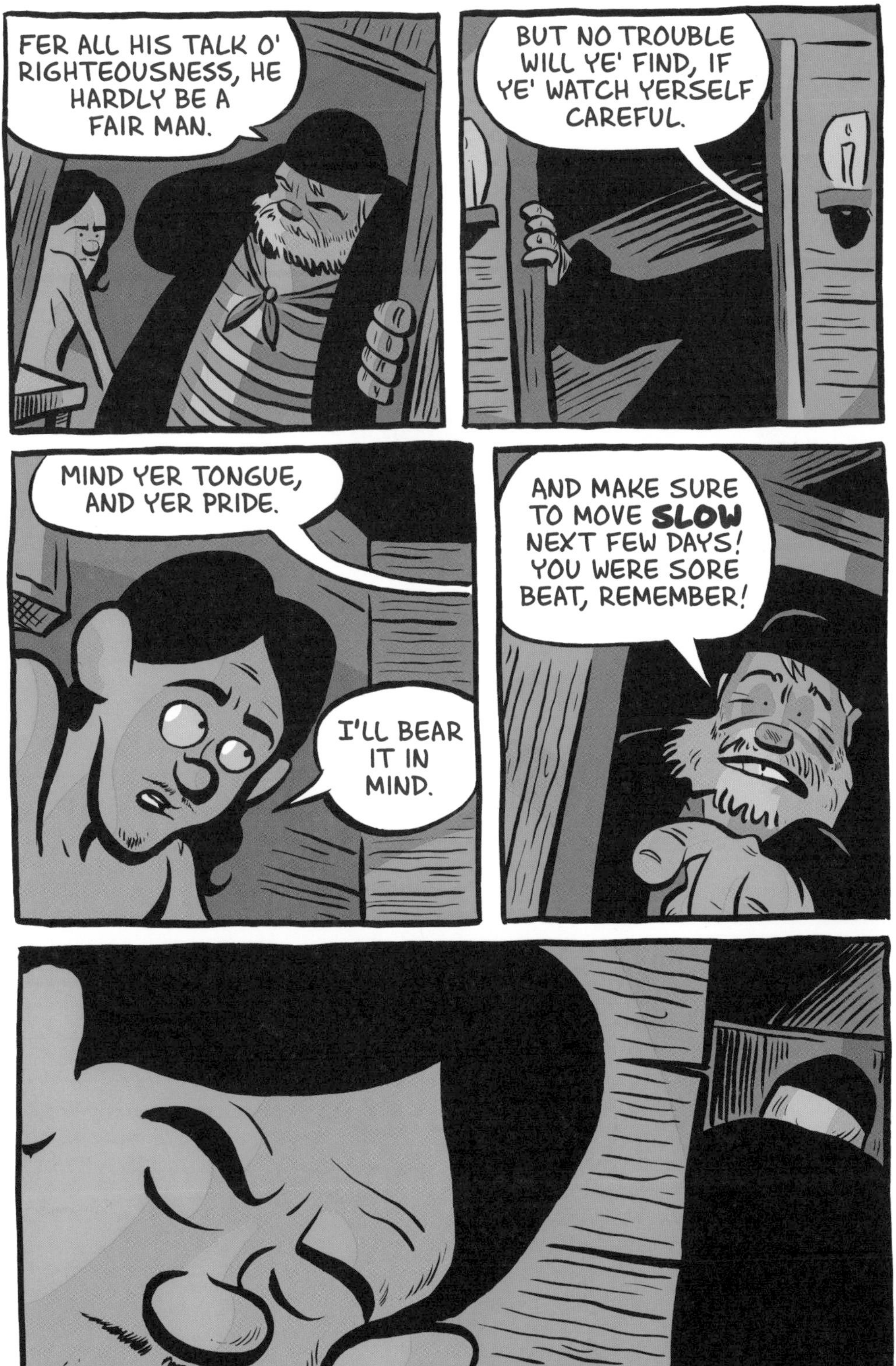

FER ALL HIS TALK O' RIGHTEOUSNESS, HE HARDLY BE A FAIR MAN.
BUT NO TROUBLE WILL YE' FIND, IF YE' WATCH YERSELF CAREFUL.
MIND YER TONGUE, AND YER PRIDE.
I'LL BEAR IT IN MIND.
AND MAKE SURE TO MOVE SLOW NEXT FEW DAYS! YOU WERE SORE BEAT, REMEMBER!

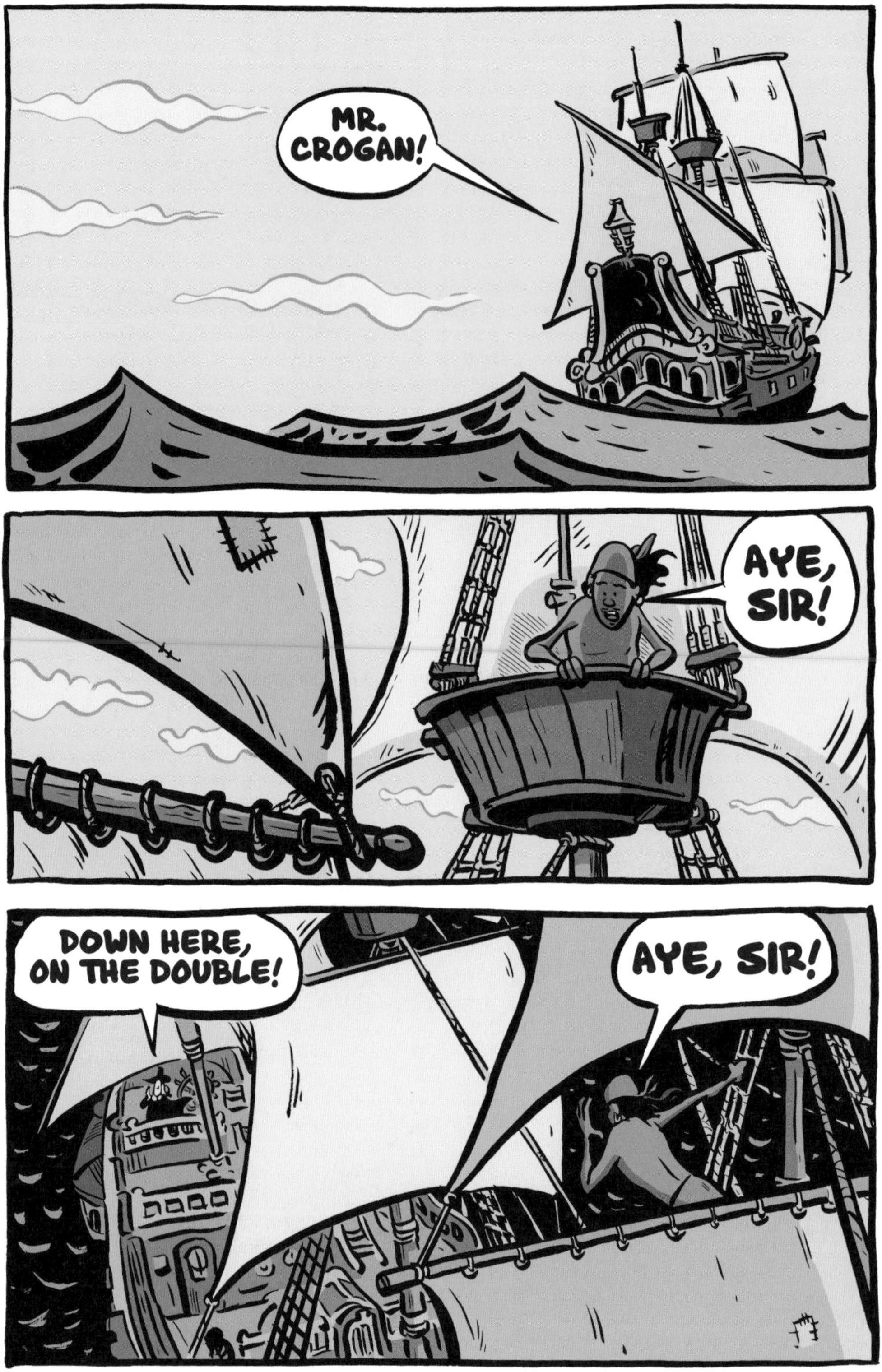
MR. CROGAN!
AYE, SIR!
DOWN HERE, ON THE DOUBLE!
AYE, SIR!

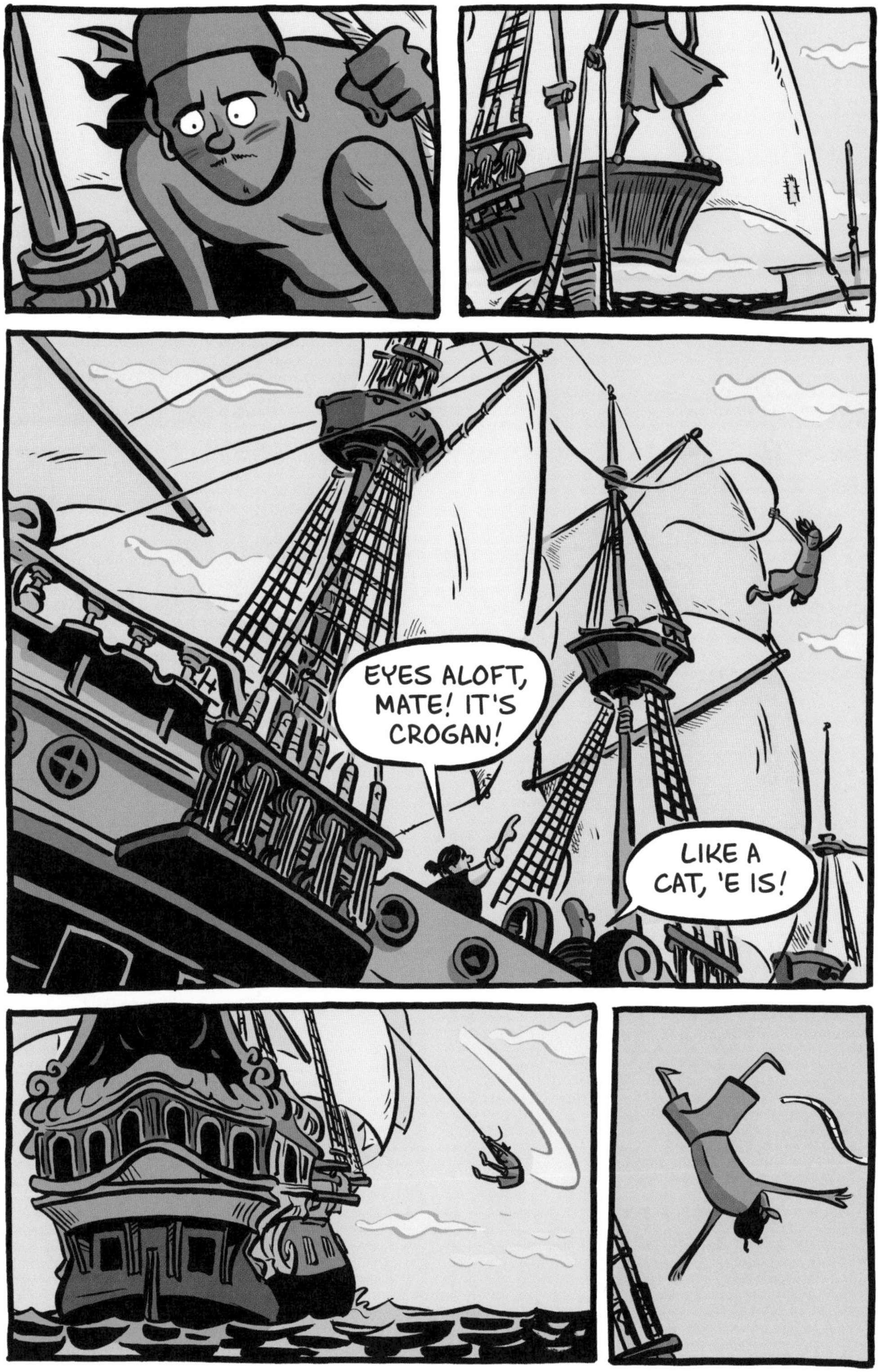
EYES ALOFT, MATE! IT'S CROGAN!
LIKE A CAT, 'E IS!

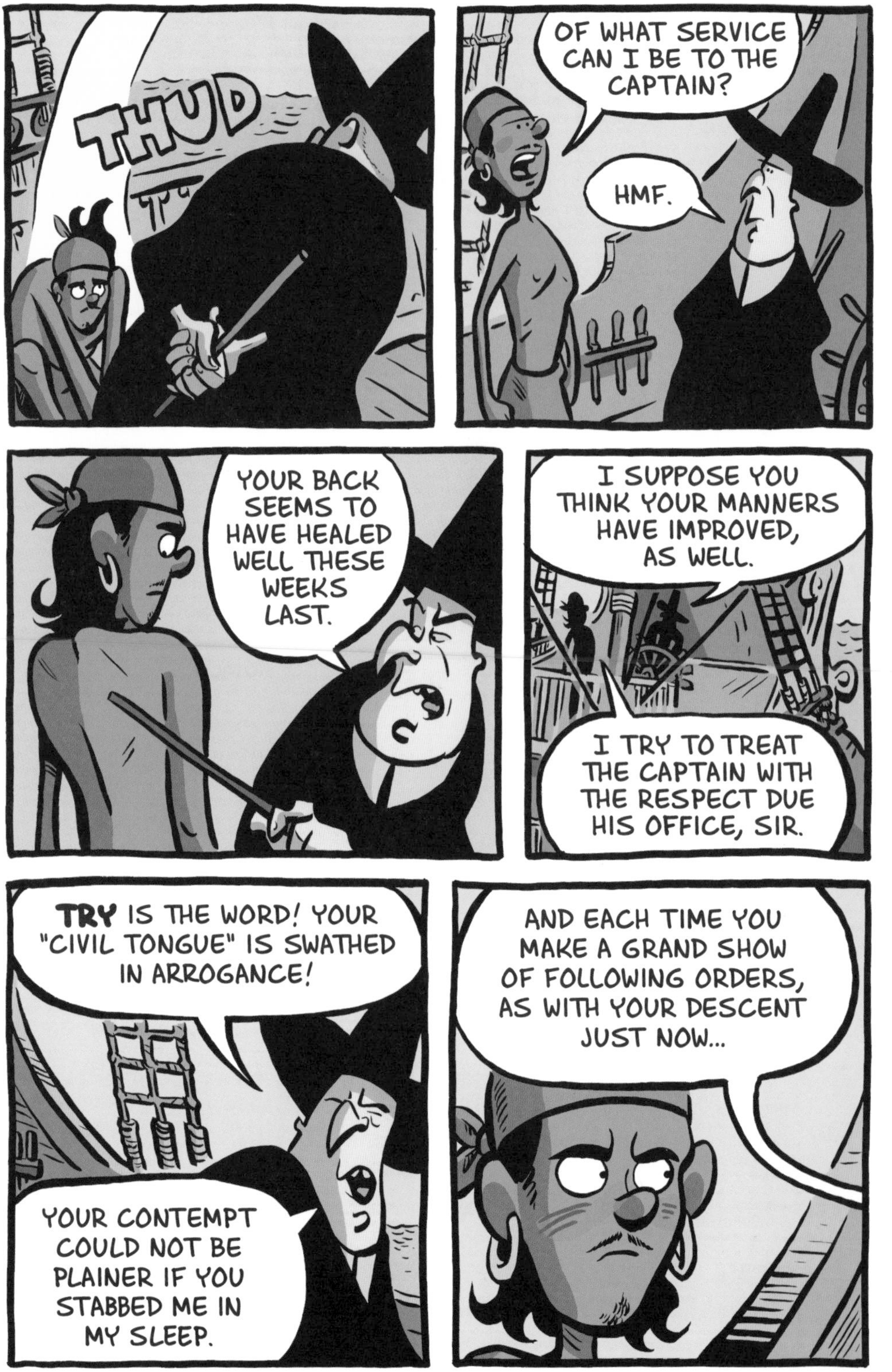
THUD
OF WHAT SERVICE CAN I BE TO THE CAPTAIN?
HMF.
YOUR BACK SEEMS TO HAVE HEALED WELL THESE WEEKS LAST.
I SUPPOSE YOU THINK YOUR MANNERS HAVE IMPROVED, AS WELL.
I TRY TO TREAT THE CAPTAIN WITH THE RESPECT DUE HIS OFFICE, SIR.
TRY IS THE WORD! YOUR "CIVIL TONGUE" IS SWATHED IN ARROGANCE!
YOUR CONTEMPT COULD NOT BE PLAINER IF YOU STABBED ME IN MY SLEEP.
AND EACH TIME YOU MAKE A GRAND SHOW OF FOLLOWING ORDERS, AS WITH YOUR DESCENT JUST NOW...

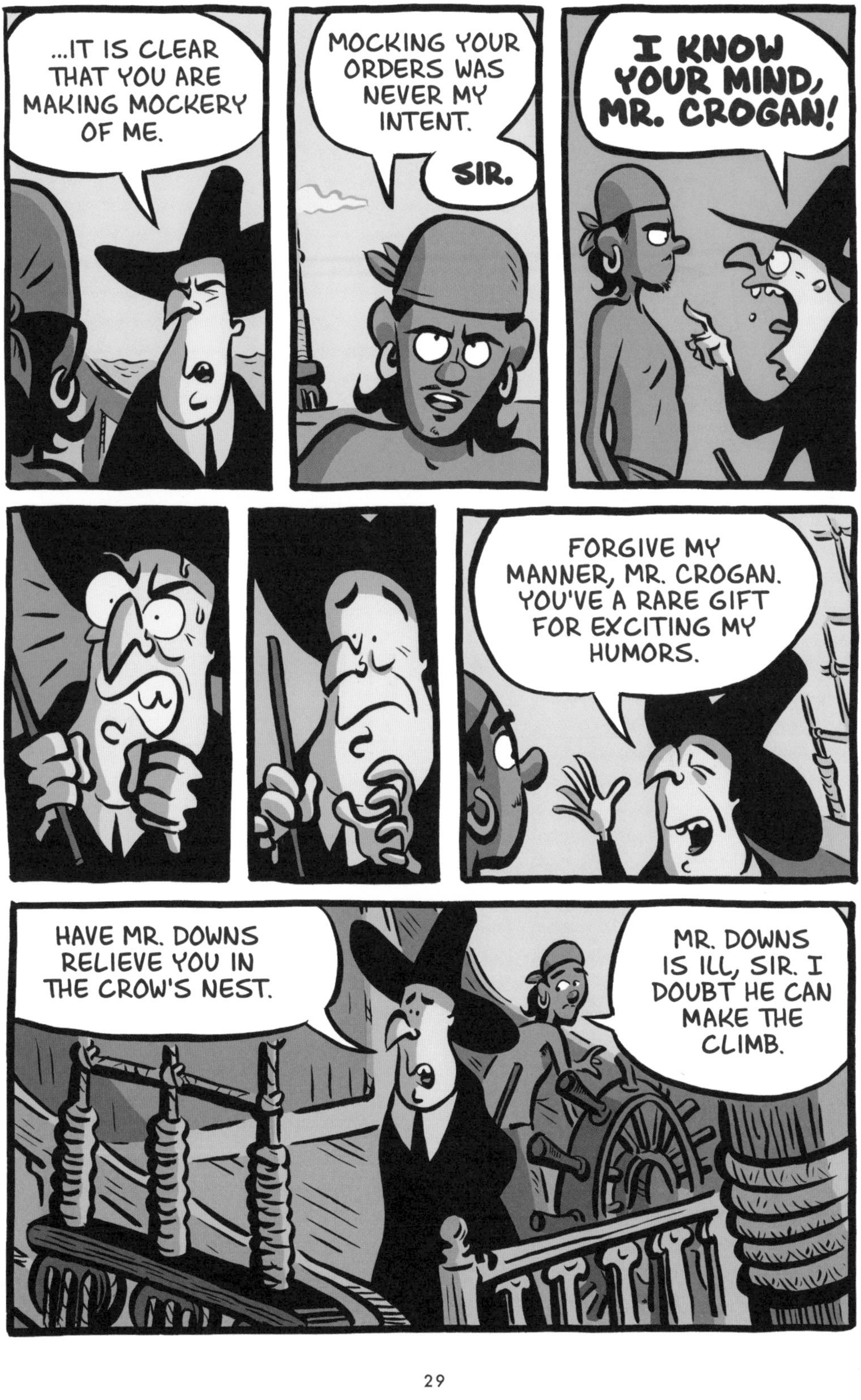
...IT IS CLEAR THAT YOU ARE MAKING MOCKERY OF ME.
MOCKING YOUR ORDERS WAS NEVER MY INTENT.
SIR.
I KNOW YOUR MIND, MR. CROGAN!
FORGIVE MY MANNER, MR. CROGAN. YOU'VE A RARE GIFT FOR EXCITING MY HUMORS.
HAVE MR. DOWNS RELIEVE YOU IN THE CROW'S NEST.
MR. DOWNS IS ILL, SIR. I DOUBT HE CAN MAKE THE CLIMB.

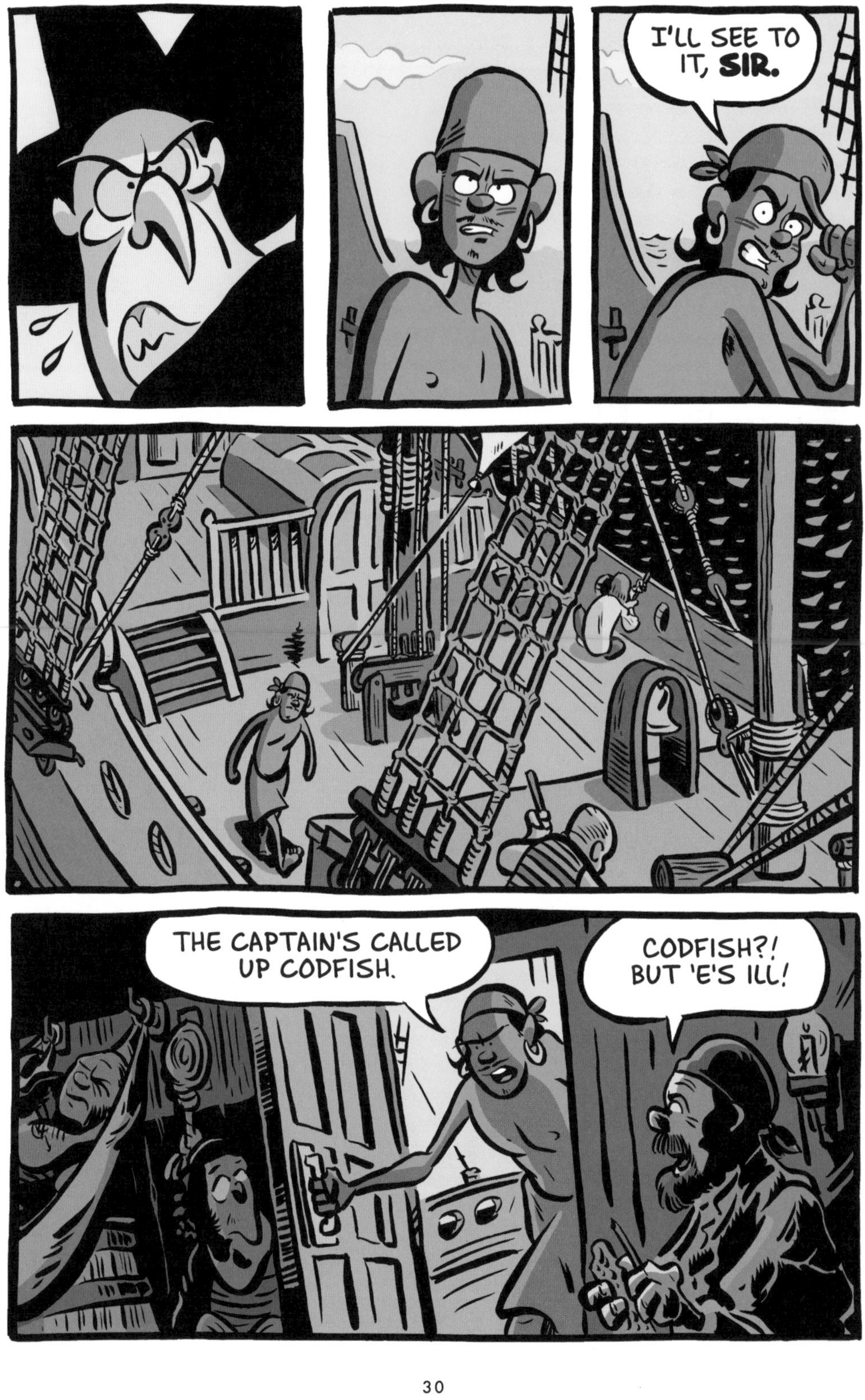
I'LL SEE TO IT, **SIR.**
THE CAPTAIN'S CALLED UP CODFISH.
CODFISH?! BUT 'E'S ILL!

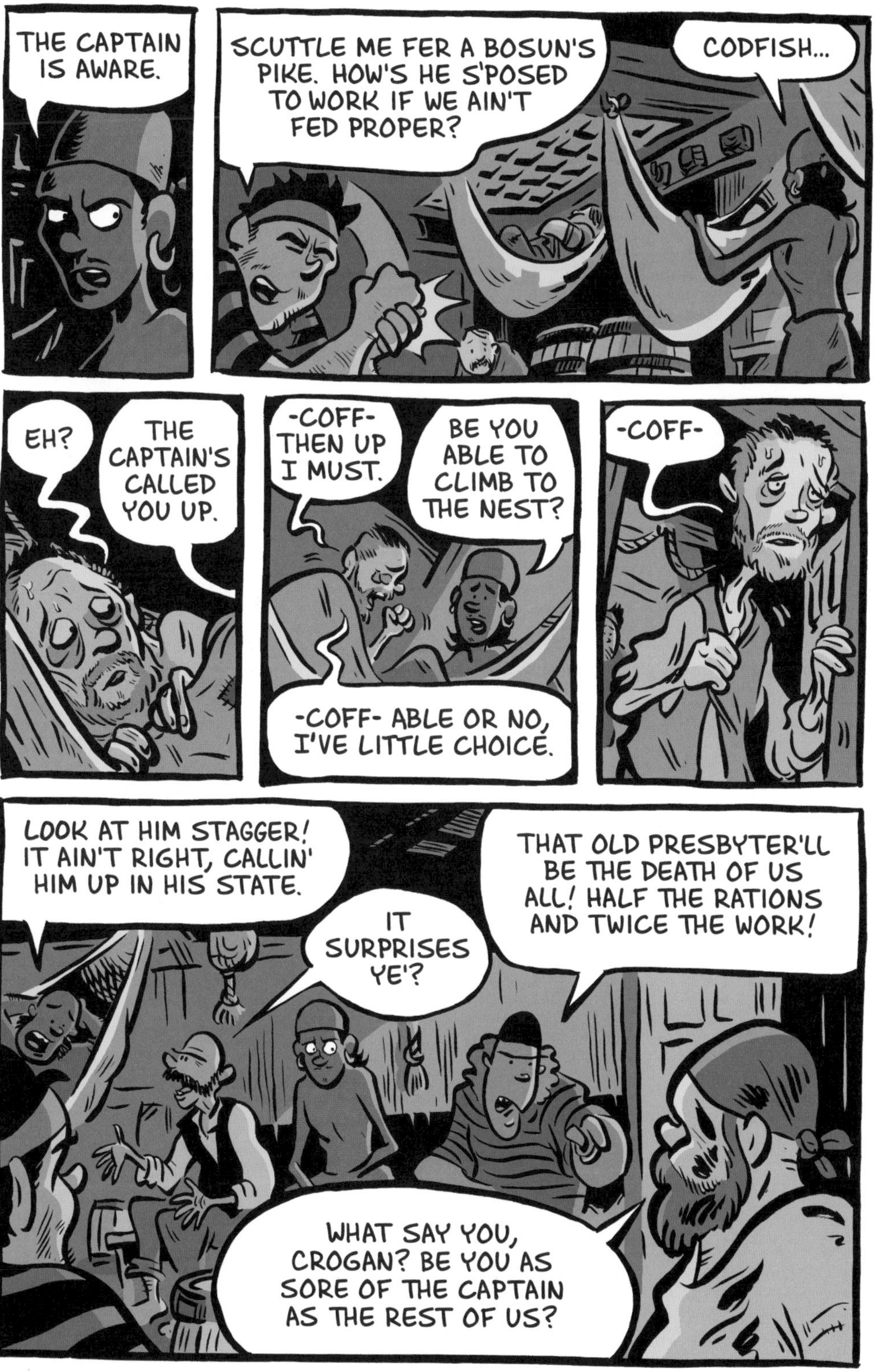
THE CAPTAIN IS AWARE.
SCUTTLE ME FER A BOSUN'S PIKE. HOW'S HE S'POSED TO WORK IF WE AIN'T FED PROPER?
CODFISH...
EH?
THE CAPTAIN'S CALLED YOU UP.
-COFF- THEN UP I MUST.
BE YOU ABLE TO CLIMB TO THE NEST?
-COFF- ABLE OR NO, I'VE LITTLE CHOICE.
-COFF-
LOOK AT HIM STAGGER! IT AIN'T RIGHT, CALLIN' HIM UP IN HIS STATE.
IT SURPRISES YE'?
THAT OLD PRESBYTER'LL BE THE DEATH OF US ALL! HALF THE RATIONS AND TWICE THE WORK!
WHAT SAY YOU, CROGAN? BE YOU AS SORE OF THE CAPTAIN AS THE REST OF US?

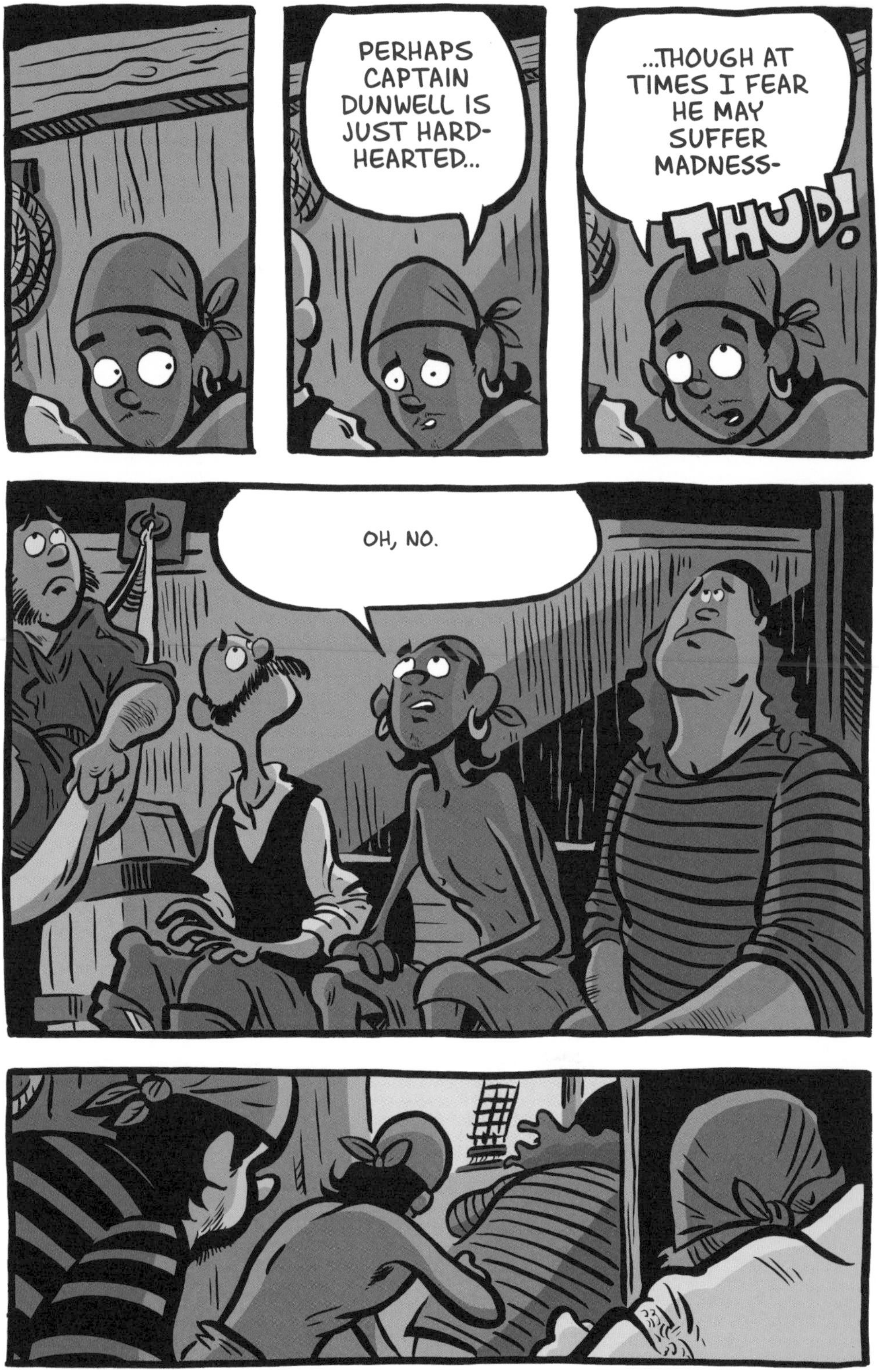
PERHAPS CAPTAIN DUNWELL IS JUST HARD-HEARTED...
...THOUGH AT TIMES I FEAR HE MAY SUFFER MADNESS-
THUD!
OH, NO.

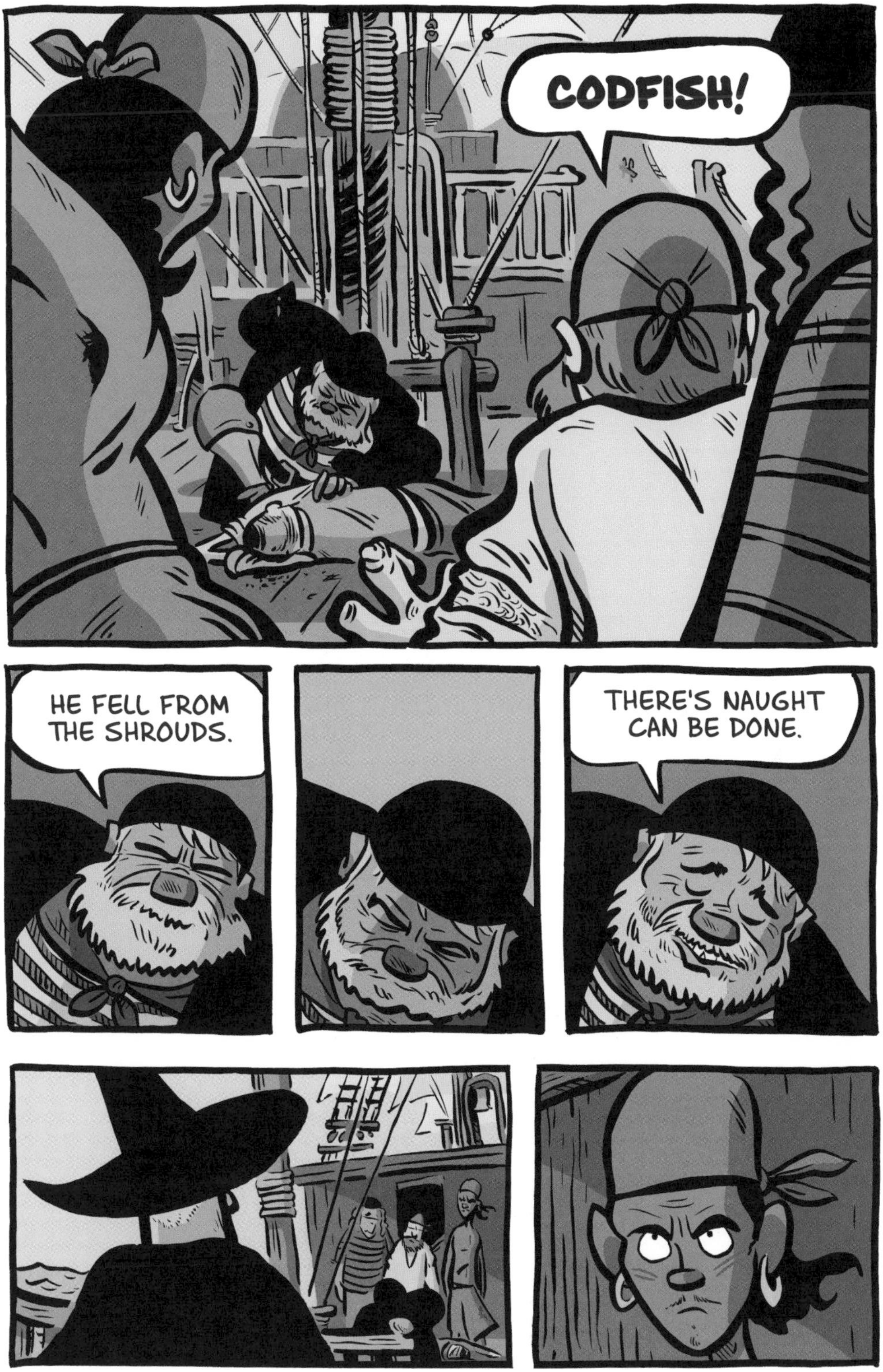
CODFISH!
HE FELL FROM THE SHROUDS.
THERE'S NAUGHT CAN BE DONE.

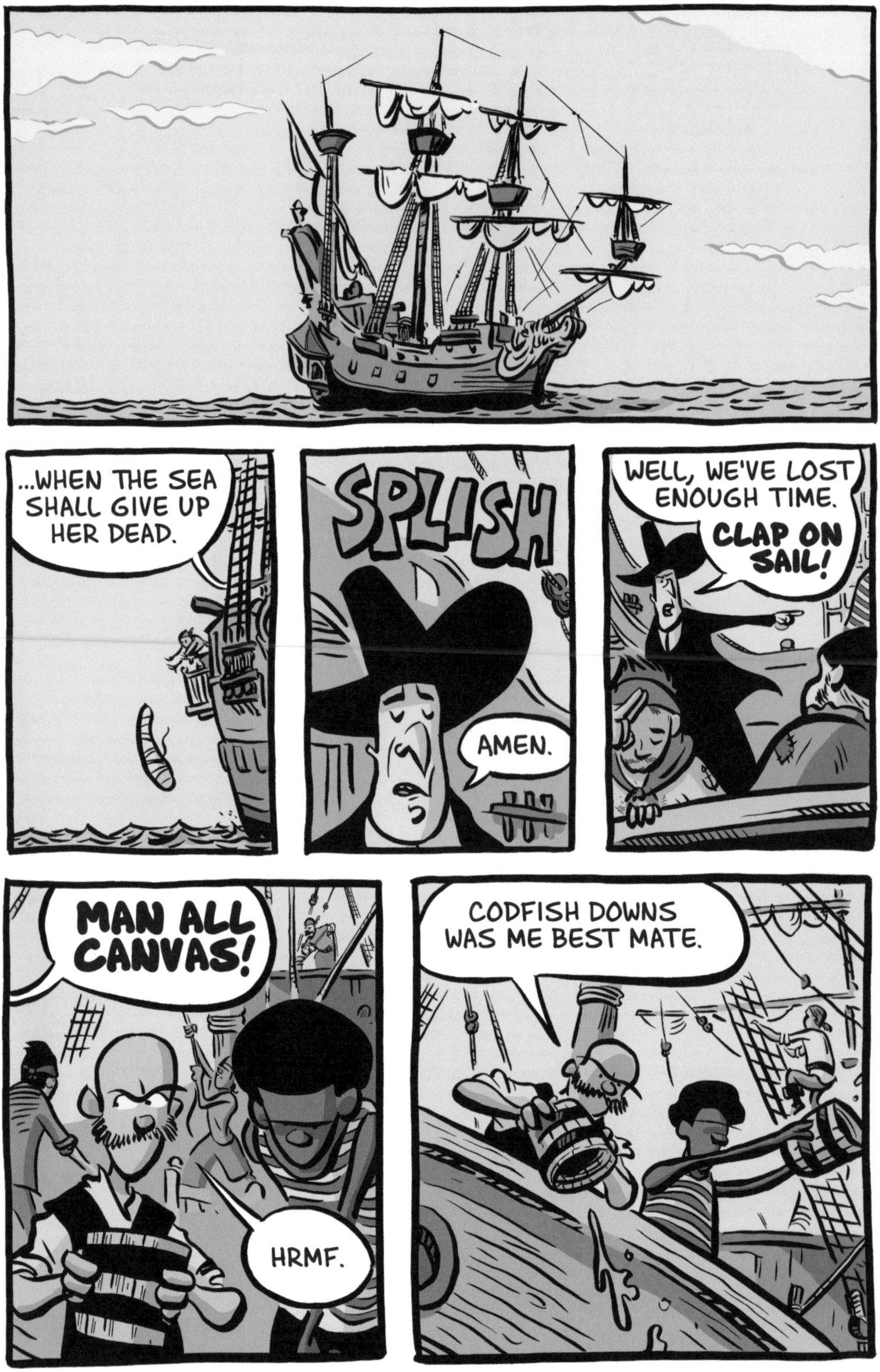
...WHEN THE SEA SHALL GIVE UP HER DEAD.
SPLISH
AMEN.
WELL, WE'VE LOST ENOUGH TIME.
CLAP ON SAIL!
MAN ALL CANVAS!
HRMF.
CODFISH DOWNS WAS ME BEST MATE.

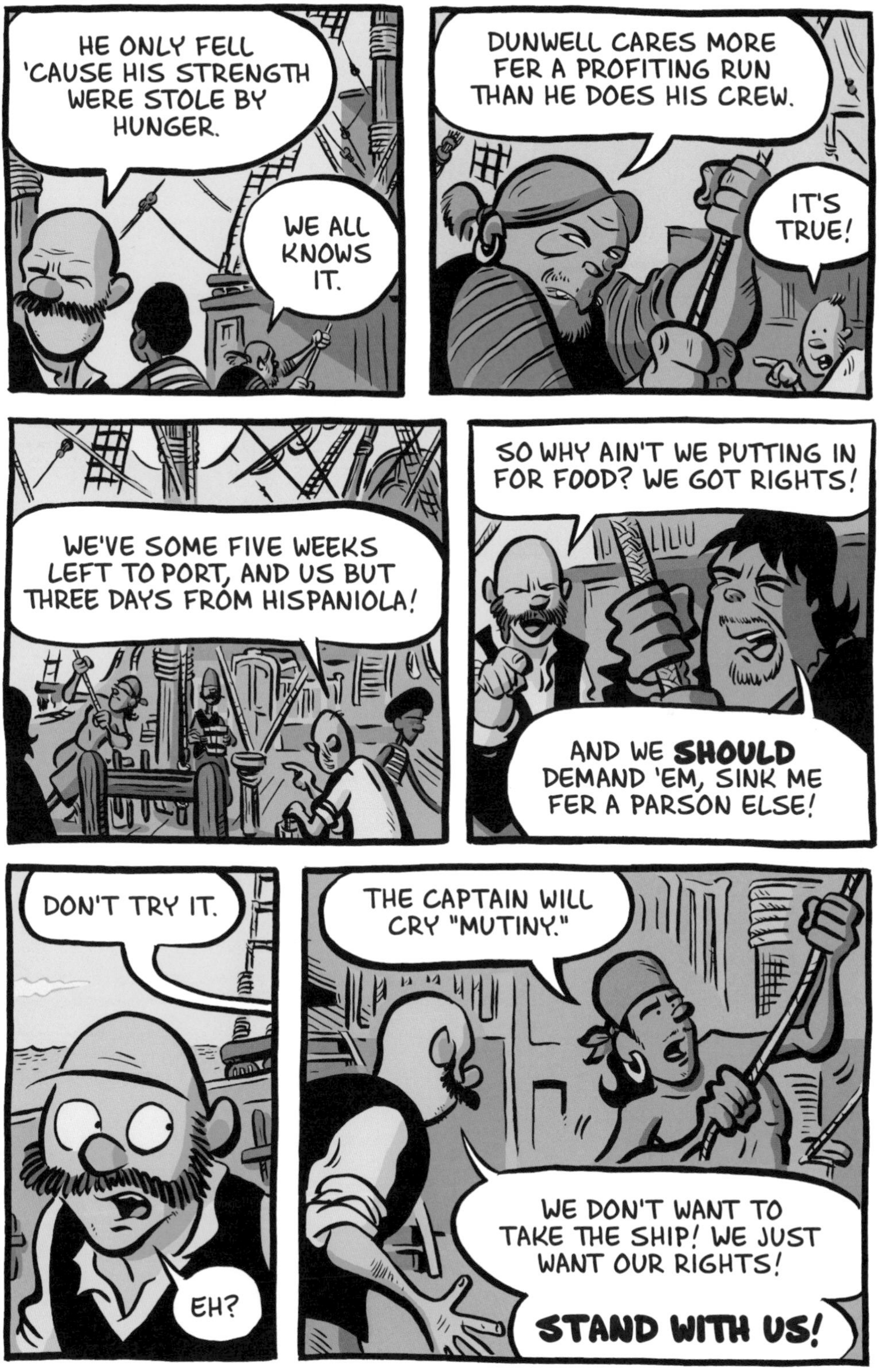
HE ONLY FELL 'CAUSE HIS STRENGTH WERE STOLE BY HUNGER.
WE ALL KNOWS IT.
DUNWELL CARES MORE FER A PROFITING RUN THAN HE DOES HIS CREW.
IT'S TRUE!
WE'VE SOME FIVE WEEKS LEFT TO PORT, AND US BUT THREE DAYS FROM HISPANIOLA!
SO WHY AIN'T WE PUTTING IN FOR FOOD? WE GOT RIGHTS!
AND WE SHOULD DEMAND 'EM, SINK ME FER A PARSON ELSE!
DON'T TRY IT.
EH?
THE CAPTAIN WILL CRY "MUTINY."
WE DON'T WANT TO TAKE THE SHIP! WE JUST WANT OUR RIGHTS!
STAND WITH US!

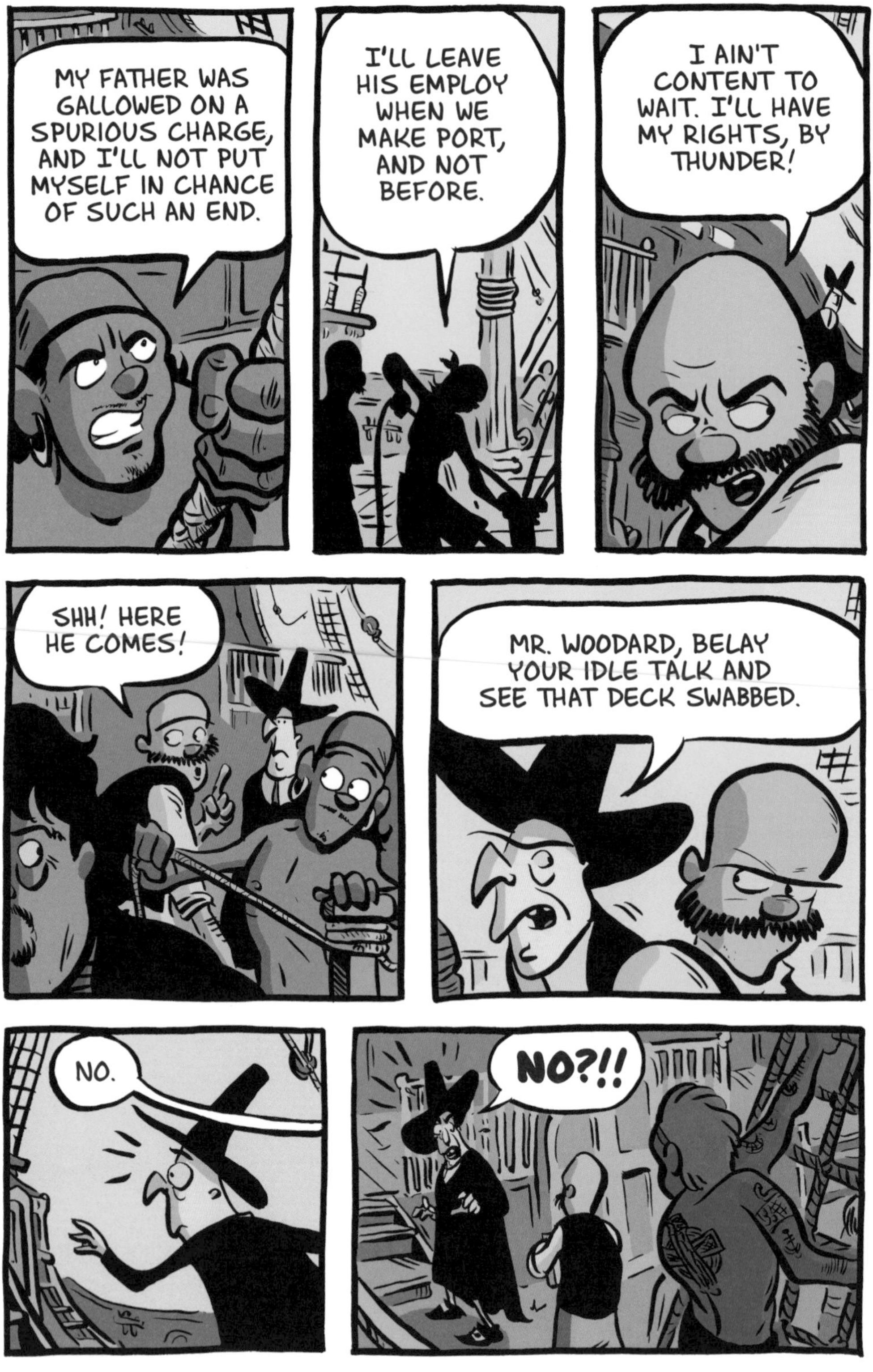
MY FATHER WAS GALLOWED ON A SPURIOUS CHARGE, AND I'LL NOT PUT MYSELF IN CHANCE OF SUCH AN END.
I'LL LEAVE HIS EMPLOY WHEN WE MAKE PORT, AND NOT BEFORE.
I AIN'T CONTENT TO WAIT. I'LL HAVE MY RIGHTS, BY THUNDER!
SHH! HERE HE COMES!
MR. WOODARD, BELAY YOUR IDLE TALK AND SEE THAT DECK SWABBED.
NO.
NO?!!

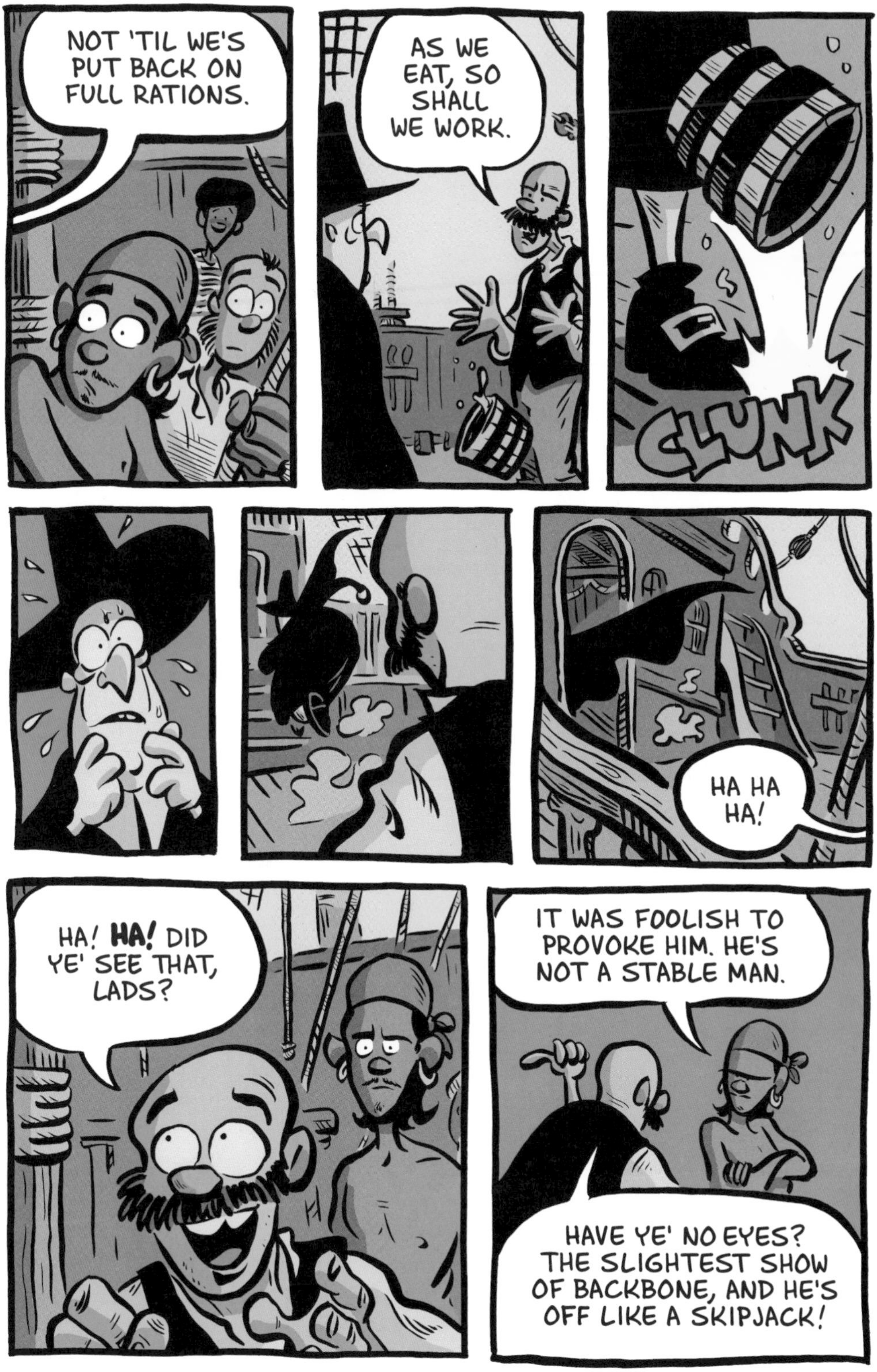
NOT 'TIL WE'S PUT BACK ON FULL RATIONS.
AS WE EAT, SO SHALL WE WORK.
CLUNK
HA HA HA!
HA! HA! DID YE' SEE THAT, LADS?
IT WAS FOOLISH TO PROVOKE HIM. HE'S NOT A STABLE MAN.
HAVE YE' NO EYES? THE SLIGHTEST SHOW OF BACKBONE, AND HE'S OFF LIKE A SKIPJACK!

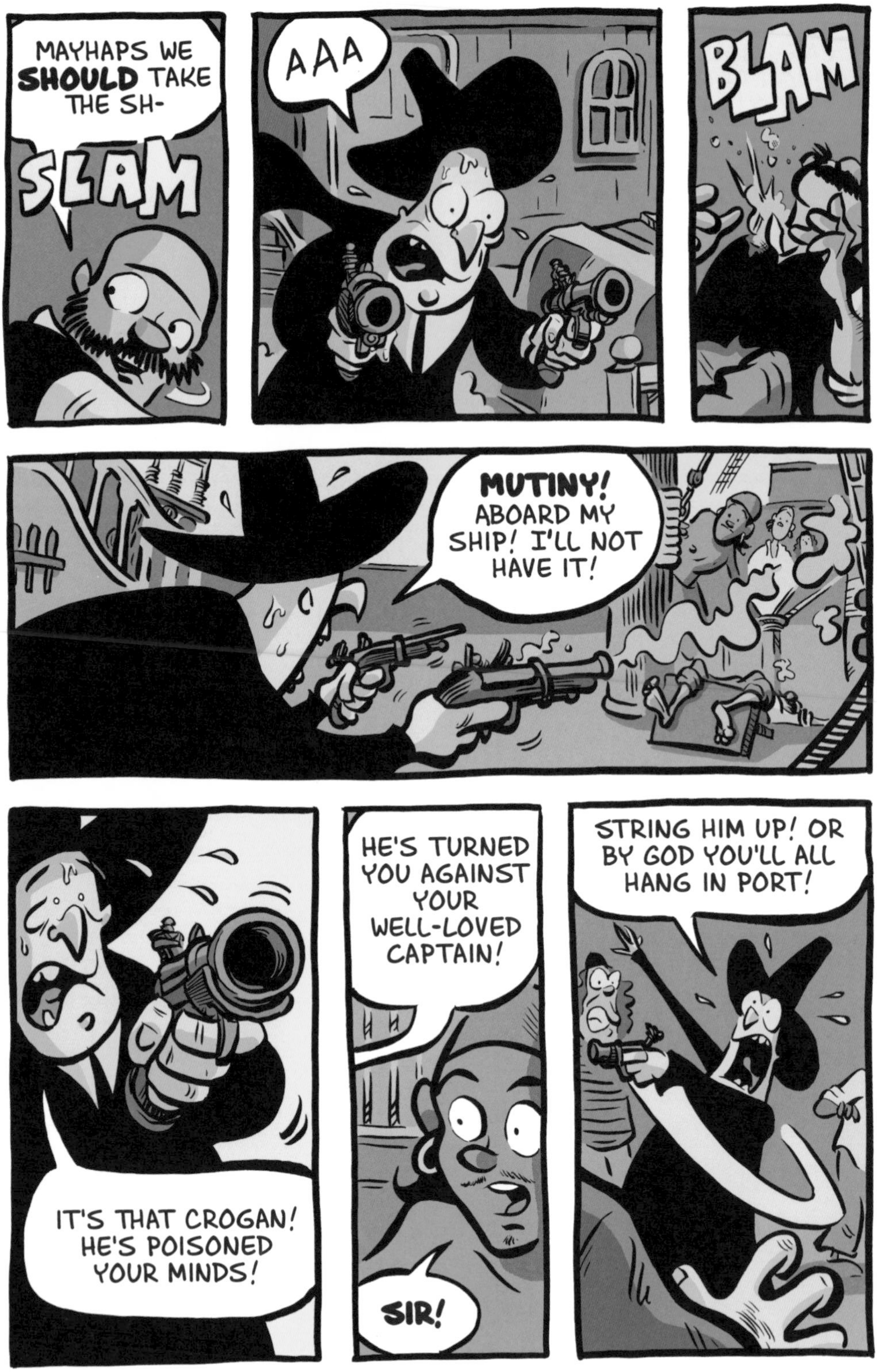
MAYHAPS WE SHOULD TAKE THE SH-
SLAM
AAA
BLAM
MUTINY! ABOARD MY SHIP! I'LL NOT HAVE IT!
IT'S THAT CROGAN! HE'S POISONED YOUR MINDS!
HE'S TURNED YOU AGAINST YOUR WELL-LOVED CAPTAIN!
SIR!
STRING HIM UP! OR BY GOD YOU'LL ALL HANG IN PORT!

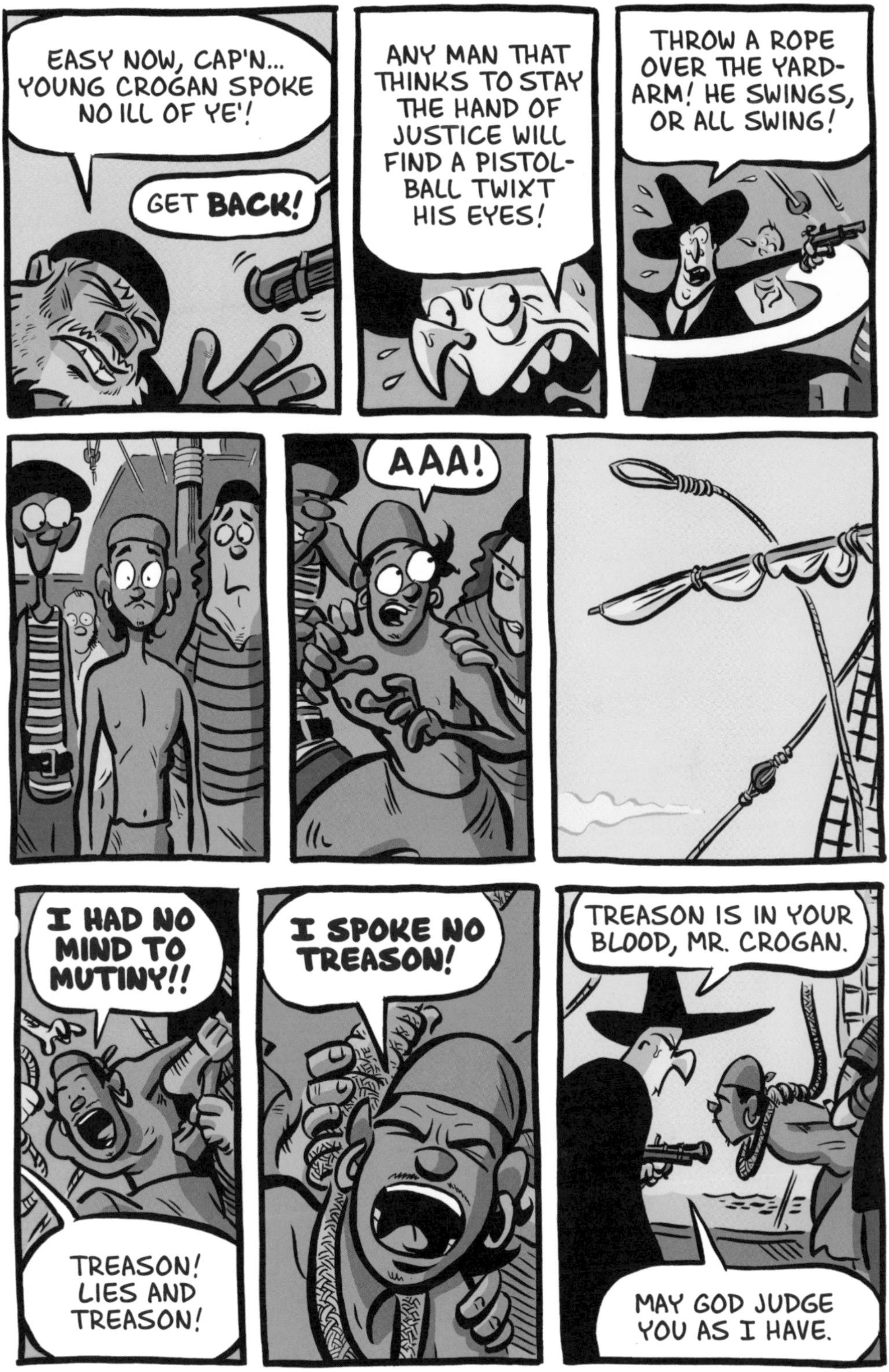
EASY NOW, CAP'N... YOUNG CROGAN SPOKE NO ILL OF YE'!
GET **BACK!**
ANY MAN THAT THINKS TO STAY THE HAND OF JUSTICE WILL FIND A PISTOL-BALL TWIXT HIS EYES!
THROW A ROPE OVER THE YARD-ARM! HE SWINGS, OR ALL SWING!
AAA!
I HAD NO MIND TO MUTINY!!
TREASON! LIES AND TREASON!
I SPOKE NO TREASON!
TREASON IS IN YOUR BLOOD, MR. CROGAN.
MAY GOD JUDGE YOU AS I HAVE.

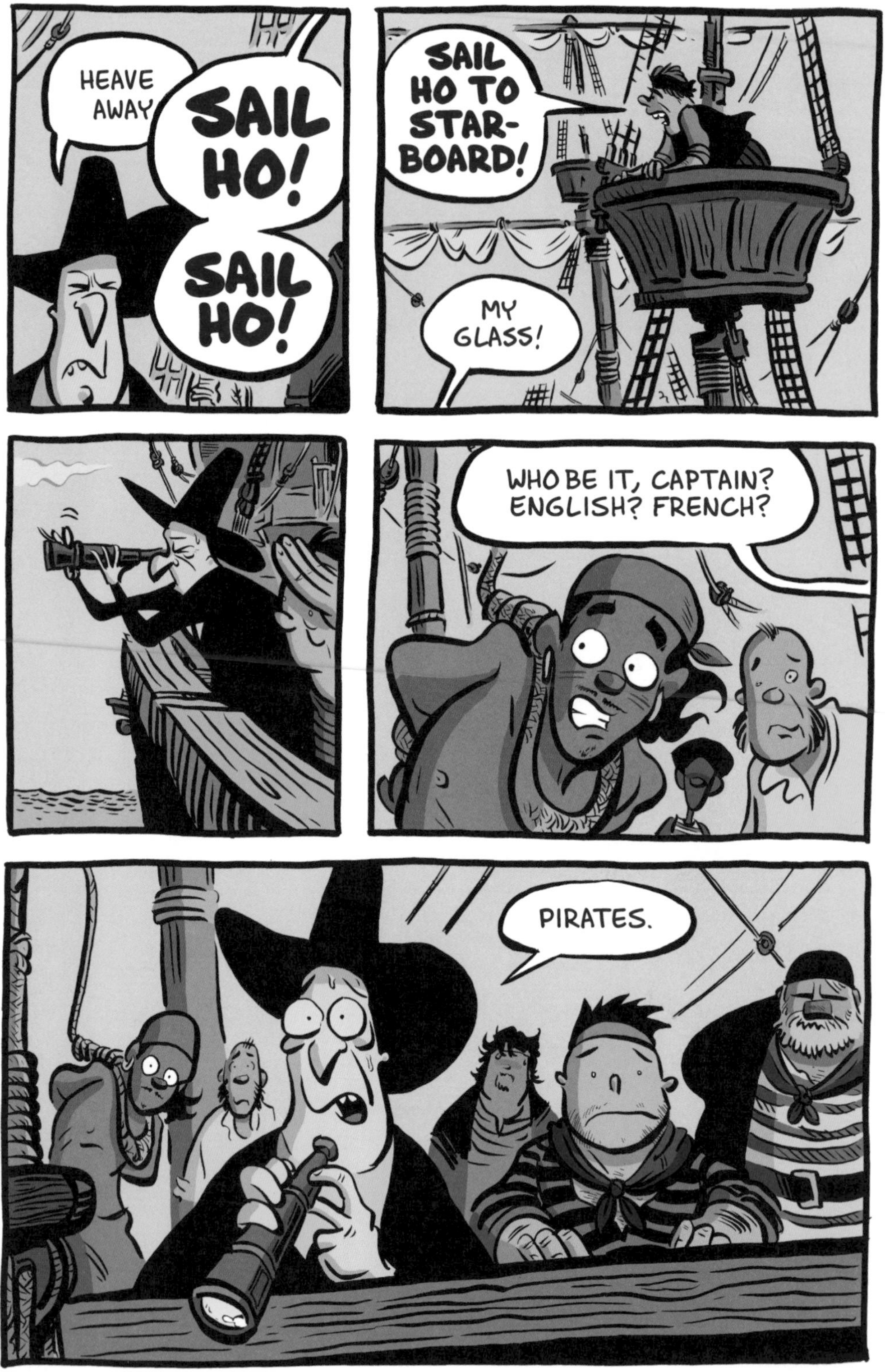
HEAVE AWAY
SAIL HO!
SAIL HO!
SAIL HO TO STAR-BOARD!
MY GLASS!
WHO BE IT, CAPTAIN? ENGLISH? FRENCH?
PIRATES.

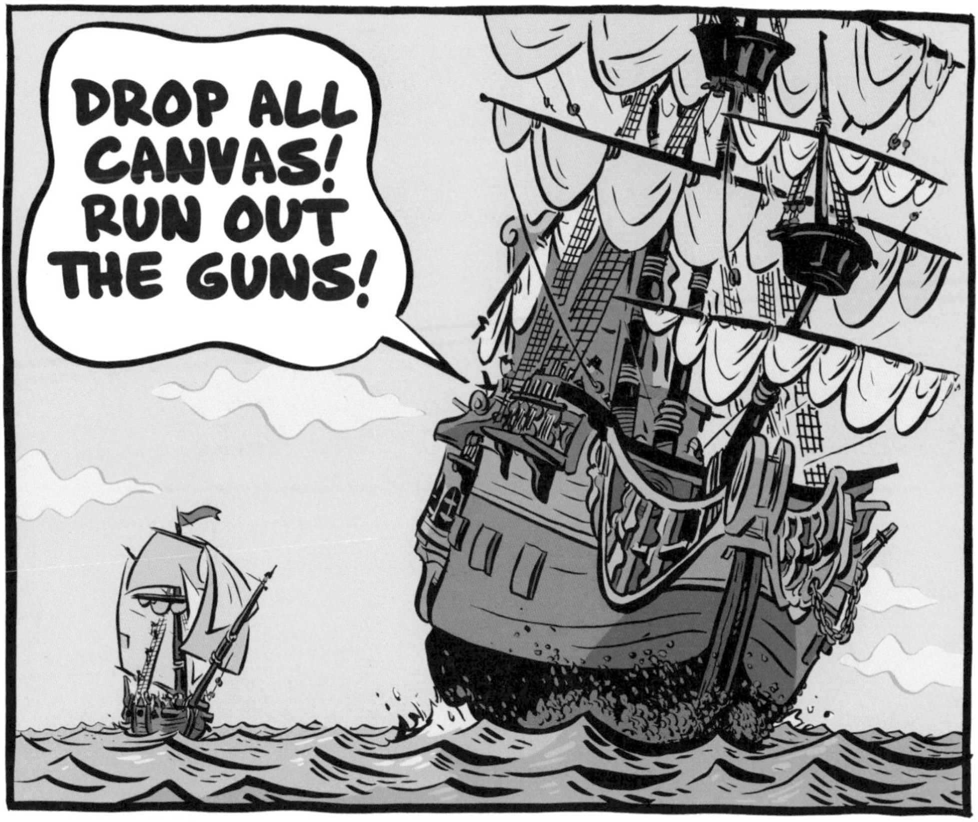
DROP ALL CANVAS! RUN OUT THE GUNS!

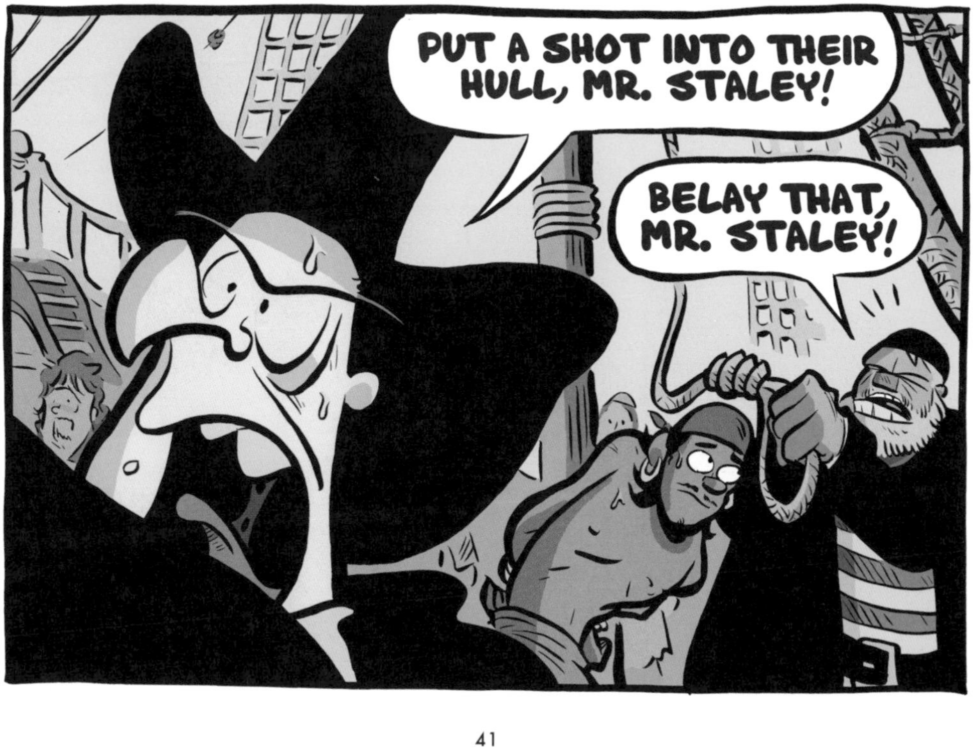
PUT A SHOT INTO THEIR HULL, MR. STALEY!
BELAY THAT, MR. STALEY!

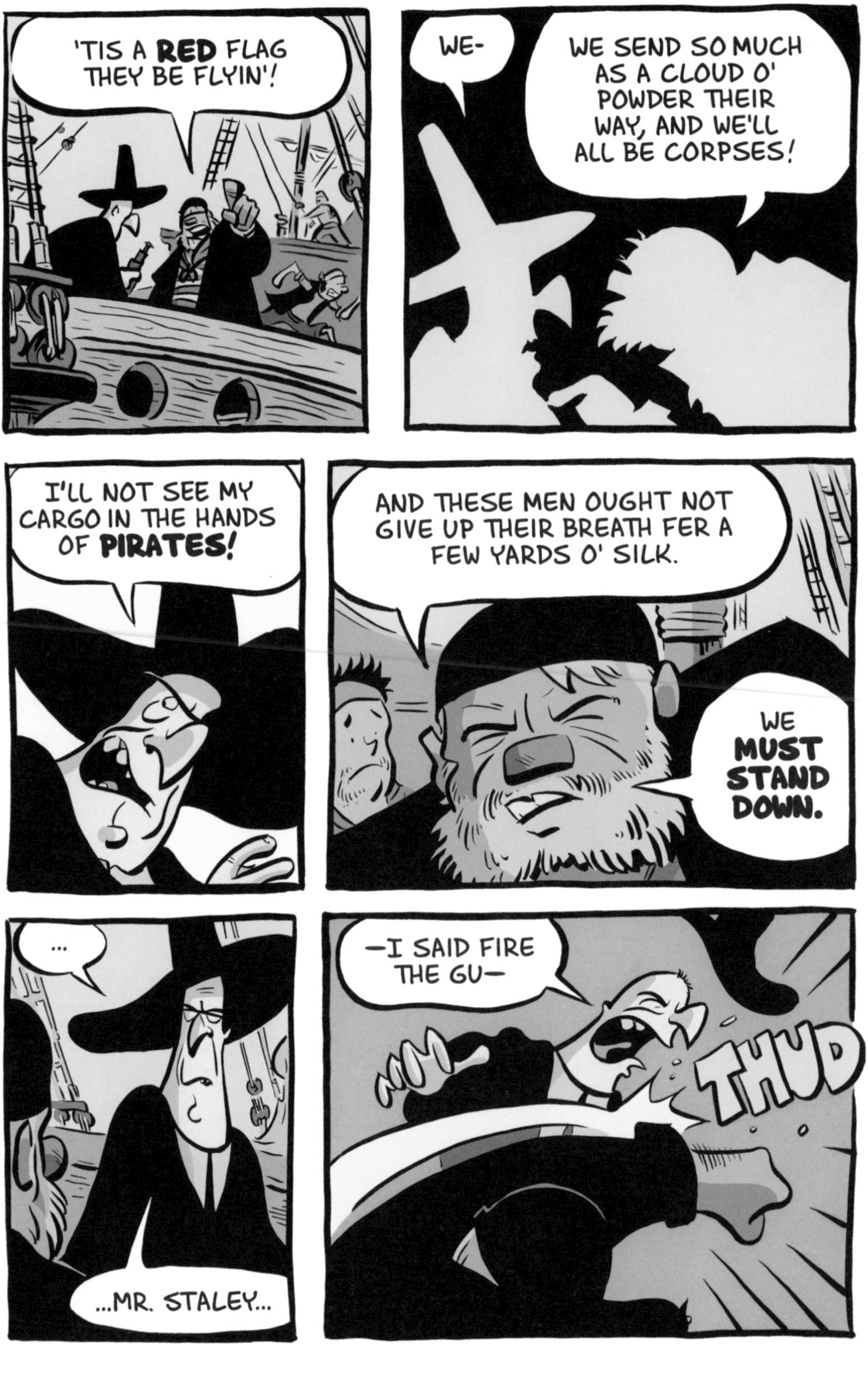
'TIS A **RED** FLAG THEY BE FLYIN'!
WE-
WE SEND SO MUCH AS A CLOUD O' POWDER THEIR WAY, AND WE'LL ALL BE CORPSES!
I'LL NOT SEE MY CARGO IN THE HANDS OF **PIRATES!**
AND THESE MEN OUGHT NOT GIVE UP THEIR BREATH FER A FEW YARDS O' SILK.
WE **MUST STAND DOWN.**
...
...MR. STALEY...
—I SAID FIRE THE GU—
THUD

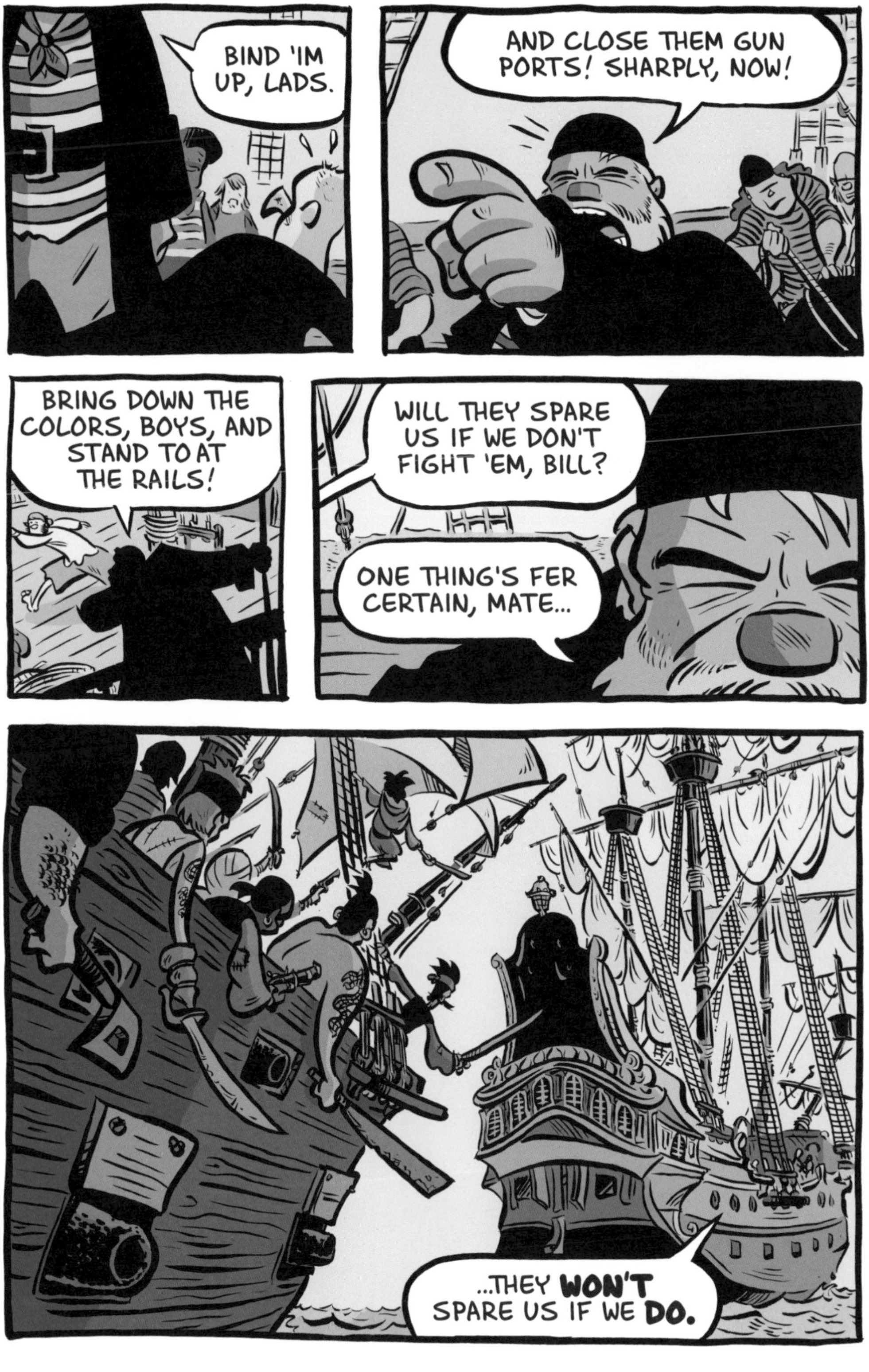
BIND 'IM UP, LADS.
AND CLOSE THEM GUN PORTS! SHARPLY, NOW!
BRING DOWN THE COLORS, BOYS, AND STAND TO AT THE RAILS!
WILL THEY SPARE US IF WE DON'T FIGHT 'EM, BILL?
ONE THING'S FER CERTAIN, MATE...
...THEY **WON'T** SPARE US IF WE **DO.**

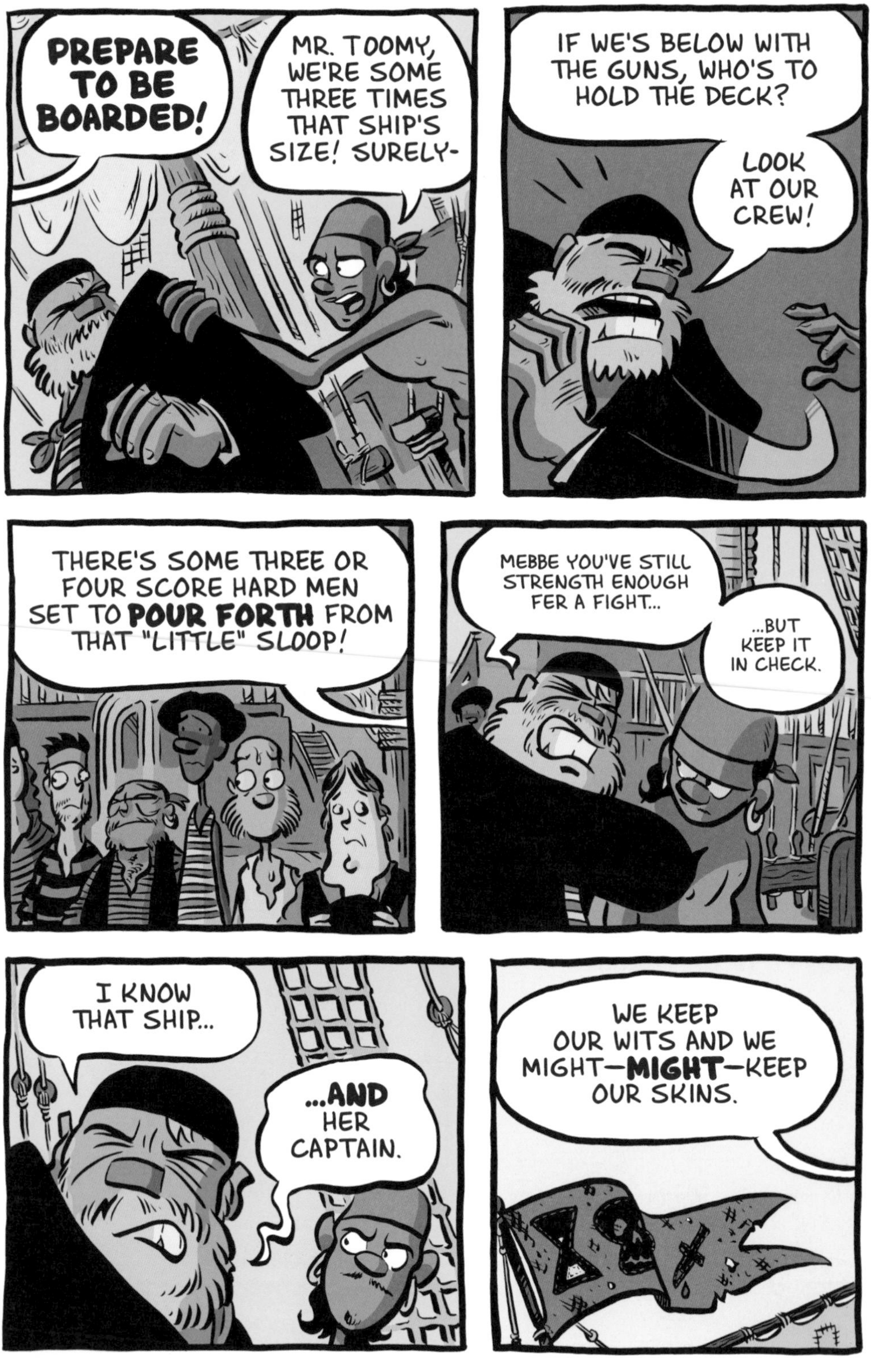
PREPARE TO BE BOARDED!
MR. TOOMY, WE'RE SOME THREE TIMES THAT SHIP'S SIZE! SURELY-
IF WE'S BELOW WITH THE GUNS, WHO'S TO HOLD THE DECK?
LOOK AT OUR CREW!
THERE'S SOME THREE OR FOUR SCORE HARD MEN SET TO POUR FORTH FROM THAT "LITTLE" SLOOP!
MEBBE YOU'VE STILL STRENGTH ENOUGH FER A FIGHT...
...BUT KEEP IT IN CHECK.
I KNOW THAT SHIP...
...AND HER CAPTAIN.
WE KEEP OUR WITS AND WE MIGHT—MIGHT—KEEP OUR SKINS.

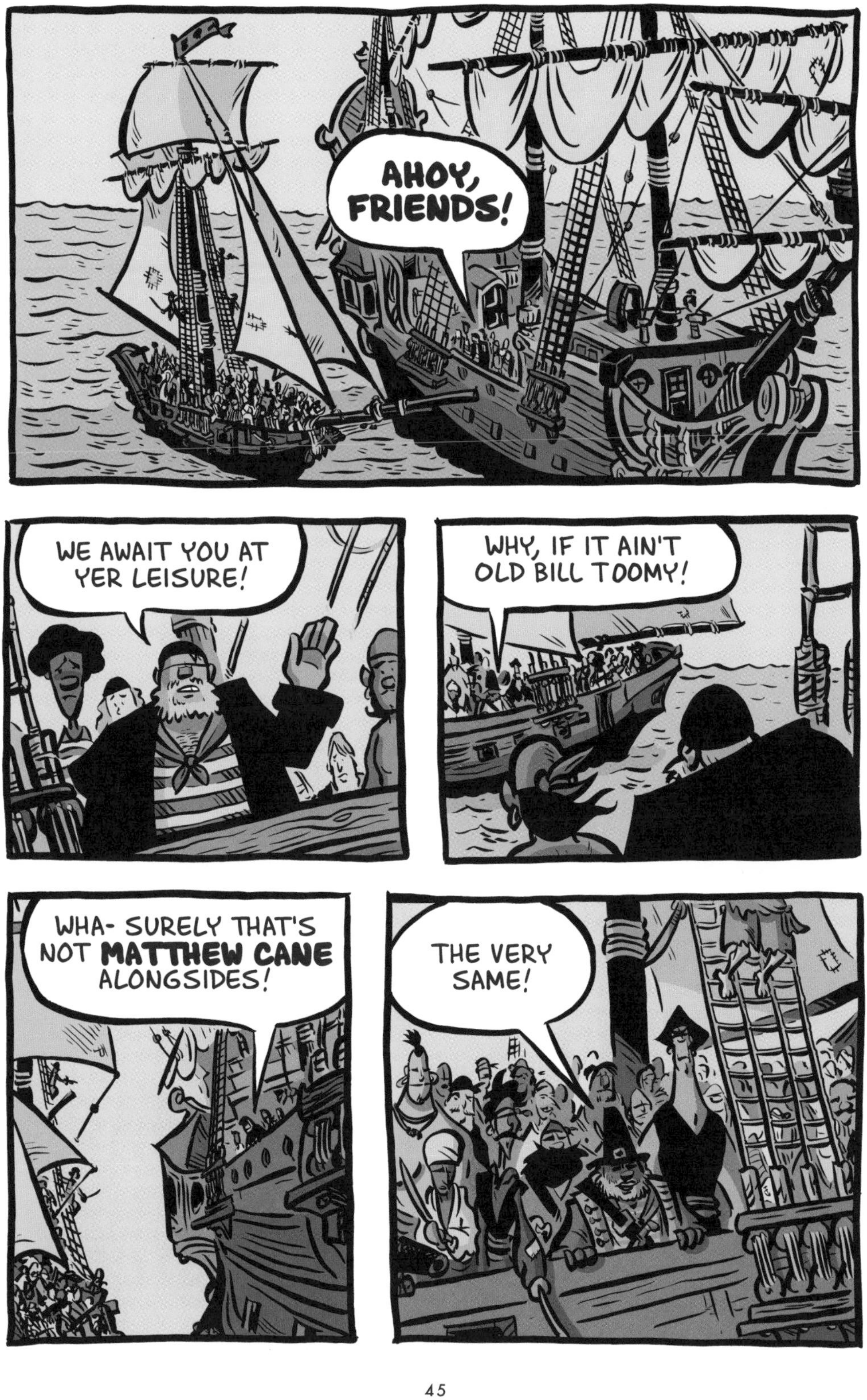
AHOY, FRIENDS!
WE AWAIT YOU AT YER LEISURE!
WHY, IF IT AIN'T OLD BILL TOOMY!
WHA- SURELY THAT'S NOT **MATTHEW CANE** ALONGSIDES!
THE VERY SAME!

WELL, SHIVER MY SIDES! **HA!**

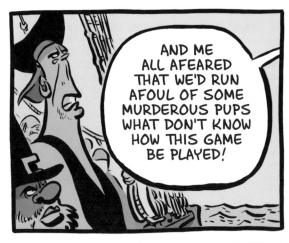

AND ME ALL AFEARED THAT WE'D RUN AFOUL OF SOME MURDEROUS PUPS WHAT DON'T KNOW HOW THIS GAME BE PLAYED!

ARE YER MEN GONNA BE TROUBLE, BILLY?

HEAVENS, NO!

EACH MAN HERE...

..SAVE OUR ERSTWHILE CAP'N..

...IS KEEN TO GO ON THE ACCOUNT!

BEST BE NO SKULLDUGGERY HERE, BILL. I'LL CUT YOU DOWN AS I WOULD A PIG.

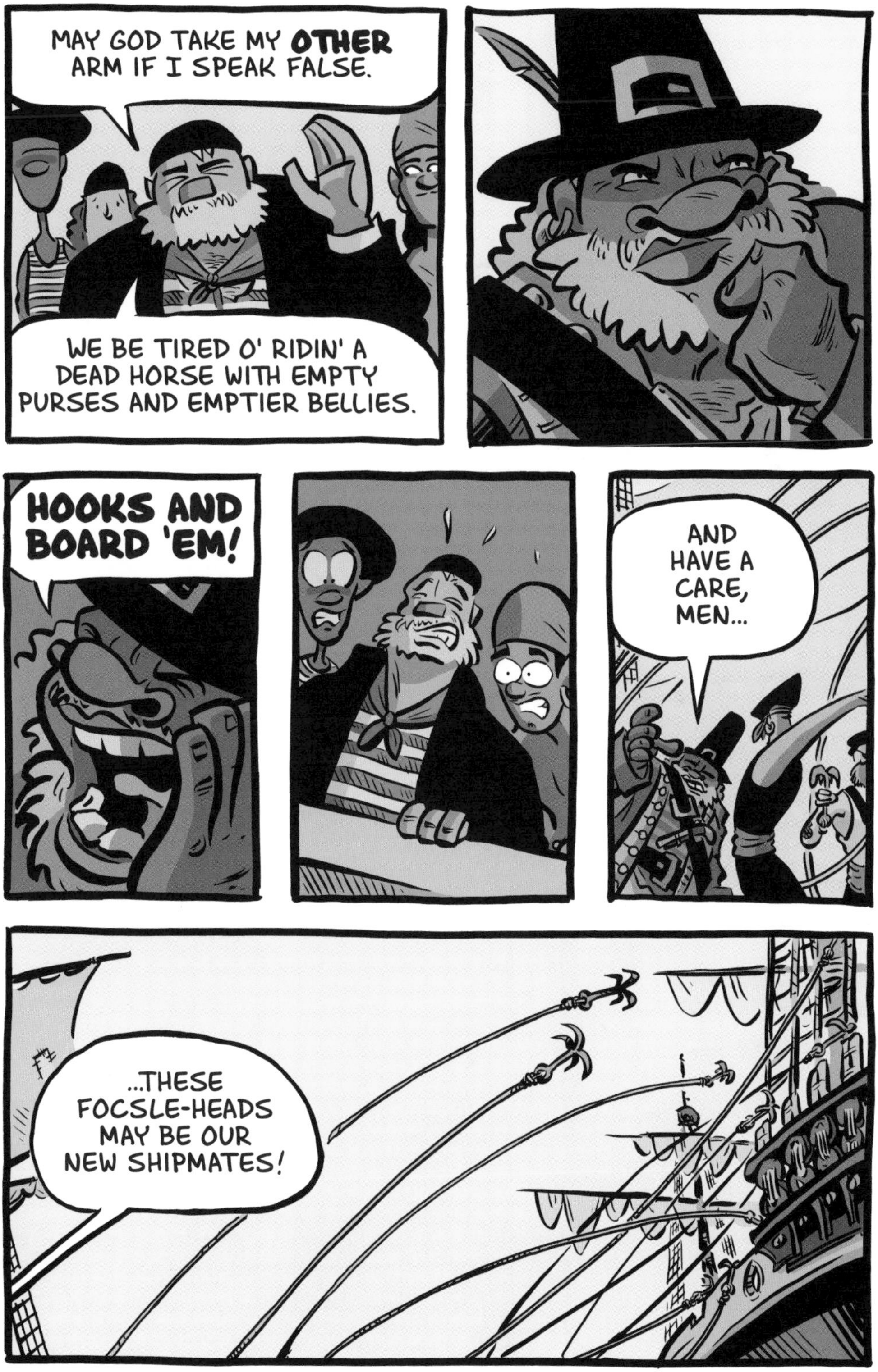
MAY GOD TAKE MY **OTHER** ARM IF I SPEAK FALSE.
WE BE TIRED O' RIDIN' A DEAD HORSE WITH EMPTY PURSES AND EMPTIER BELLIES.
HOOKS AND BOARD 'EM!
AND HAVE A CARE, MEN...
...THESE FOCSLE-HEADS MAY BE OUR NEW SHIPMATES!

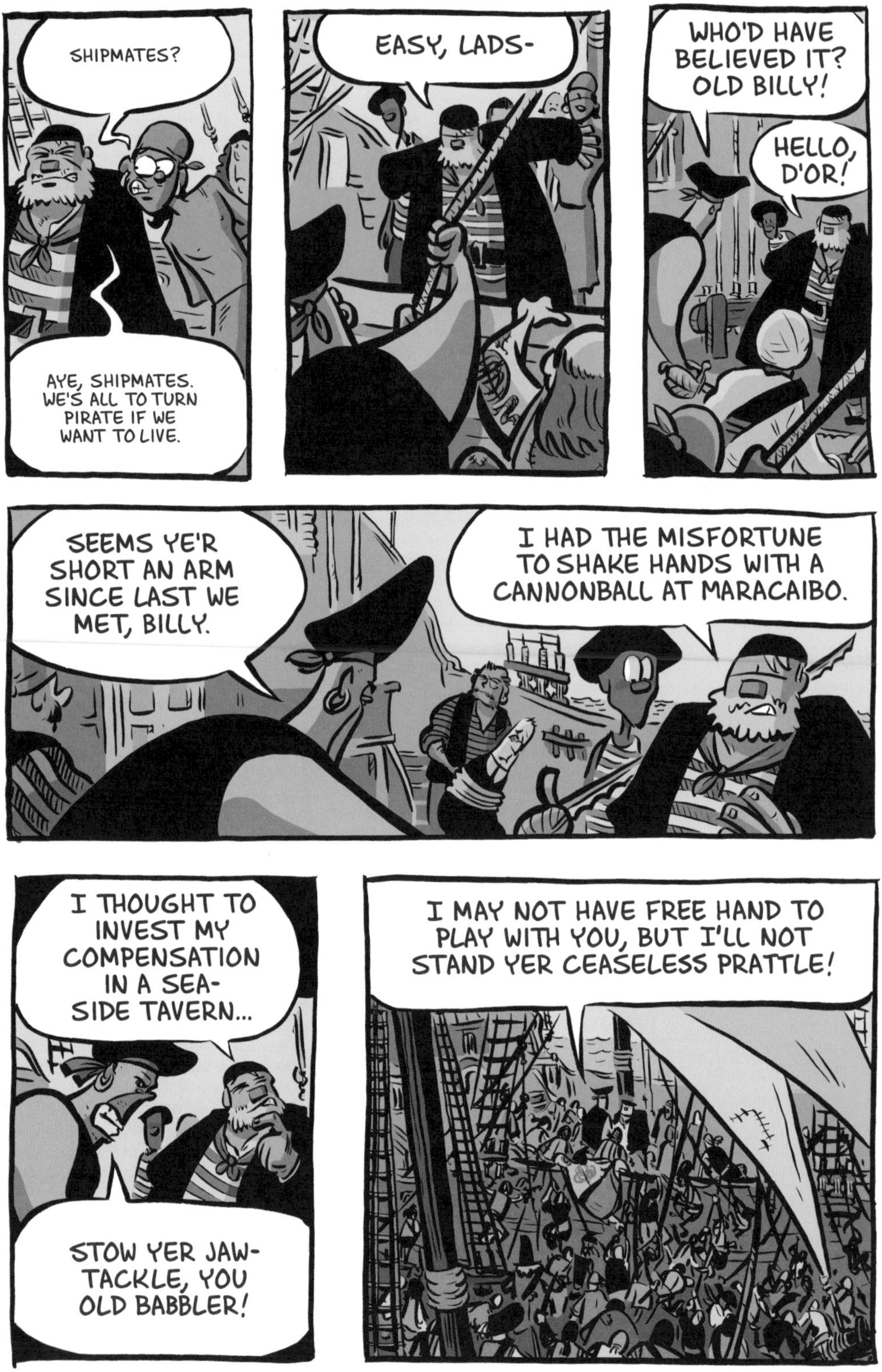
SHIPMATES?
AYE, SHIPMATES. WE'S ALL TO TURN PIRATE IF WE WANT TO LIVE.
EASY, LADS-
WHO'D HAVE BELIEVED IT? OLD BILLY!
HELLO, D'OR!
SEEMS YE'R SHORT AN ARM SINCE LAST WE MET, BILLY.
I HAD THE MISFORTUNE TO SHAKE HANDS WITH A CANNONBALL AT MARACAIBO.
I THOUGHT TO INVEST MY COMPENSATION IN A SEA-SIDE TAVERN...
STOW YER JAW-TACKLE, YOU OLD BABBLER!
I MAY NOT HAVE FREE HAND TO PLAY WITH YOU, BUT I'LL NOT STAND YER CEASELESS PRATTLE!

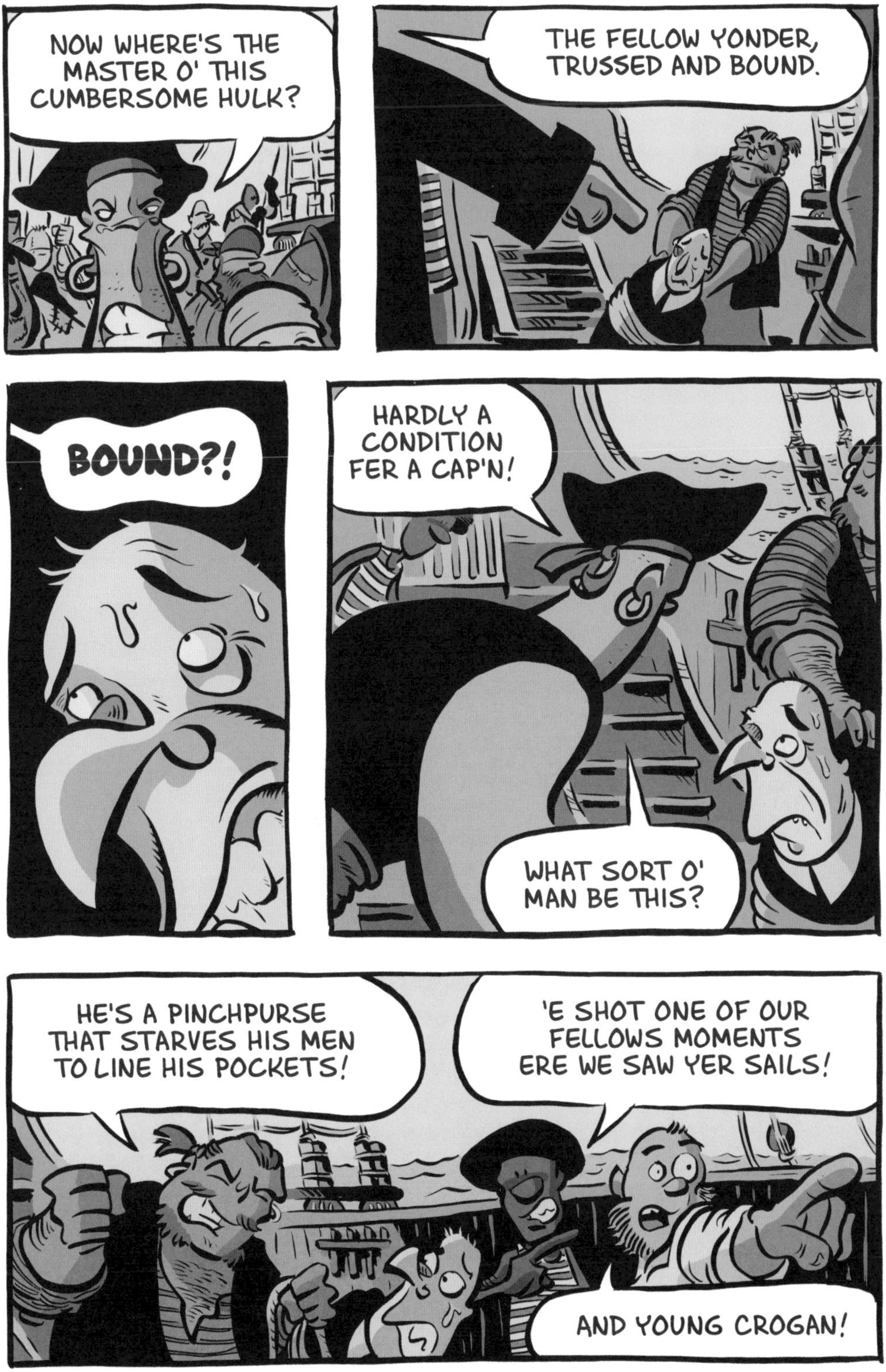
NOW WHERE'S THE MASTER O' THIS CUMBERSOME HULK?
THE FELLOW YONDER, TRUSSED AND BOUND.
BOUND?!
HARDLY A CONDITION FER A CAP'N!
WHAT SORT O' MAN BE THIS?
HE'S A PINCHPURSE THAT STARVES HIS MEN TO LINE HIS POCKETS!
'E SHOT ONE OF OUR FELLOWS MOMENTS ERE WE SAW YER SAILS!
AND YOUNG CROGAN!

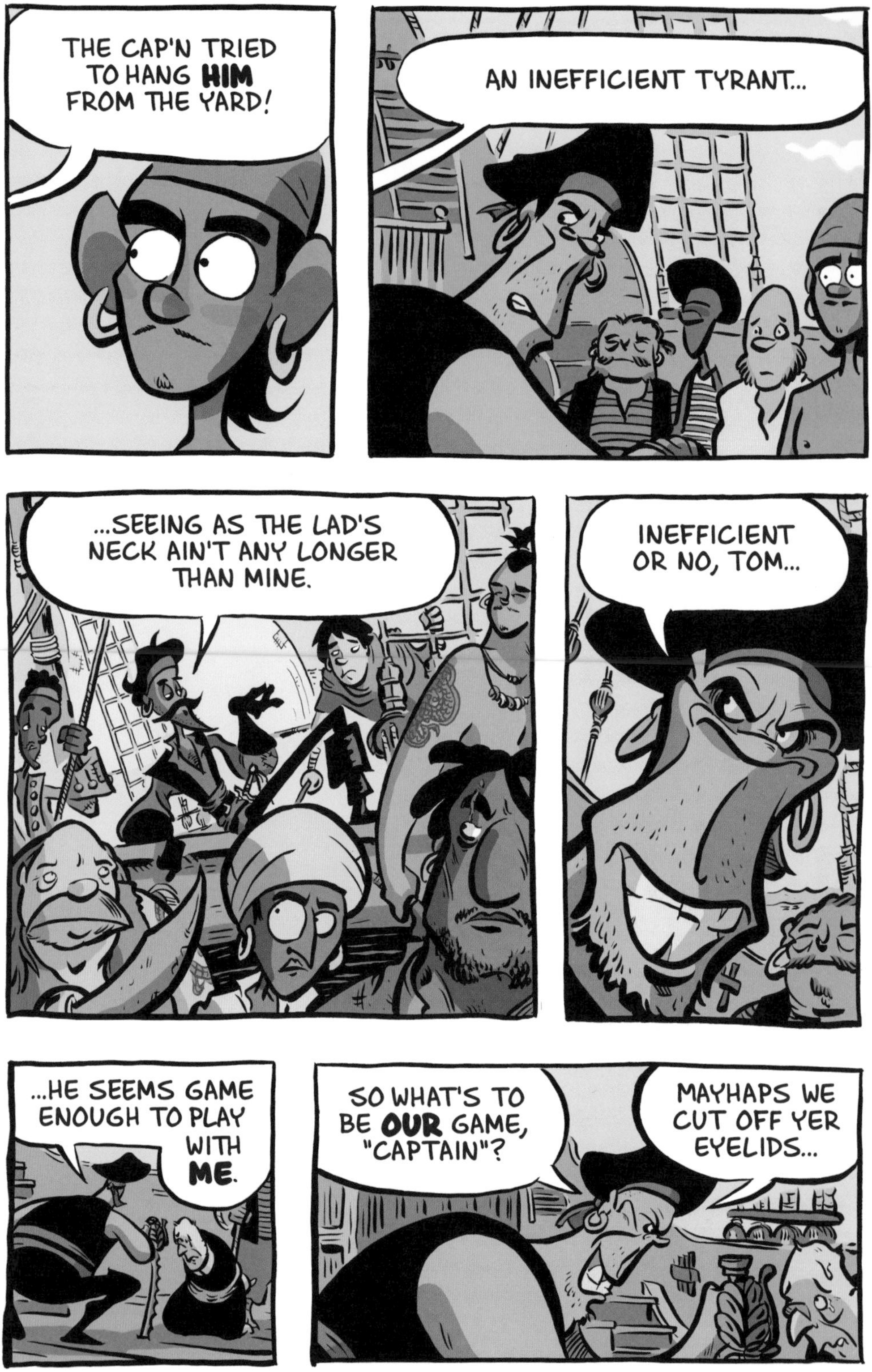
THE CAP'N TRIED TO HANG **HIM** FROM THE YARD!
AN INEFFICIENT TYRANT...
...SEEING AS THE LAD'S NECK AIN'T ANY LONGER THAN MINE.
INEFFICIENT OR NO, TOM...
...HE SEEMS GAME ENOUGH TO PLAY WITH **ME**.
SO WHAT'S TO BE **OUR** GAME, "CAPTAIN"?
MAYHAPS WE CUT OFF YER EYELIDS...

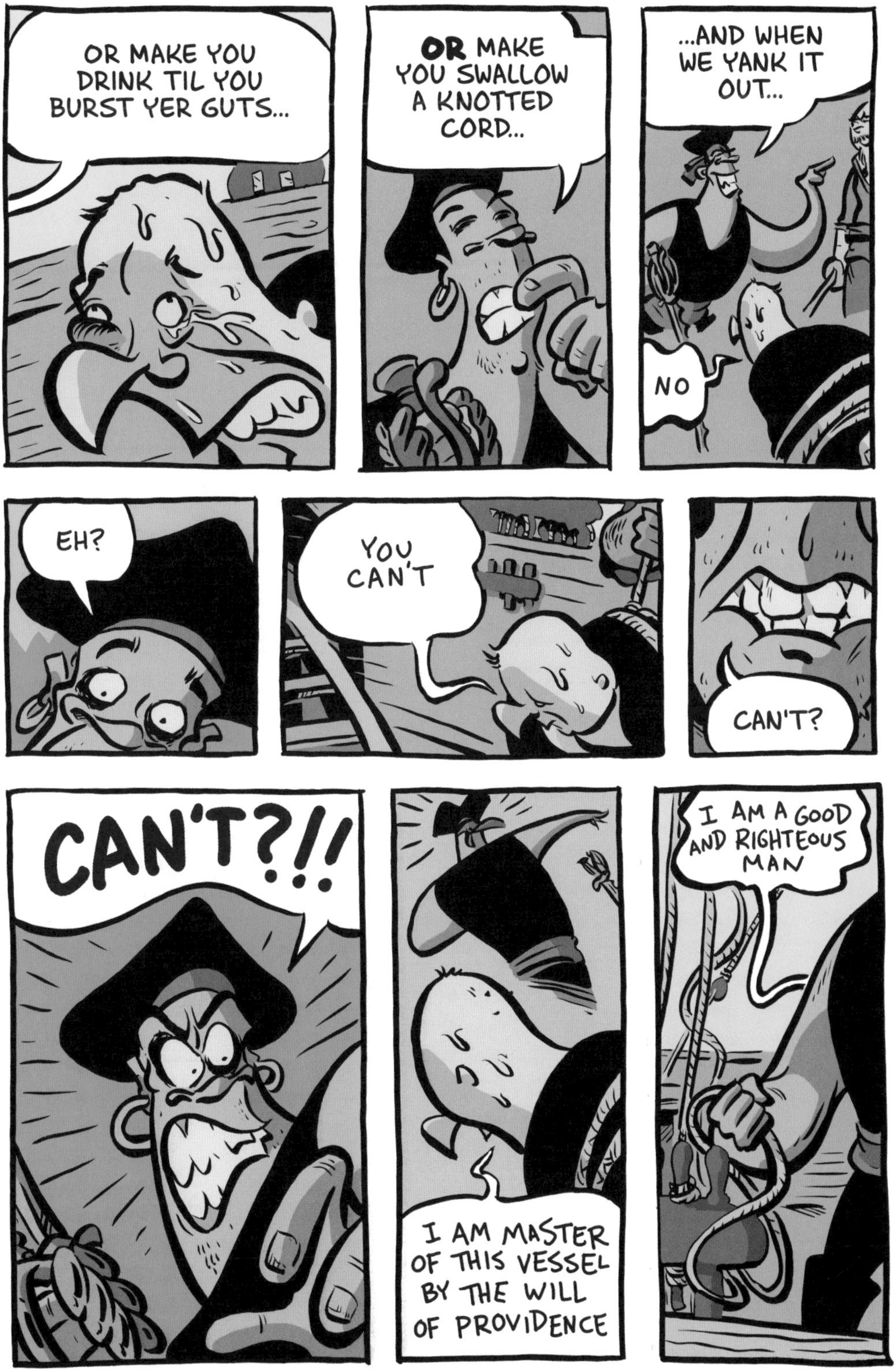
OR MAKE YOU DRINK TIL YOU BURST YER GUTS...
OR MAKE YOU SWALLOW A KNOTTED CORD...
...AND WHEN WE YANK IT OUT...
NO
EH?
YOU CAN'T
CAN'T?
CAN'T?!!
I AM MASTER OF THIS VESSEL BY THE WILL OF PROVIDENCE
I AM A GOOD AND RIGHTEOUS MAN

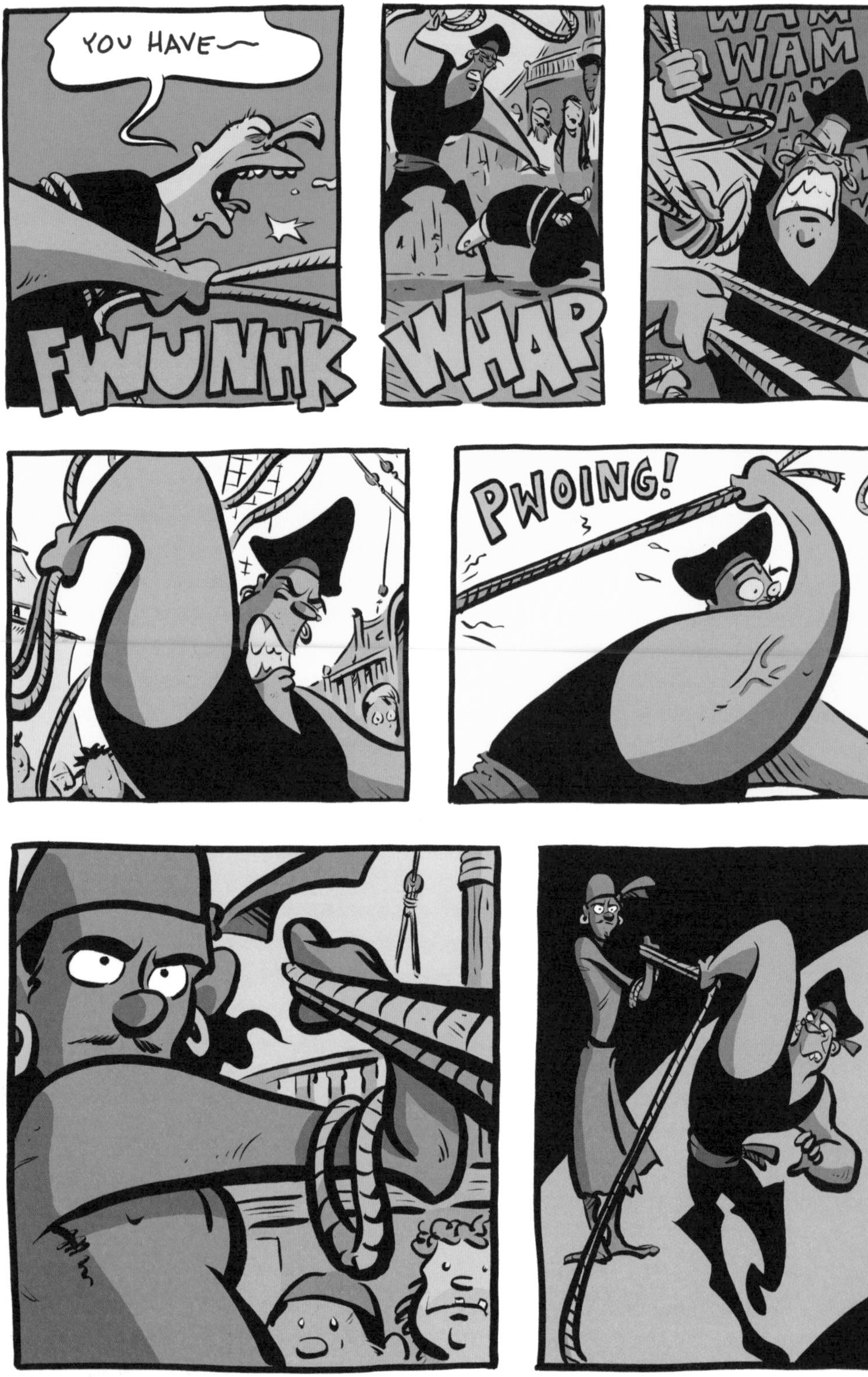
YOU HAVE—
FWUNHK
WHAP
WAM
PWOING!

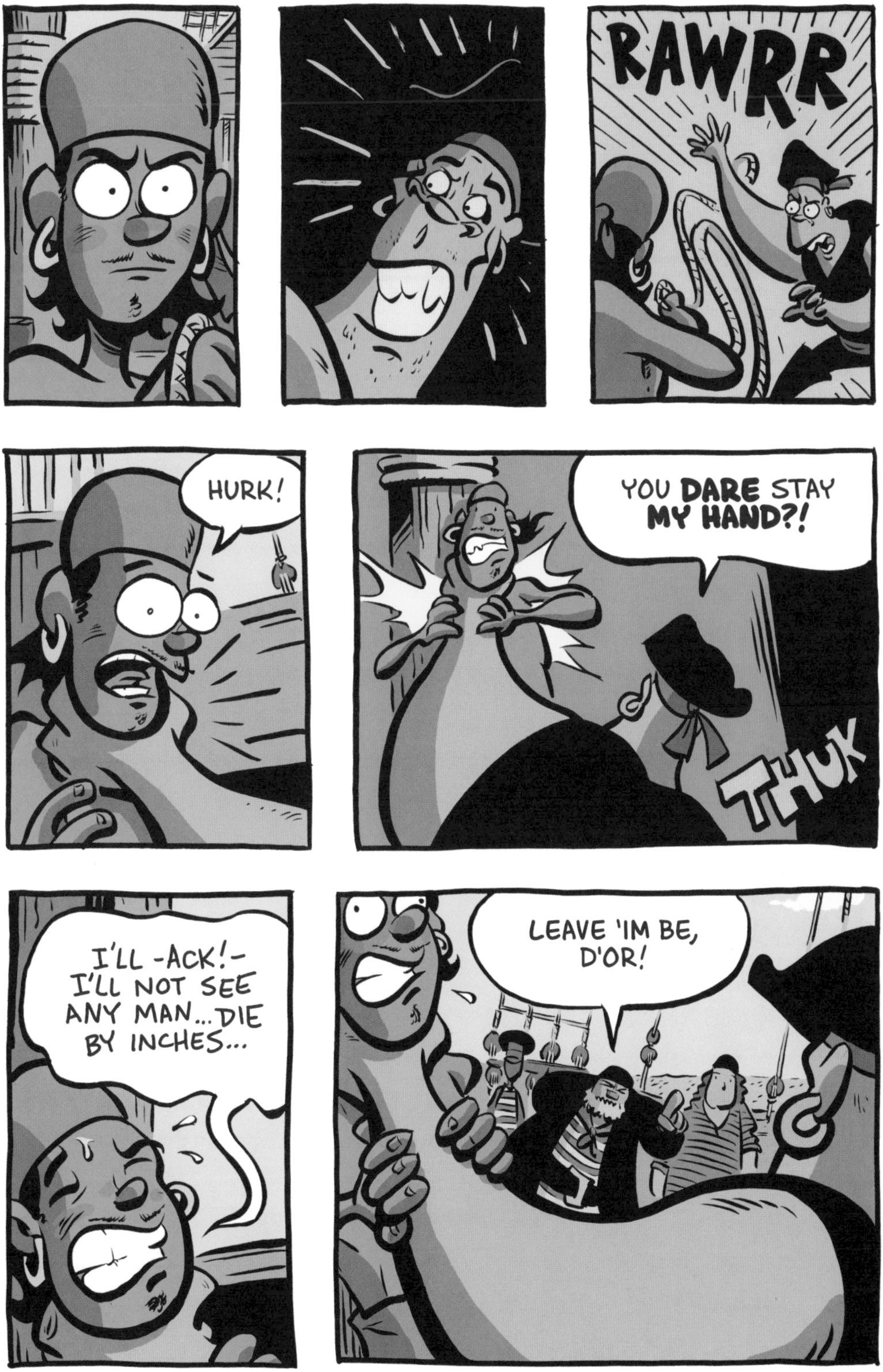
RAWRR
HURK!
YOU DARE STAY MY HAND?!
THUK
I'LL -ACK!- I'LL NOT SEE ANY MAN... DIE BY INCHES...
LEAVE 'IM BE, D'OR!

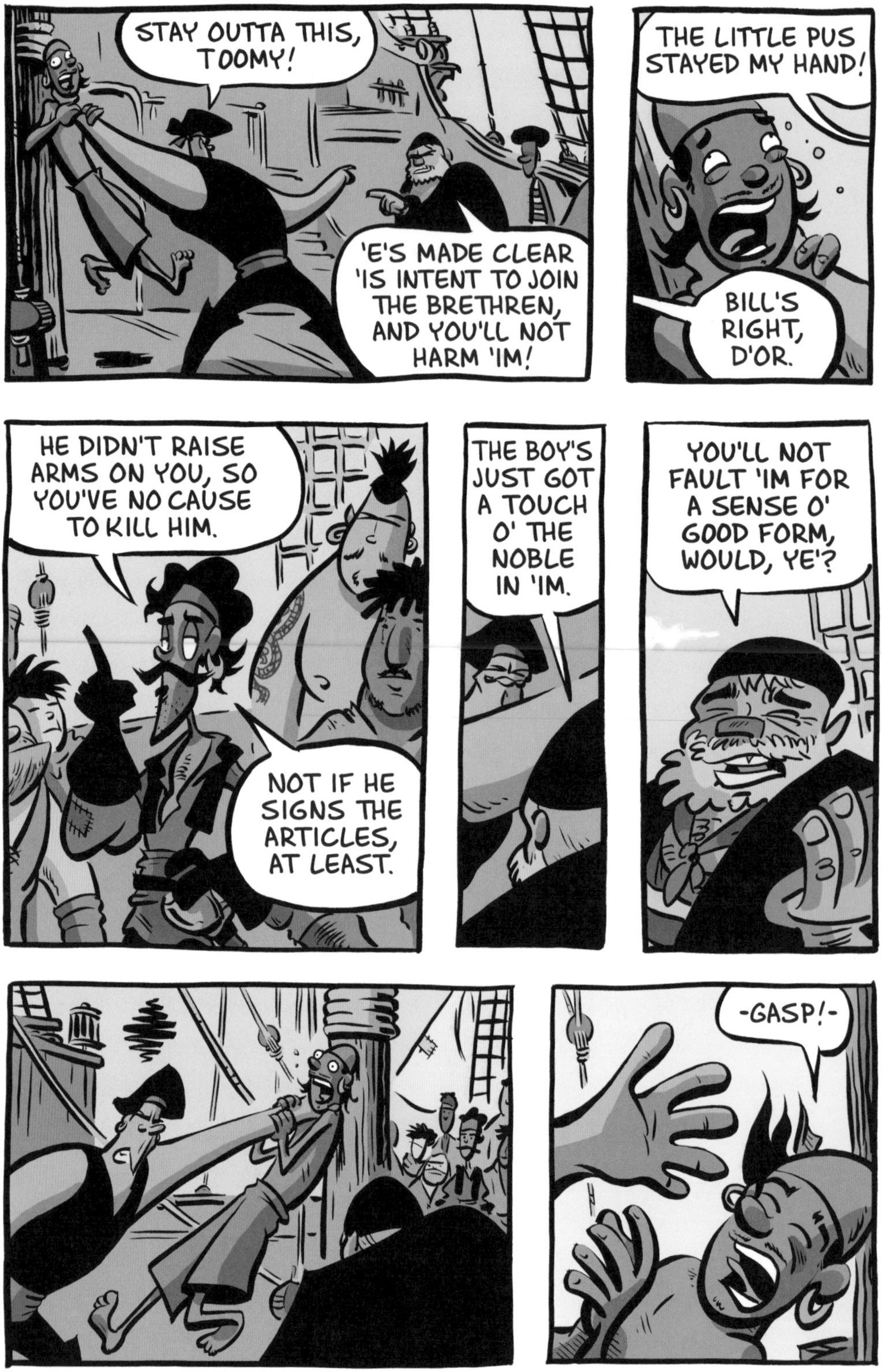
STAY OUTTA THIS, TOOMY!
'E'S MADE CLEAR 'IS INTENT TO JOIN THE BRETHREN, AND YOU'LL NOT HARM 'IM!
THE LITTLE PUS STAYED MY HAND!
BILL'S RIGHT, D'OR.
HE DIDN'T RAISE ARMS ON YOU, SO YOU'VE NO CAUSE TO KILL HIM.
NOT IF HE SIGNS THE ARTICLES, AT LEAST.
THE BOY'S JUST GOT A TOUCH O' THE NOBLE IN 'IM.
YOU'LL NOT FAULT 'IM FOR A SENSE O' GOOD FORM, WOULD, YE'?
-GASP!-

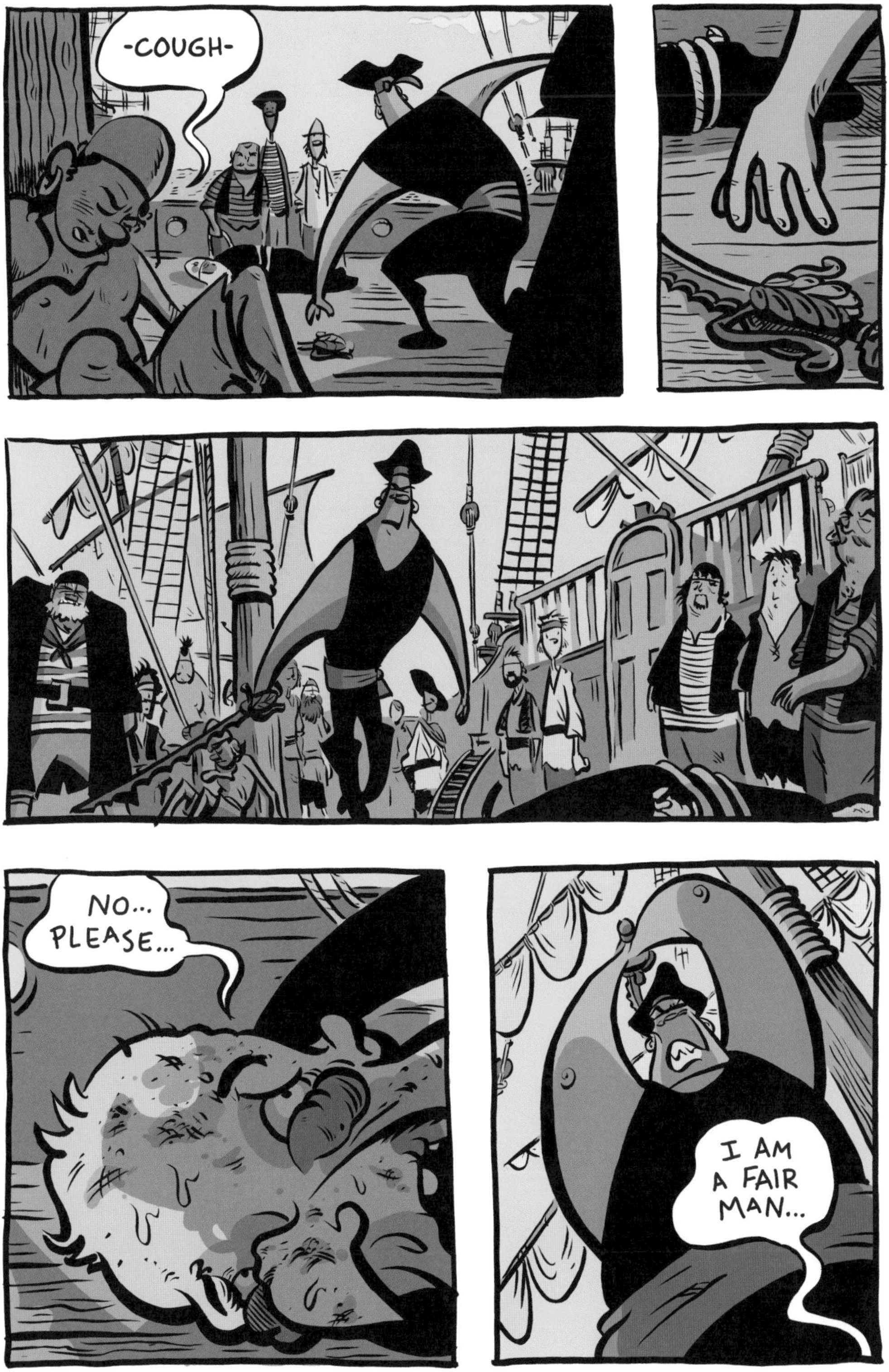
-COUGH-
NO... PLEASE...
I AM A FAIR MAN...

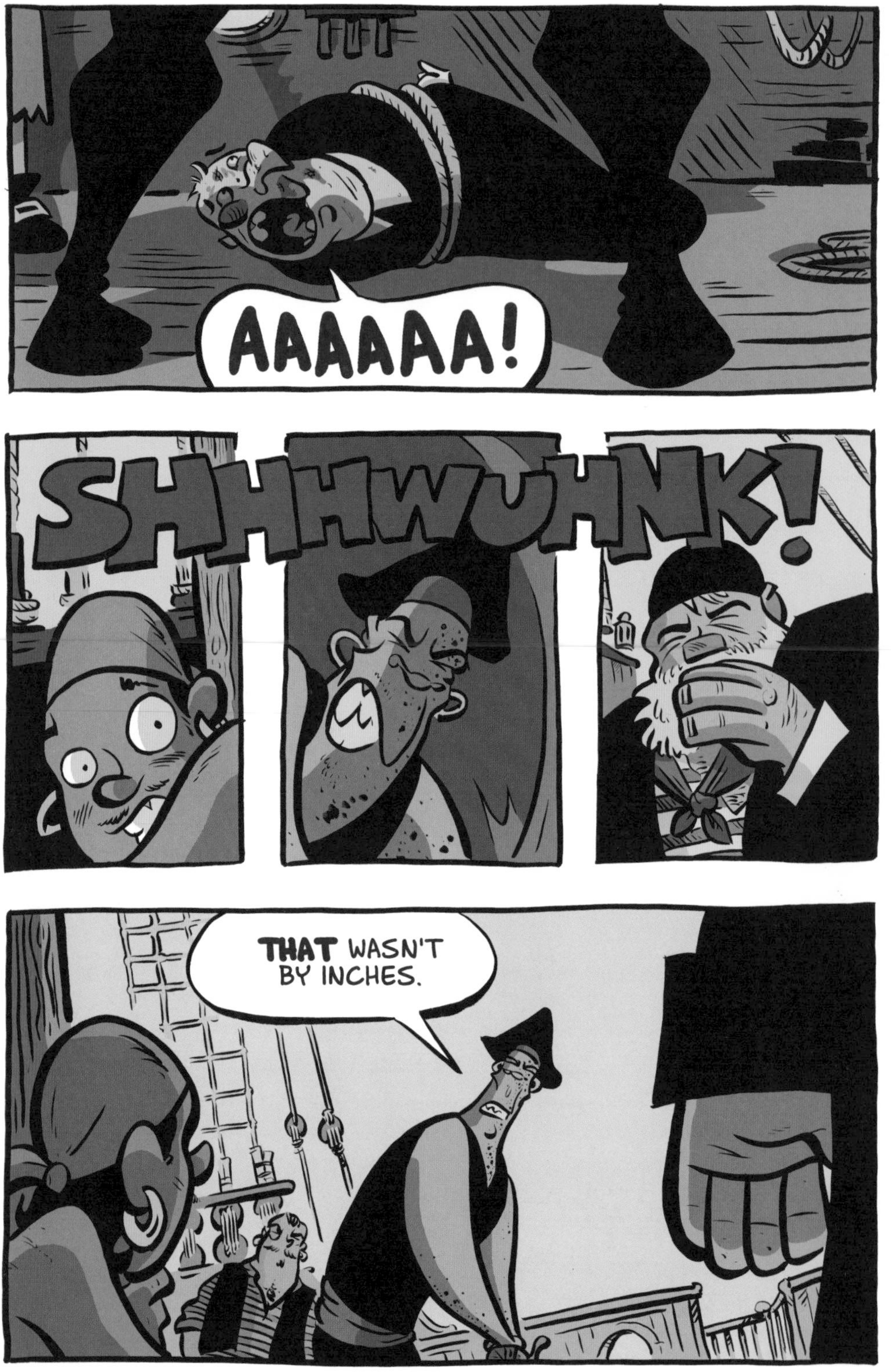
AAAAAA!
SHHHWUHNK!
THAT WASN'T BY INCHES.

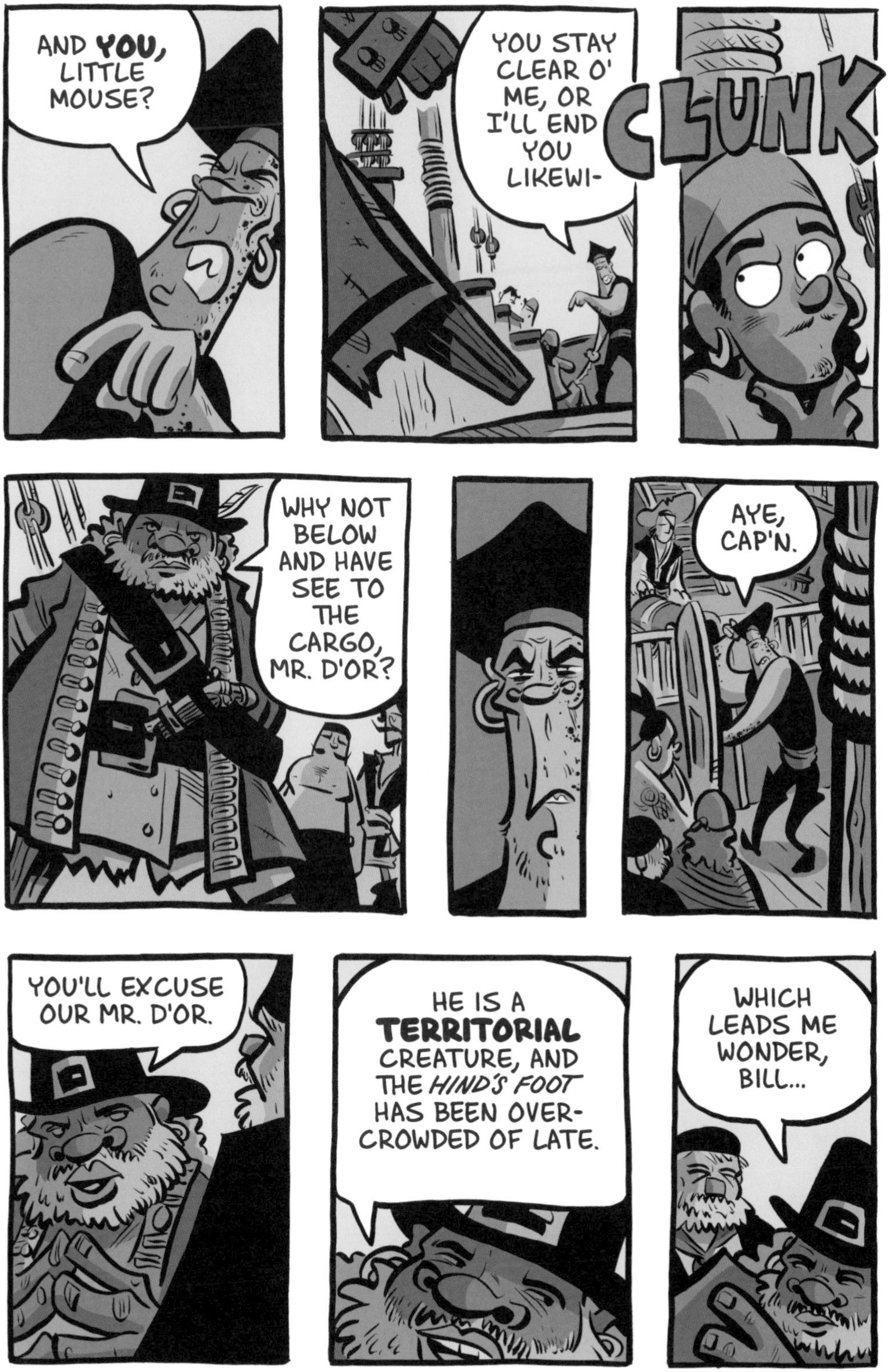

AND **YOU**, LITTLE MOUSE?
YOU STAY CLEAR O' ME, OR I'LL END YOU LIKEWI-
CLUNK
WHY NOT BELOW AND HAVE SEE TO THE CARGO, MR. D'OR?
AYE, CAP'N.
YOU'LL EXCUSE OUR MR. D'OR.
HE IS A **TERRITORIAL** CREATURE, AND THE *HIND'S FOOT* HAS BEEN OVER-CROWDED OF LATE.
WHICH LEADS ME WONDER, BILL...

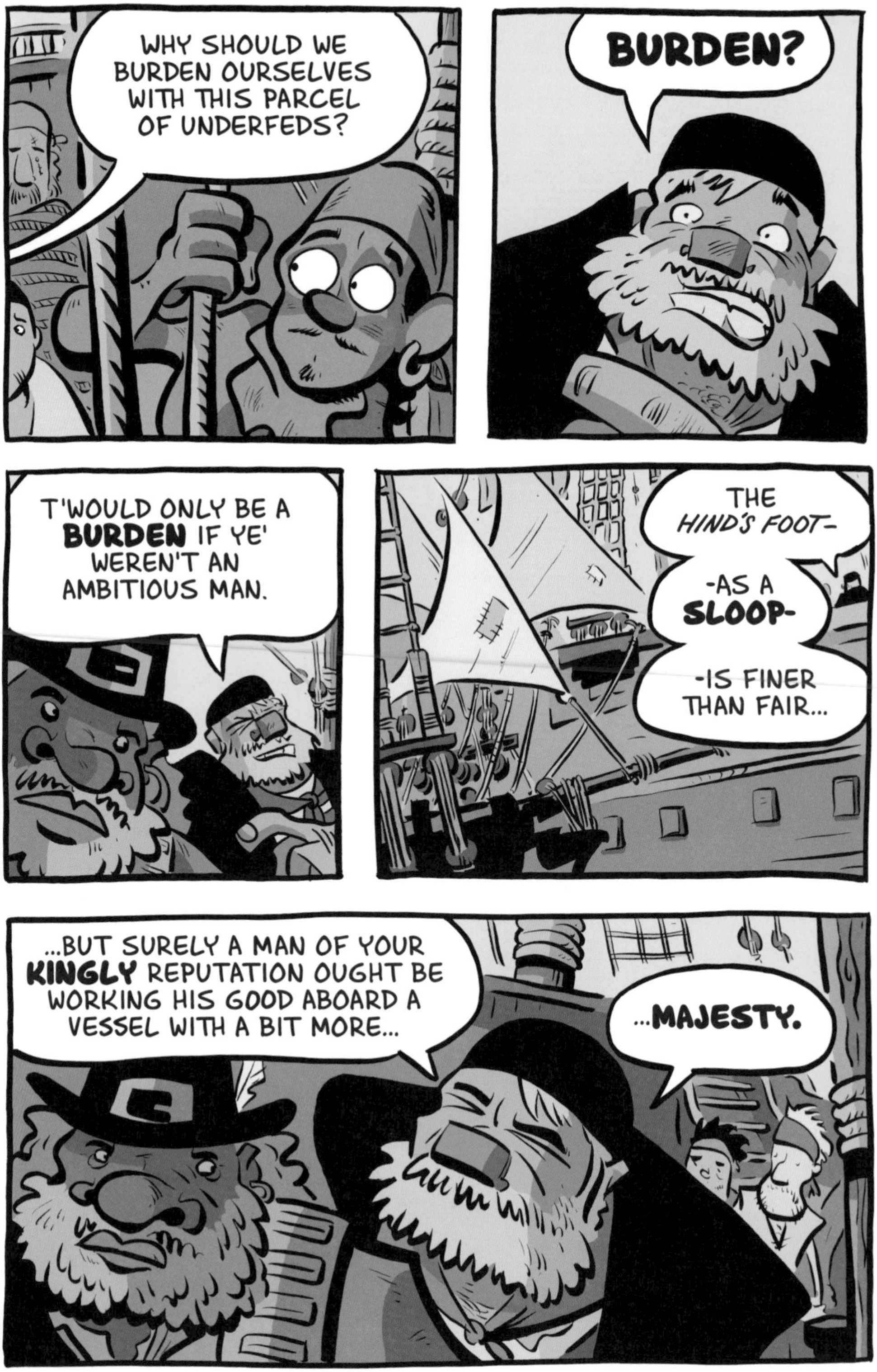
WHY SHOULD WE BURDEN OURSELVES WITH THIS PARCEL OF UNDERFEDS?
BURDEN?
T'WOULD ONLY BE A BURDEN IF YE' WEREN'T AN AMBITIOUS MAN.
THE HIND'S FOOT-
-AS A SLOOP-
-IS FINER THAN FAIR...
...BUT SURELY A MAN OF YOUR KINGLY REPUTATION OUGHT BE WORKING HIS GOOD ABOARD A VESSEL WITH A BIT MORE...
...MAJESTY.

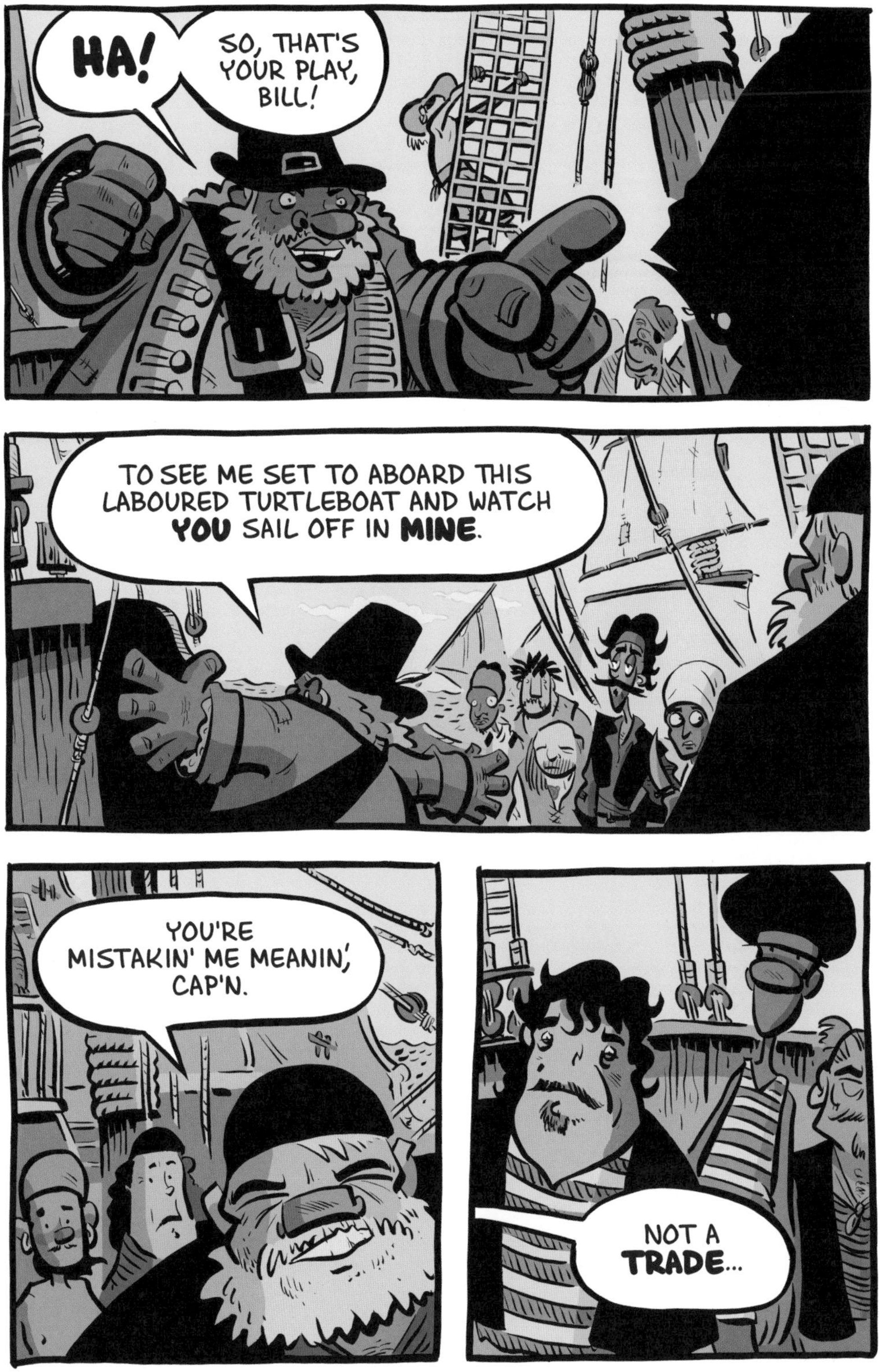
HA!
SO, THAT'S YOUR PLAY, BILL!
TO SEE ME SET TO ABOARD THIS LABOURED TURTLEBOAT AND WATCH **YOU** SAIL OFF IN **MINE**.
YOU'RE MISTAKIN' ME MEANIN', CAP'N.
NOT A **TRADE**...

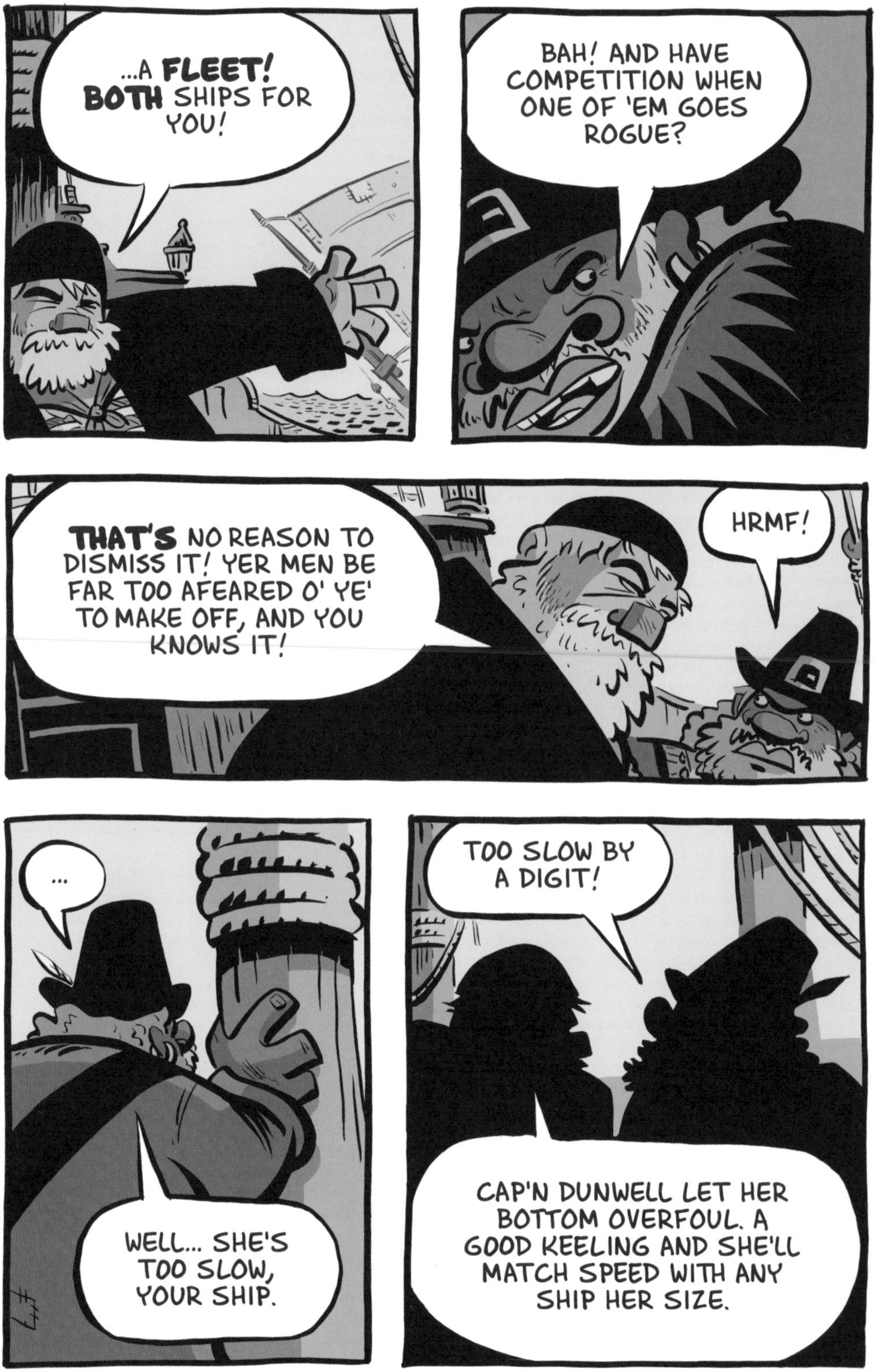
...A **FLEET!** **BOTH** SHIPS FOR YOU!
BAH! AND HAVE COMPETITION WHEN ONE OF 'EM GOES ROGUE?
THAT'S NO REASON TO DISMISS IT! YER MEN BE FAR TOO AFEARED O' YE' TO MAKE OFF, AND YOU KNOWS IT!
HRMF!
...
WELL... SHE'S TOO SLOW, YOUR SHIP.
TOO SLOW BY A DIGIT!
CAP'N DUNWELL LET HER BOTTOM OVERFOUL. A GOOD KEELING AND SHE'LL MATCH SPEED WITH ANY SHIP HER SIZE.

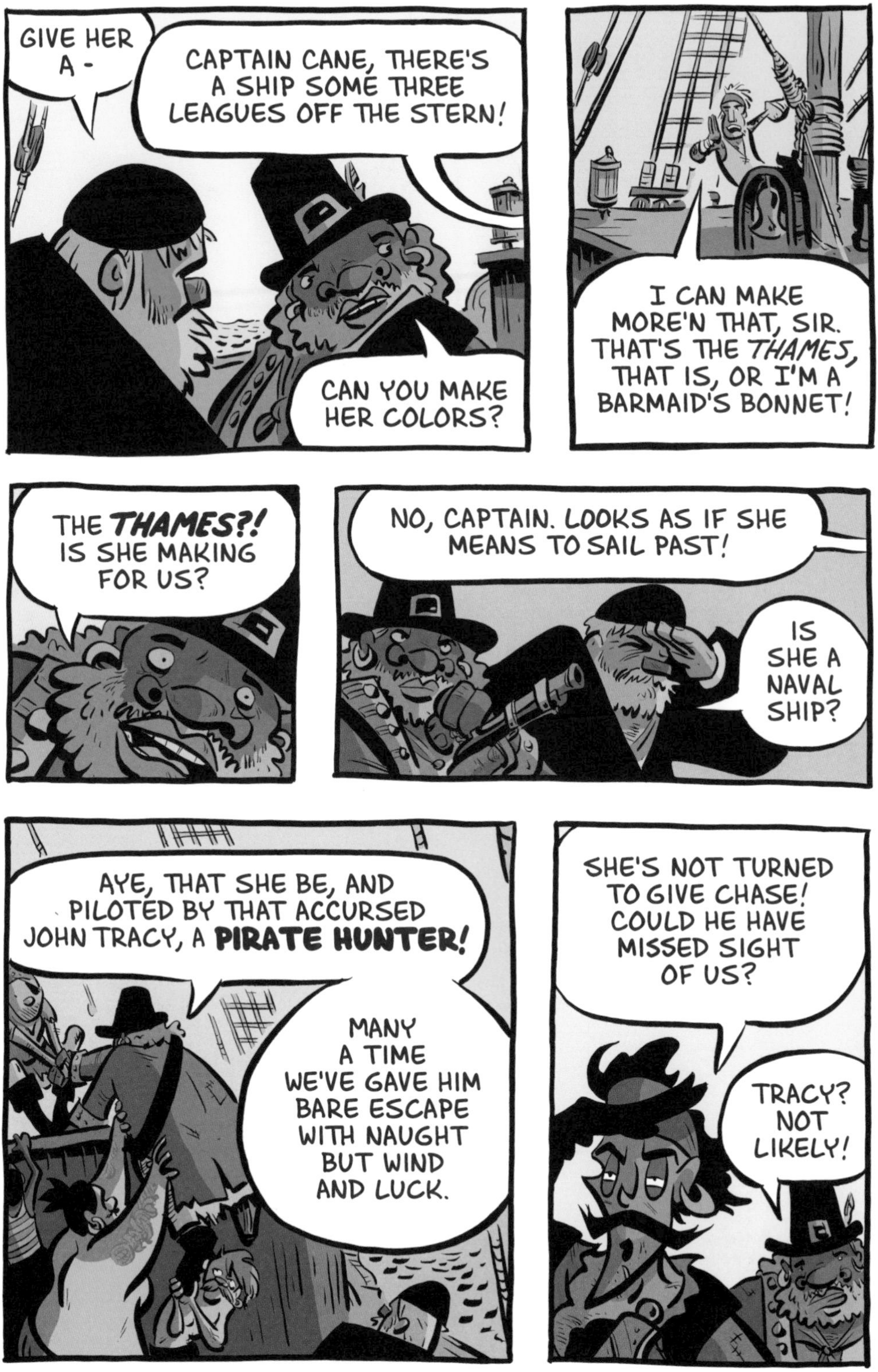
GIVE HER A -
CAPTAIN CANE, THERE'S A SHIP SOME THREE LEAGUES OFF THE STERN!
CAN YOU MAKE HER COLORS?
I CAN MAKE MORE'N THAT, SIR. THAT'S THE *THAMES*, THAT IS, OR I'M A BARMAID'S BONNET!
THE ***THAMES?!*** IS SHE MAKING FOR US?
NO, CAPTAIN. LOOKS AS IF SHE MEANS TO SAIL PAST!
IS SHE A NAVAL SHIP?
AYE, THAT SHE BE, AND PILOTED BY THAT ACCURSED JOHN TRACY, A **PIRATE HUNTER!**
MANY A TIME WE'VE GAVE HIM BARE ESCAPE WITH NAUGHT BUT WIND AND LUCK.
SHE'S NOT TURNED TO GIVE CHASE! COULD HE HAVE MISSED SIGHT OF US?
TRACY? NOT LIKELY!

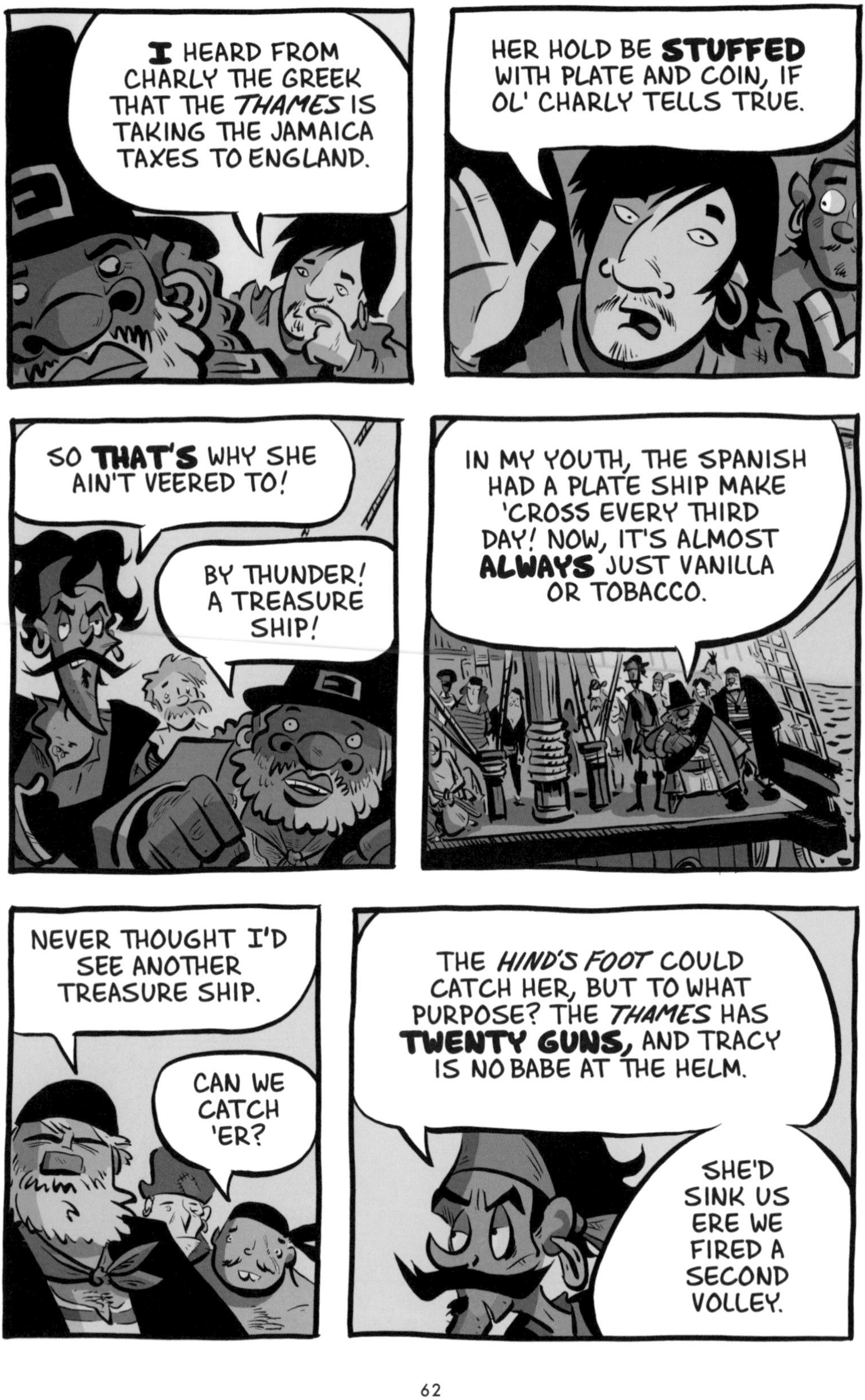
I HEARD FROM CHARLY THE GREEK THAT THE *THAMES* IS TAKING THE JAMAICA TAXES TO ENGLAND.
HER HOLD BE **STUFFED** WITH PLATE AND COIN, IF OL' CHARLY TELLS TRUE.
SO **THAT'S** WHY SHE AIN'T VEERED TO!
BY THUNDER! A TREASURE SHIP!
IN MY YOUTH, THE SPANISH HAD A PLATE SHIP MAKE 'CROSS EVERY THIRD DAY! NOW, IT'S ALMOST **ALWAYS** JUST VANILLA OR TOBACCO.
NEVER THOUGHT I'D SEE ANOTHER TREASURE SHIP.
CAN WE CATCH 'ER?
THE *HIND'S FOOT* COULD CATCH HER, BUT TO WHAT PURPOSE? THE *THAMES* HAS **TWENTY GUNS,** AND TRACY IS NO BABE AT THE HELM.
SHE'D SINK US ERE WE FIRED A SECOND VOLLEY.

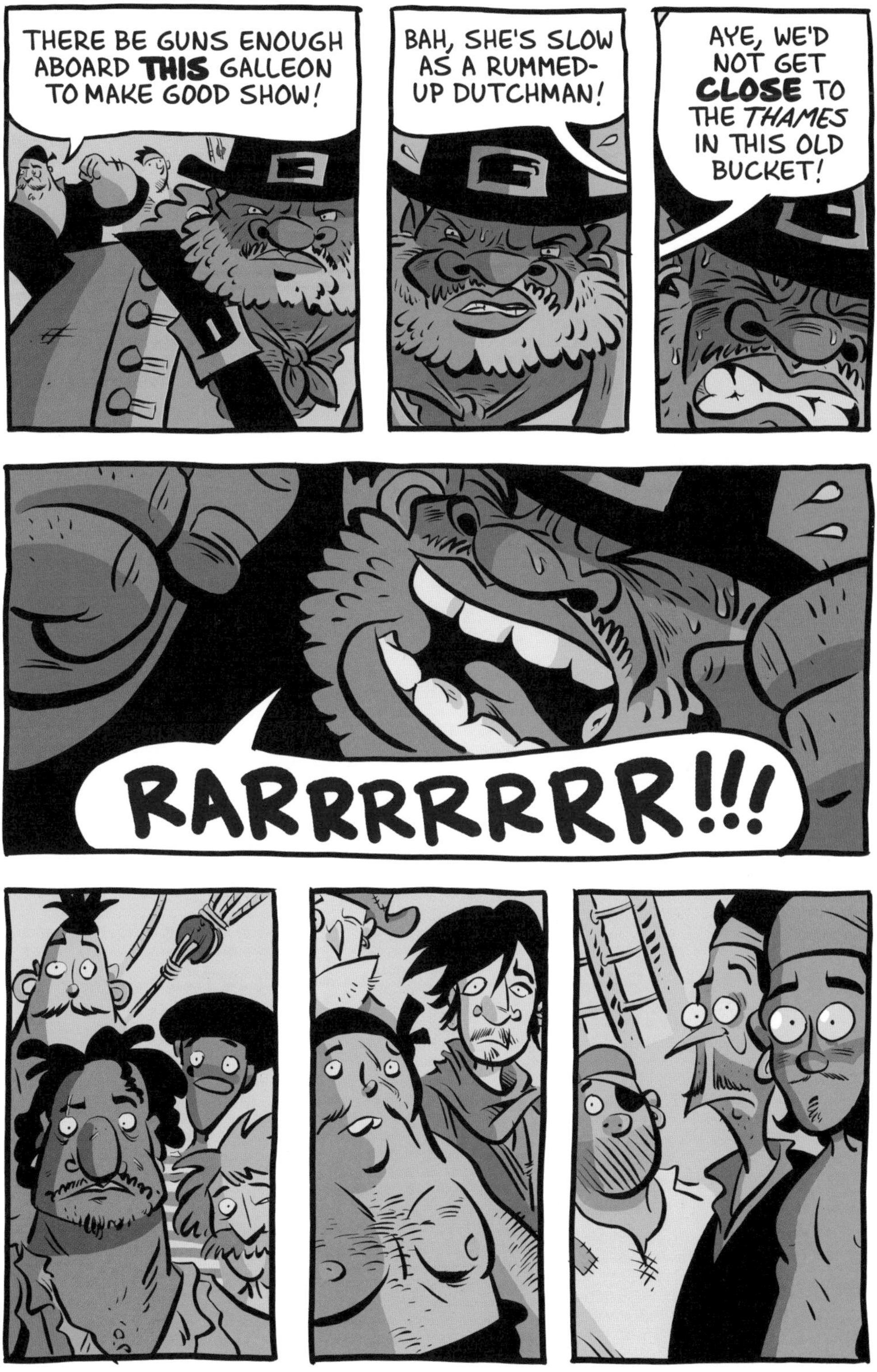
THERE BE GUNS ENOUGH ABOARD **THIS** GALLEON TO MAKE GOOD SHOW!
BAH, SHE'S SLOW AS A RUMMED-UP DUTCHMAN!
AYE, WE'D NOT GET **CLOSE** TO THE *THAMES* IN THIS OLD BUCKET!
RARRRRRRR!!!

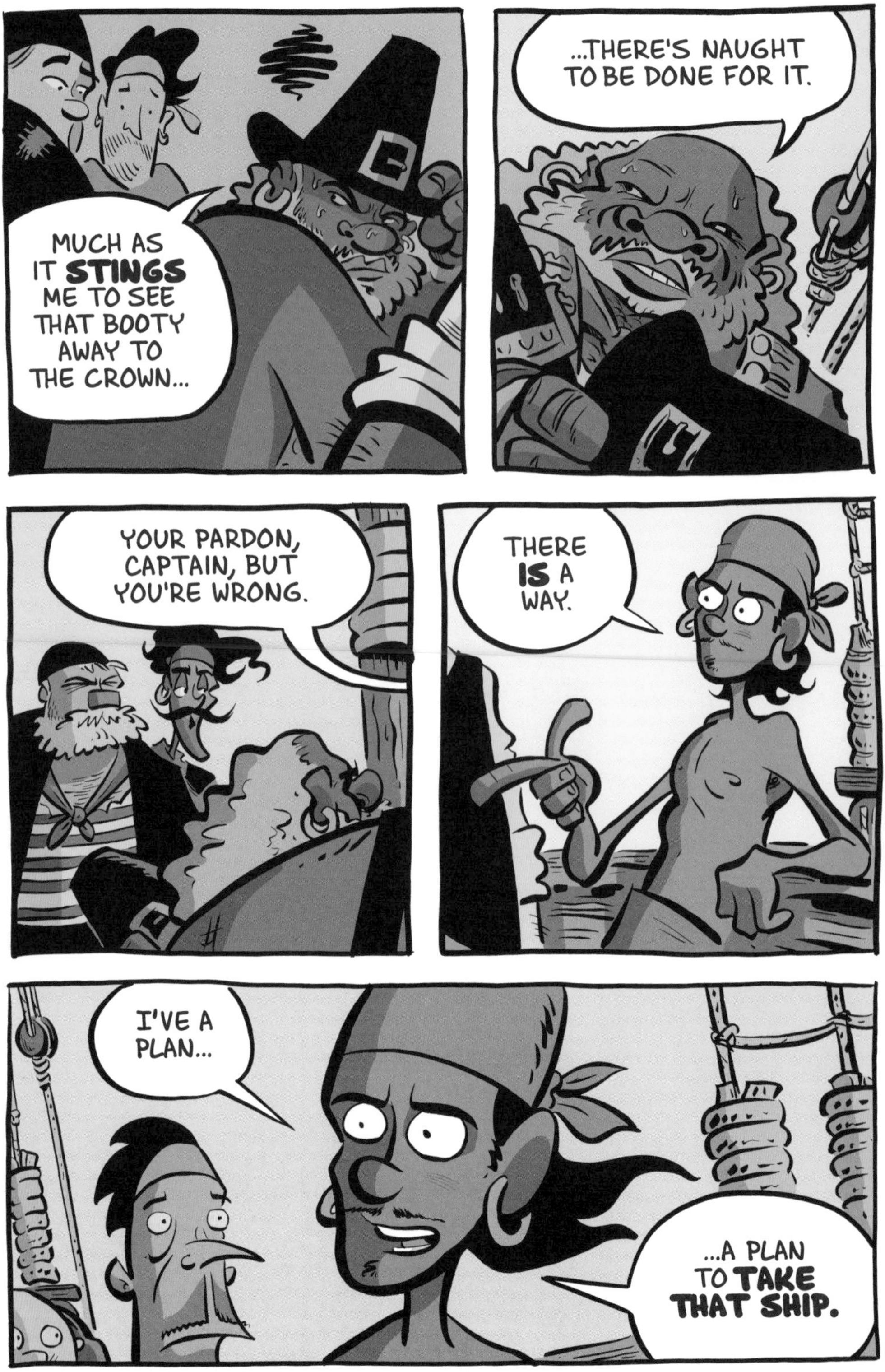
MUCH AS IT **STINGS** ME TO SEE THAT BOOTY AWAY TO THE CROWN...
...THERE'S NAUGHT TO BE DONE FOR IT.
YOUR PARDON, CAPTAIN, BUT YOU'RE WRONG.
THERE **IS** A WAY.
I'VE A PLAN...
...A PLAN TO **TAKE THAT SHIP.**

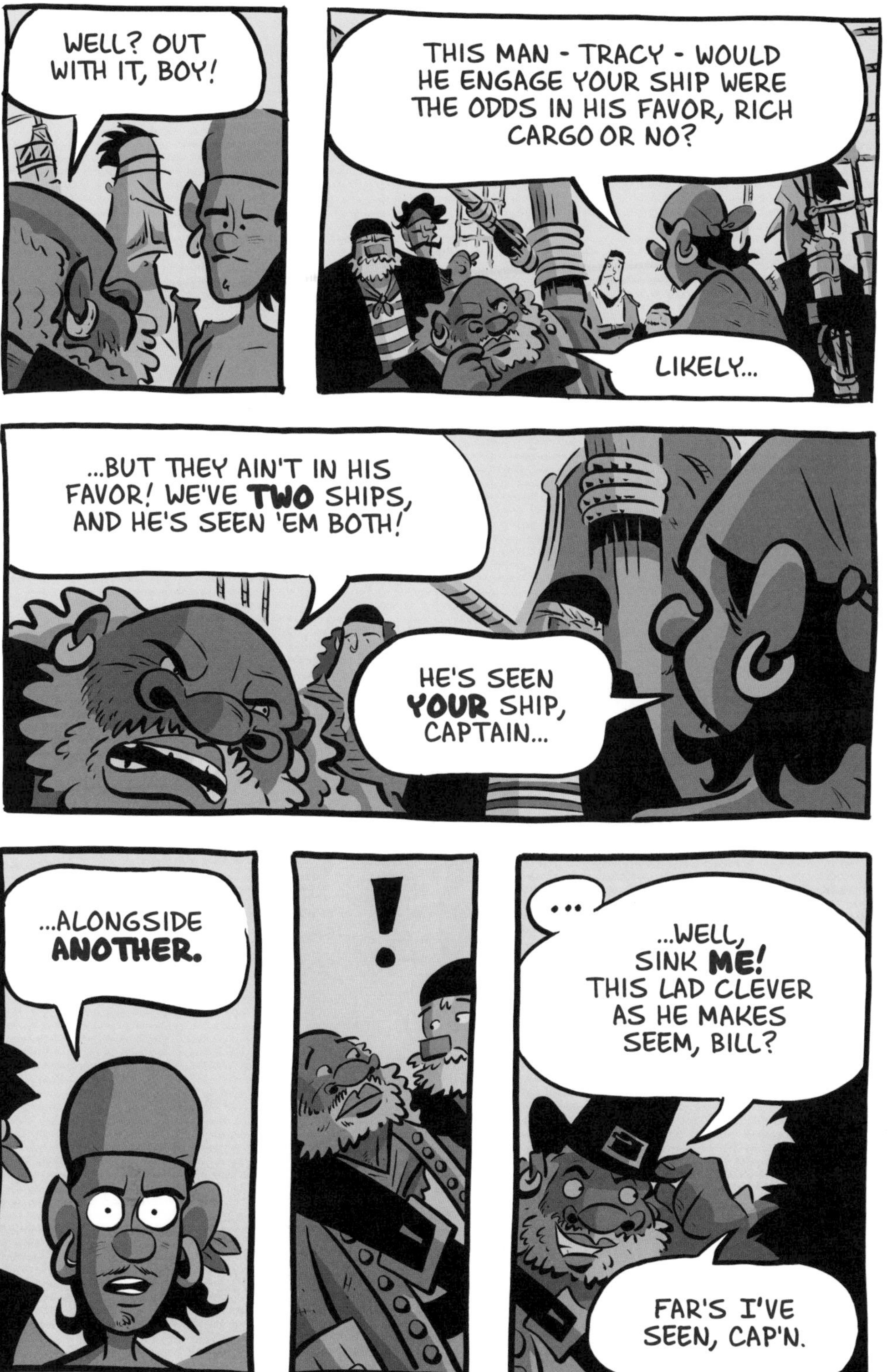
WELL? OUT WITH IT, BOY!
THIS MAN - TRACY - WOULD HE ENGAGE YOUR SHIP WERE THE ODDS IN HIS FAVOR, RICH CARGO OR NO?
LIKELY...
...BUT THEY AIN'T IN HIS FAVOR! WE'VE TWO SHIPS, AND HE'S SEEN 'EM BOTH!
HE'S SEEN YOUR SHIP, CAPTAIN...
...ALONGSIDE ANOTHER.
!
...
...WELL, SINK ME! THIS LAD CLEVER AS HE MAKES SEEM, BILL?
FAR'S I'VE SEEN, CAP'N.

WELL, MISTER...

CROGAN.

WELL, MR. CROGAN...

...HAVE SEE TO THIS PLAN OF YOURS.

UM... ALL RIGHT.

THE FLAGS!

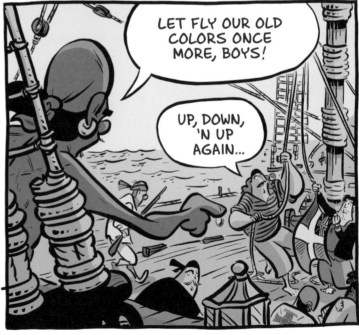

LET FLY OUR OLD COLORS ONCE MORE, BOYS!

UP, DOWN, 'N UP AGAIN...

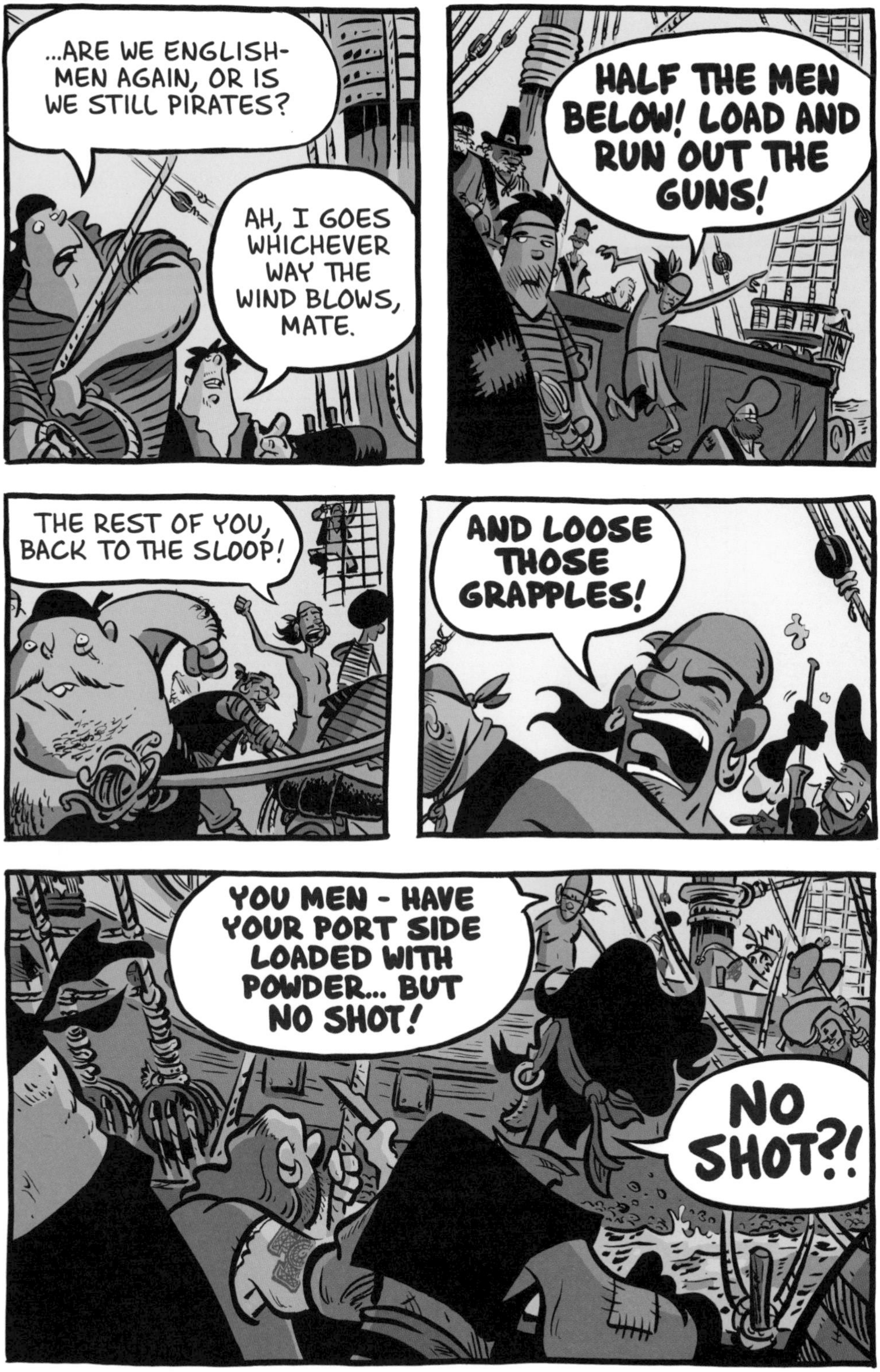
...ARE WE ENGLISH-MEN AGAIN, OR IS WE STILL PIRATES?
AH, I GOES WHICHEVER WAY THE WIND BLOWS, MATE.
HALF THE MEN BELOW! LOAD AND RUN OUT THE GUNS!
THE REST OF YOU, BACK TO THE SLOOP!
AND LOOSE THOSE GRAPPLES!
YOU MEN - HAVE YOUR PORT SIDE LOADED WITH POWDER... BUT NO SHOT!
NO SHOT?!

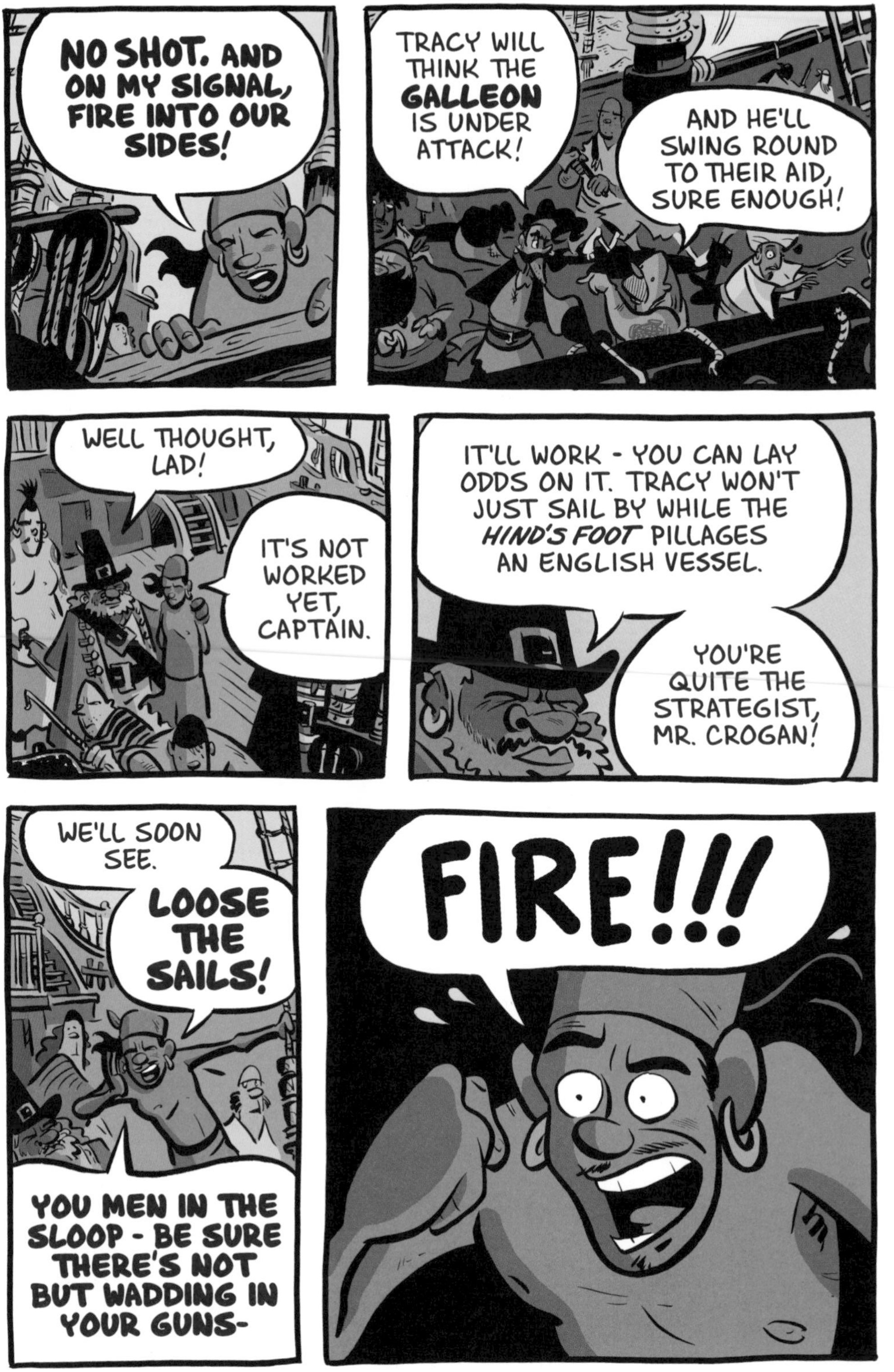
NO SHOT. AND ON MY SIGNAL, FIRE INTO OUR SIDES!
TRACY WILL THINK THE GALLEON IS UNDER ATTACK!
AND HE'LL SWING ROUND TO THEIR AID, SURE ENOUGH!
WELL THOUGHT, LAD!
IT'S NOT WORKED YET, CAPTAIN.
IT'LL WORK - YOU CAN LAY ODDS ON IT. TRACY WON'T JUST SAIL BY WHILE THE *HIND'S FOOT* PILLAGES AN ENGLISH VESSEL.
YOU'RE QUITE THE STRATEGIST, MR. CROGAN!
WE'LL SOON SEE.
LOOSE THE SAILS!
YOU MEN IN THE SLOOP - BE SURE THERE'S NOT BUT WADDING IN YOUR GUNS-
FIRE!!!

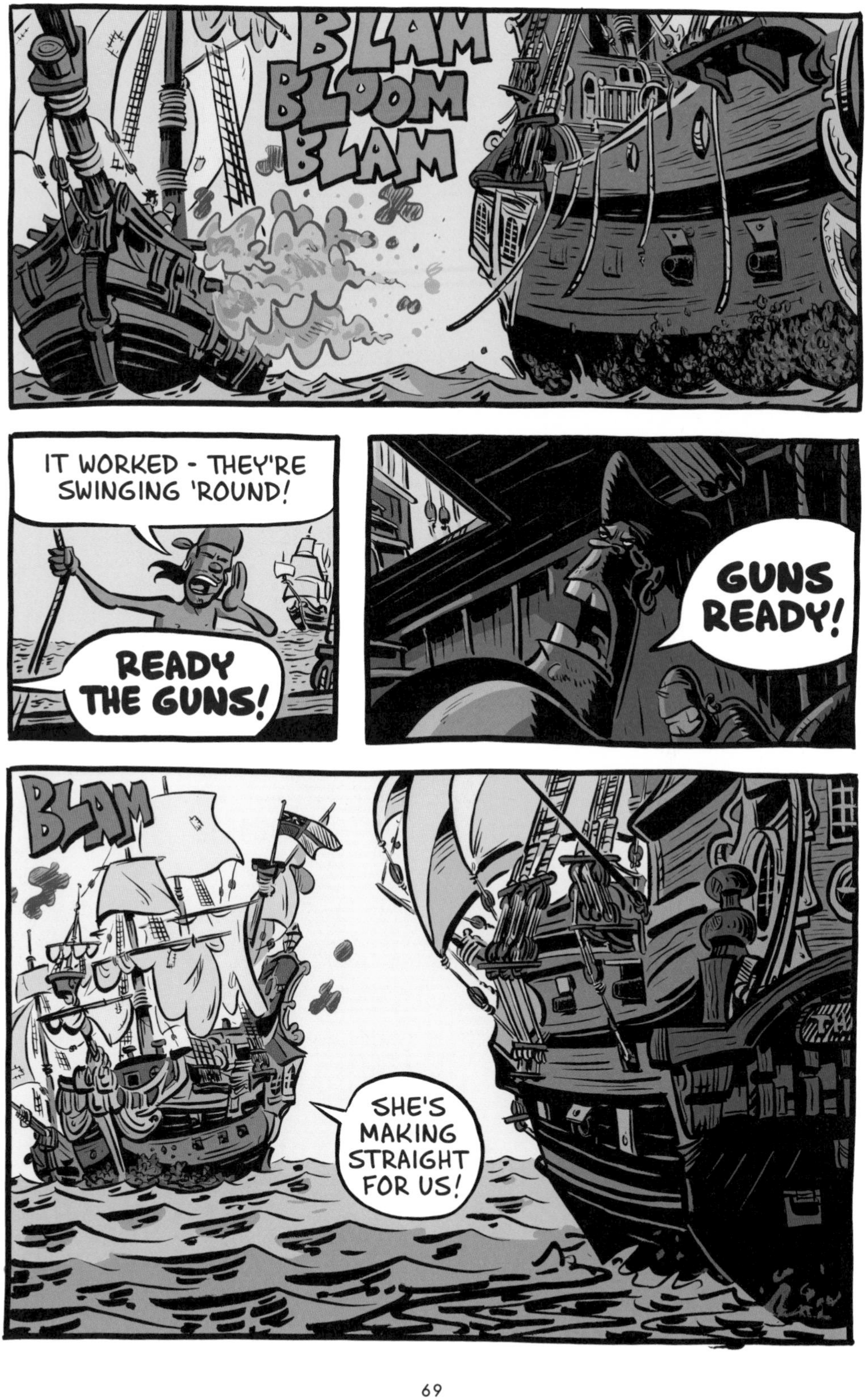
BLAM
BLOOM
BLAM
IT WORKED - THEY'RE SWINGING 'ROUND!
READY THE GUNS!
GUNS READY!
BLAM
SHE'S MAKING STRAIGHT FOR US!

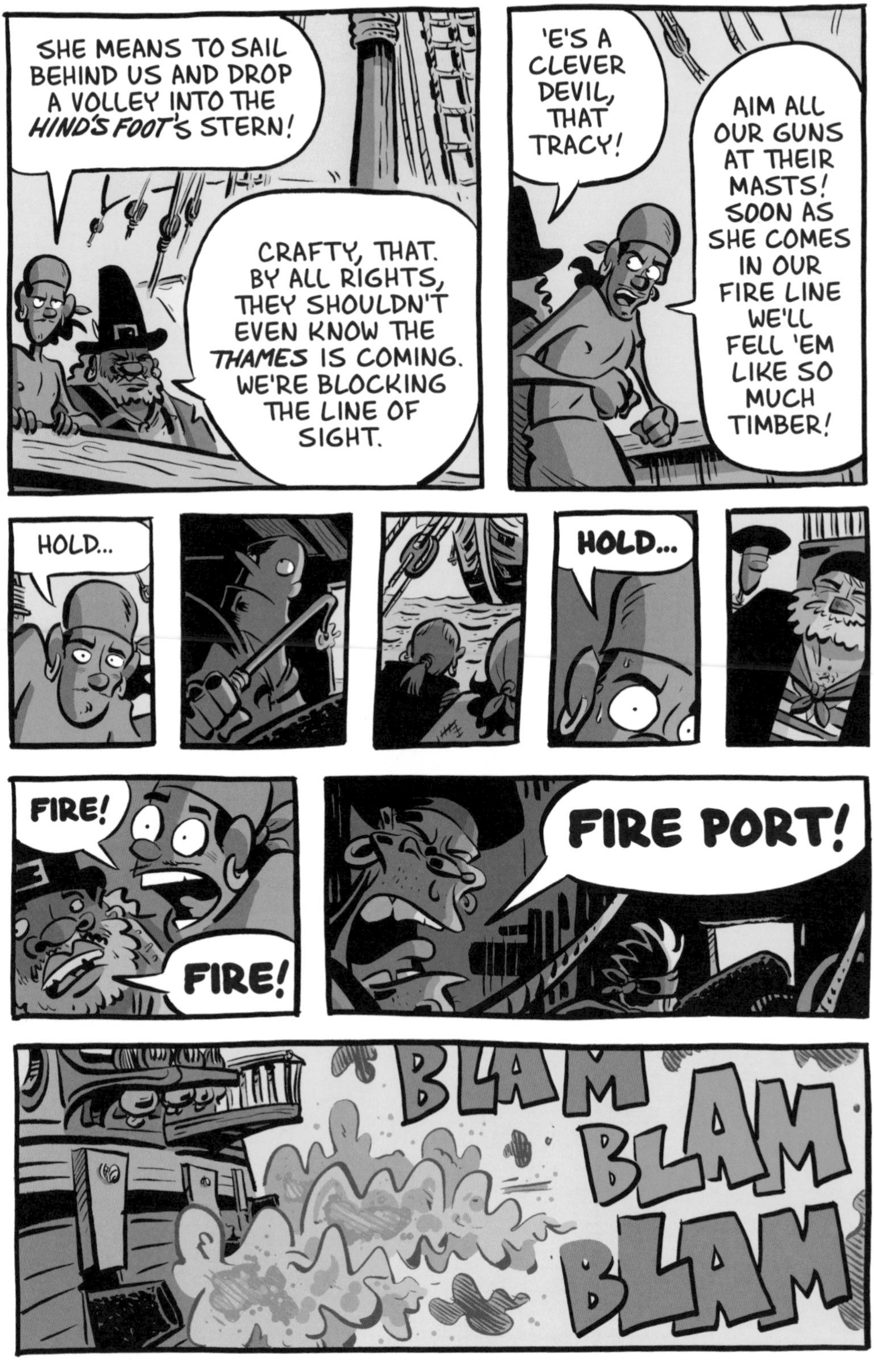
SHE MEANS TO SAIL BEHIND US AND DROP A VOLLEY INTO THE *HIND'S FOOT*'S STERN!
CRAFTY, THAT. BY ALL RIGHTS, THEY SHOULDN'T EVEN KNOW THE *THAMES* IS COMING. WE'RE BLOCKING THE LINE OF SIGHT.
'E'S A CLEVER DEVIL, THAT TRACY!
AIM ALL OUR GUNS AT THEIR MASTS! SOON AS SHE COMES IN OUR FIRE LINE WE'LL FELL 'EM LIKE SO MUCH TIMBER!
HOLD...
HOLD...
FIRE!
FIRE!
FIRE PORT!
BLAM
BLAM
BLAM

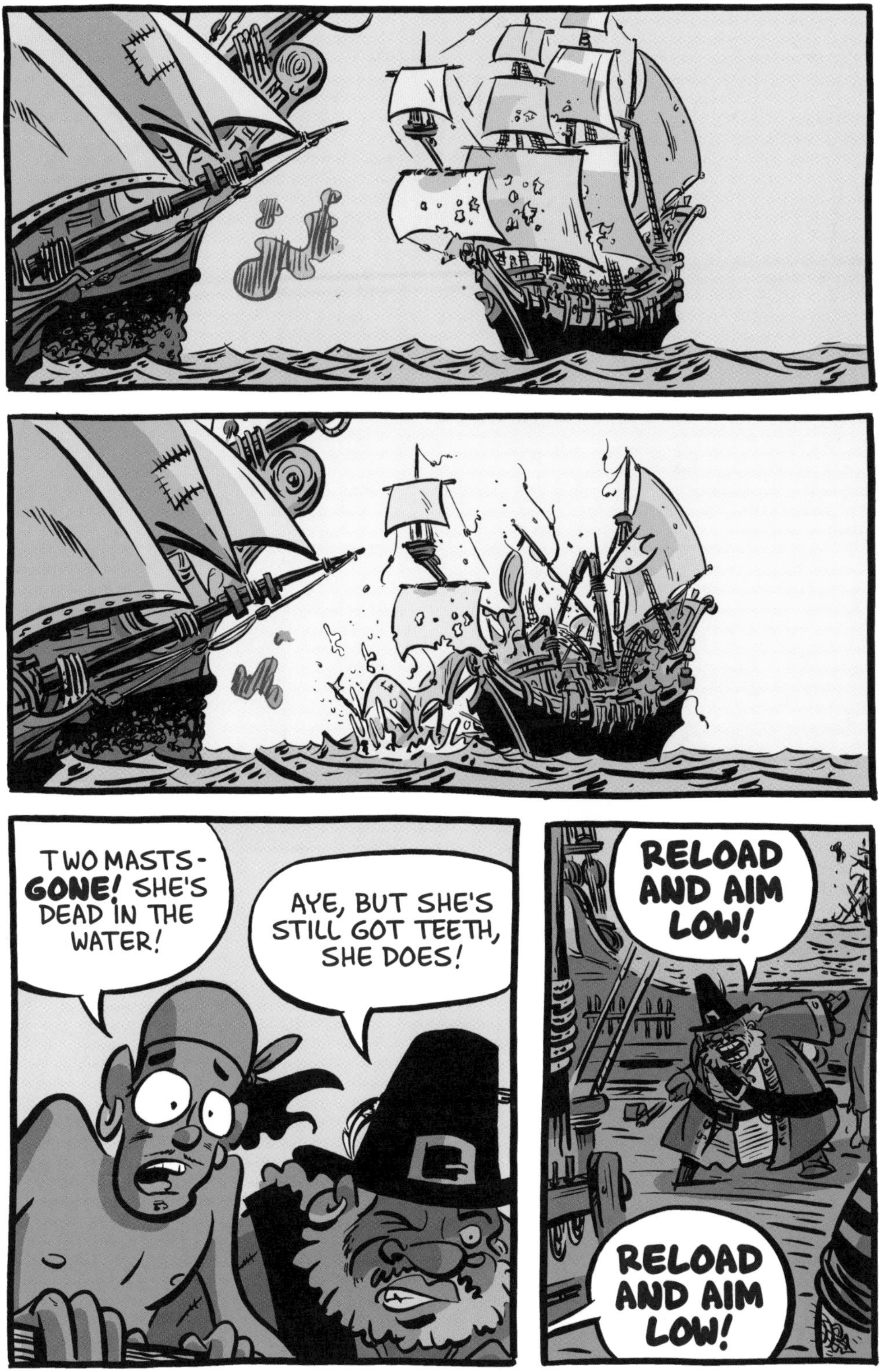
TWO MASTS- GONE! SHE'S DEAD IN THE WATER!
AYE, BUT SHE'S STILL GOT TEETH, SHE DOES!
RELOAD AND AIM LOW!
RELOAD AND AIM LOW!

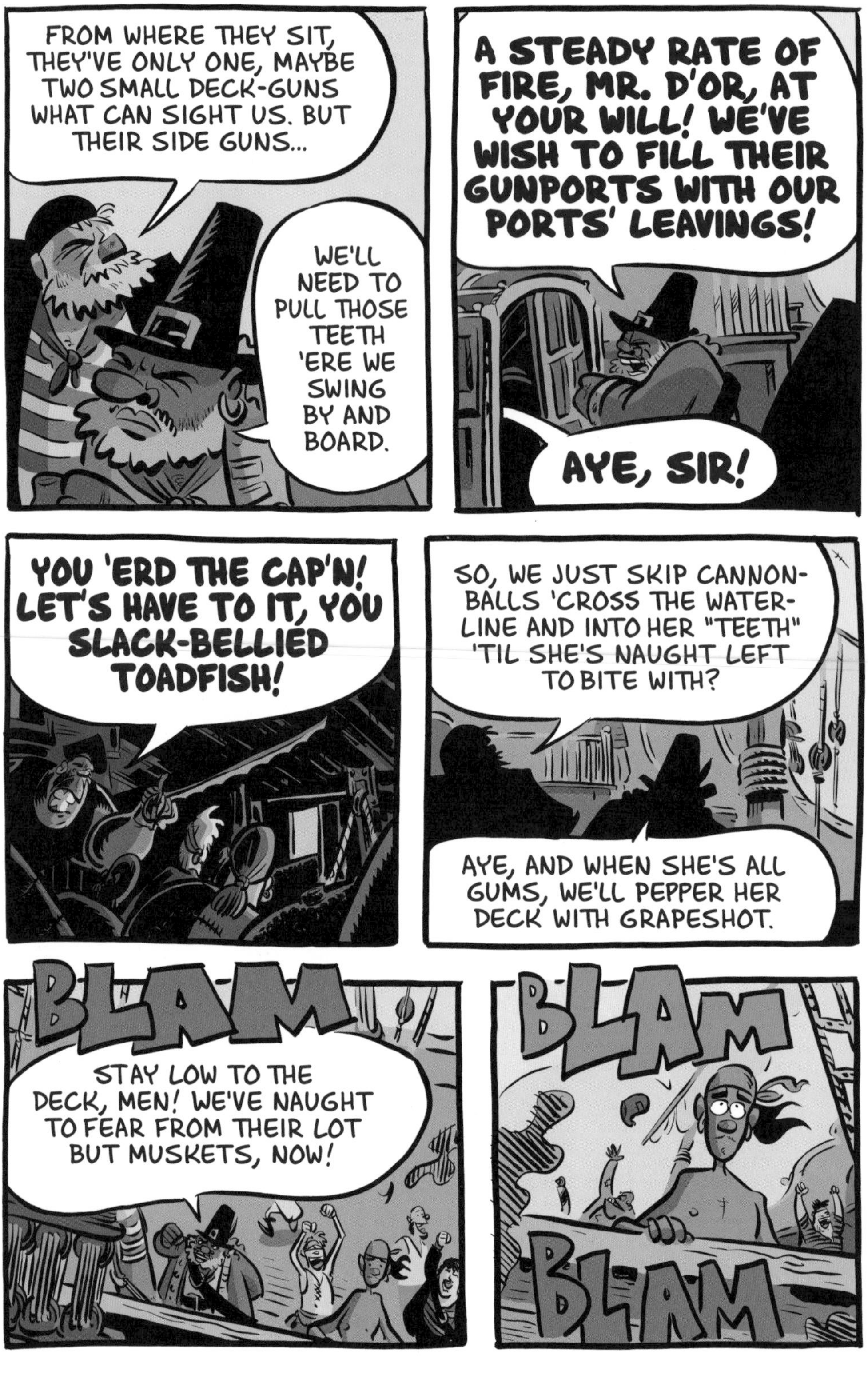
FROM WHERE THEY SIT, THEY'VE ONLY ONE, MAYBE TWO SMALL DECK-GUNS WHAT CAN SIGHT US. BUT THEIR SIDE GUNS...
WE'LL NEED TO PULL THOSE TEETH 'ERE WE SWING BY AND BOARD.
A STEADY RATE OF FIRE, MR. D'OR, AT YOUR WILL! WE'VE WISH TO FILL THEIR GUNPORTS WITH OUR PORTS' LEAVINGS!
AYE, SIR!
YOU 'ERD THE CAP'N! LET'S HAVE TO IT, YOU SLACK-BELLIED TOADFISH!
SO, WE JUST SKIP CANNON-BALLS 'CROSS THE WATER-LINE AND INTO HER "TEETH" 'TIL SHE'S NAUGHT LEFT TO BITE WITH?
AYE, AND WHEN SHE'S ALL GUMS, WE'LL PEPPER HER DECK WITH GRAPESHOT.
BLAM
STAY LOW TO THE DECK, MEN! WE'VE NAUGHT TO FEAR FROM THEIR LOT BUT MUSKETS, NOW!
BLAM
BLAM

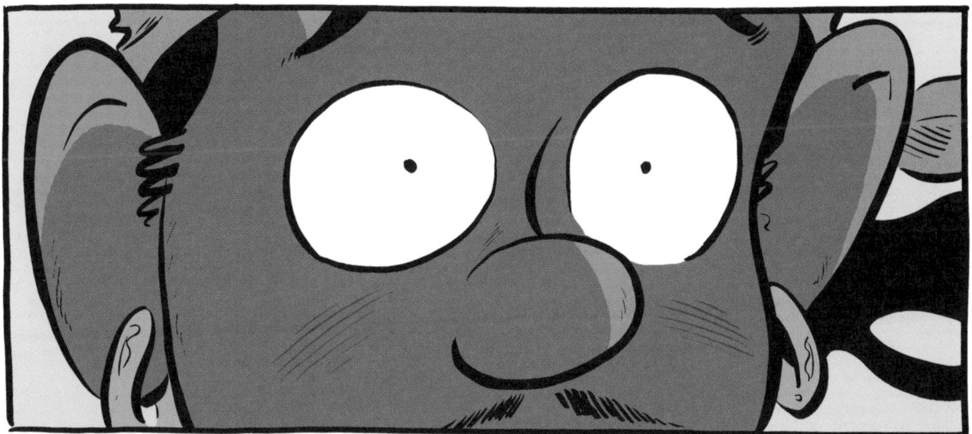

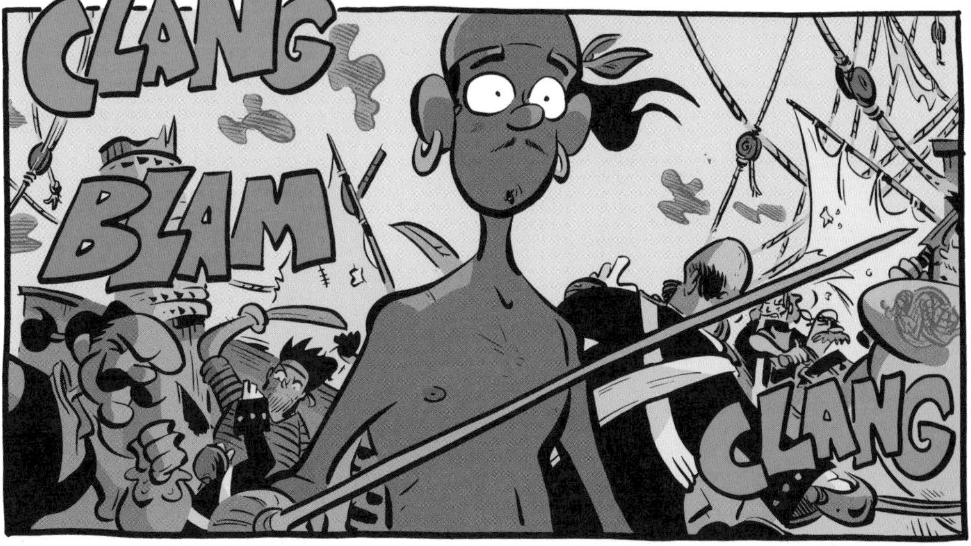
CLANG
BLAM
CLANG

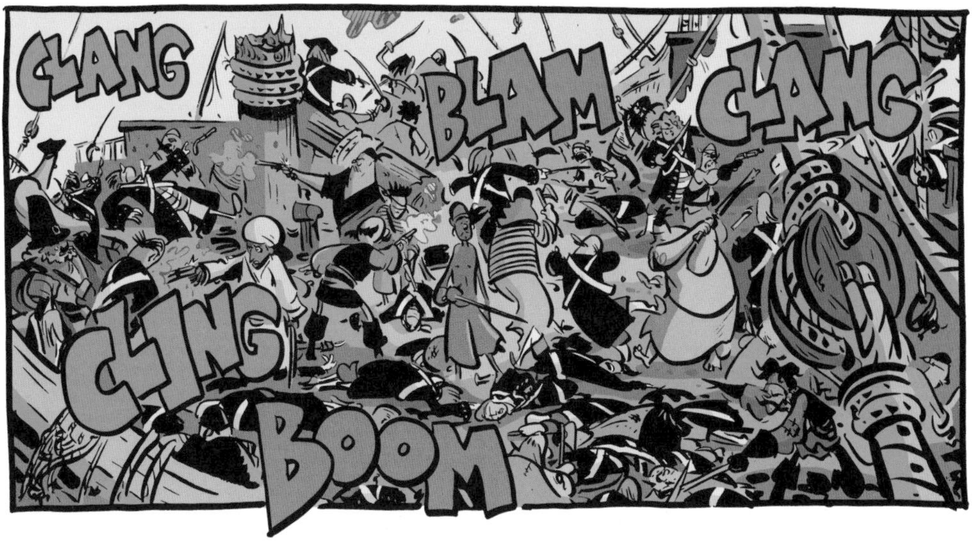
CLANG
BLAM
CLANG
CLING
BOOM

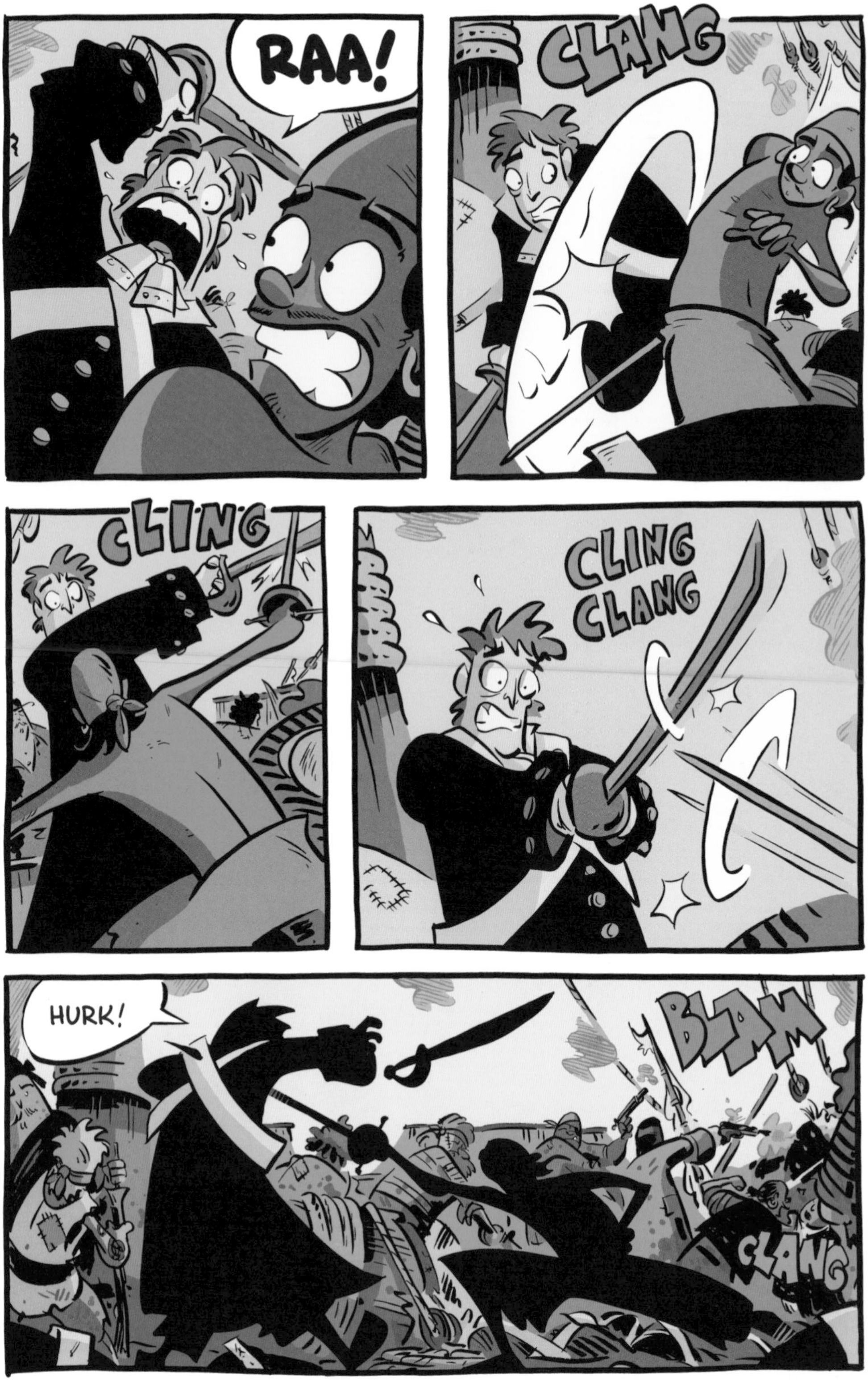
RAA!
CLANG
CLING
CLING
CLANG
HURK!
BLAM
CLANG

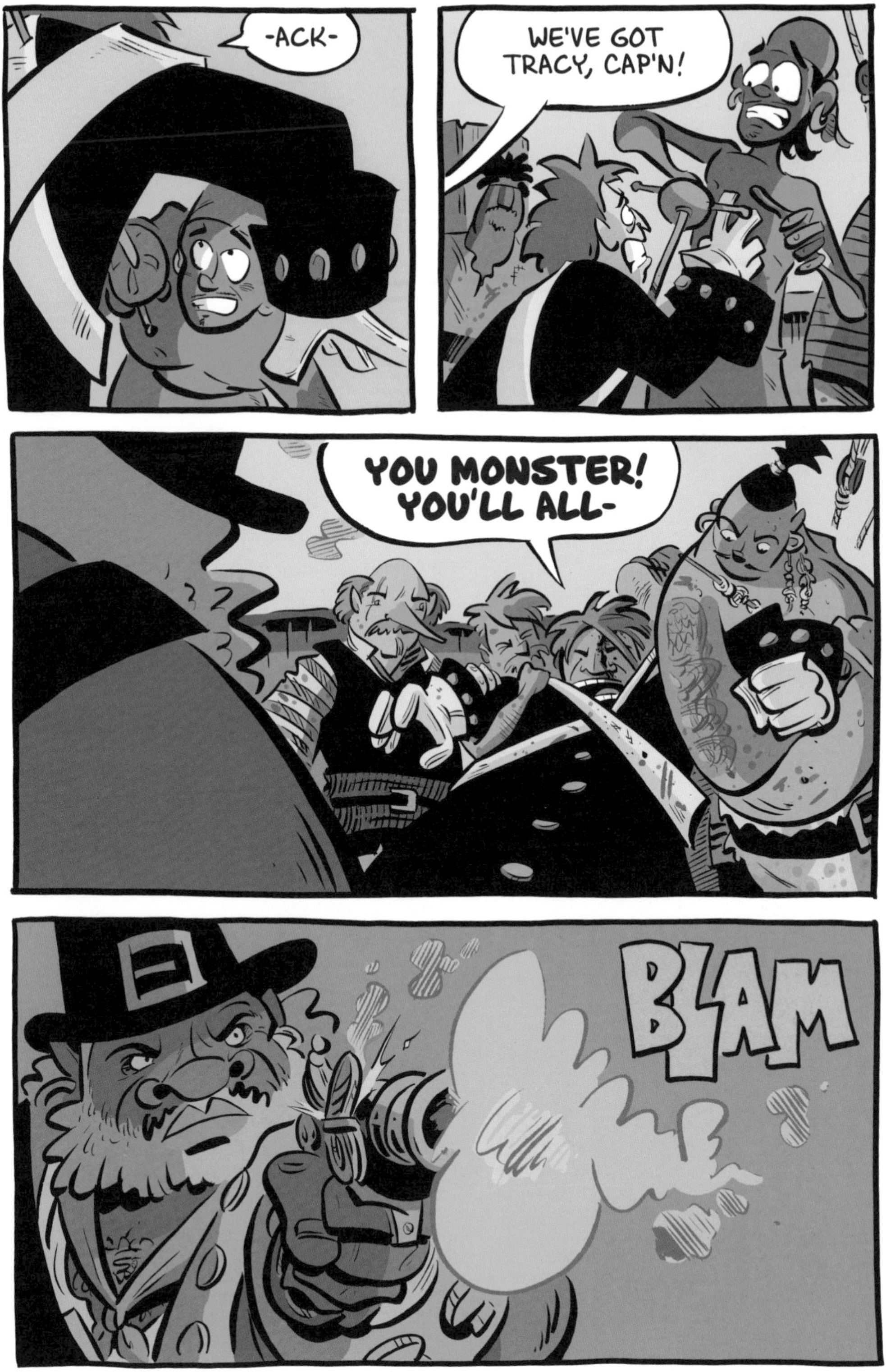
-ACK-
WE'VE GOT TRACY, CAP'N!
YOU MONSTER! YOU'LL ALL-
BLAM

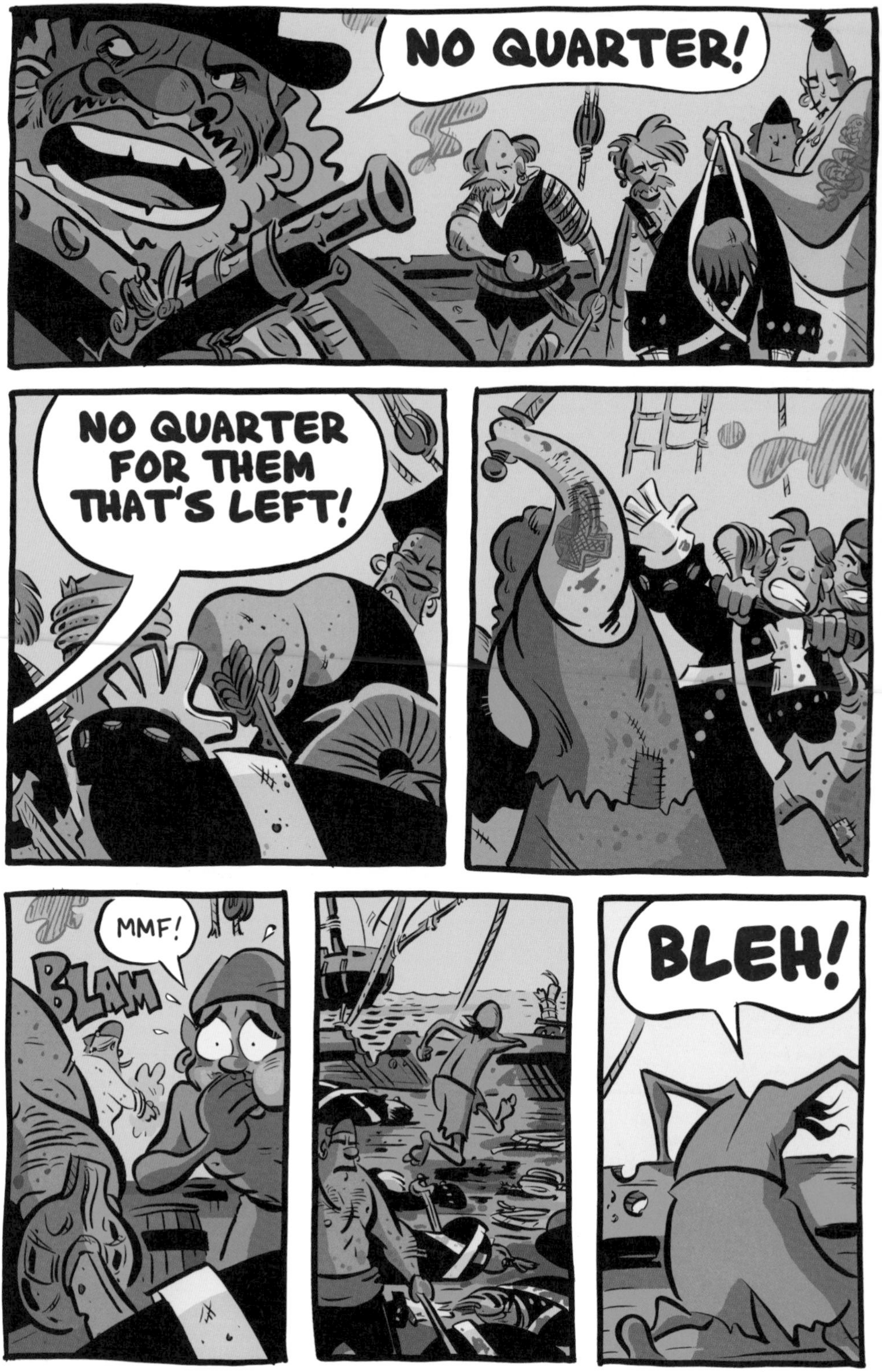
NO QUARTER!
NO QUARTER FOR THEM THAT'S LEFT!
MMF!
BLAM
BLEH!

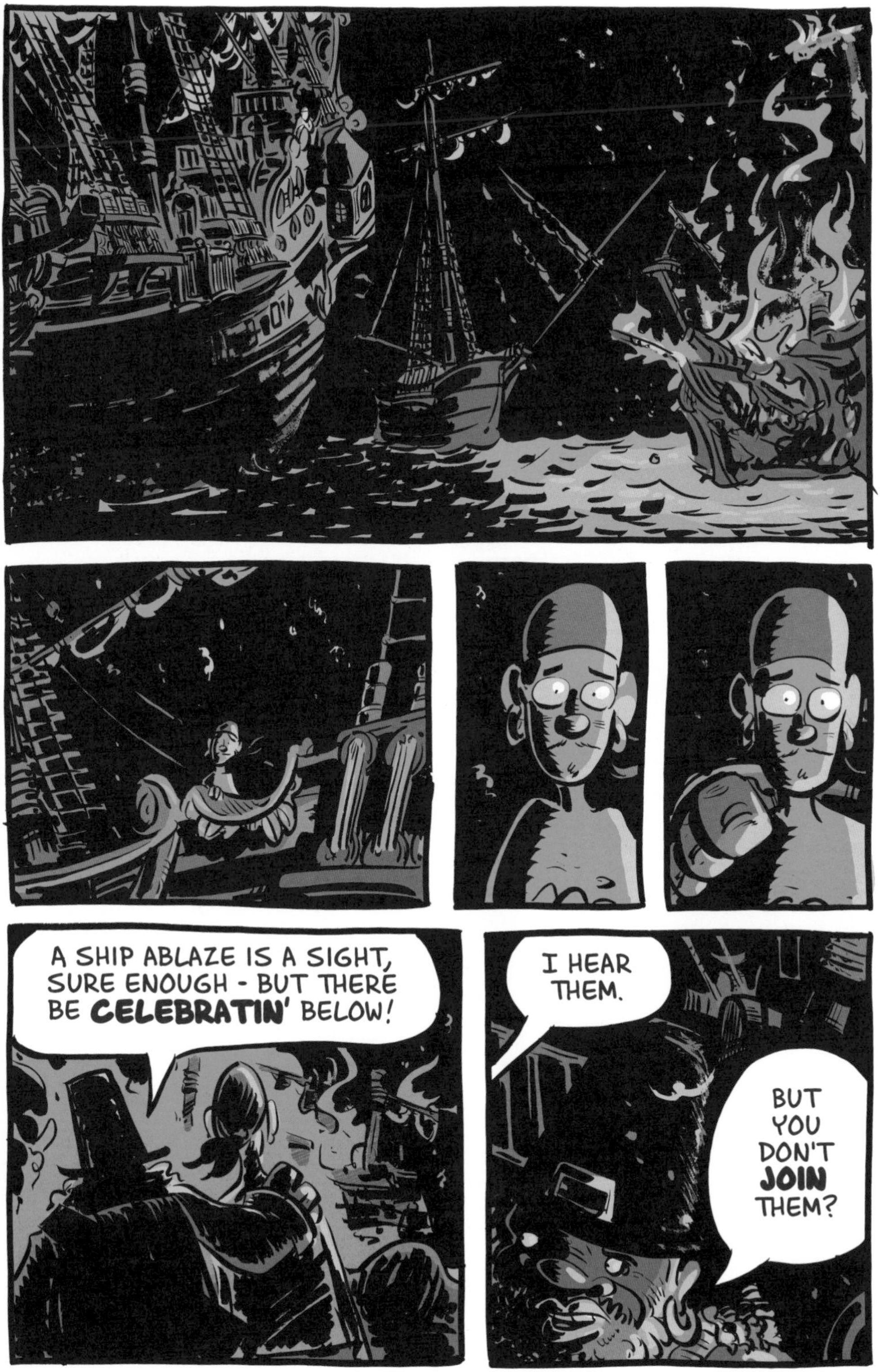
A SHIP ABLAZE IS A SIGHT, SURE ENOUGH - BUT THERE BE **CELEBRATIN'** BELOW!
I HEAR THEM.
BUT YOU DON'T **JOIN** THEM?

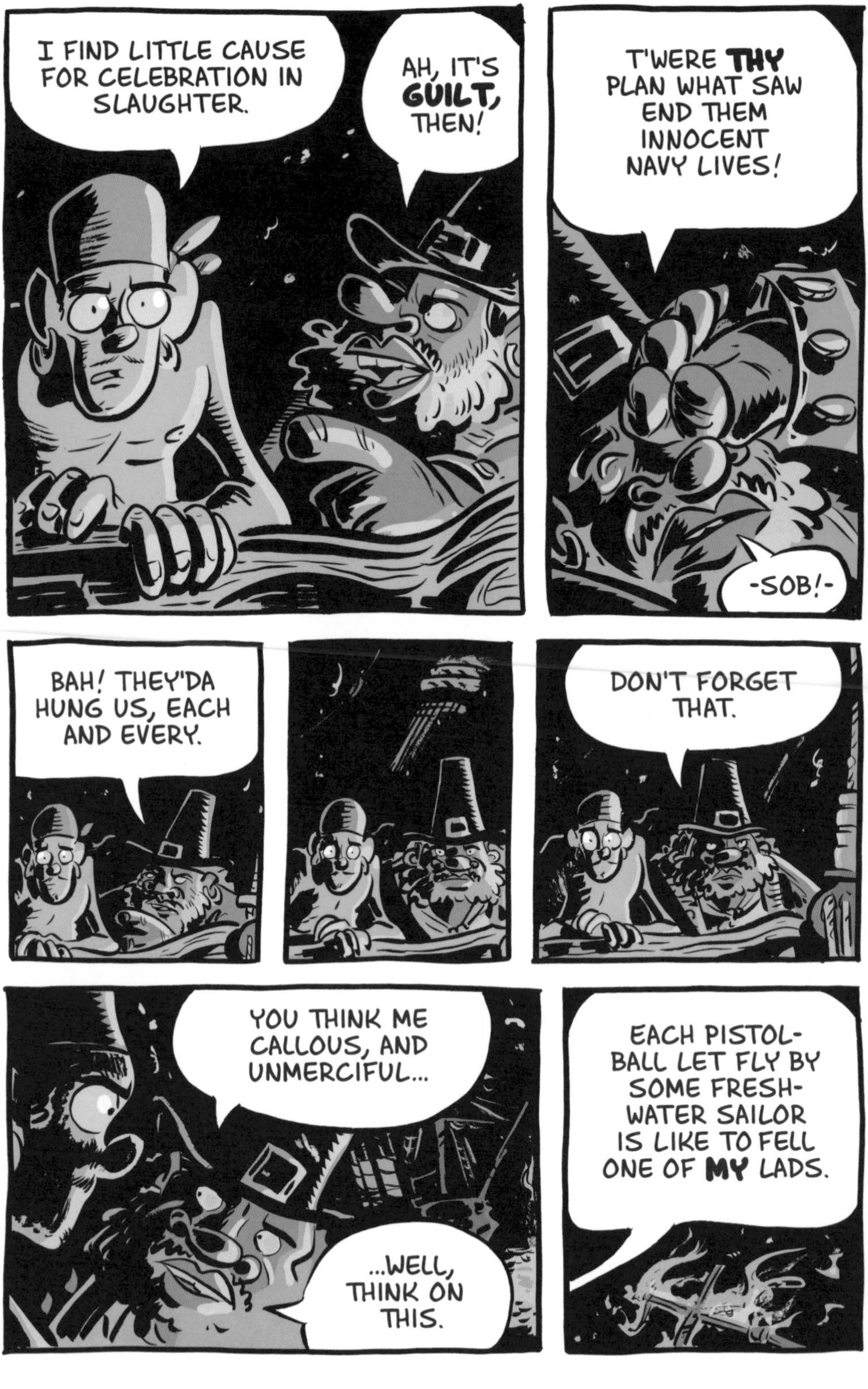
I FIND LITTLE CAUSE FOR CELEBRATION IN SLAUGHTER.
AH, IT'S **GUILT**, THEN!
T'WERE **THY** PLAN WHAT SAW END THEM INNOCENT NAVY LIVES!
-SOB!-
BAH! THEY'DA HUNG US, EACH AND EVERY.
DON'T FORGET THAT.
YOU THINK ME CALLOUS, AND UNMERCIFUL...
...WELL, THINK ON THIS.
EACH PISTOL-BALL LET FLY BY SOME FRESH-WATER SAILOR IS LIKE TO FELL ONE OF **MY** LADS.

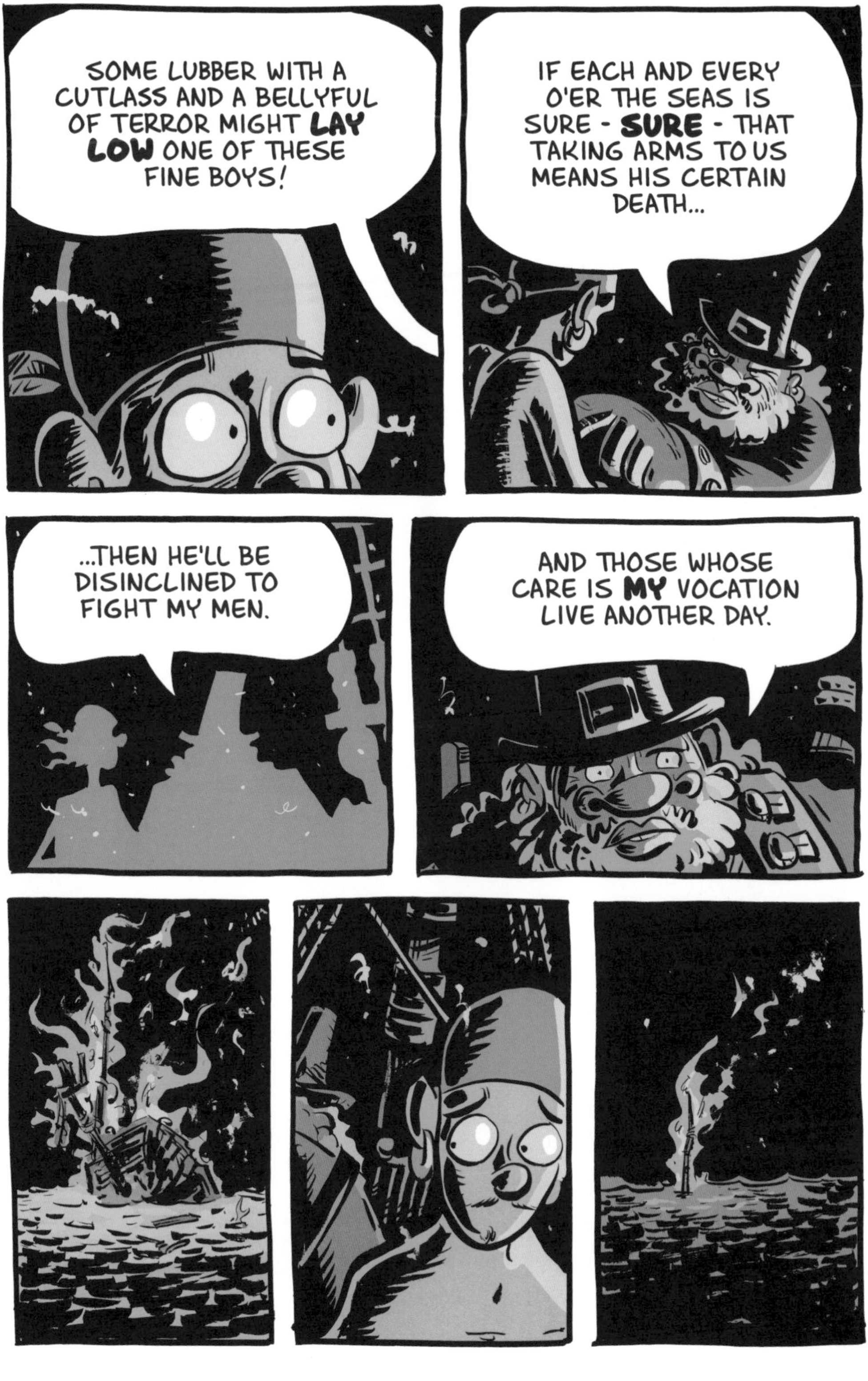
SOME LUBBER WITH A CUTLASS AND A BELLYFUL OF TERROR MIGHT LAY LOW ONE OF THESE FINE BOYS!
IF EACH AND EVERY O'ER THE SEAS IS SURE - SURE - THAT TAKING ARMS TO US MEANS HIS CERTAIN DEATH...
...THEN HE'LL BE DISINCLINED TO FIGHT MY MEN.
AND THOSE WHOSE CARE IS MY VOCATION LIVE ANOTHER DAY.

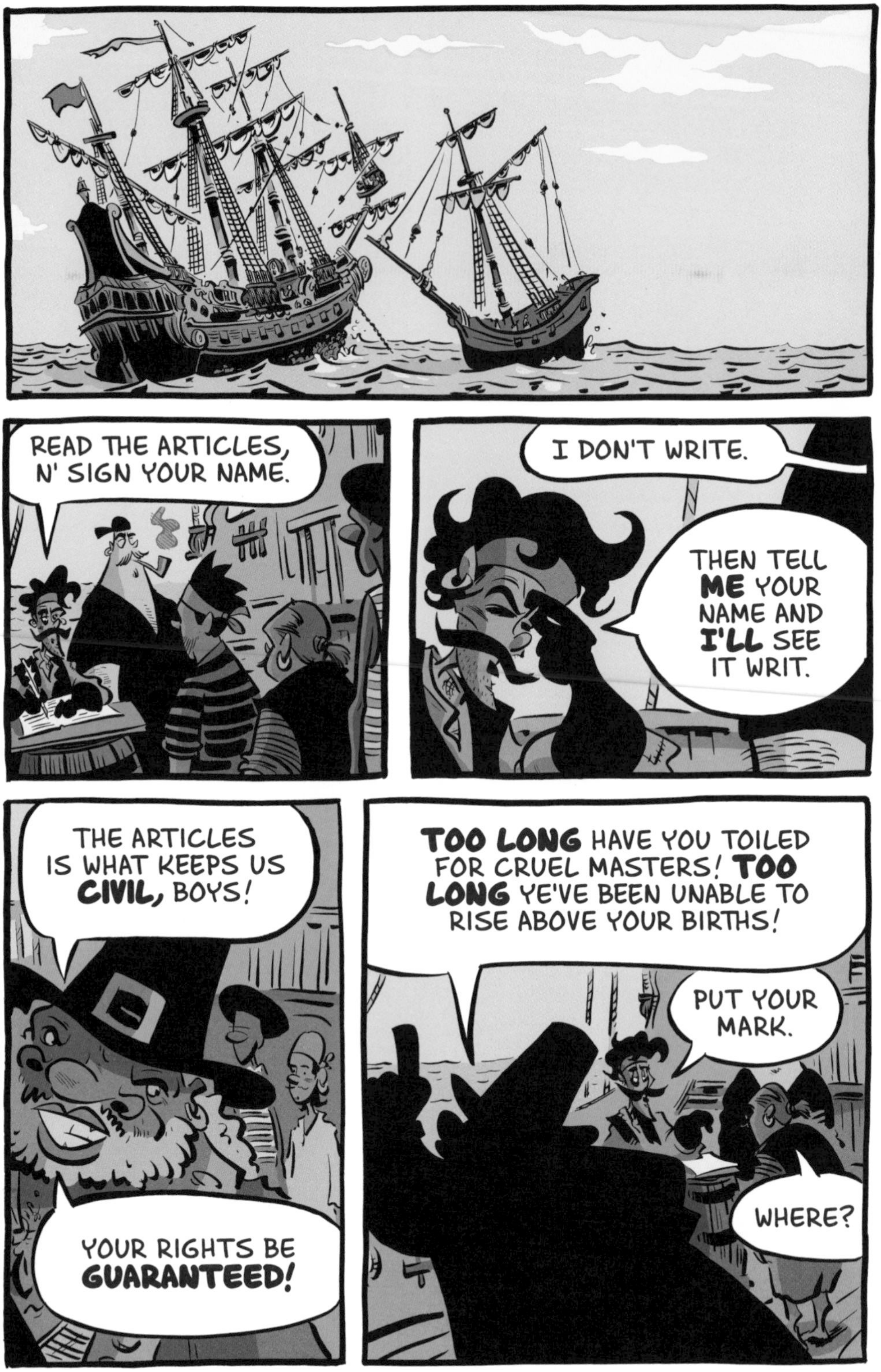
READ THE ARTICLES, N' SIGN YOUR NAME.
I DON'T WRITE.
THEN TELL ME YOUR NAME AND I'LL SEE IT WRIT.
THE ARTICLES IS WHAT KEEPS US CIVIL, BOYS!
YOUR RIGHTS BE GUARANTEED!
TOO LONG HAVE YOU TOILED FOR CRUEL MASTERS! TOO LONG YE'VE BEEN UNABLE TO RISE ABOVE YOUR BIRTHS!
PUT YOUR MARK.
WHERE?

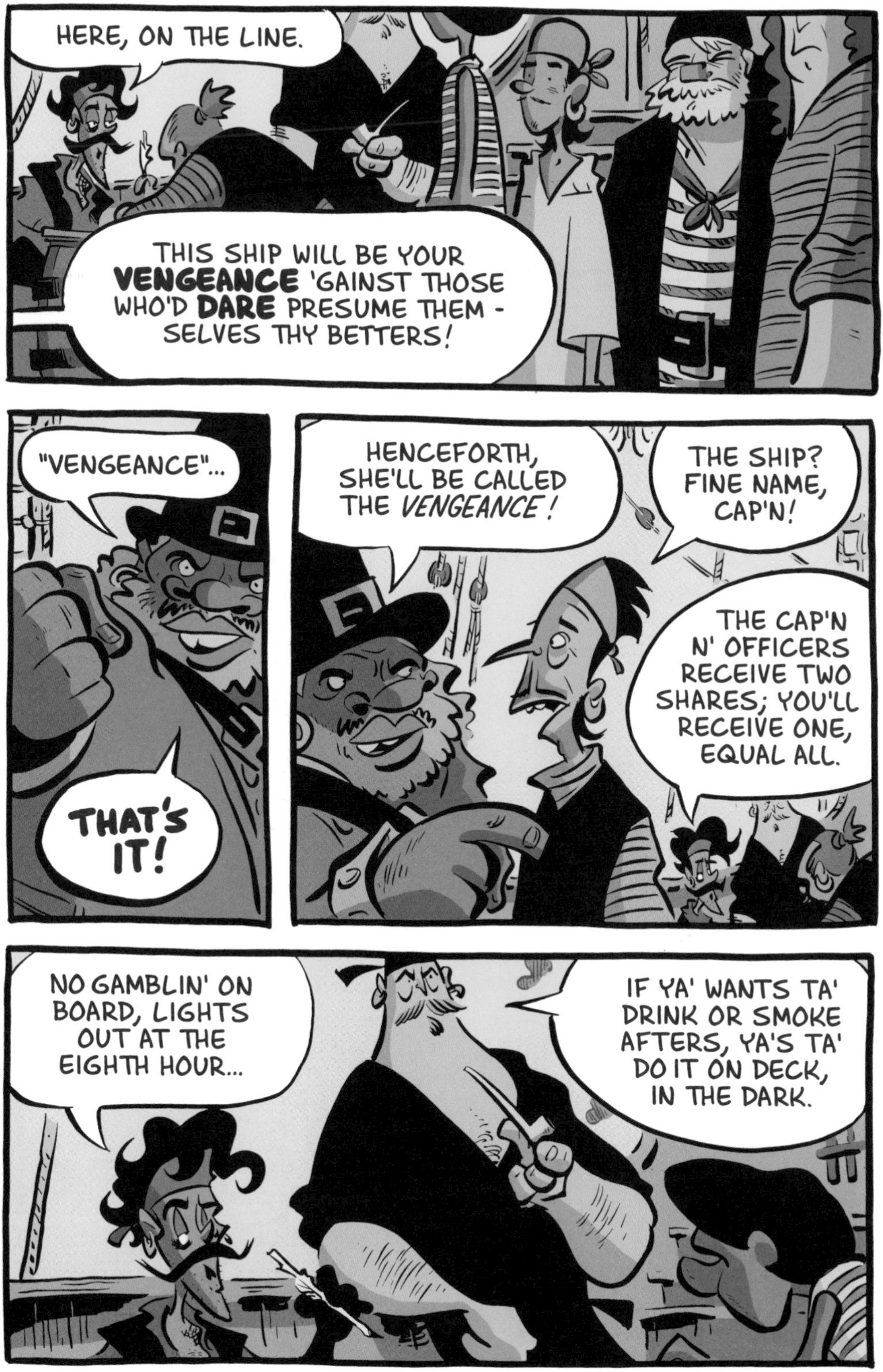
HERE, ON THE LINE.
THIS SHIP WILL BE YOUR **VENGEANCE** 'GAINST THOSE WHO'D **DARE** PRESUME THEM - SELVES THY BETTERS!
"VENGEANCE"...
THAT'S IT!
HENCEFORTH, SHE'LL BE CALLED THE *VENGEANCE*!
THE SHIP? FINE NAME, CAP'N!
THE CAP'N N' OFFICERS RECEIVE TWO SHARES; YOU'LL RECEIVE ONE, EQUAL ALL.
NO GAMBLIN' ON BOARD, LIGHTS OUT AT THE EIGHTH HOUR...
IF YA' WANTS TA' DRINK OR SMOKE AFTERS, YA'S TA' DO IT ON DECK, IN THE DARK.

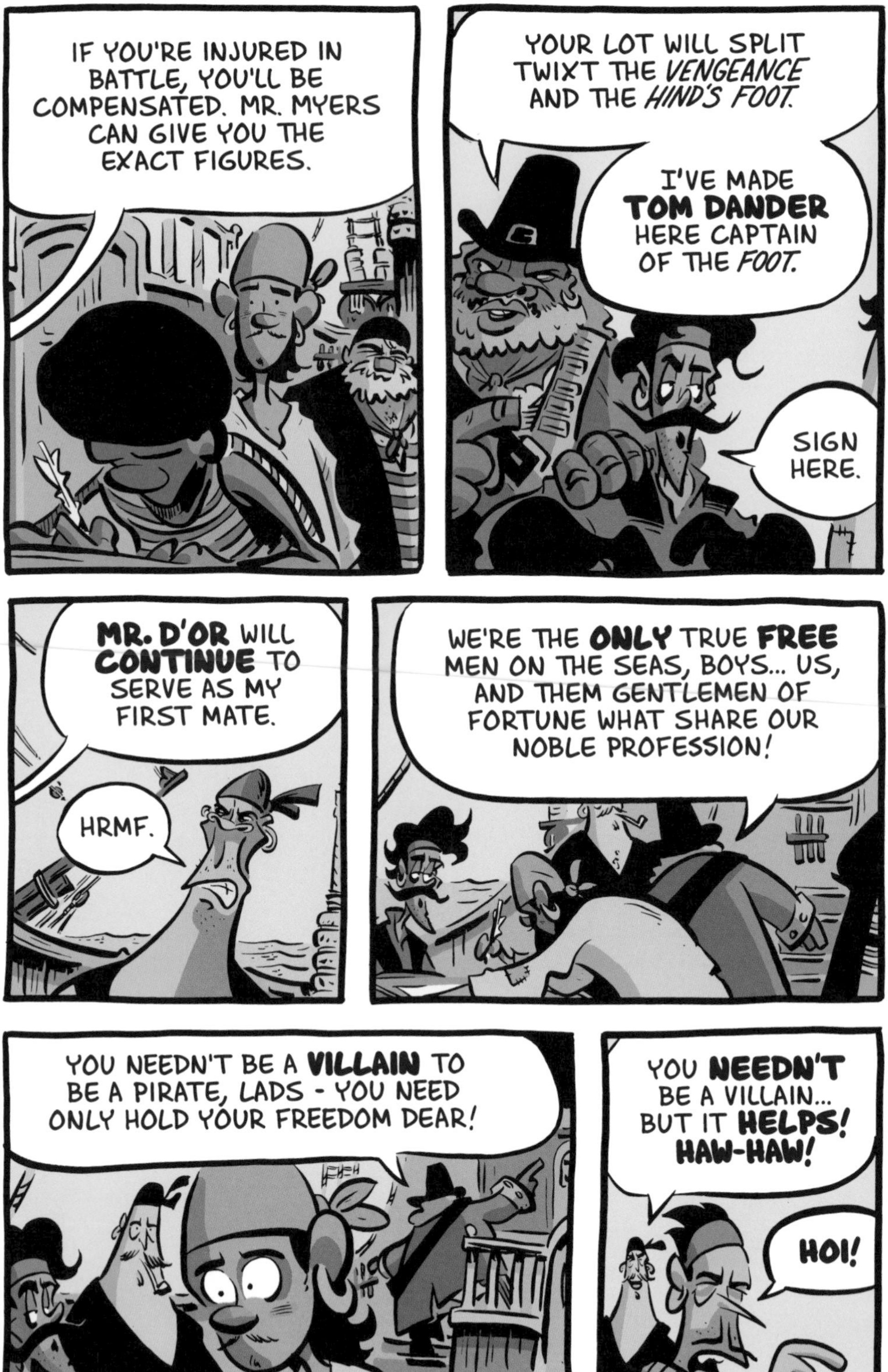
IF YOU'RE INJURED IN BATTLE, YOU'LL BE COMPENSATED. MR. MYERS CAN GIVE YOU THE EXACT FIGURES.
YOUR LOT WILL SPLIT TWIXT THE *VENGEANCE* AND THE *HIND'S FOOT.*
I'VE MADE **TOM DANDER** HERE CAPTAIN OF THE *FOOT.*
SIGN HERE.
MR. D'OR WILL **CONTINUE** TO SERVE AS MY FIRST MATE.
HRMF.
WE'RE THE **ONLY** TRUE **FREE** MEN ON THE SEAS, BOYS... US, AND THEM GENTLEMEN OF FORTUNE WHAT SHARE OUR NOBLE PROFESSION!
YOU NEEDN'T BE A **VILLAIN** TO BE A PIRATE, LADS - YOU NEED ONLY HOLD YOUR FREEDOM DEAR!
YOU **NEEDN'T** BE A VILLAIN... BUT IT **HELPS! HAW-HAW!**
HOI!

YOU'S THE FELLA 'SPOSED TO BE CLEVER, EH?

SEE TO WRAPPIN' YER FORMIDABLE MIND 'ROUND THE TASK OF SWABBIN' THE QUARTERDECK.

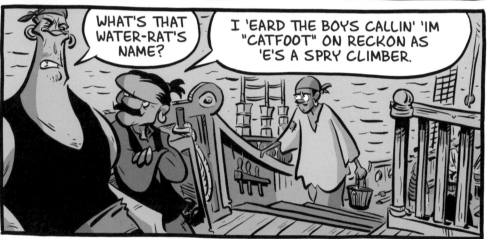

WHAT'S THAT WATER-RAT'S NAME?

I 'EARD THE BOYS CALLIN' 'IM "CATFOOT" ON RECKON AS 'E'S A SPRY CLIMBER.

"CATFOOT," EH?

OOF!

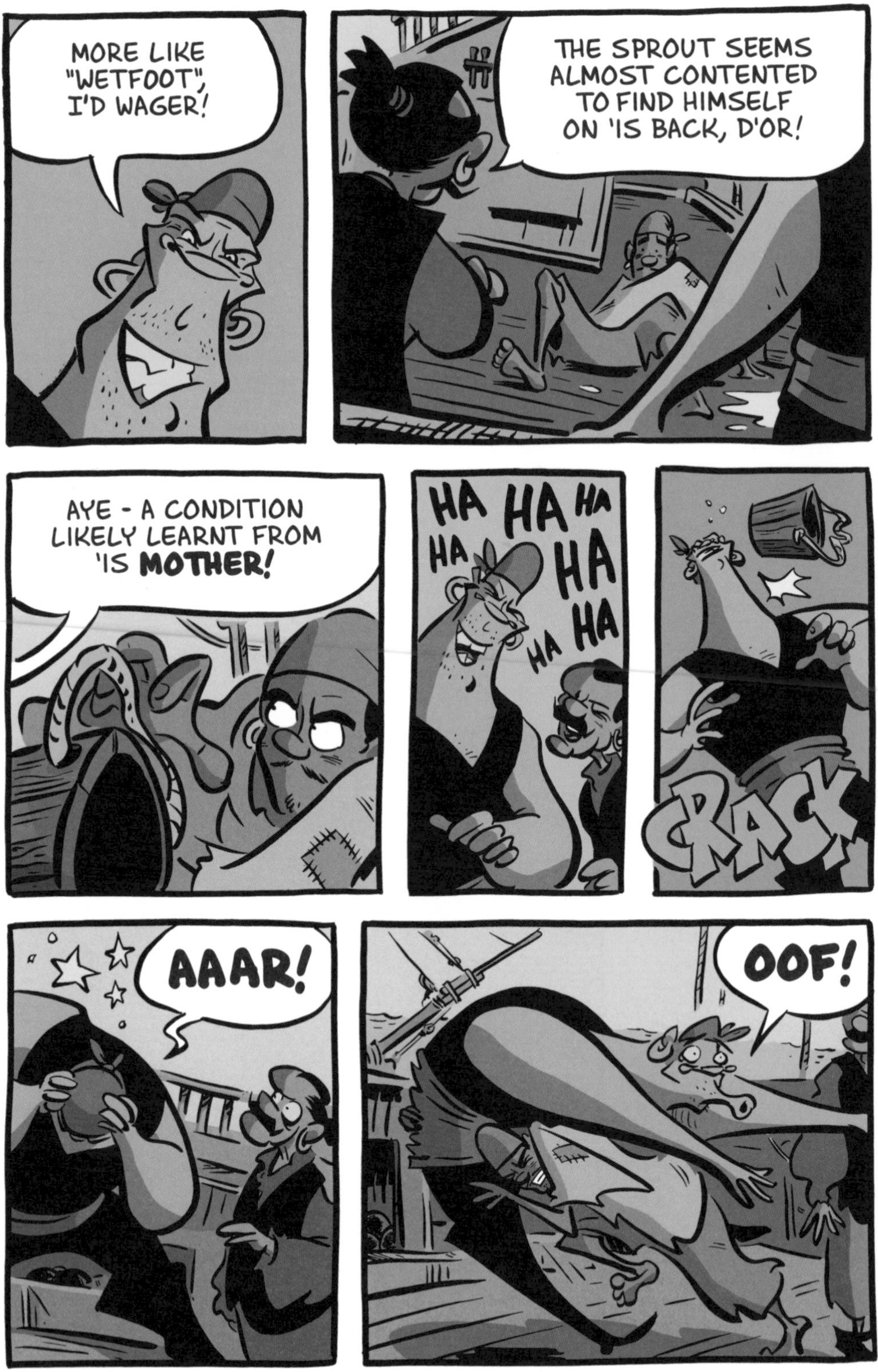
MORE LIKE "WETFOOT", I'D WAGER!
THE SPROUT SEEMS ALMOST CONTENTED TO FIND HIMSELF ON 'IS BACK, D'OR!
AYE - A CONDITION LIKELY LEARNT FROM 'IS **MOTHER**!
HA HA HA HA HA HA HA HA
CRACK
AAAR!
OOF!

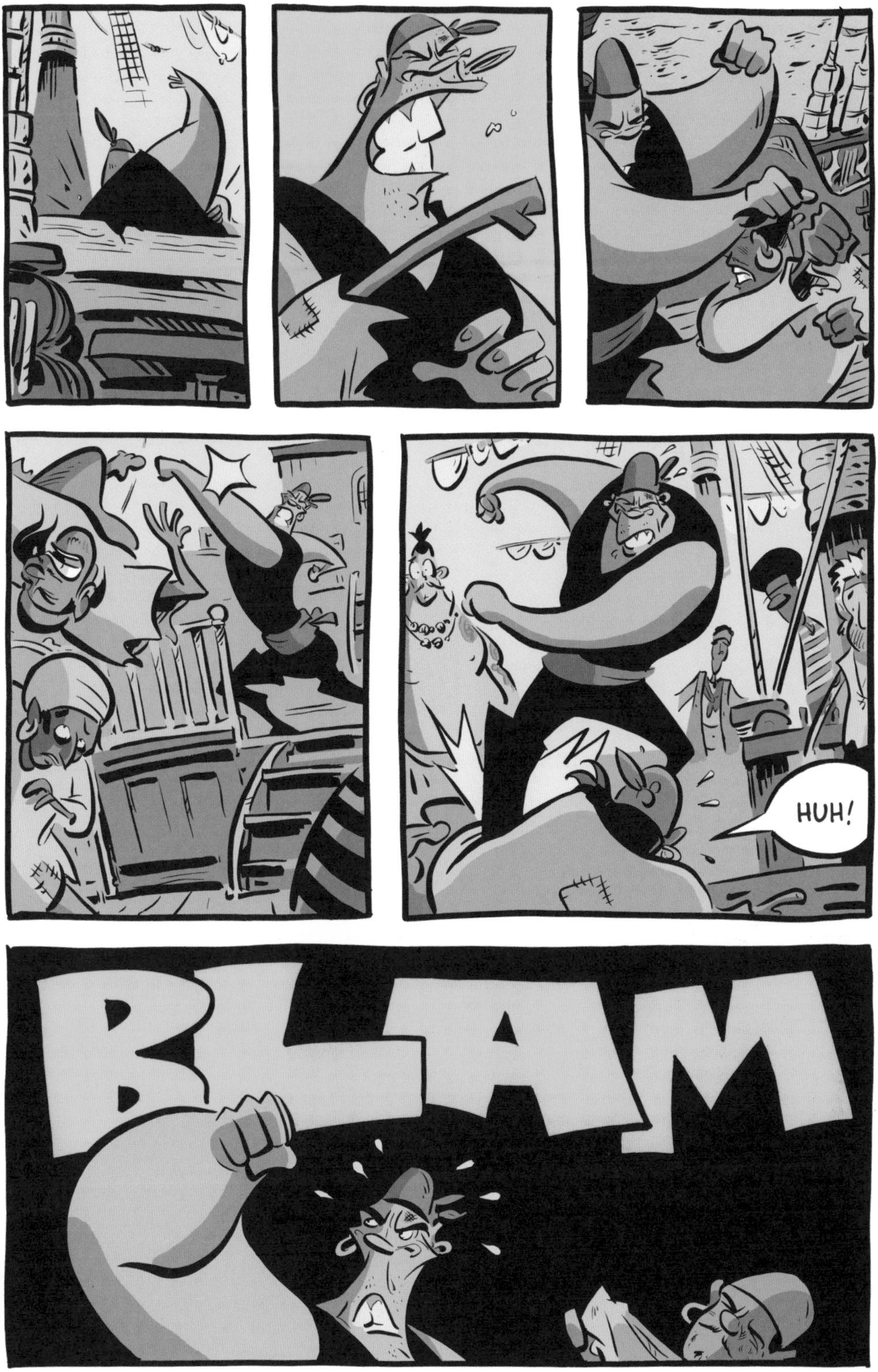
HUH!
BLAM

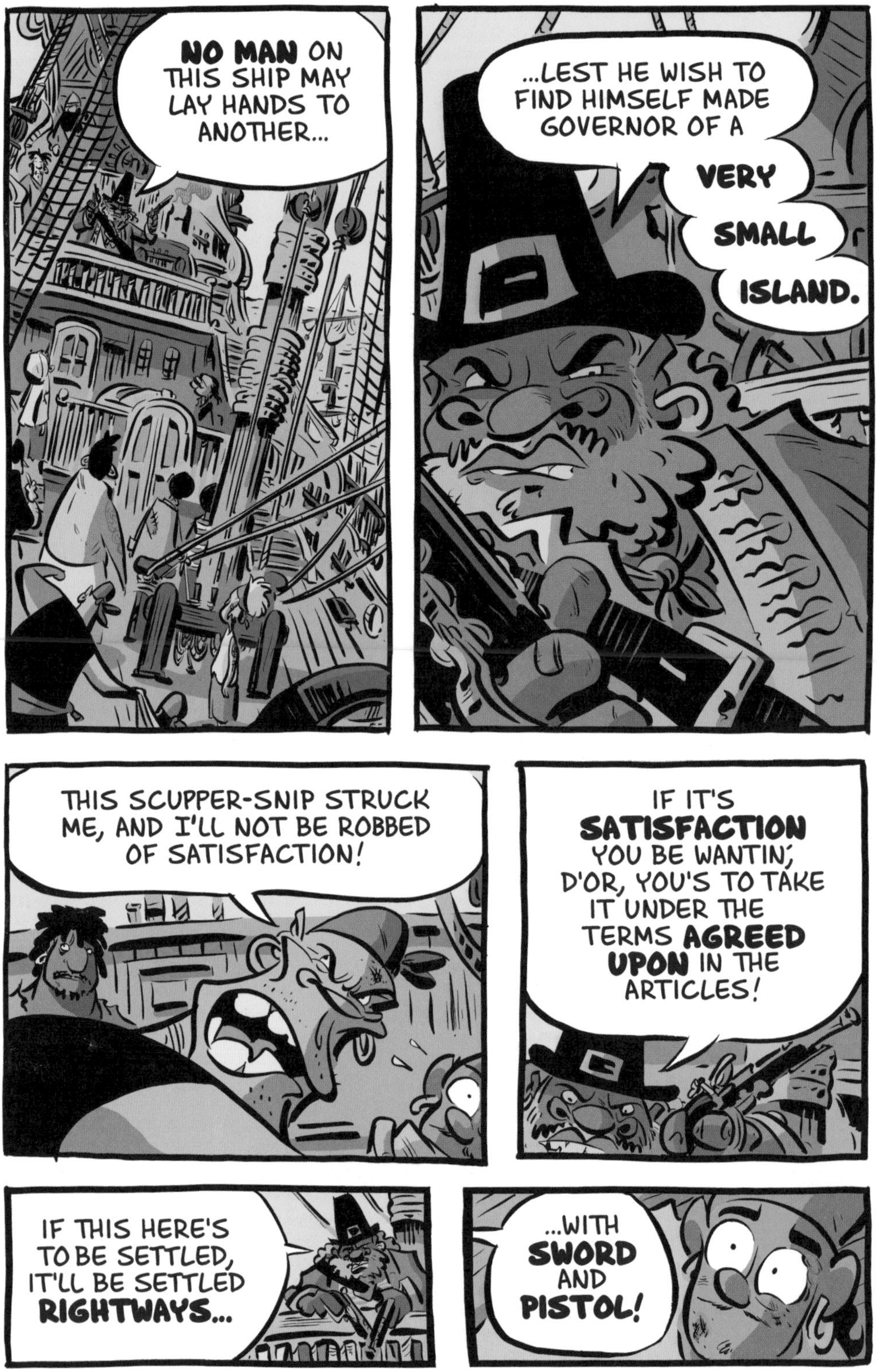
NO MAN ON THIS SHIP MAY LAY HANDS TO ANOTHER...
...LEST HE WISH TO FIND HIMSELF MADE GOVERNOR OF A
VERY
SMALL
ISLAND.
THIS SCUPPER-SNIP STRUCK ME, AND I'LL NOT BE ROBBED OF SATISFACTION!
IF IT'S SATISFACTION YOU BE WANTIN', D'OR, YOU'S TO TAKE IT UNDER THE TERMS AGREED UPON IN THE ARTICLES!
IF THIS HERE'S TO BE SETTLED, IT'LL BE SETTLED RIGHTWAYS...
...WITH SWORD AND PISTOL!

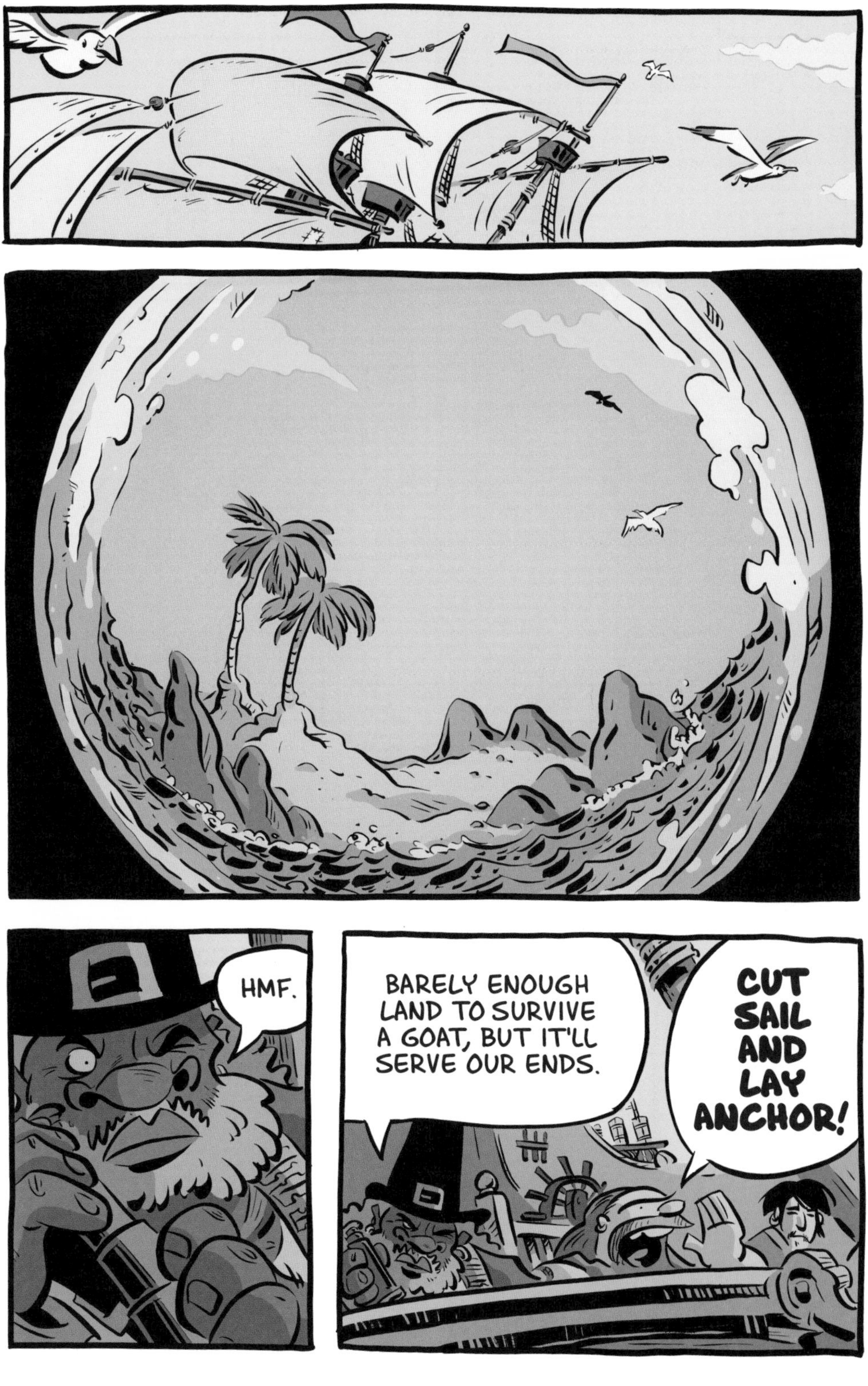
HMF.
BARELY ENOUGH LAND TO SURVIVE A GOAT, BUT IT'LL SERVE OUR ENDS.
CUT SAIL AND LAY ANCHOR!

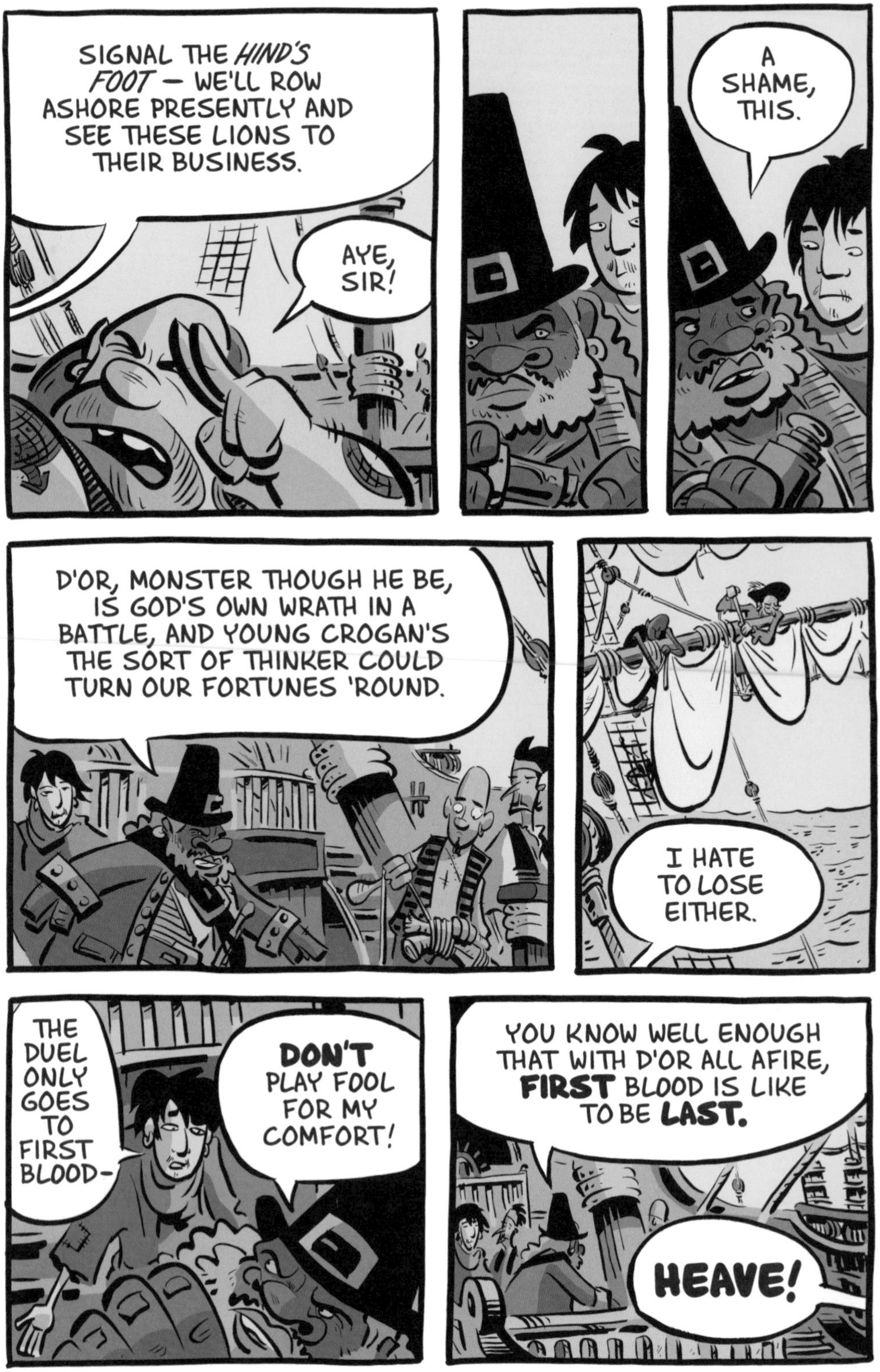
SIGNAL THE *HIND'S FOOT* — WE'LL ROW ASHORE PRESENTLY AND SEE THESE LIONS TO THEIR BUSINESS.
AYE, SIR!
A SHAME, THIS.
D'OR, MONSTER THOUGH HE BE, IS GOD'S OWN WRATH IN A BATTLE, AND YOUNG CROGAN'S THE SORT OF THINKER COULD TURN OUR FORTUNES 'ROUND.
I HATE TO LOSE EITHER.
THE DUEL ONLY GOES TO FIRST BLOOD-
DON'T PLAY FOOL FOR MY COMFORT!
YOU KNOW WELL ENOUGH THAT WITH D'OR ALL AFIRE, **FIRST** BLOOD IS LIKE TO BE **LAST.**
HEAVE!

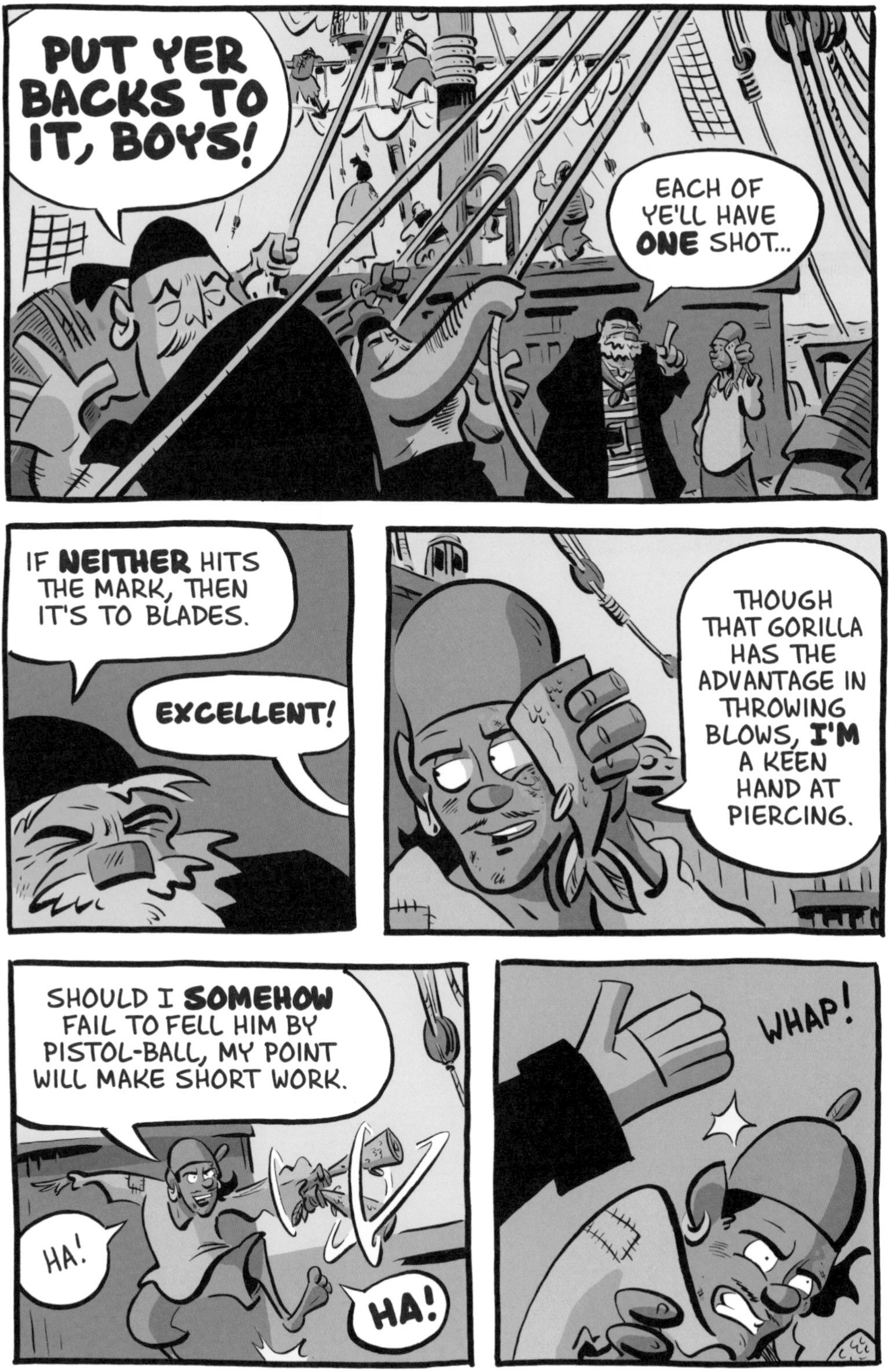
PUT YER BACKS TO IT, BOYS!
EACH OF YE'LL HAVE ONE SHOT...
IF NEITHER HITS THE MARK, THEN IT'S TO BLADES.
EXCELLENT!
THOUGH THAT GORILLA HAS THE ADVANTAGE IN THROWING BLOWS, I'M A KEEN HAND AT PIERCING.
SHOULD I SOMEHOW FAIL TO FELL HIM BY PISTOL-BALL, MY POINT WILL MAKE SHORT WORK.
HA!
HA!
WHAP!

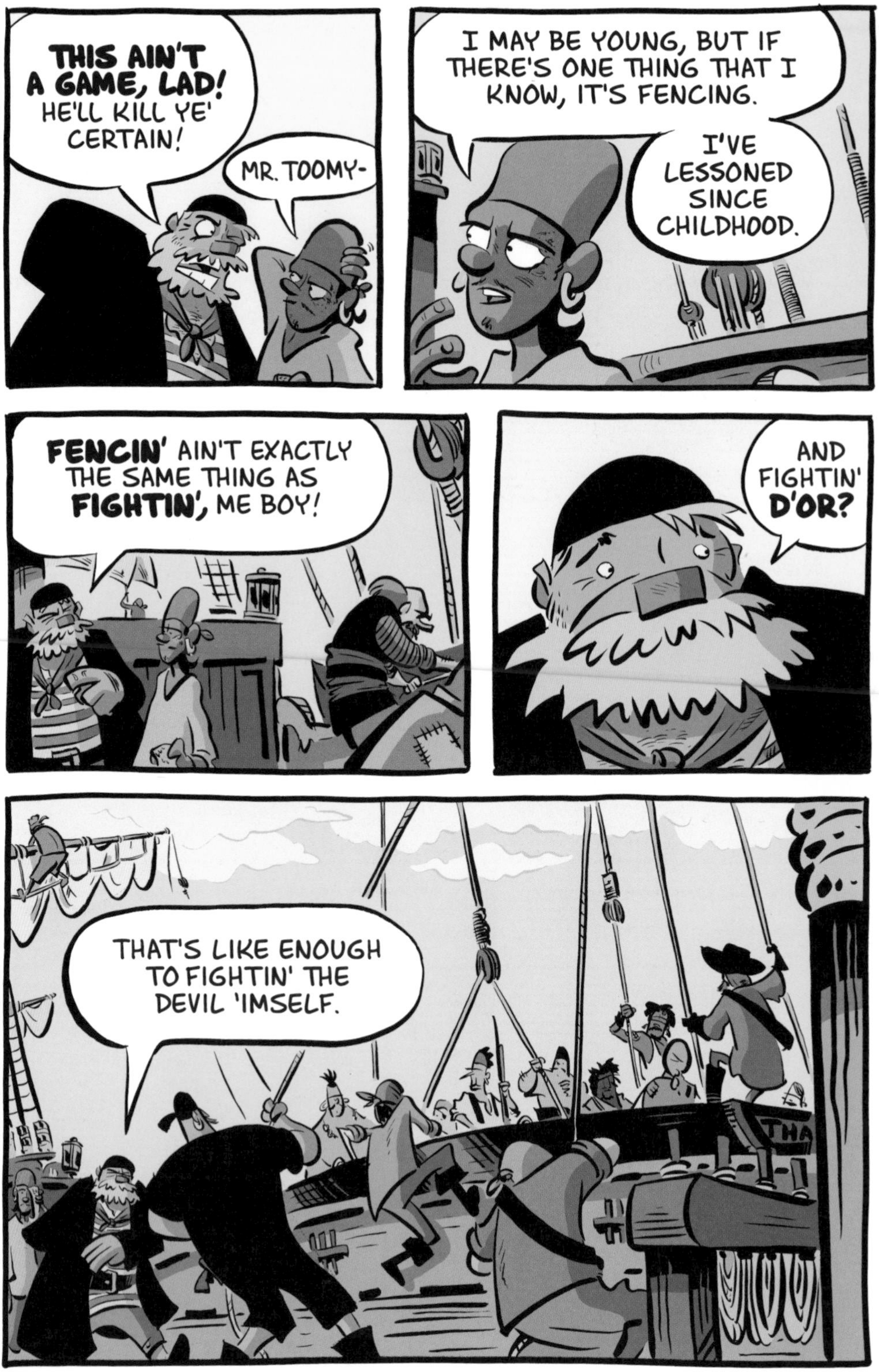
THIS AIN'T A GAME, LAD! HE'LL KILL YE' CERTAIN!
MR. TOOMY-
I MAY BE YOUNG, BUT IF THERE'S ONE THING THAT I KNOW, IT'S FENCING.
I'VE LESSONED SINCE CHILDHOOD.
FENCIN' AIN'T EXACTLY THE SAME THING AS FIGHTIN', ME BOY!
AND FIGHTIN' D'OR?
THAT'S LIKE ENOUGH TO FIGHTIN' THE DEVIL 'IMSELF.
THA

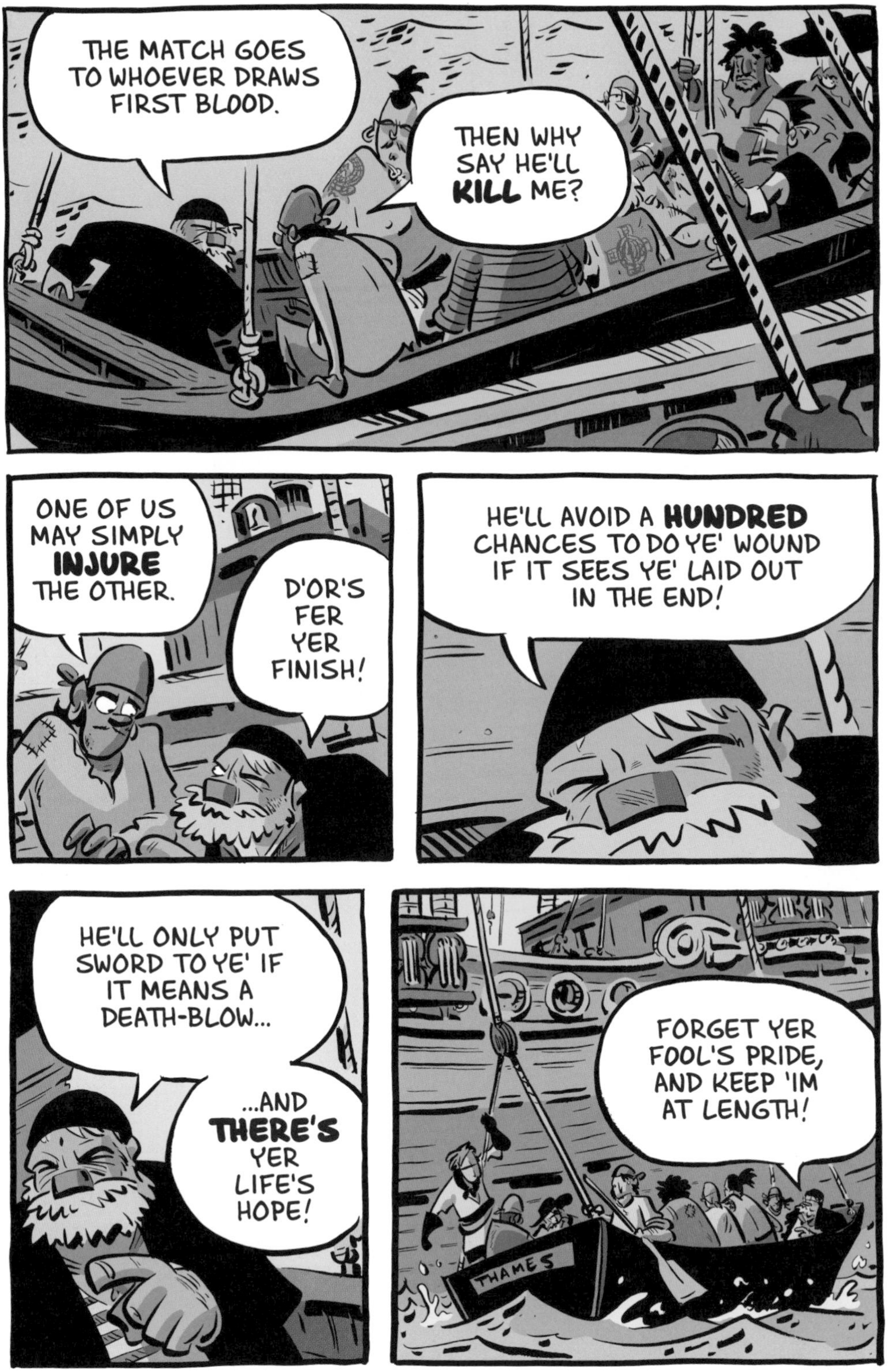
THE MATCH GOES TO WHOEVER DRAWS FIRST BLOOD.
THEN WHY SAY HE'LL **KILL** ME?
ONE OF US MAY SIMPLY **INJURE** THE OTHER.
D'OR'S FER YER FINISH!
HE'LL AVOID A **HUNDRED** CHANCES TO DO YE' WOUND IF IT SEES YE' LAID OUT IN THE END!
HE'LL ONLY PUT SWORD TO YE' IF IT MEANS A DEATH-BLOW...
...AND **THERE'S** YER LIFE'S HOPE!
FORGET YER FOOL'S PRIDE, AND KEEP 'IM AT LENGTH!
THAMES

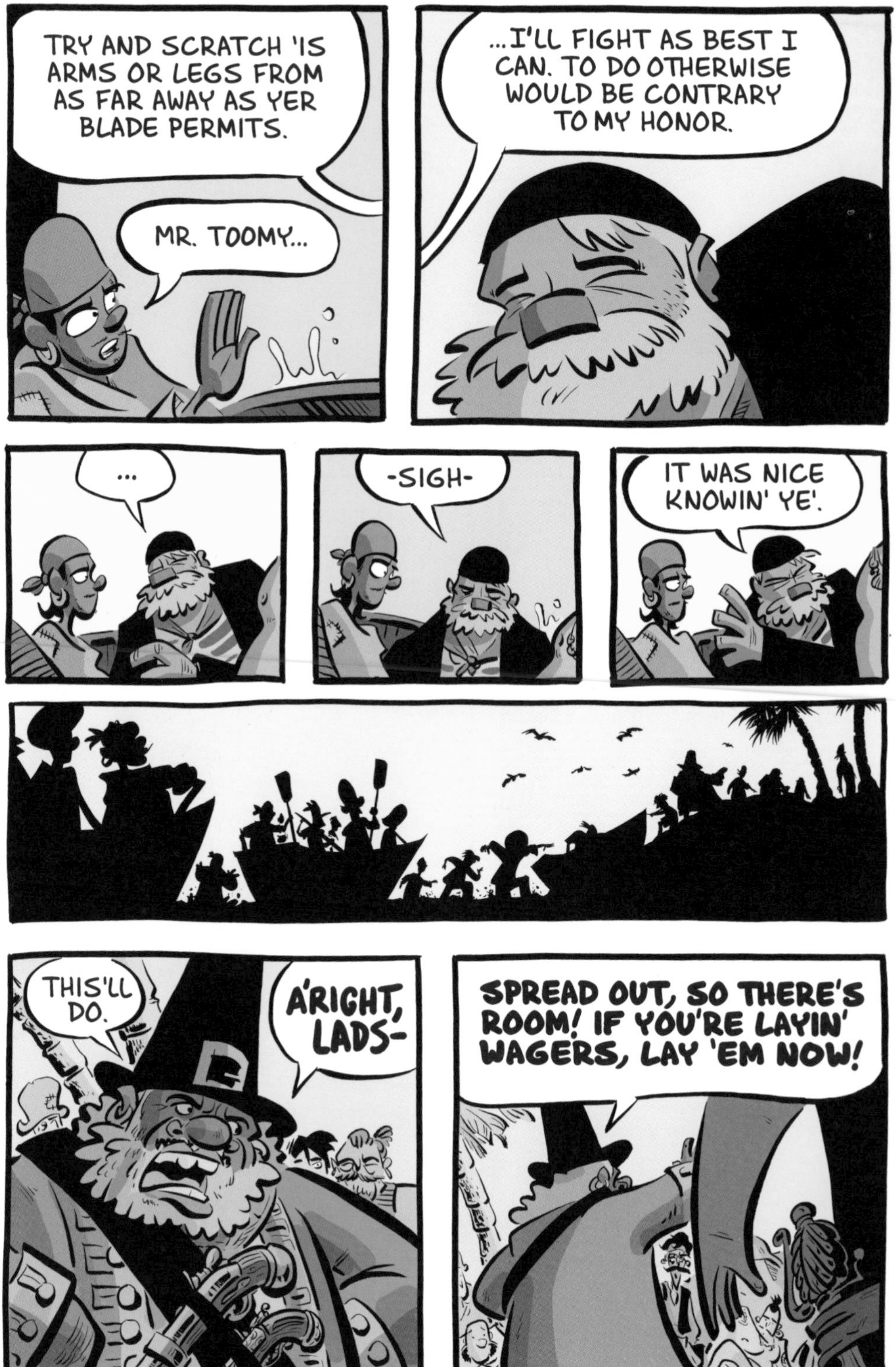
TRY AND SCRATCH 'IS ARMS OR LEGS FROM AS FAR AWAY AS YER BLADE PERMITS.
MR. TOOMY...
...I'LL FIGHT AS BEST I CAN. TO DO OTHERWISE WOULD BE CONTRARY TO MY HONOR.
...
-SIGH-
IT WAS NICE KNOWIN' YE'.
THIS'LL DO.
A'RIGHT, LADS-
SPREAD OUT, SO THERE'S ROOM! IF YOU'RE LAYIN' WAGERS, LAY 'EM NOW!

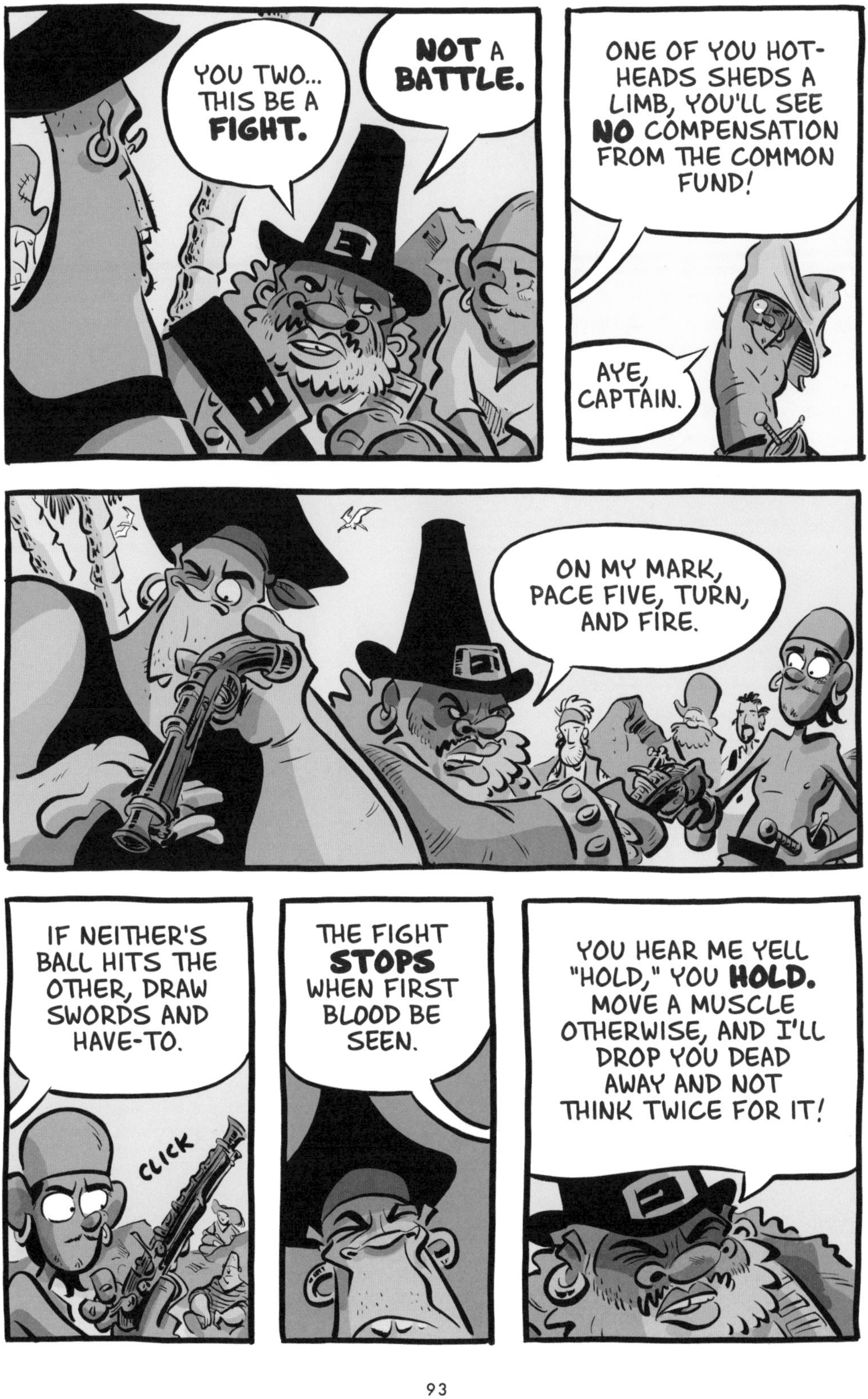
YOU TWO... THIS BE A **FIGHT.**
NOT A **BATTLE.**
ONE OF YOU HOT-HEADS SHEDS A LIMB, YOU'LL SEE **NO** COMPENSATION FROM THE COMMON FUND!
AYE, CAPTAIN.
ON MY MARK, PACE FIVE, TURN, AND FIRE.
IF NEITHER'S BALL HITS THE OTHER, DRAW SWORDS AND HAVE-TO.
CLICK
THE FIGHT **STOPS** WHEN FIRST BLOOD BE SEEN.
YOU HEAR ME YELL "HOLD," YOU **HOLD.** MOVE A MUSCLE OTHERWISE, AND I'LL DROP YOU DEAD AWAY AND NOT THINK TWICE FOR IT!

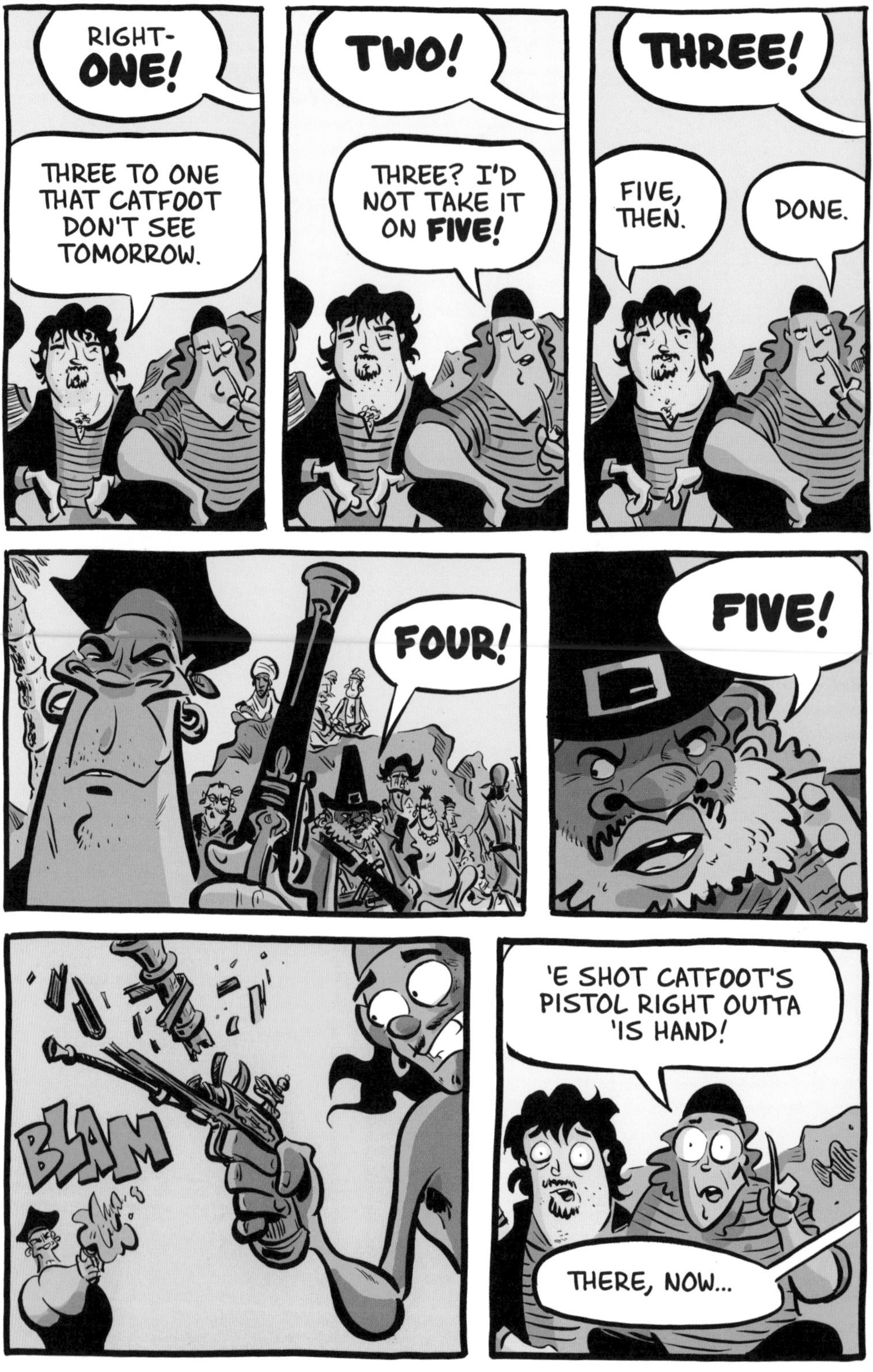
RIGHT-
ONE!
THREE TO ONE THAT CATFOOT DON'T SEE TOMORROW.
TWO!
THREE? I'D NOT TAKE IT ON FIVE!
THREE!
FIVE, THEN.
DONE.
FOUR!
FIVE!
BLAM
'E SHOT CATFOOT'S PISTOL RIGHT OUTTA 'IS HAND!
THERE, NOW...

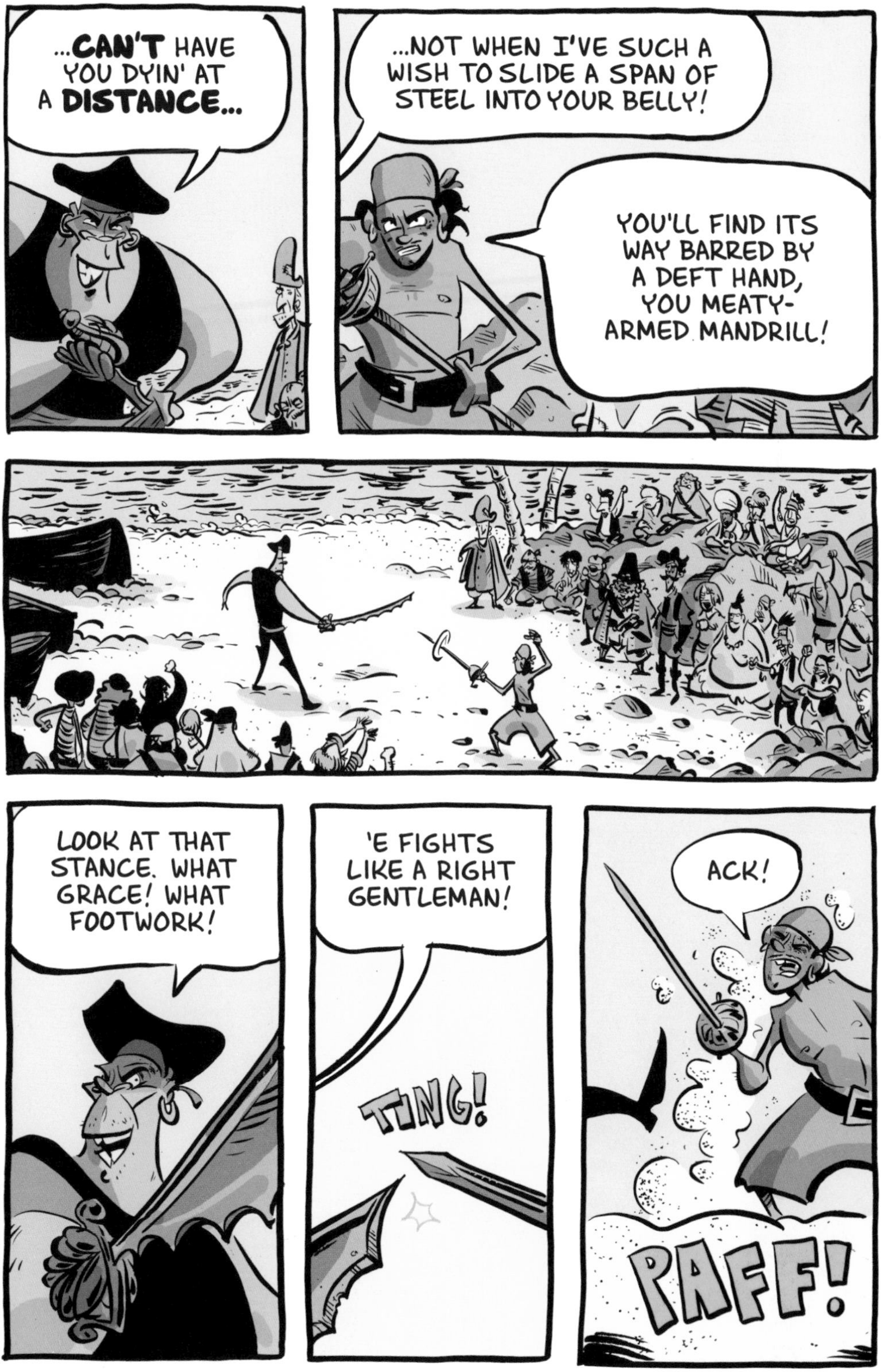
...**CAN'T** HAVE YOU DYIN' AT A **DISTANCE**...
...NOT WHEN I'VE SUCH A WISH TO SLIDE A SPAN OF STEEL INTO YOUR BELLY!
YOU'LL FIND ITS WAY BARRED BY A DEFT HAND, YOU MEATY-ARMED MANDRILL!
LOOK AT THAT STANCE. WHAT GRACE! WHAT FOOTWORK!
'E FIGHTS LIKE A RIGHT GENTLEMAN!
TING!
ACK!
PAFF!

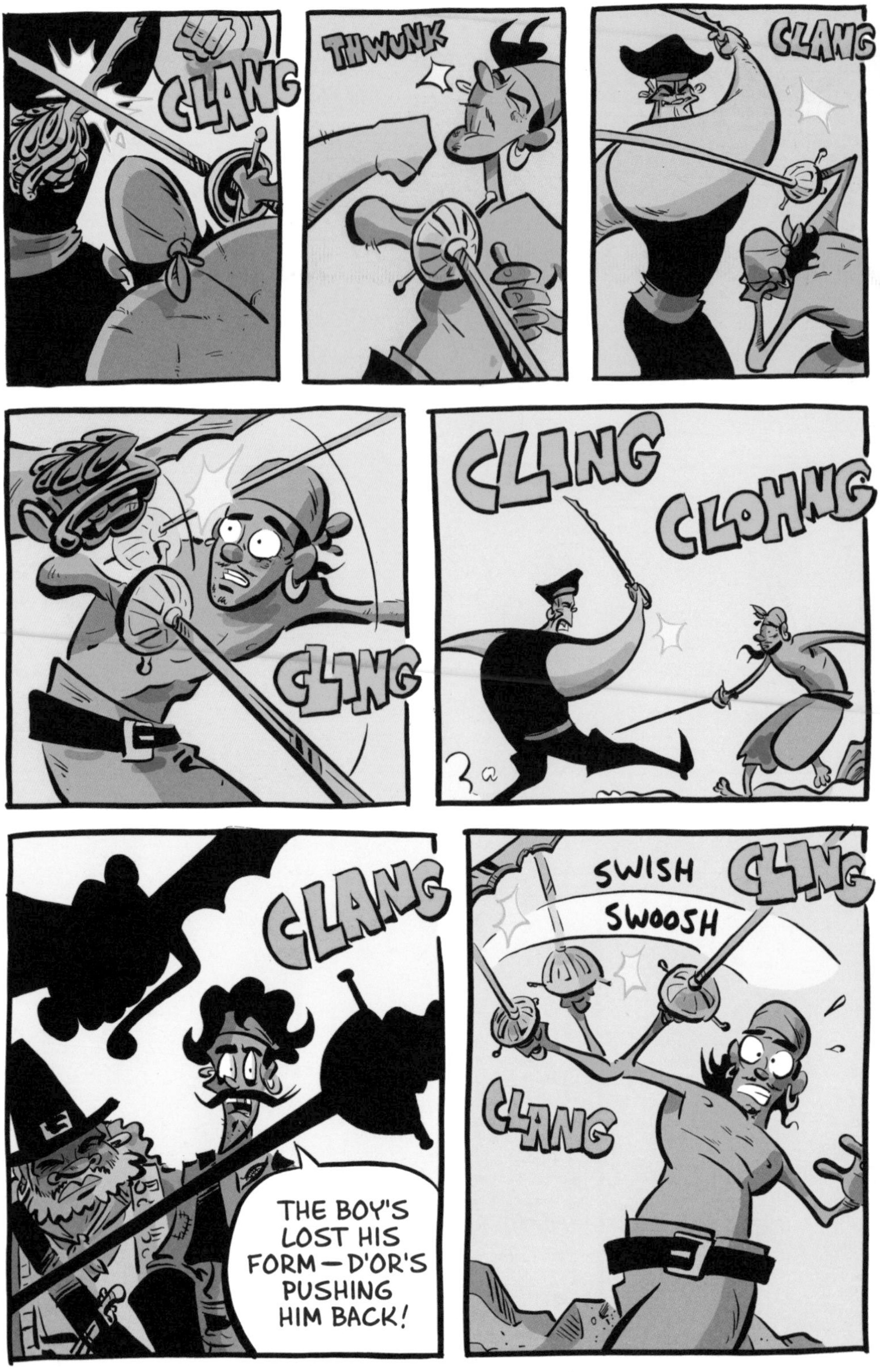
CLANG
THWUNK
CLANG
CLANG
CLING
CLOHNG
CLANG
THE BOY'S LOST HIS FORM—D'OR'S PUSHING HIM BACK!
SWISH
SWOOSH
CLING
CLANG

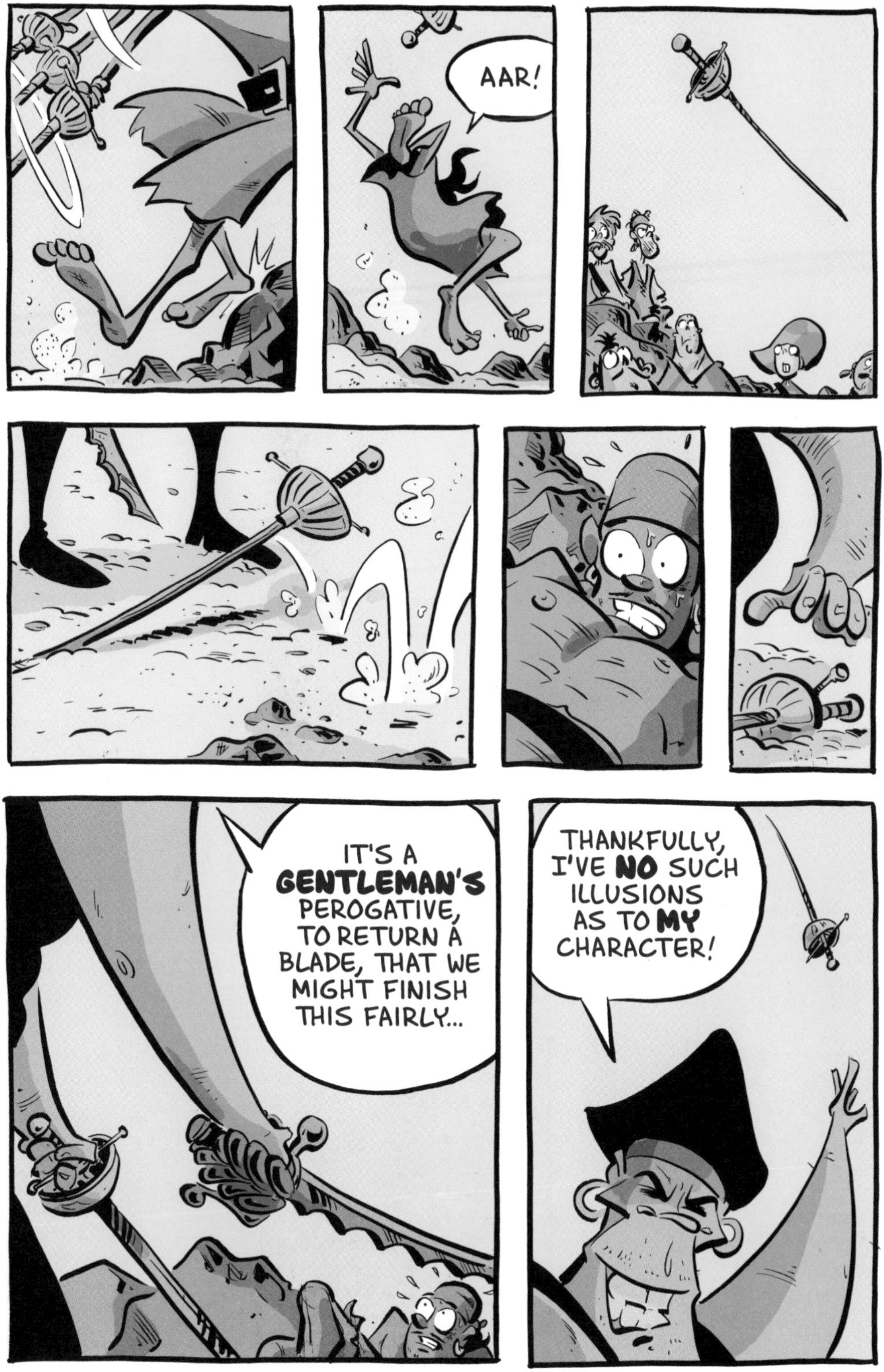
AAR!
IT'S A GENTLEMAN'S PEROGATIVE, TO RETURN A BLADE, THAT WE MIGHT FINISH THIS FAIRLY...
THANKFULLY, I'VE NO SUCH ILLUSIONS AS TO MY CHARACTER!

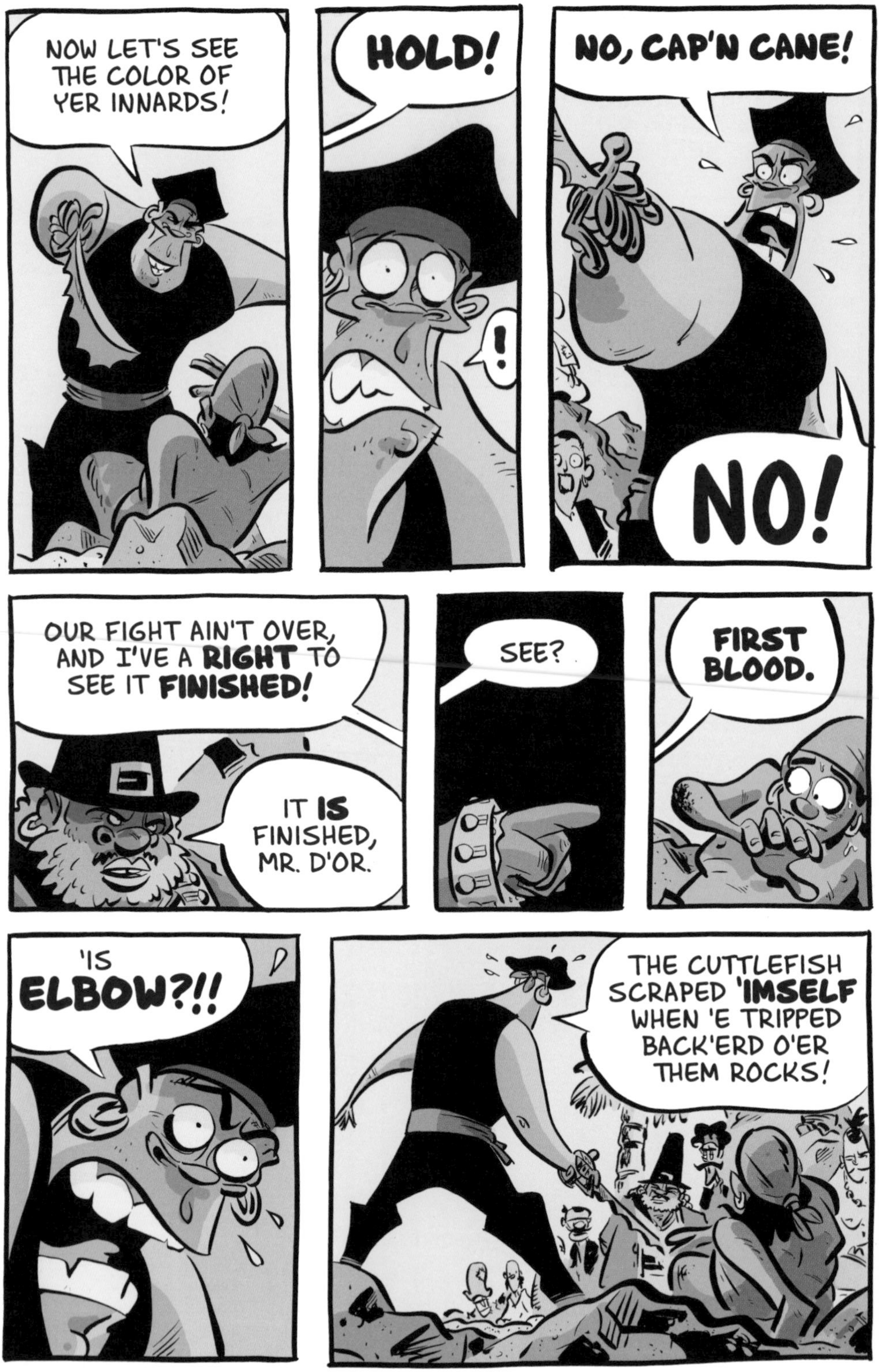
NOW LET'S SEE THE COLOR OF YER INNARDS!
HOLD!
!
NO, CAP'N CANE!
NO!
OUR FIGHT AIN'T OVER, AND I'VE A RIGHT TO SEE IT FINISHED!
IT IS FINISHED, MR. D'OR.
SEE?
FIRST BLOOD.
'IS ELBOW?!!
THE CUTTLEFISH SCRAPED 'IMSELF WHEN 'E TRIPPED BACK'ERD O'ER THEM ROCKS!

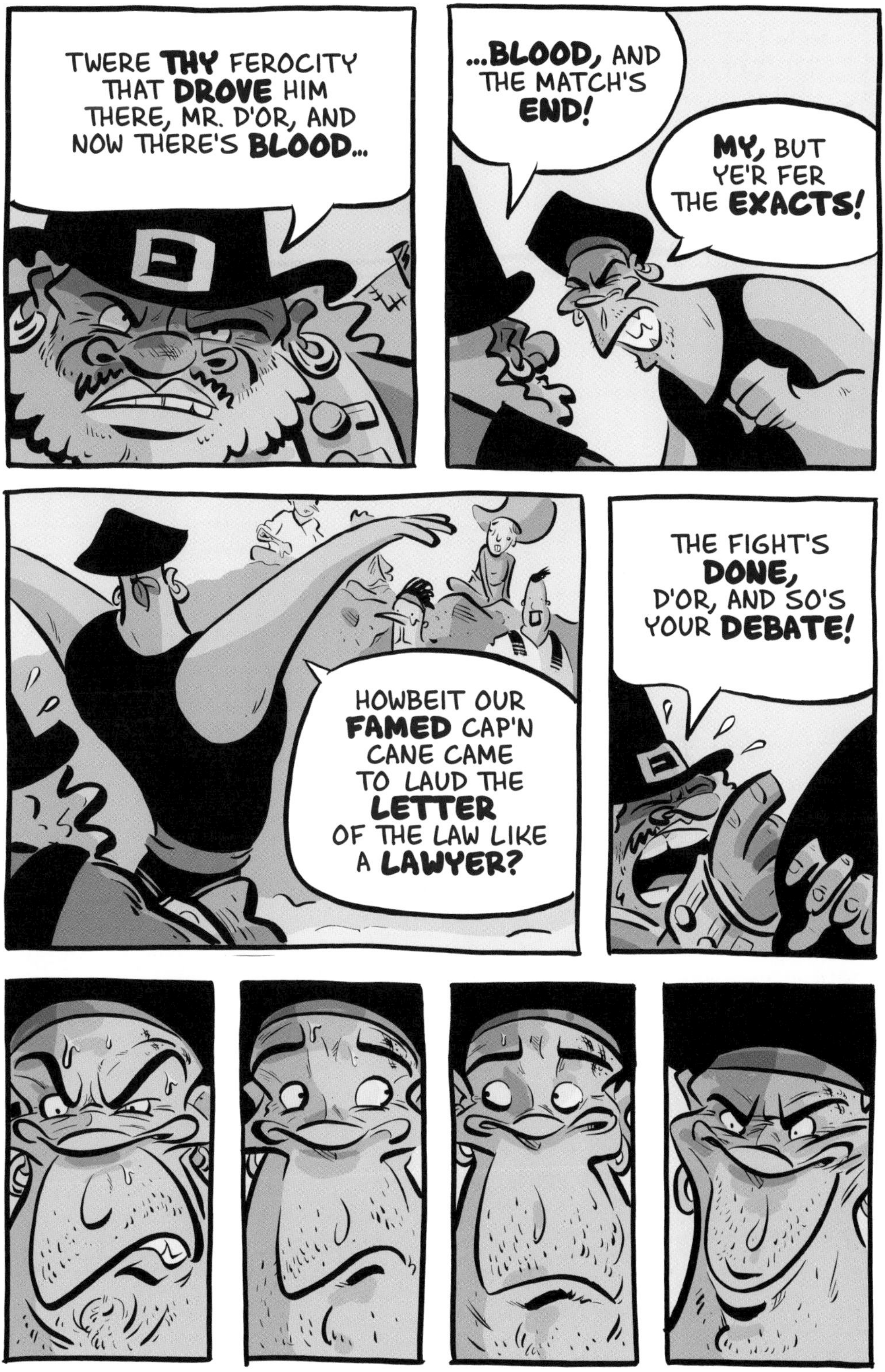
TWERE THY FEROCITY THAT DROVE HIM THERE, MR. D'OR, AND NOW THERE'S BLOOD...
...BLOOD, AND THE MATCH'S END!
MY, BUT YE'R FER THE EXACTS!
HOWBEIT OUR FAMED CAP'N CANE CAME TO LAUD THE LETTER OF THE LAW LIKE A LAWYER?
THE FIGHT'S DONE, D'OR, AND SO'S YOUR DEBATE!

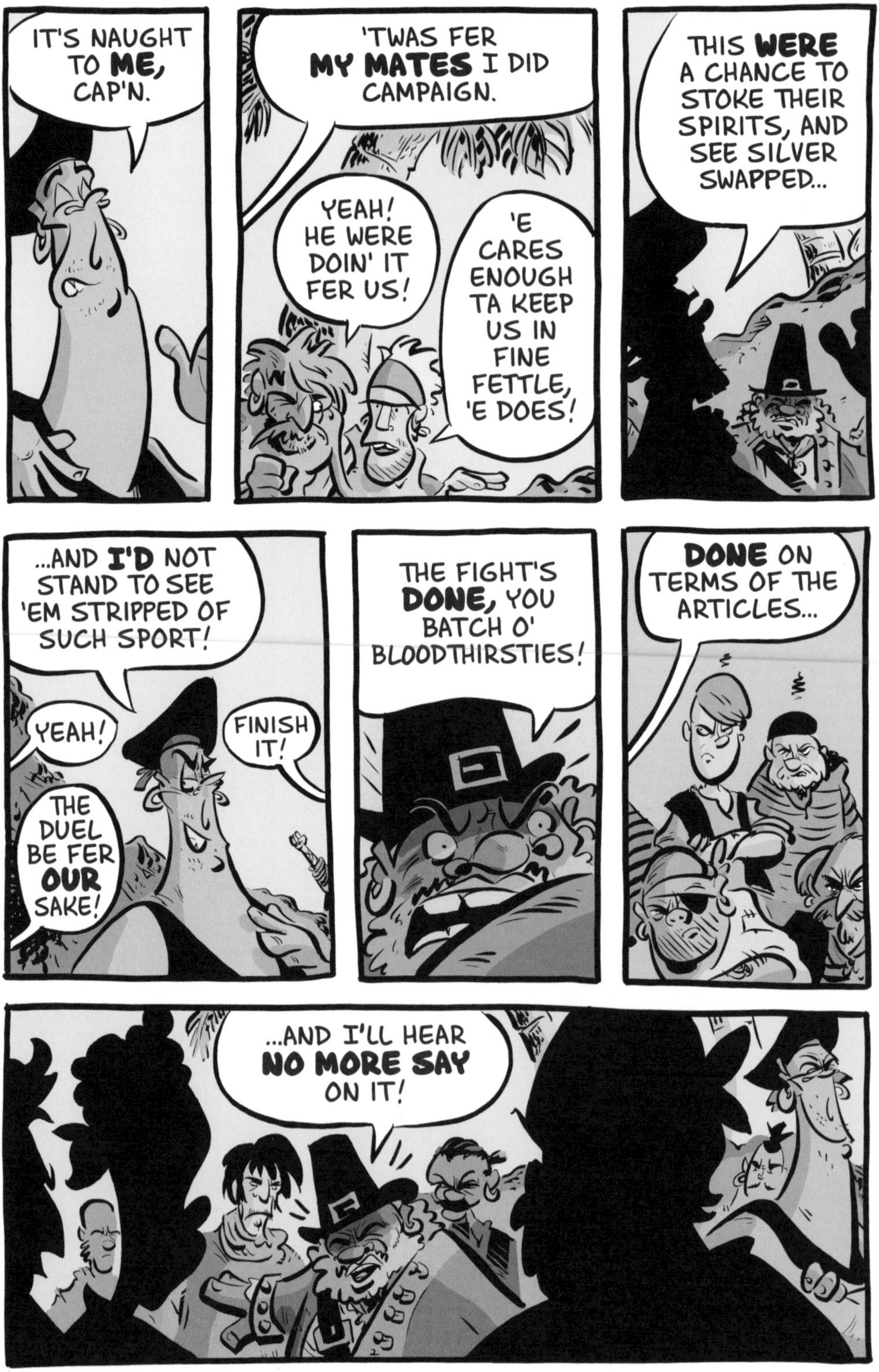

IT'S NAUGHT TO ME, CAP'N.
'TWAS FER MY MATES I DID CAMPAIGN.
YEAH! HE WERE DOIN' IT FER US!
'E CARES ENOUGH TA KEEP US IN FINE FETTLE, 'E DOES!
THIS WERE A CHANCE TO STOKE THEIR SPIRITS, AND SEE SILVER SWAPPED...
...AND I'D NOT STAND TO SEE 'EM STRIPPED OF SUCH SPORT!
YEAH!
FINISH IT!
THE DUEL BE FER OUR SAKE!
THE FIGHT'S DONE, YOU BATCH O' BLOODTHIRSTIES!
DONE ON TERMS OF THE ARTICLES...
...AND I'LL HEAR NO MORE SAY ON IT!

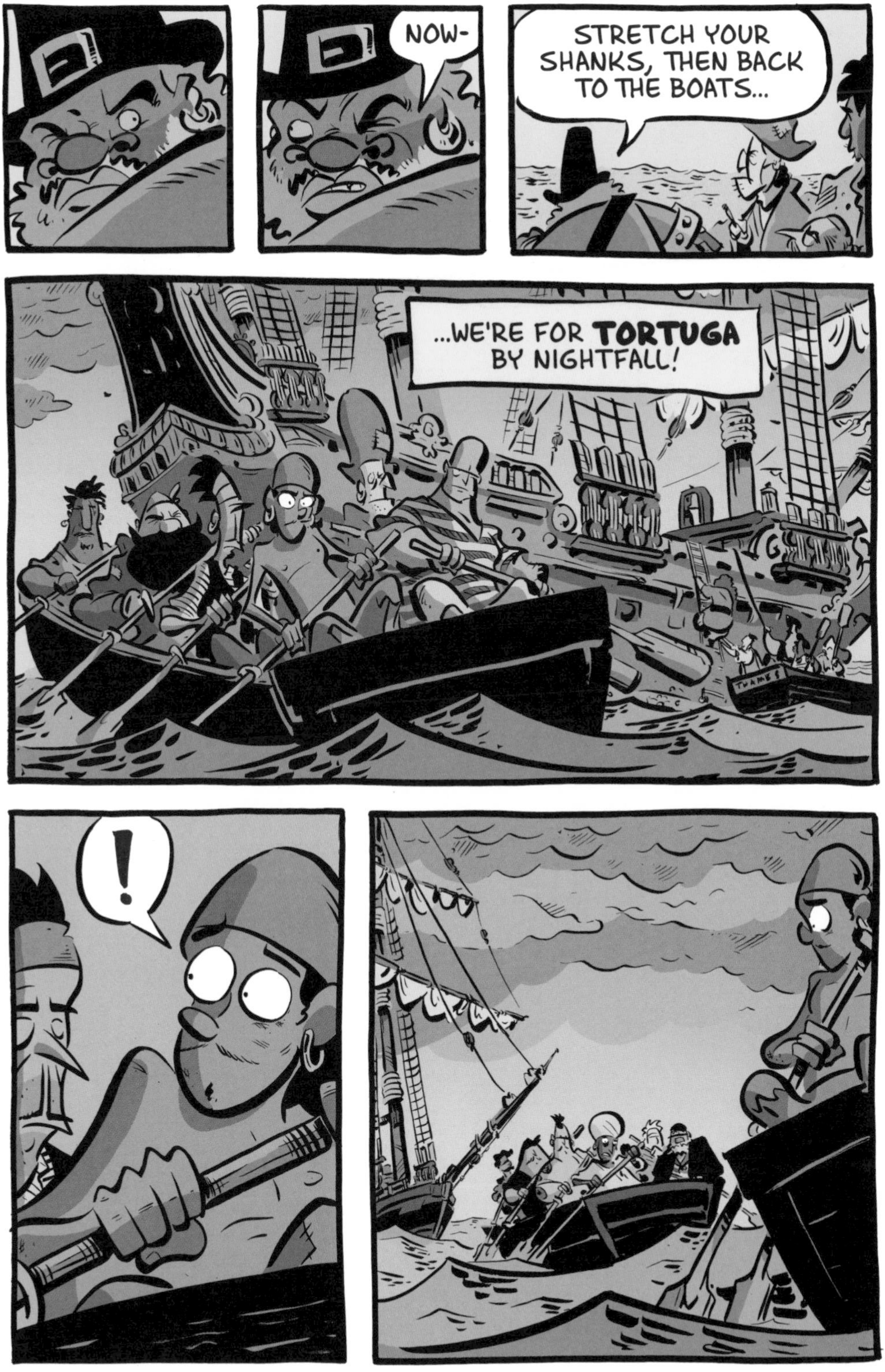
NOW-
STRETCH YOUR SHANKS, THEN BACK TO THE BOATS...
...WE'RE FOR **TORTUGA** BY NIGHTFALL!
!

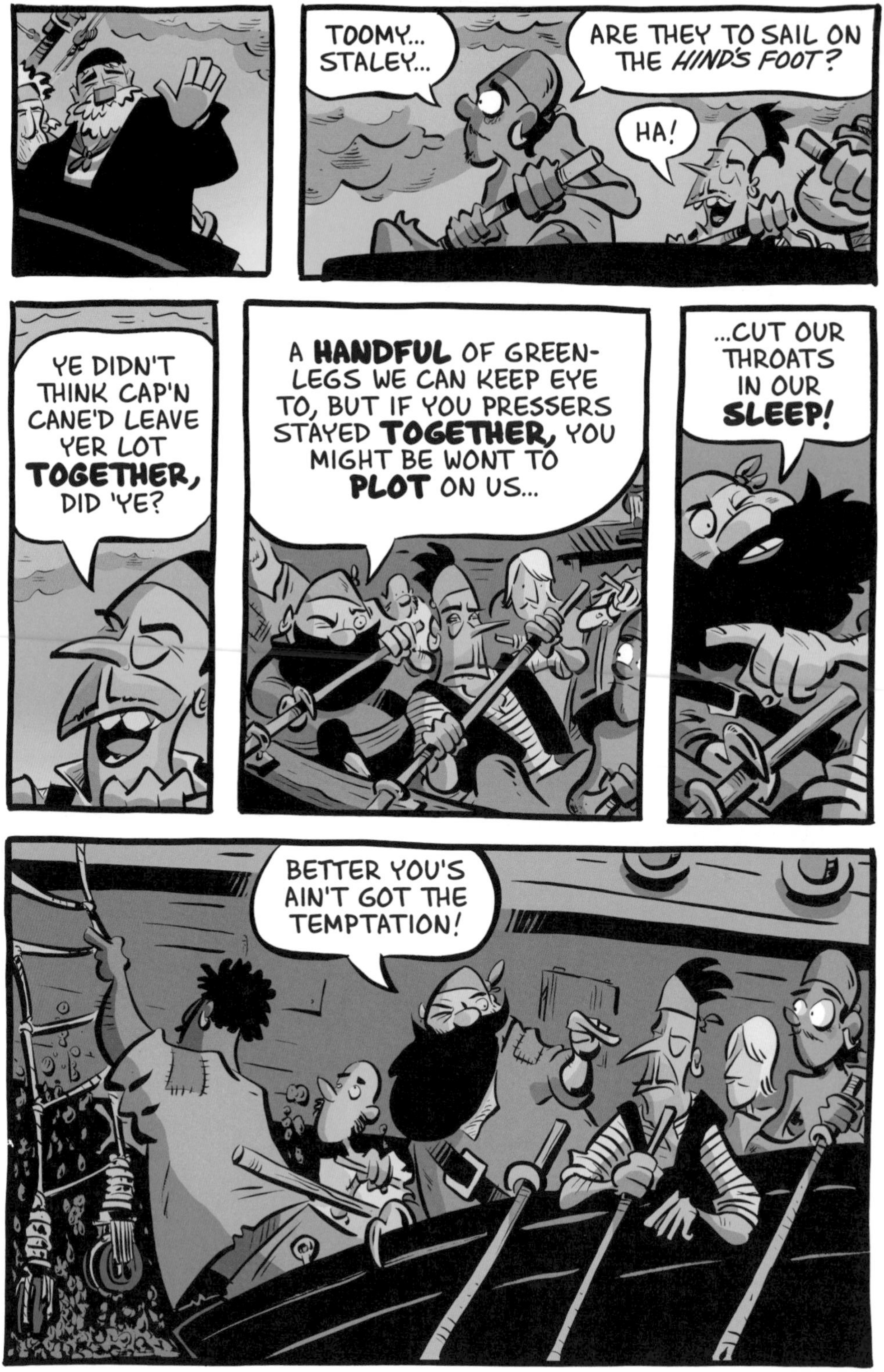
TOOMY... STALEY...
ARE THEY TO SAIL ON THE *HIND'S FOOT*?
HA!
YE DIDN'T THINK CAP'N CANE'D LEAVE YER LOT **TOGETHER**, DID 'YE?
A **HANDFUL** OF GREEN-LEGS WE CAN KEEP EYE TO, BUT IF YOU PRESSERS STAYED **TOGETHER**, YOU MIGHT BE WONT TO **PLOT** ON US...
...CUT OUR THROATS IN OUR **SLEEP**!
BETTER YOU'S AIN'T GOT THE TEMPTATION!

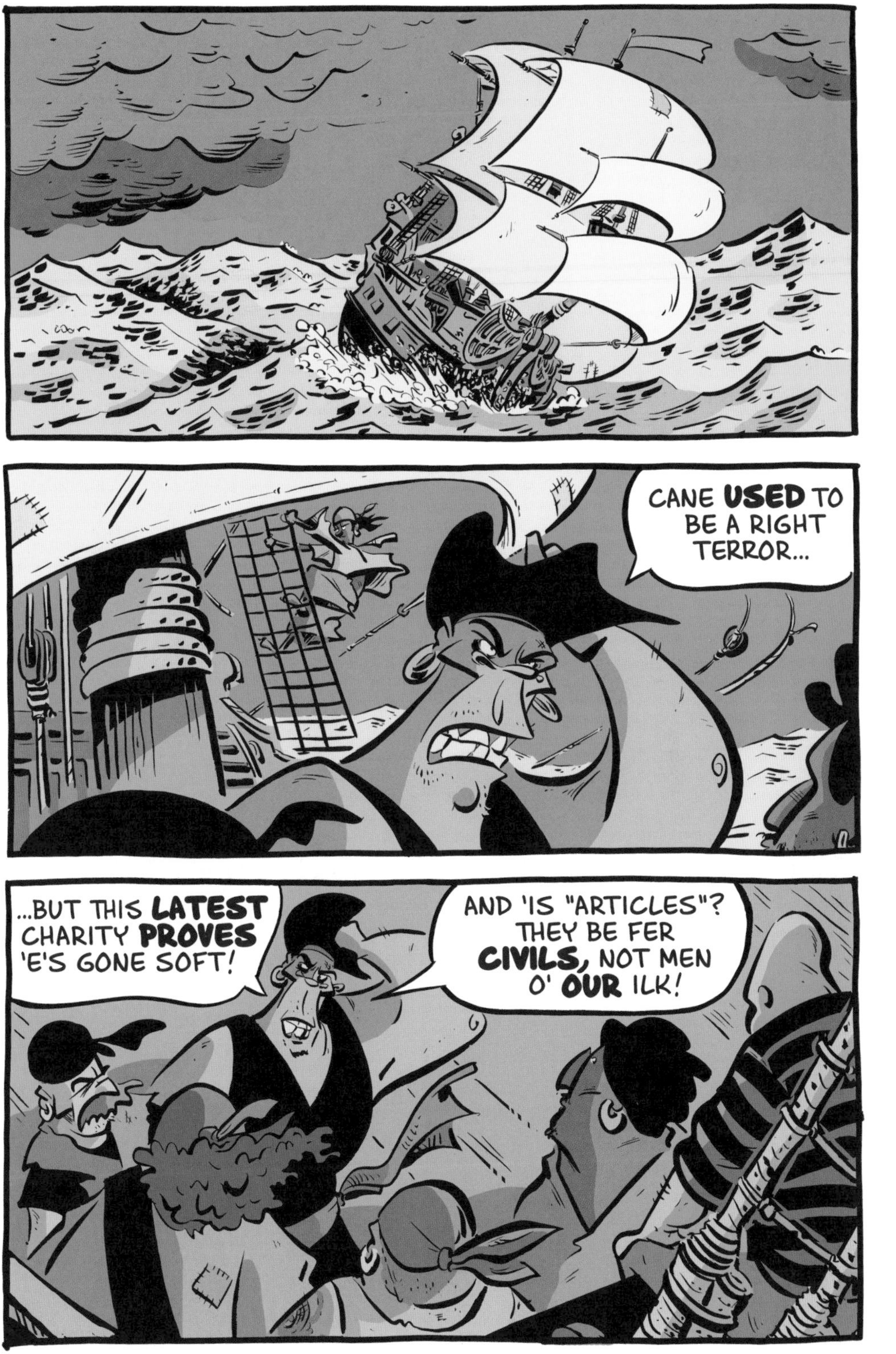
CANE USED TO BE A RIGHT TERROR...
...BUT THIS LATEST CHARITY PROVES 'E'S GONE SOFT!
AND 'IS "ARTICLES"? THEY BE FER CIVILS, NOT MEN O' OUR ILK!

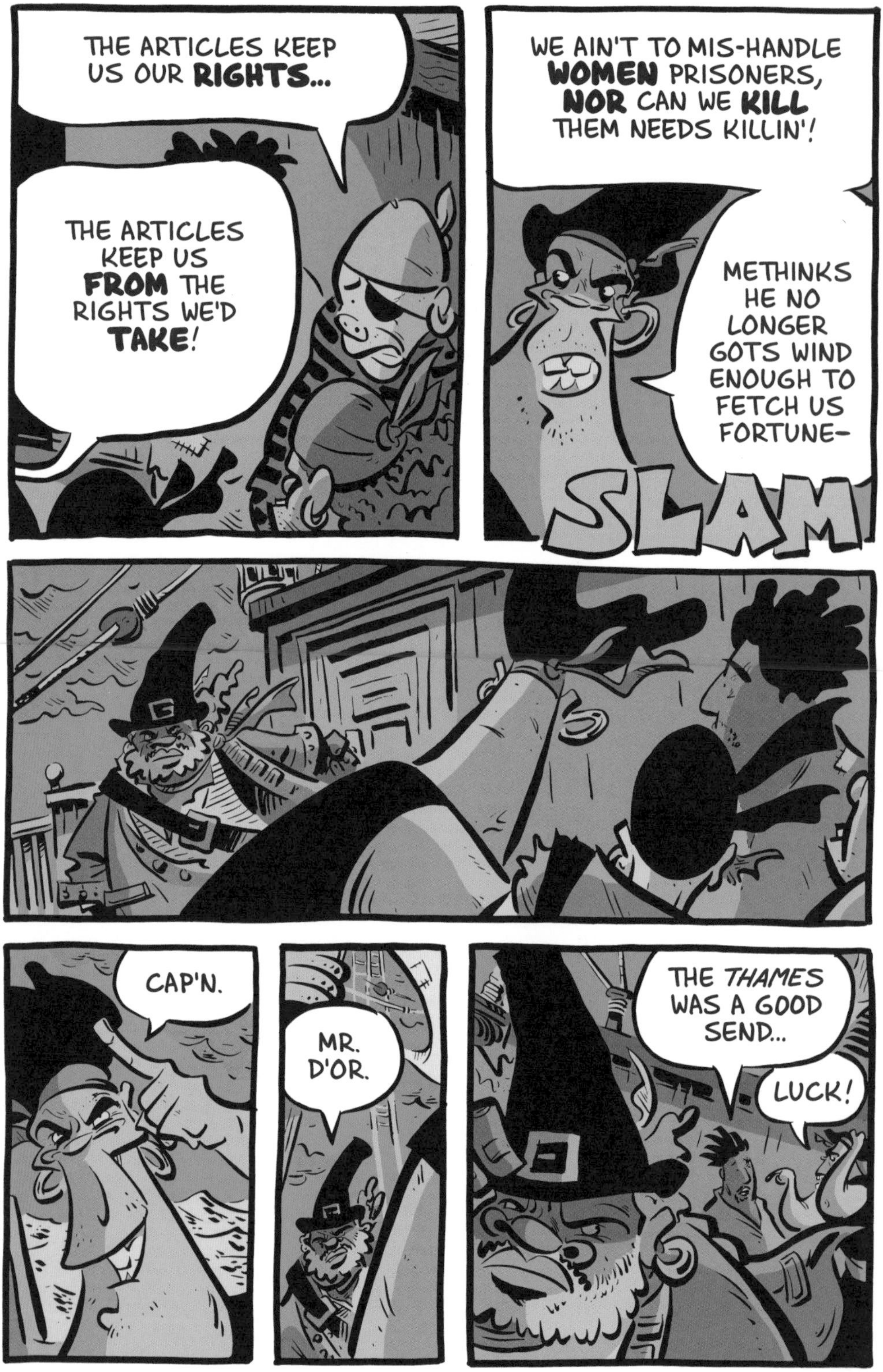
THE ARTICLES KEEP US OUR **RIGHTS...**
THE ARTICLES KEEP US **FROM** THE RIGHTS WE'D **TAKE**!
WE AIN'T TO MIS-HANDLE **WOMEN** PRISONERS, **NOR** CAN WE **KILL** THEM NEEDS KILLIN'!
METHINKS HE NO LONGER GOTS WIND ENOUGH TO FETCH US FORTUNE-
SLAM
CAP'N.
MR. D'OR.
THE *THAMES* WAS A GOOD SEND...
LUCK!

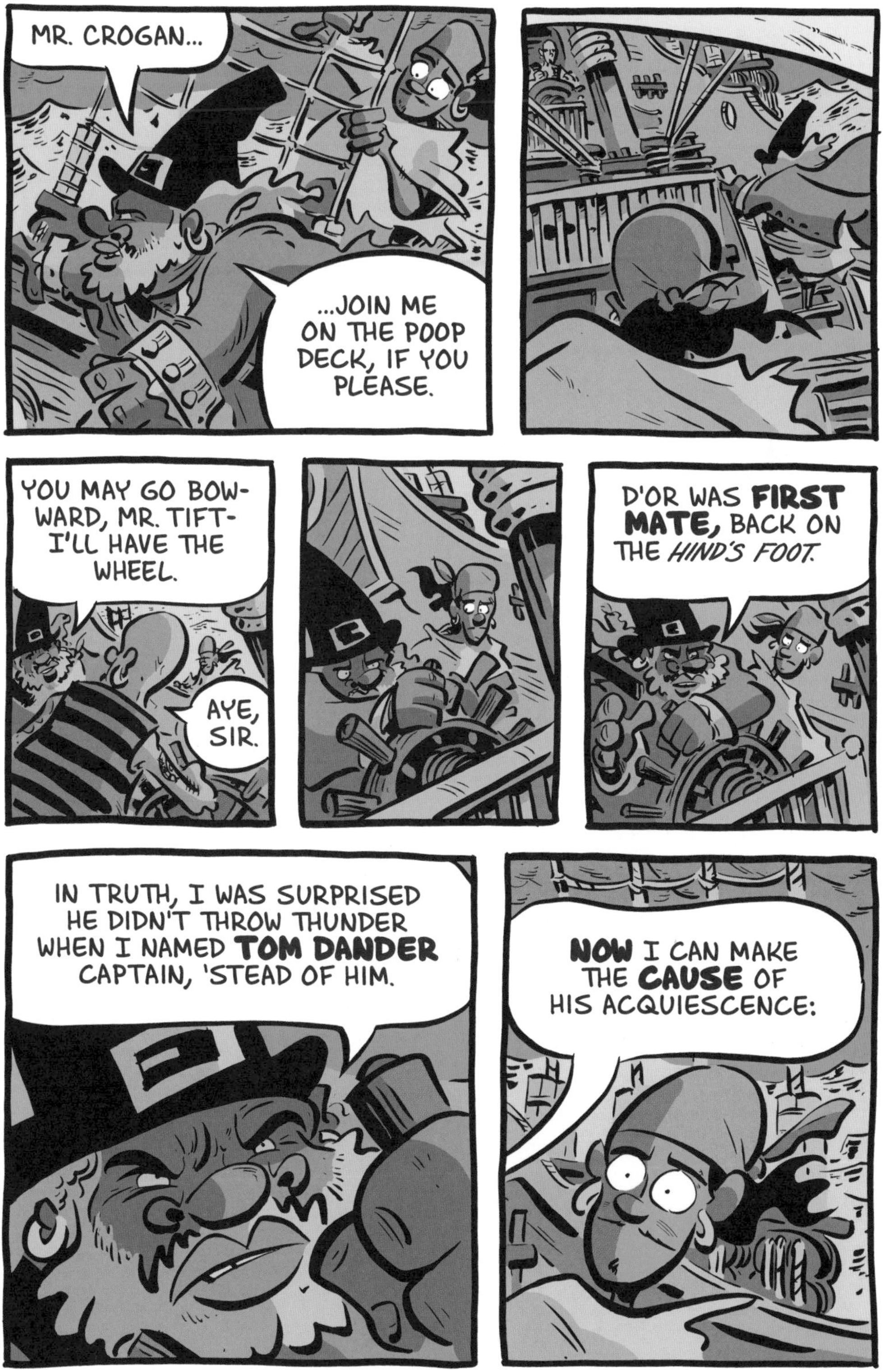
MR. CROGAN...
...JOIN ME ON THE POOP DECK, IF YOU PLEASE.
YOU MAY GO BOW-WARD, MR. TIFT-I'LL HAVE THE WHEEL.
AYE, SIR.
D'OR WAS FIRST MATE, BACK ON THE HIND'S FOOT.
IN TRUTH, I WAS SURPRISED HE DIDN'T THROW THUNDER WHEN I NAMED TOM DANDER CAPTAIN, 'STEAD OF HIM.
NOW I CAN MAKE THE CAUSE OF HIS ACQUIESCENCE:

HE WANTS THE *VENGEANCE* FOR HIMSELF...

...AND **HAS**, I'D WAGER, SINCE HE FIRST LAID EYES TO HER.

DOES HE MEAN TO LEAD A MUTINY?

NO...

...**NO**. HE'S TURNING THE CREW, AND HE'LL RAISE A VOTE ON ME SHOULD THE OPPORTUNITY PRESENT ITSELF.

D'OR WINS THE VOTE...

...**HE** BECOMES CAPTAIN.

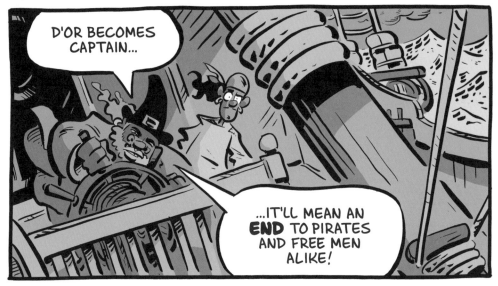

D'OR BECOMES CAPTAIN...

...IT'LL MEAN AN **END** TO PIRATES AND FREE MEN ALIKE!

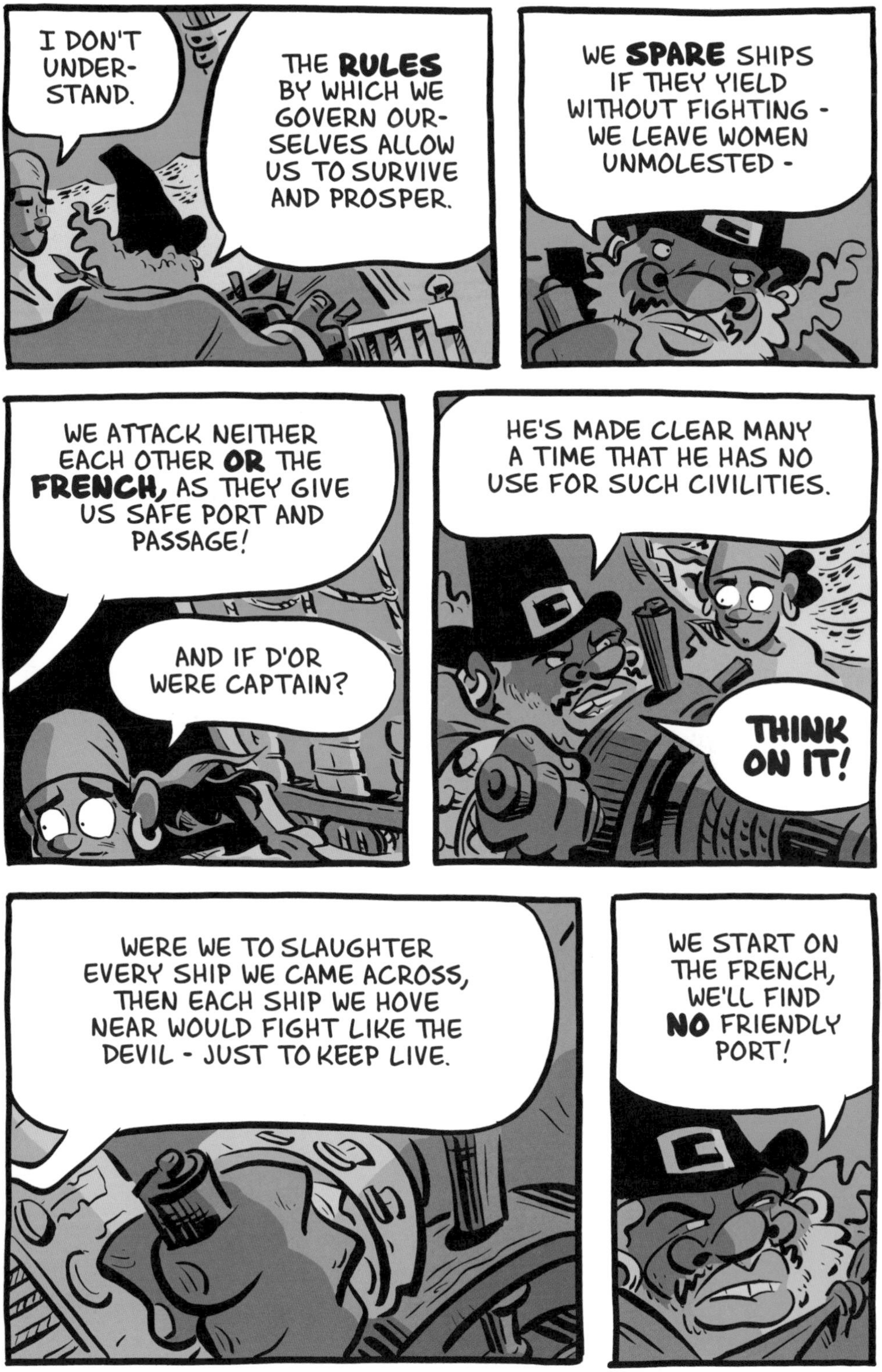
I DON'T UNDER-STAND.
THE RULES BY WHICH WE GOVERN OUR-SELVES ALLOW US TO SURVIVE AND PROSPER.
WE SPARE SHIPS IF THEY YIELD WITHOUT FIGHTING - WE LEAVE WOMEN UNMOLESTED -
WE ATTACK NEITHER EACH OTHER OR THE FRENCH, AS THEY GIVE US SAFE PORT AND PASSAGE!
AND IF D'OR WERE CAPTAIN?
HE'S MADE CLEAR MANY A TIME THAT HE HAS NO USE FOR SUCH CIVILITIES.
THINK ON IT!
WERE WE TO SLAUGHTER EVERY SHIP WE CAME ACROSS, THEN EACH SHIP WE HOVE NEAR WOULD FIGHT LIKE THE DEVIL - JUST TO KEEP LIVE.
WE START ON THE FRENCH, WE'LL FIND NO FRIENDLY PORT!

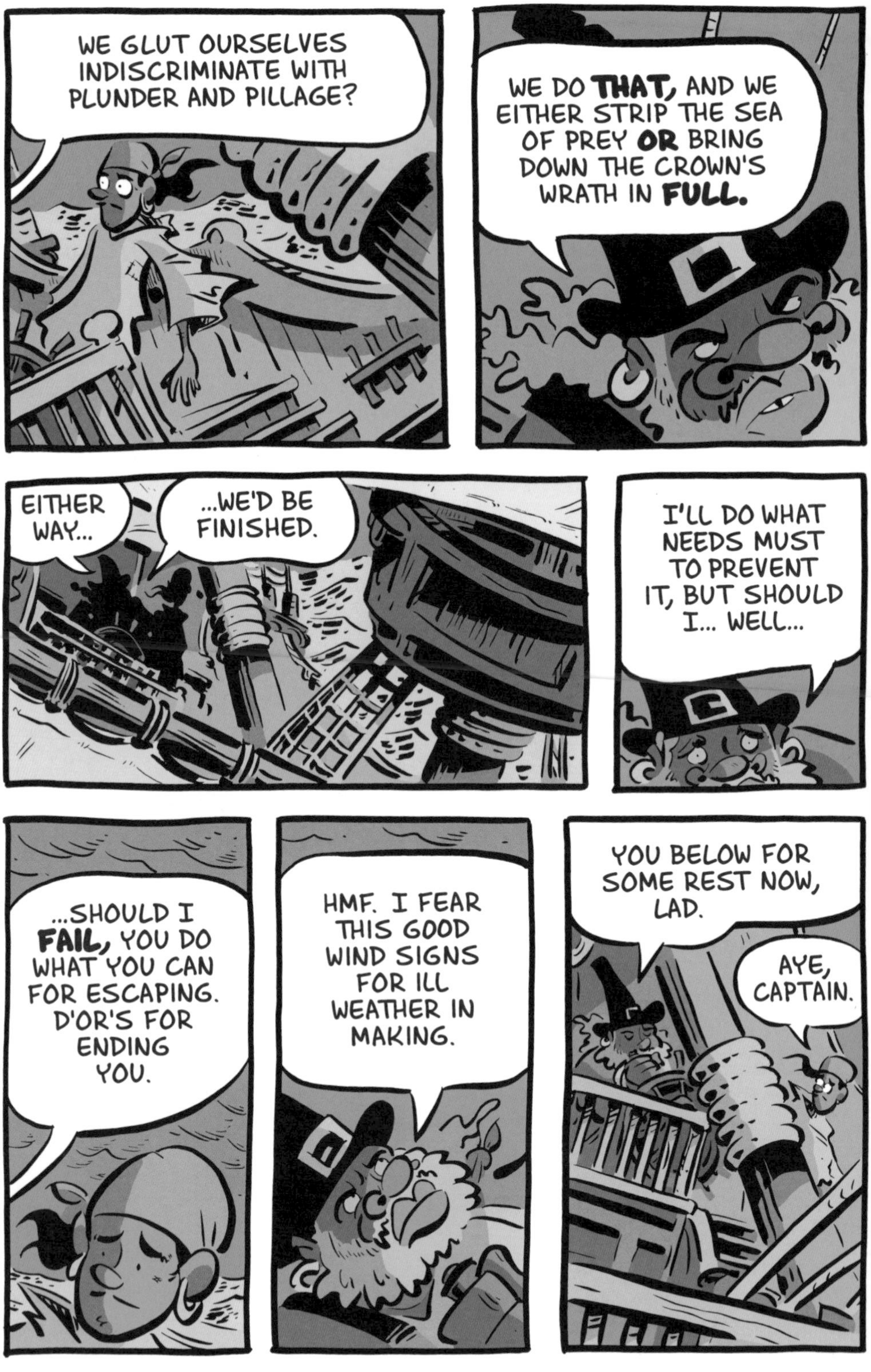
WE GLUT OURSELVES INDISCRIMINATE WITH PLUNDER AND PILLAGE?
WE DO **THAT,** AND WE EITHER STRIP THE SEA OF PREY **OR** BRING DOWN THE CROWN'S WRATH IN **FULL.**
EITHER WAY...
...WE'D BE FINISHED.
I'LL DO WHAT NEEDS MUST TO PREVENT IT, BUT SHOULD I... WELL...
...SHOULD I **FAIL,** YOU DO WHAT YOU CAN FOR ESCAPING. D'OR'S FOR ENDING YOU.
HMF. I FEAR THIS GOOD WIND SIGNS FOR ILL WEATHER IN MAKING.
YOU BELOW FOR SOME REST NOW, LAD.
AYE, CAPTAIN.

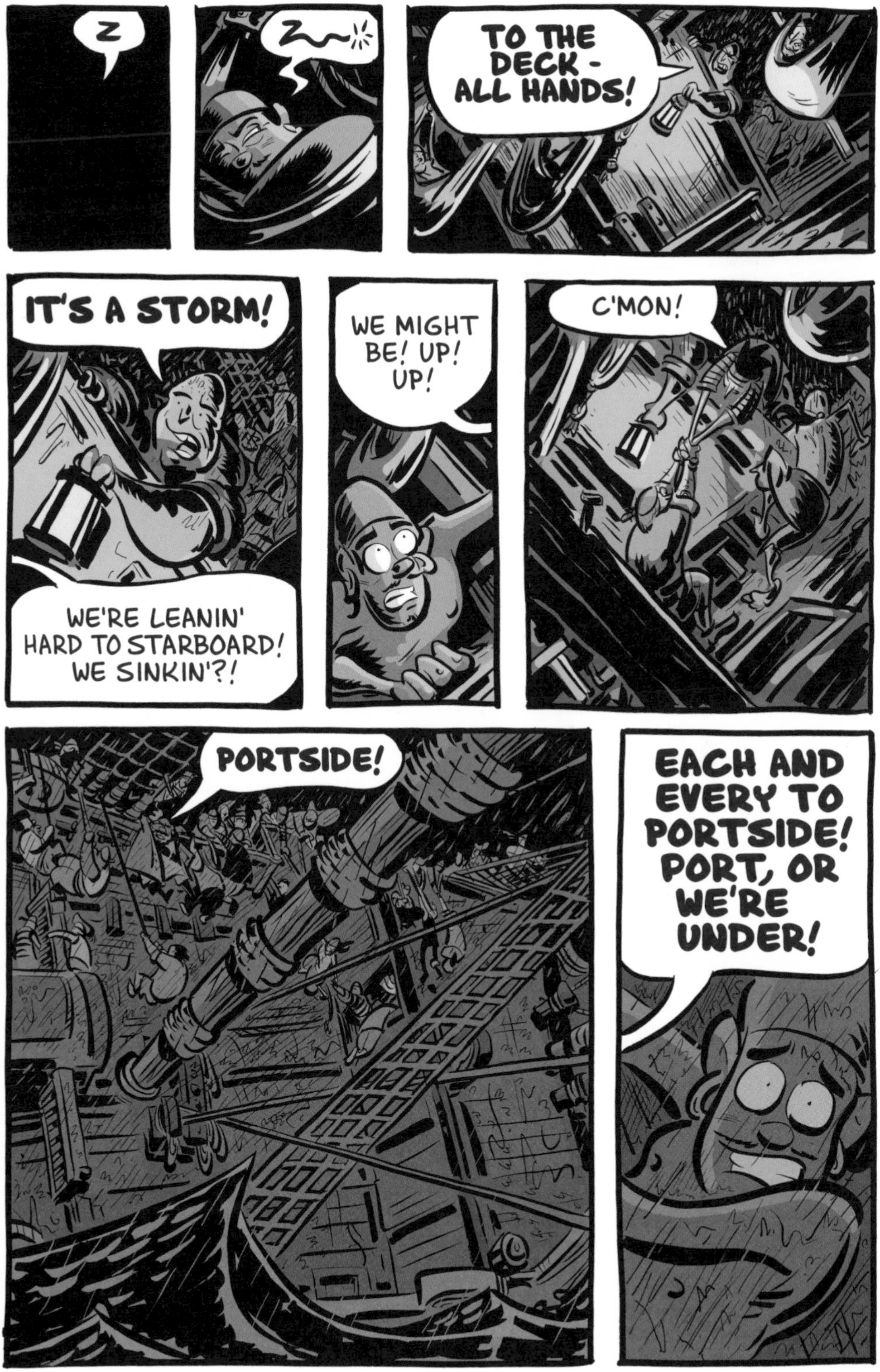
Z
Z~~
TO THE DECK - ALL HANDS!
IT'S A STORM!
WE'RE LEANIN' HARD TO STARBOARD! WE SINKIN'?!
WE MIGHT BE! UP! UP!
C'MON!
PORTSIDE!
EACH AND EVERY TO PORTSIDE! PORT, OR WE'RE UNDER!

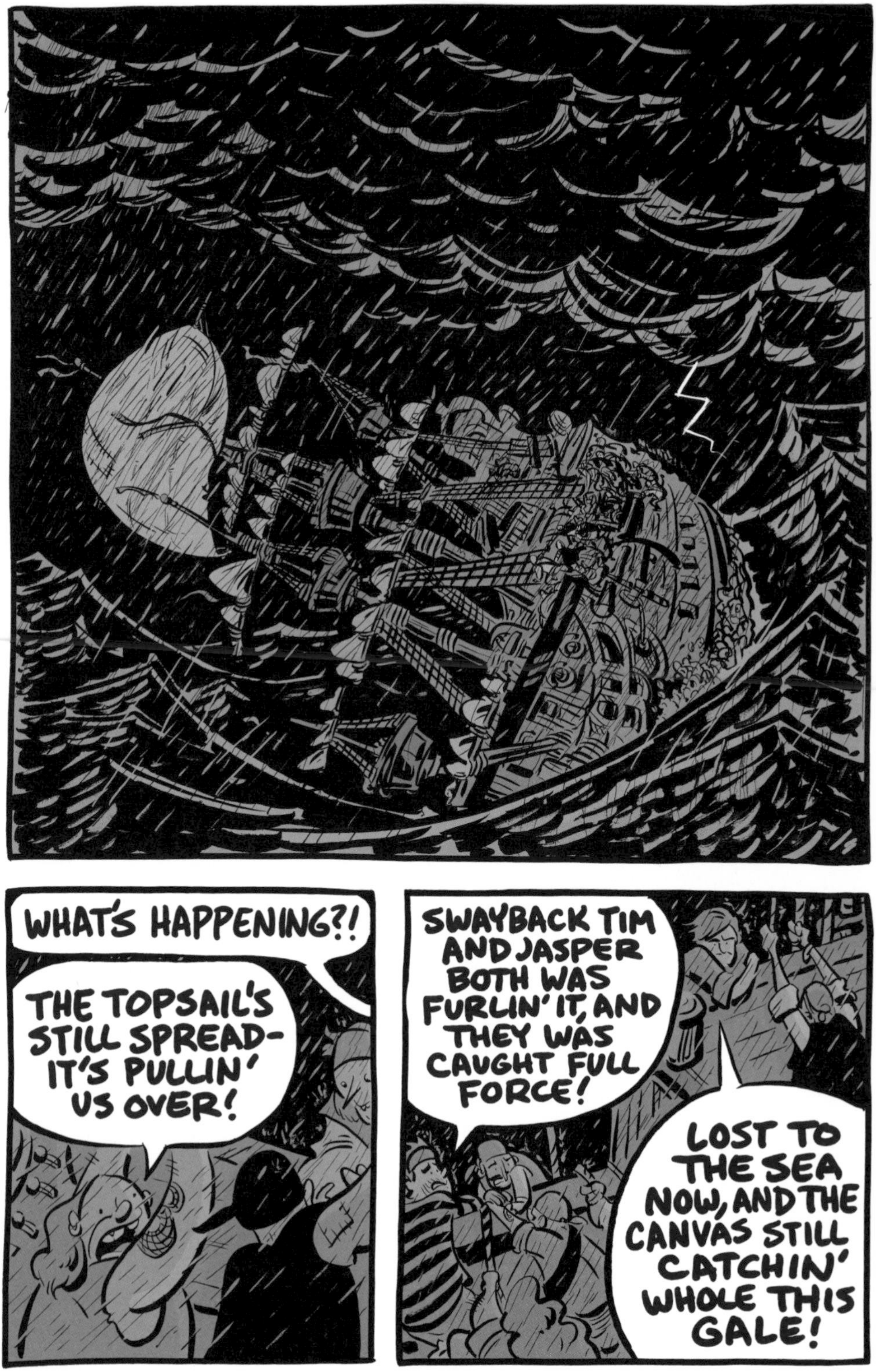
WHAT'S HAPPENING?!
THE TOPSAIL'S STILL SPREAD- IT'S PULLIN' US OVER!
SWAYBACK TIM AND JASPER BOTH WAS FURLIN' IT, AND THEY WAS CAUGHT FULL FORCE!
LOST TO THE SEA NOW, AND THE CANVAS STILL CATCHIN' WHOLE THIS GALE!

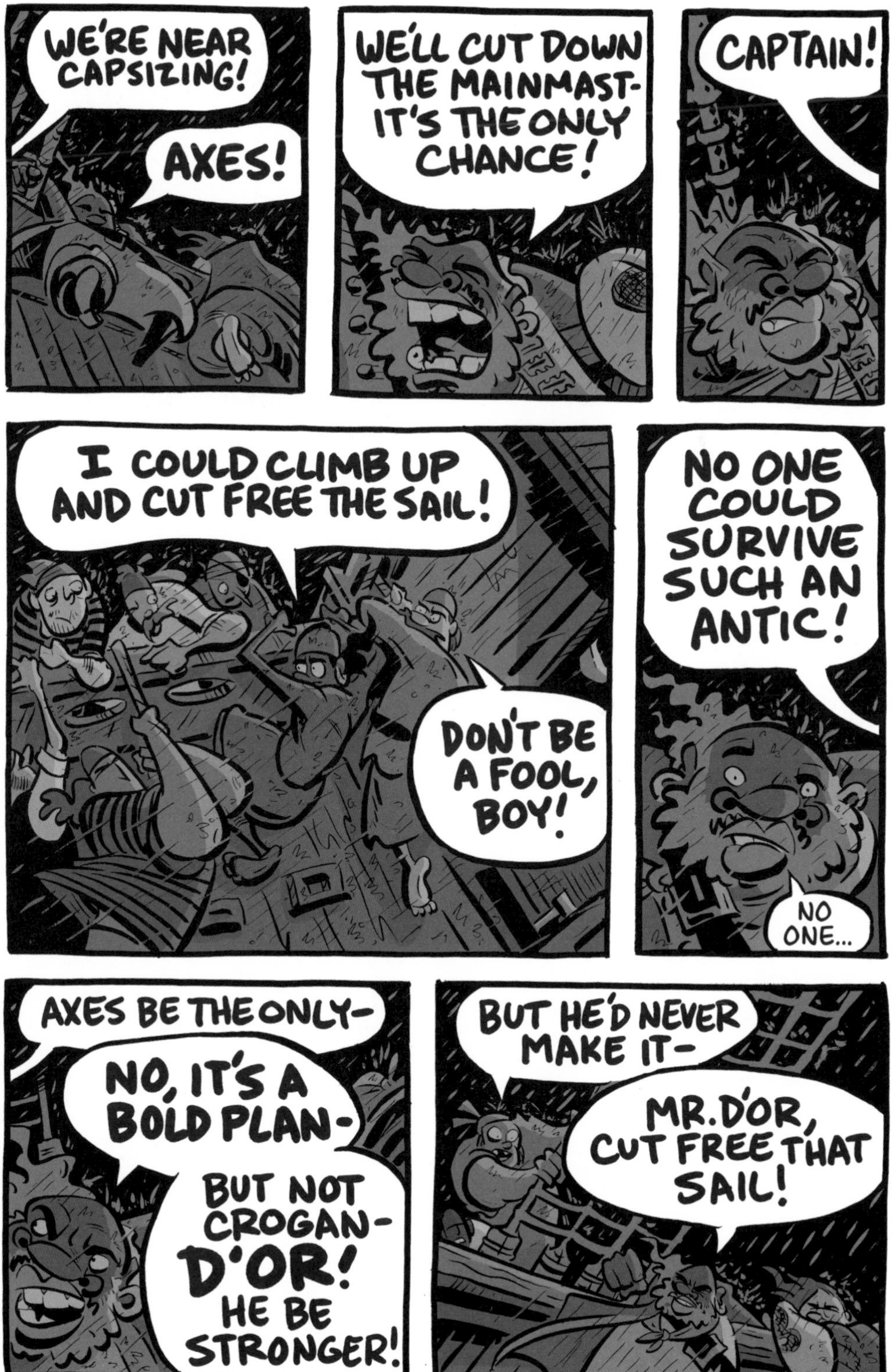
WE'RE NEAR CAPSIZING!
AXES!
WE'LL CUT DOWN THE MAINMAST- IT'S THE ONLY CHANCE!
CAPTAIN!
I COULD CLIMB UP AND CUT FREE THE SAIL!
DON'T BE A FOOL, BOY!
NO ONE COULD SURVIVE SUCH AN ANTIC!
NO ONE...
AXES BE THE ONLY-
NO, IT'S A BOLD PLAN-
BUT NOT CROGAN-D'OR! HE BE STRONGER!
BUT HE'D NEVER MAKE IT-
MR. D'OR, CUT FREE THAT SAIL!

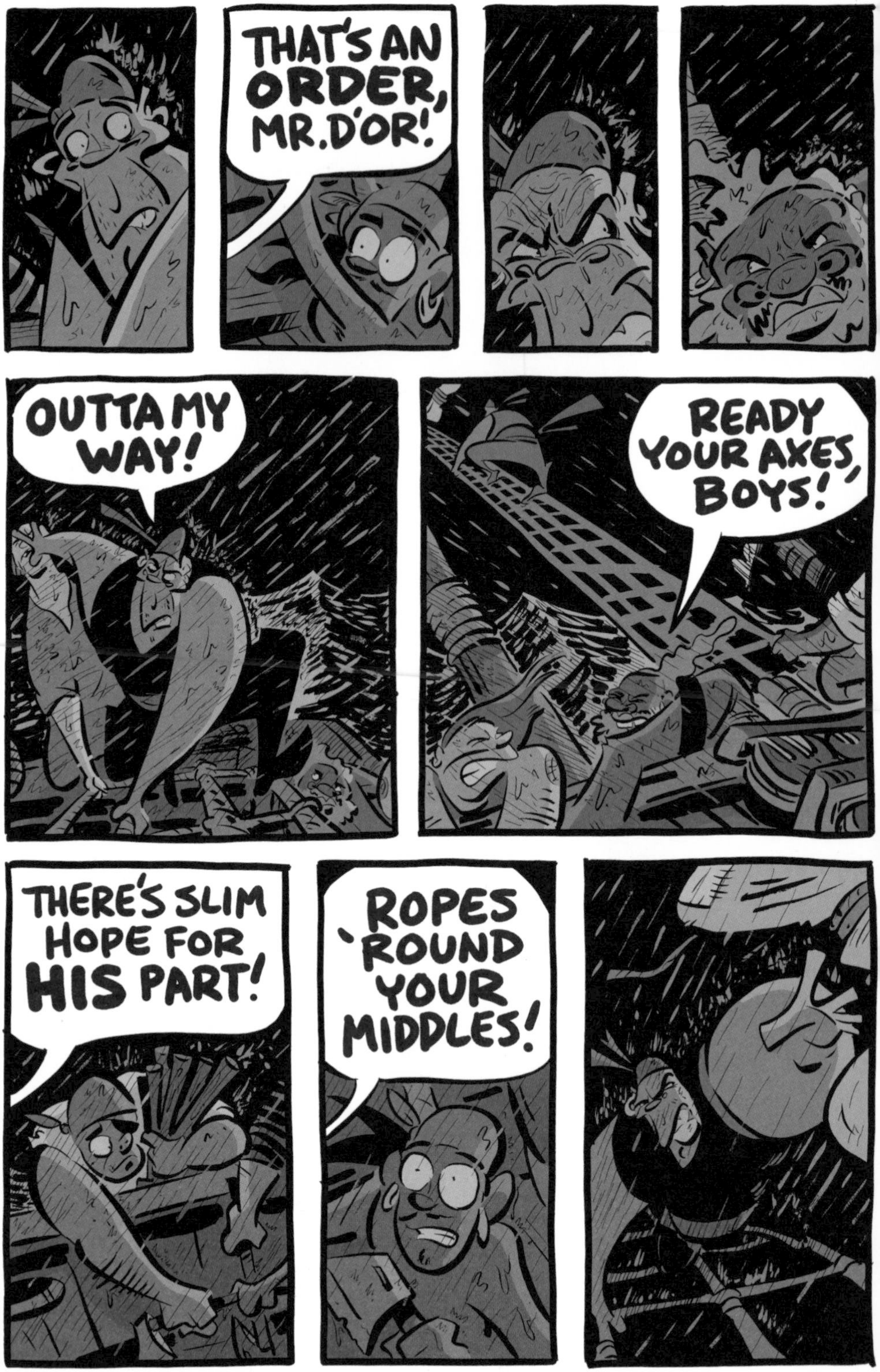
THAT'S AN ORDER, MR. D'OR!
OUTTA MY WAY!
READY YOUR AXES, BOYS!
THERE'S SLIM HOPE FOR HIS PART!
ROPES 'ROUND YOUR MIDDLES!

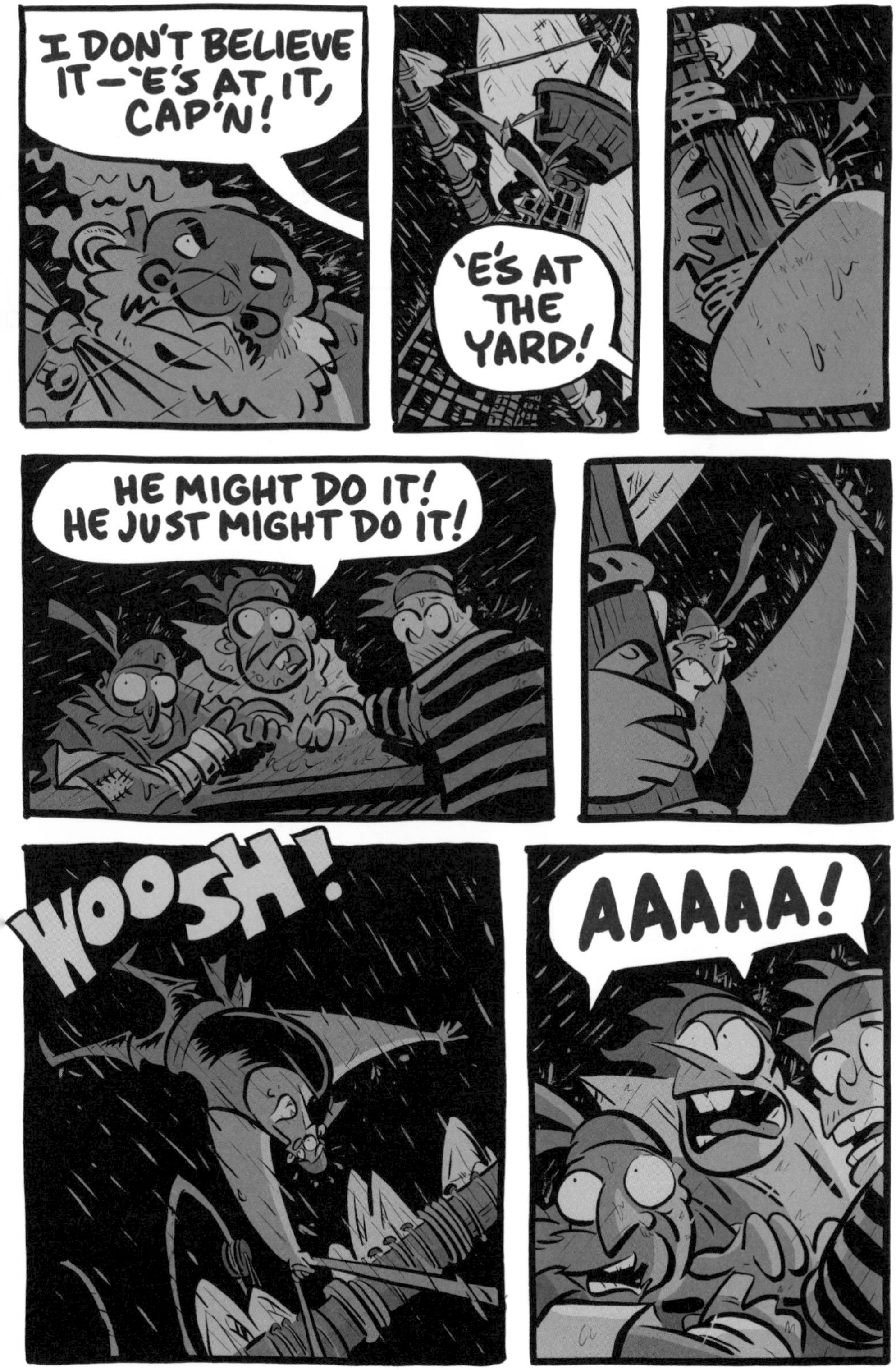
I DON'T BELIEVE IT—'E'S AT IT, CAP'N!
'E'S AT THE YARD!
HE MIGHT DO IT! HE JUST MIGHT DO IT!
WOOSH!
AAAAA!

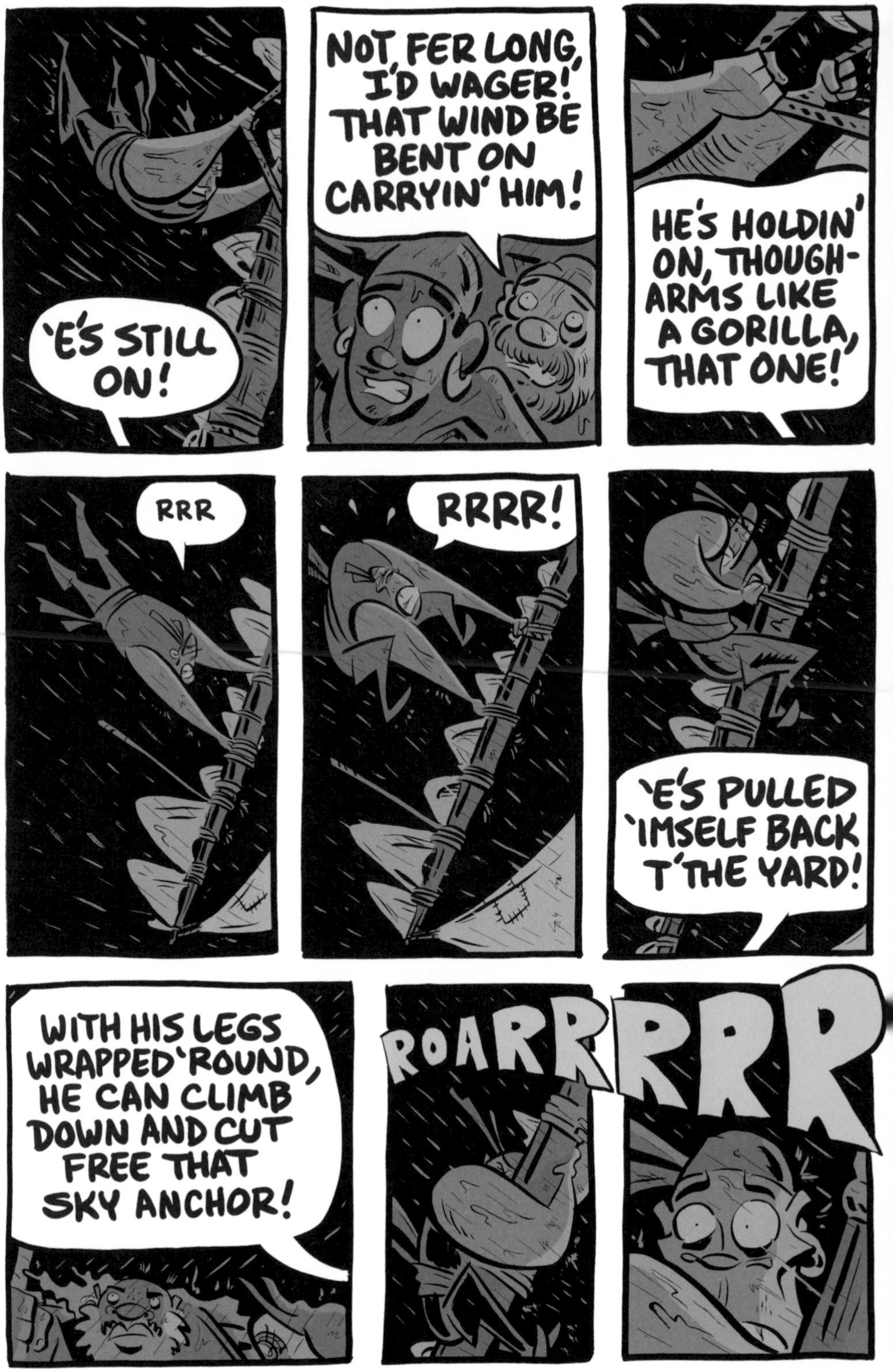
'E'S STILL ON!
NOT FER LONG, I'D WAGER! THAT WIND BE BENT ON CARRYIN' HIM!
HE'S HOLDIN' ON, THOUGH- ARMS LIKE A GORILLA, THAT ONE!
RRR
RRRR!
'E'S PULLED 'IMSELF BACK T'THE YARD!
WITH HIS LEGS WRAPPED 'ROUND, HE CAN CLIMB DOWN AND CUT FREE THAT SKY ANCHOR!
ROARRRRR

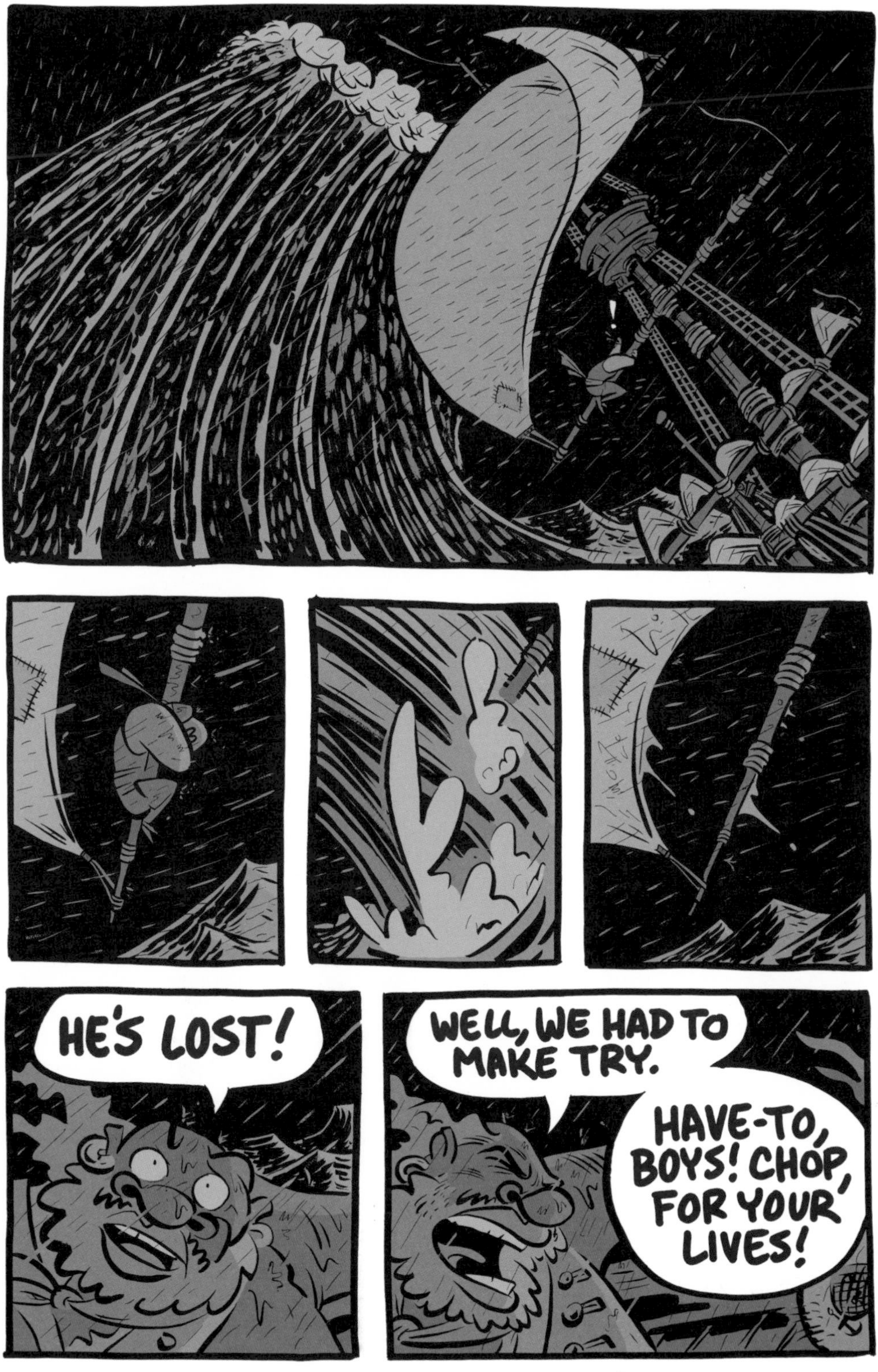
HE'S LOST!
WELL, WE HAD TO MAKE TRY.
HAVE-TO, BOYS! CHOP, FOR YOUR LIVES!

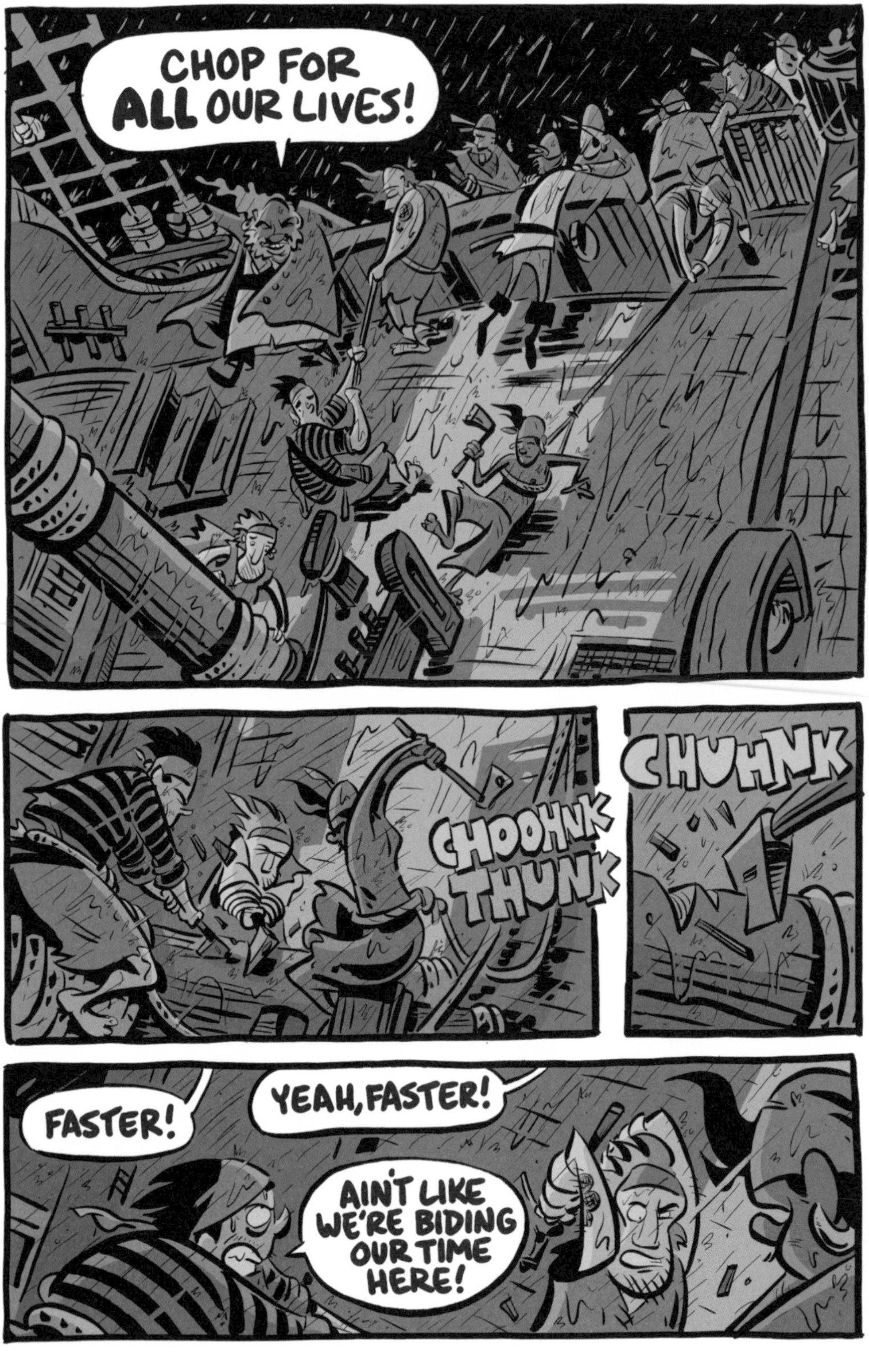
CHOP FOR ALL OUR LIVES!
CHUHNK
CHOOHNK
THUNK
FASTER!
YEAH, FASTER!
AIN'T LIKE WE'RE BIDING OUR TIME HERE!

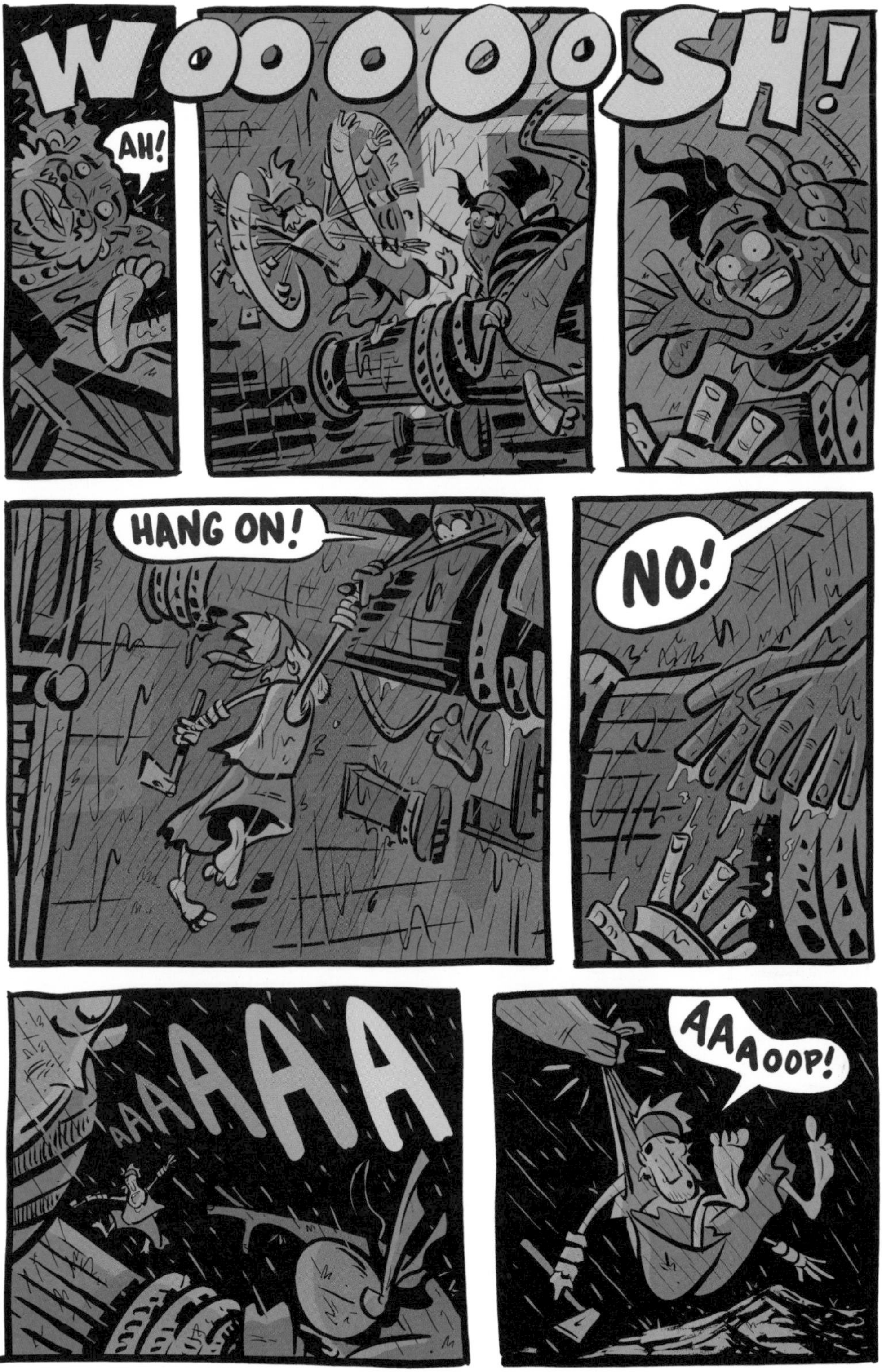
WOOOOOSH!
AH!
HANG ON!
NO!
AAAAAA
AAAOOP!

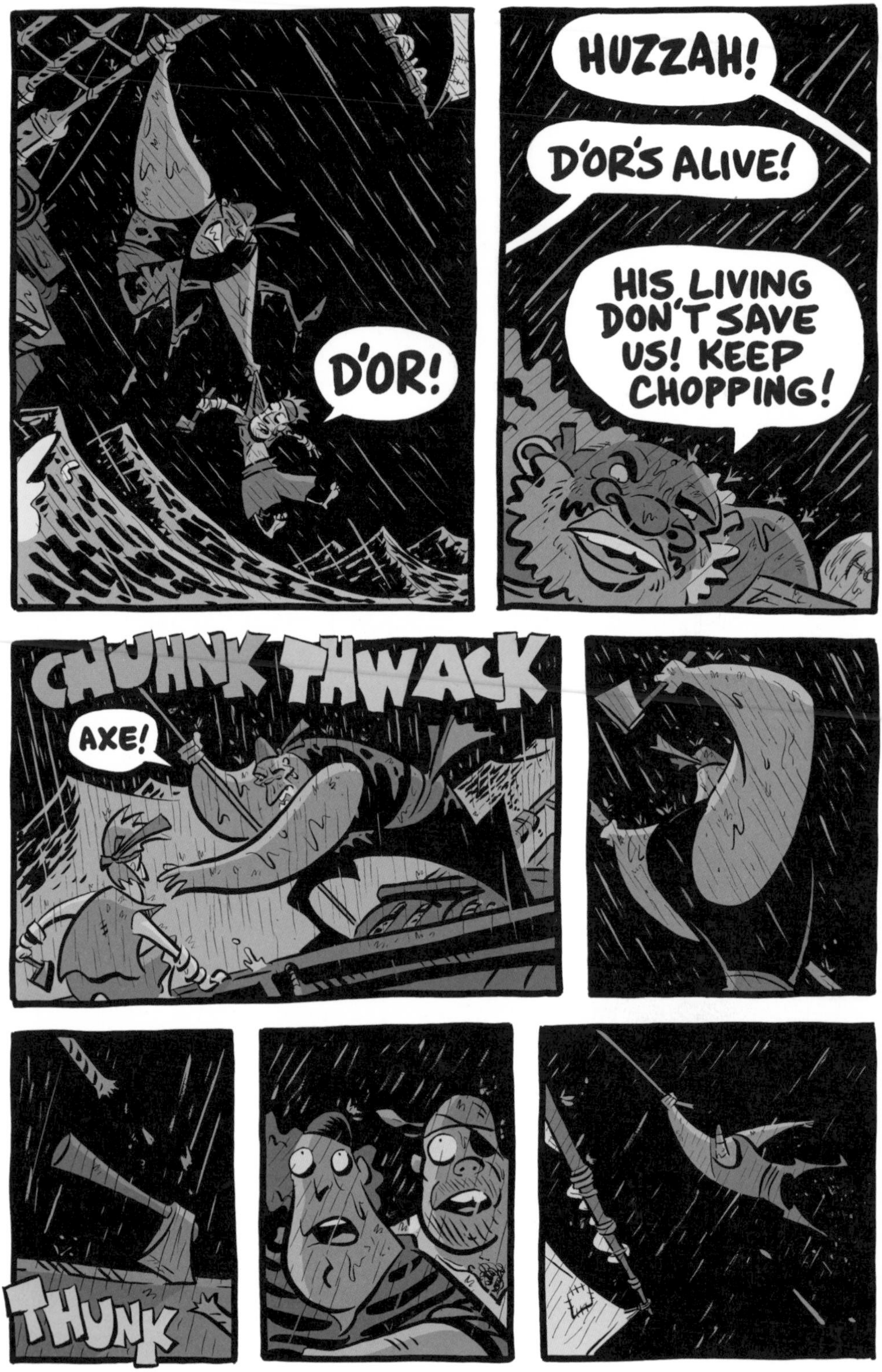
D'OR!
HUZZAH!
D'OR'S ALIVE!
HIS LIVING DON'T SAVE US! KEEP CHOPPING!
CHUHNK THWACK
AXE!
THUNK

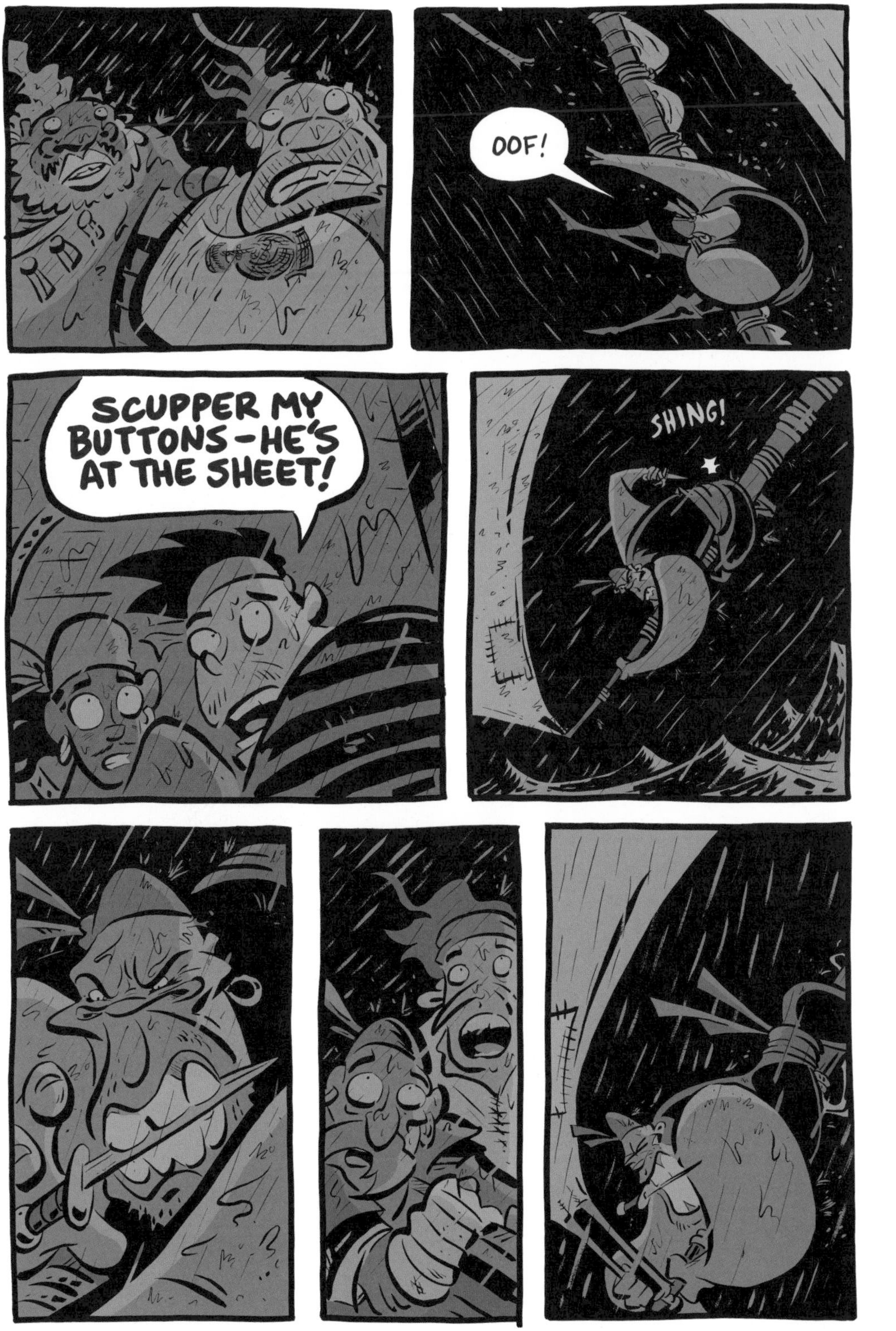
OOF!
SCUPPER MY BUTTONS - HE'S AT THE SHEET!
SHING!

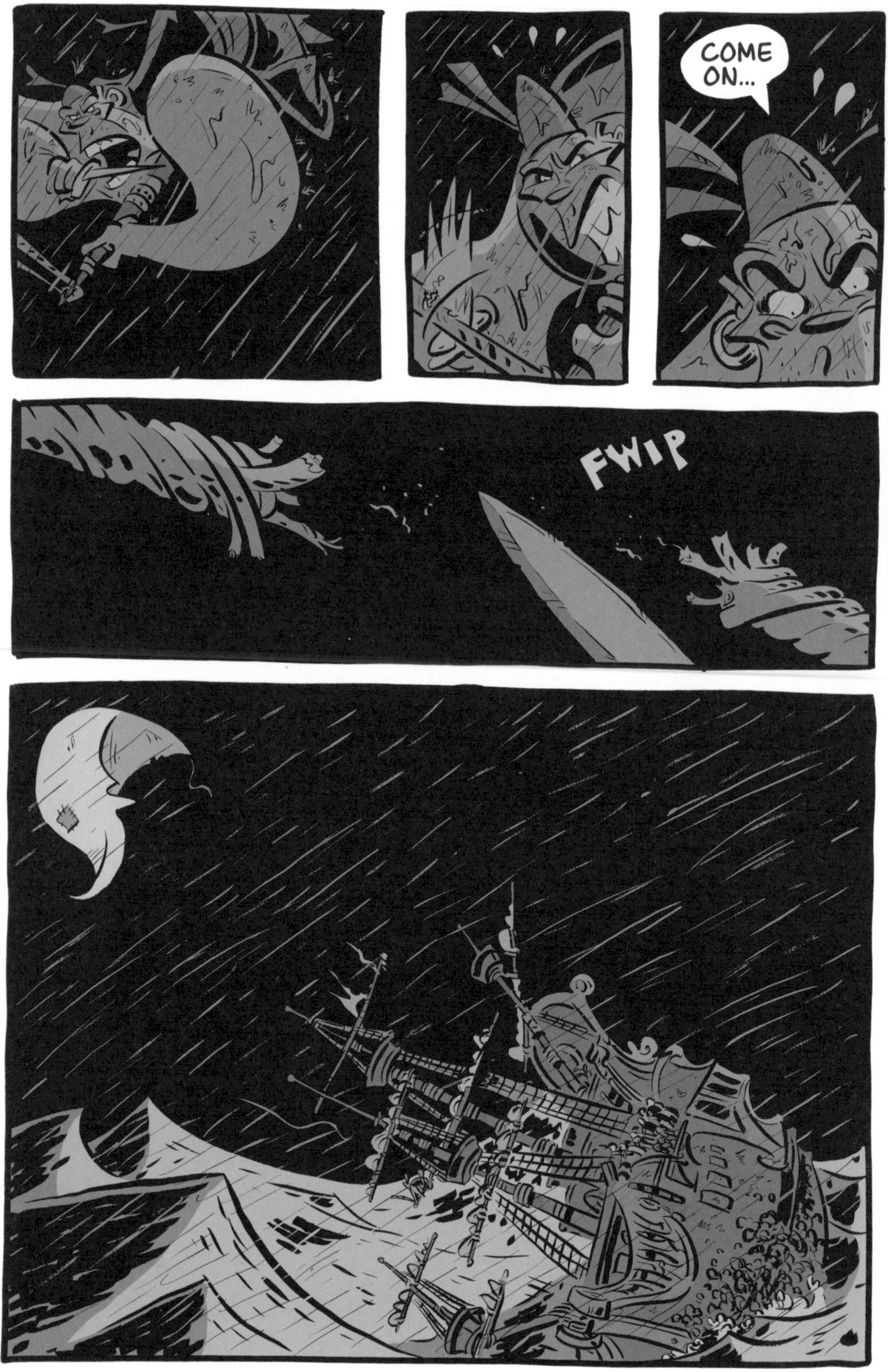
COME ON...
FWIP

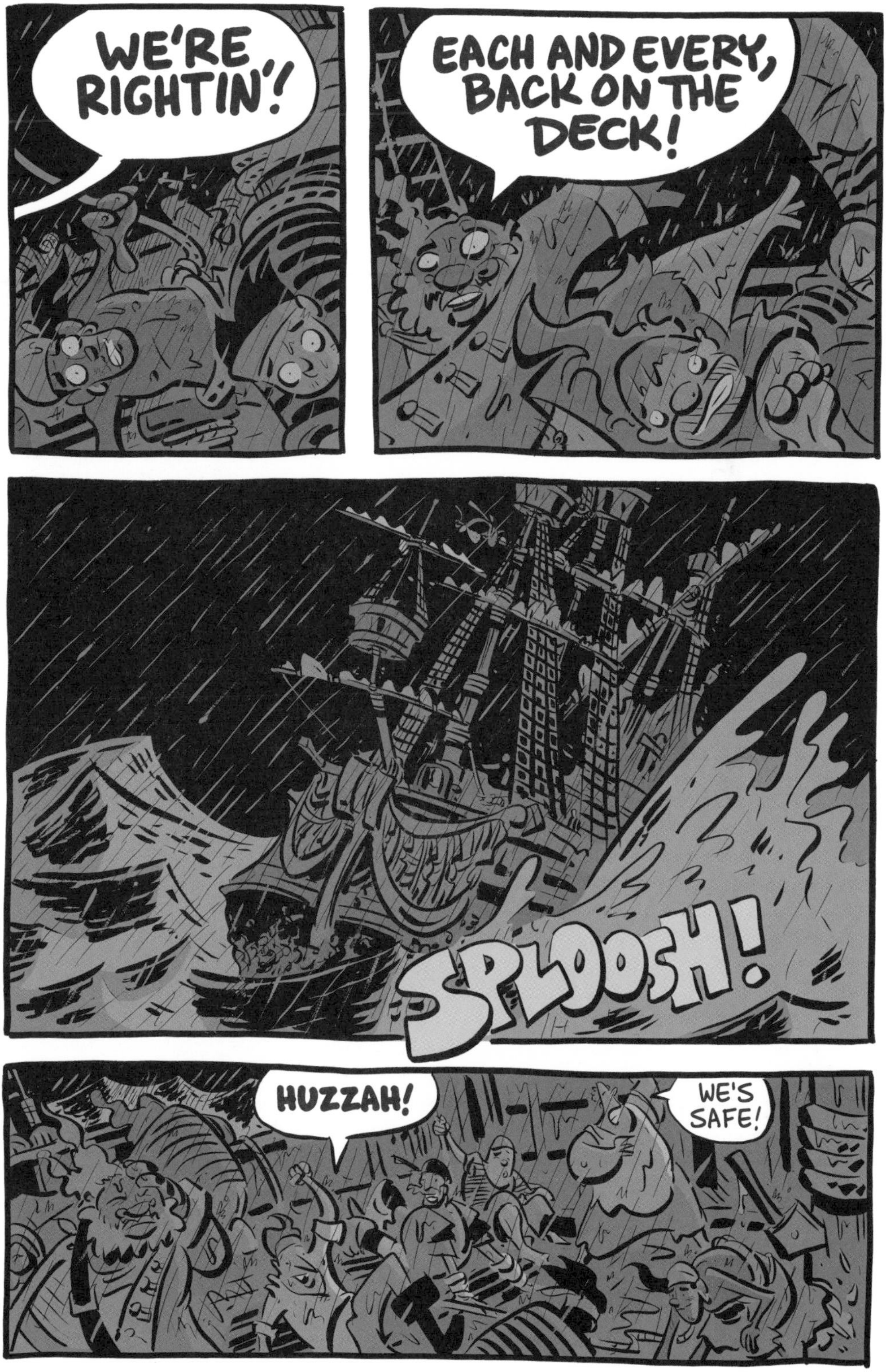
WE'RE RIGHTIN'!
EACH AND EVERY, BACK ON THE DECK!
SPLOOSH!
HUZZAH!
WE'S SAFE!

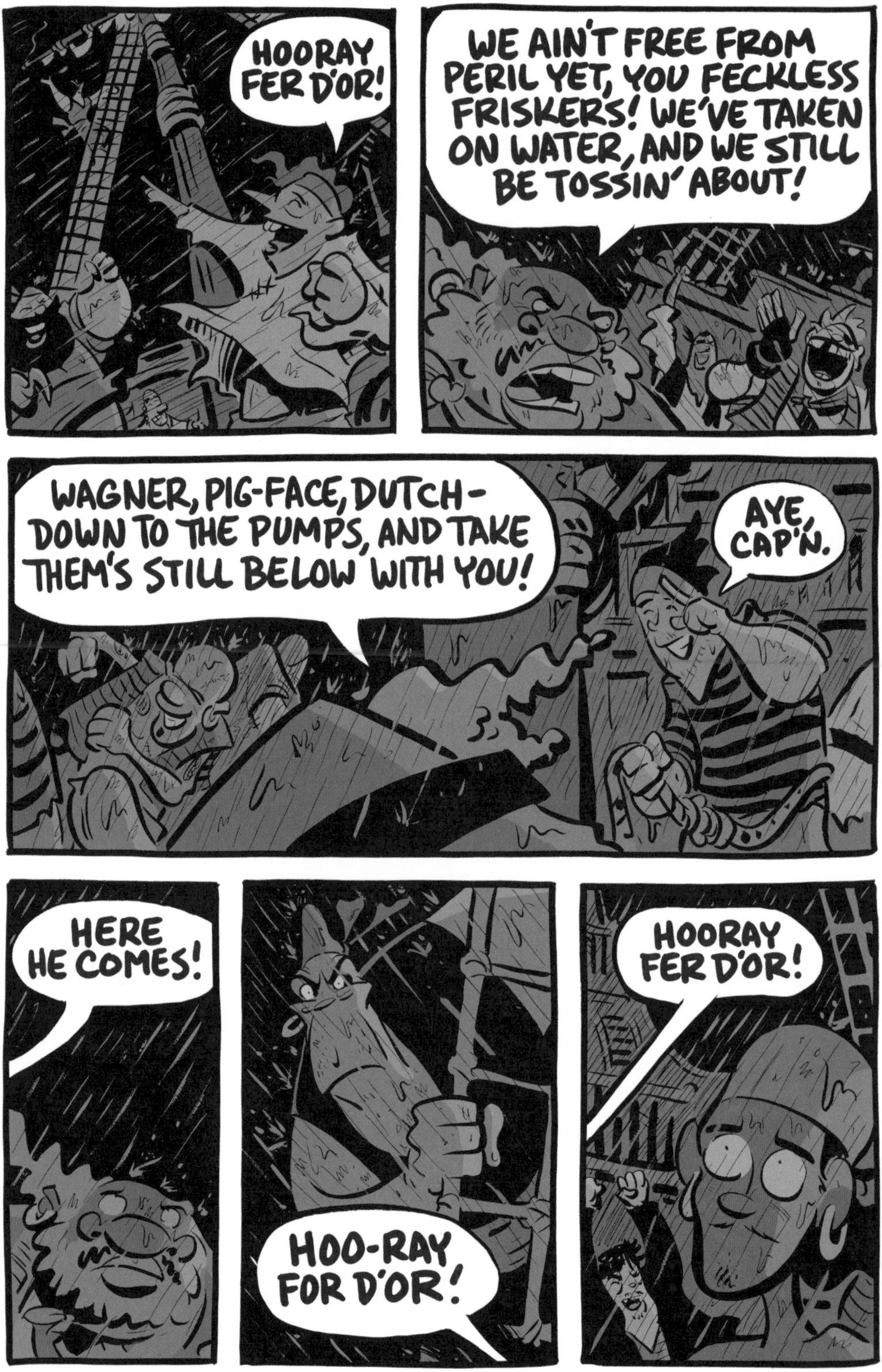
HOORAY FER D'OR!
WE AIN'T FREE FROM PERIL YET, YOU FECKLESS FRISKERS! WE'VE TAKEN ON WATER, AND WE STILL BE TOSSIN' ABOUT!
WAGNER, PIG-FACE, DUTCH-DOWN TO THE PUMPS, AND TAKE THEM'S STILL BELOW WITH YOU!
AYE, CAP'N.
HERE HE COMES!
HOO-RAY FOR D'OR!
HOORAY FER D'OR!

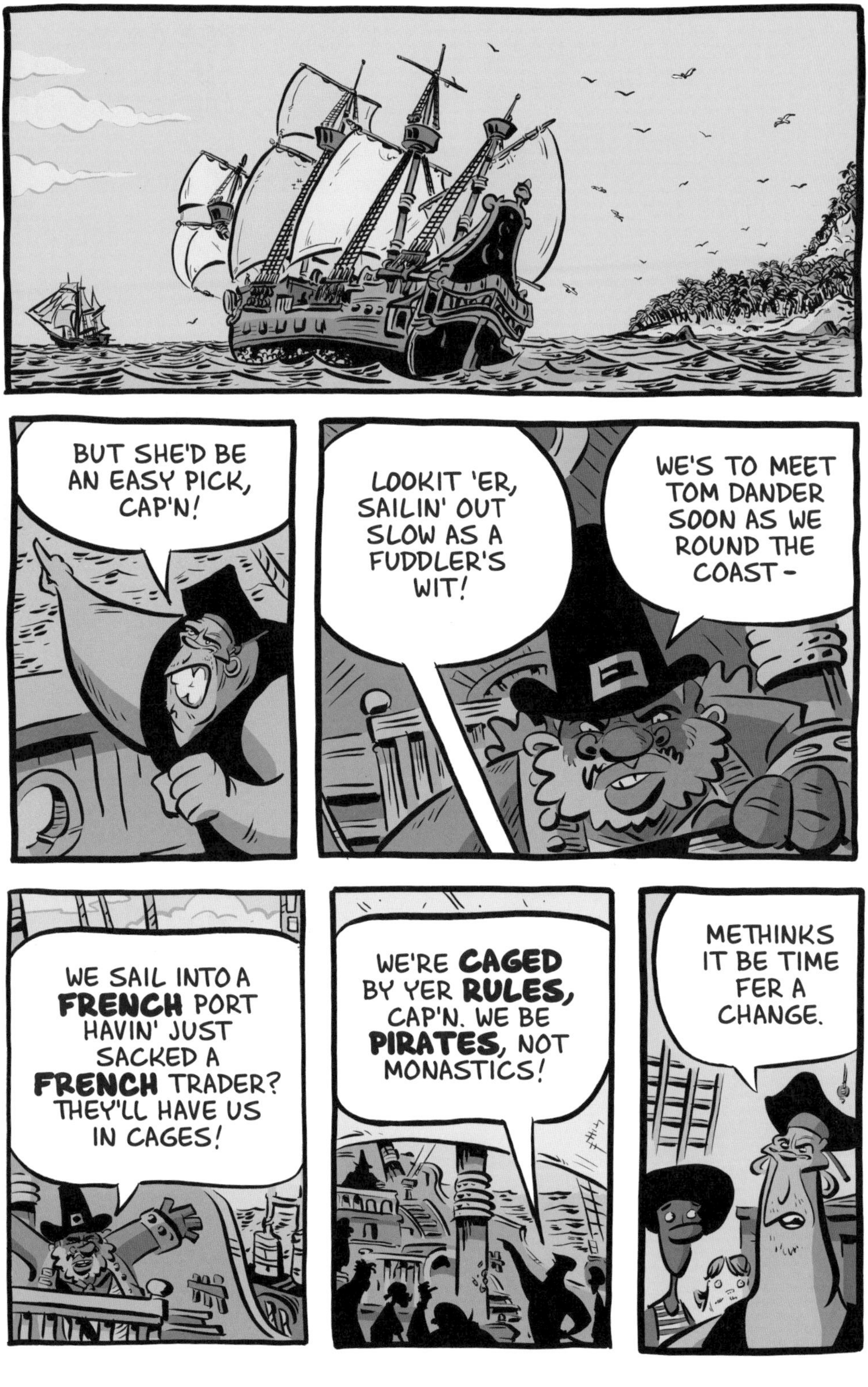
BUT SHE'D BE AN EASY PICK, CAP'N!
LOOKIT 'ER, SAILIN' OUT SLOW AS A FUDDLER'S WIT!
WE'S TO MEET TOM DANDER SOON AS WE ROUND THE COAST-
WE SAIL INTO A FRENCH PORT HAVIN' JUST SACKED A FRENCH TRADER? THEY'LL HAVE US IN CAGES!
WE'RE CAGED BY YER RULES, CAP'N. WE BE PIRATES, NOT MONASTICS!
METHINKS IT BE TIME FER A CHANGE.

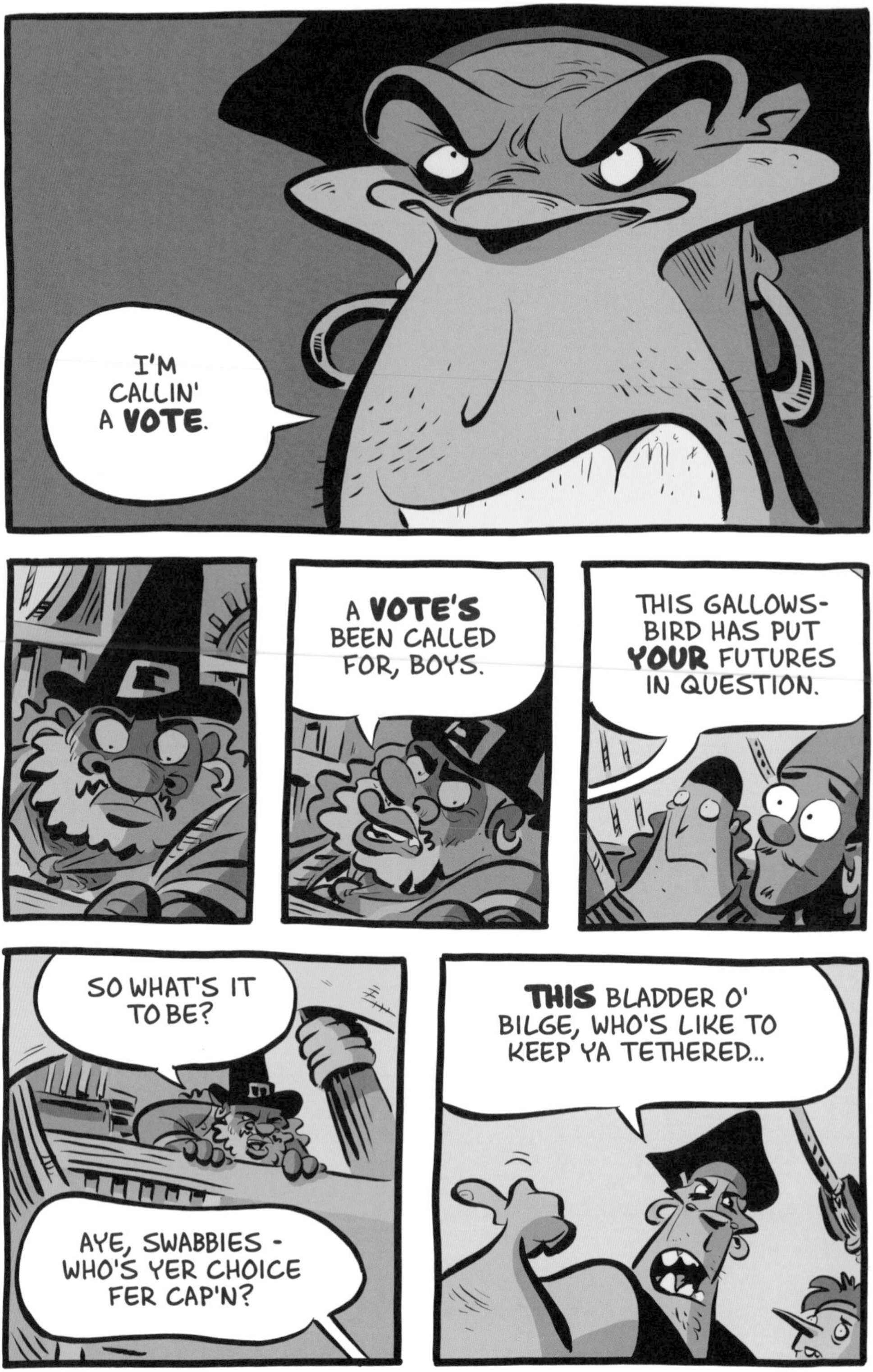
I'M CALLIN' A VOTE.
A VOTE'S BEEN CALLED FOR, BOYS.
THIS GALLOWS-BIRD HAS PUT YOUR FUTURES IN QUESTION.
SO WHAT'S IT TO BE?
AYE, SWABBIES - WHO'S YER CHOICE FER CAP'N?
THIS BLADDER O' BILGE, WHO'S LIKE TO KEEP YA TETHERED...

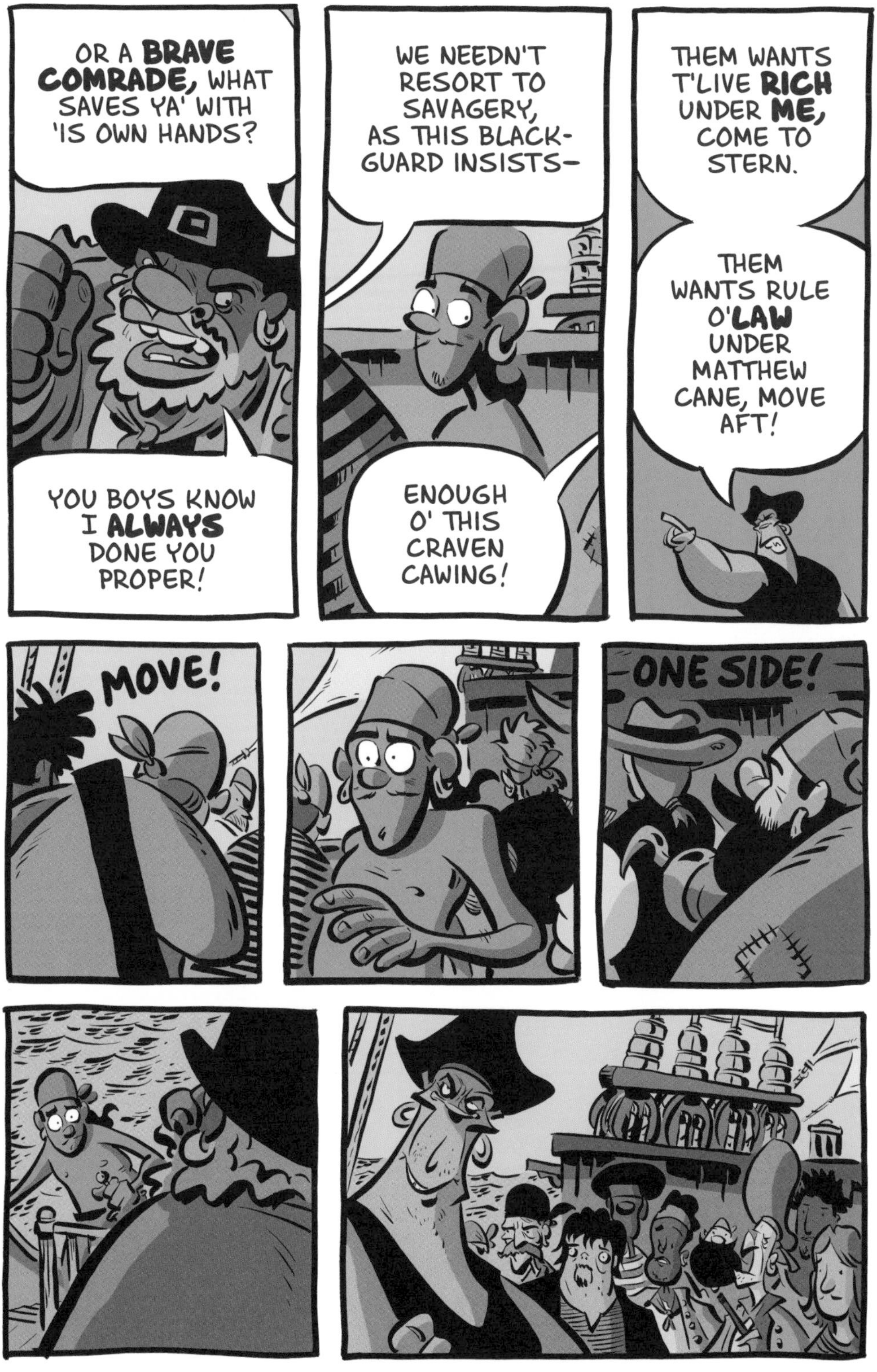
OR A **BRAVE COMRADE,** WHAT SAVES YA' WITH 'IS OWN HANDS?
YOU BOYS KNOW I **ALWAYS** DONE YOU PROPER!
WE NEEDN'T RESORT TO SAVAGERY, AS THIS BLACK-GUARD INSISTS–
ENOUGH O' THIS CRAVEN CAWING!
THEM WANTS T'LIVE **RICH** UNDER **ME,** COME TO STERN.
THEM WANTS RULE O'**LAW** UNDER MATTHEW CANE, MOVE AFT!
MOVE!
ONE SIDE!

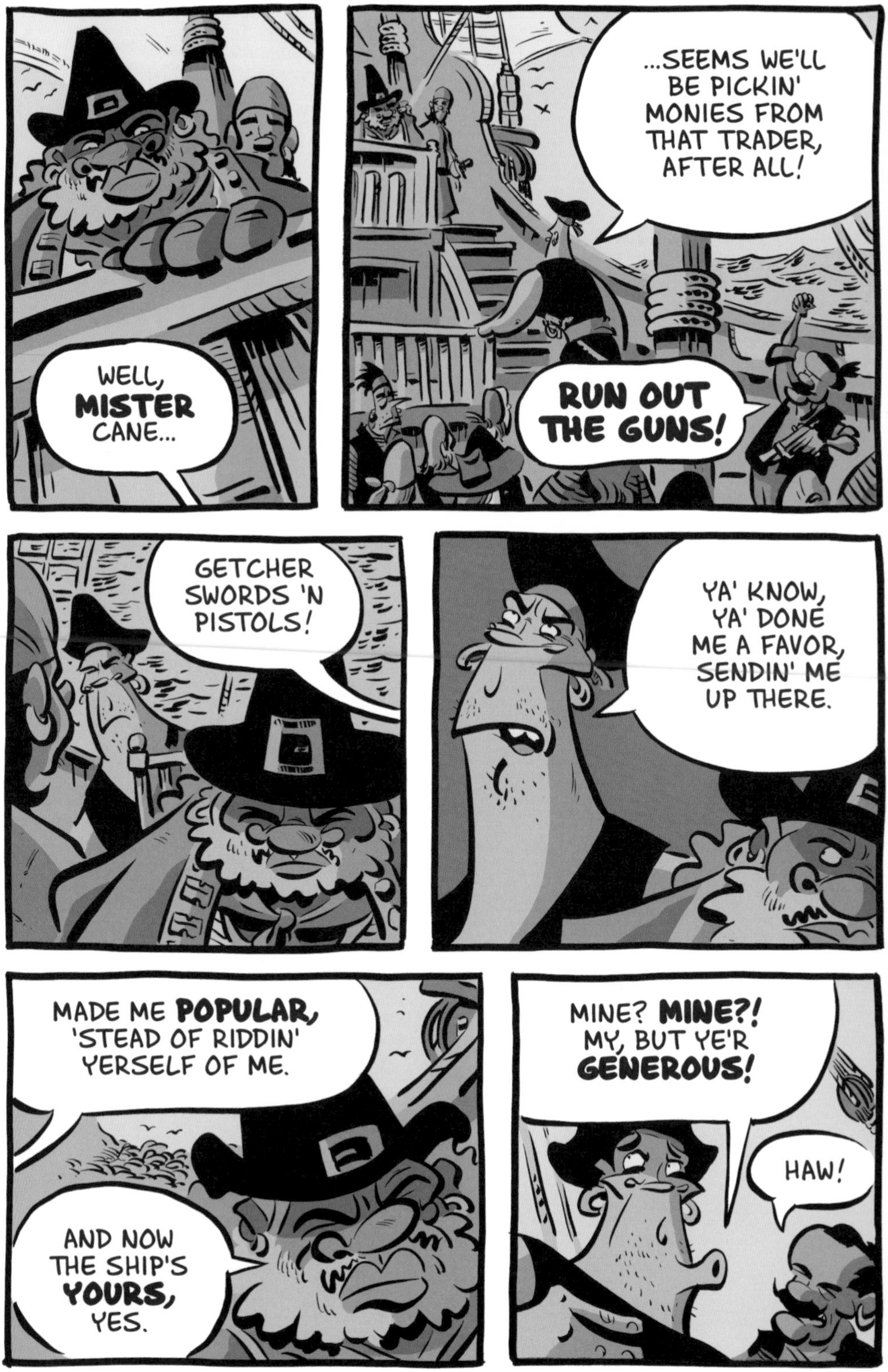
WELL, **MISTER** CANE...
...SEEMS WE'LL BE PICKIN' MONIES FROM THAT TRADER, AFTER ALL!
RUN OUT THE GUNS!
GETCHER SWORDS 'N PISTOLS!
YA' KNOW, YA' DONE ME A FAVOR, SENDIN' ME UP THERE.
MADE ME **POPULAR,** 'STEAD OF RIDDIN' YERSELF OF ME.
AND NOW THE SHIP'S **YOURS,** YES.
MINE? **MINE?!** MY, BUT YE'R **GENEROUS!**
HAW!

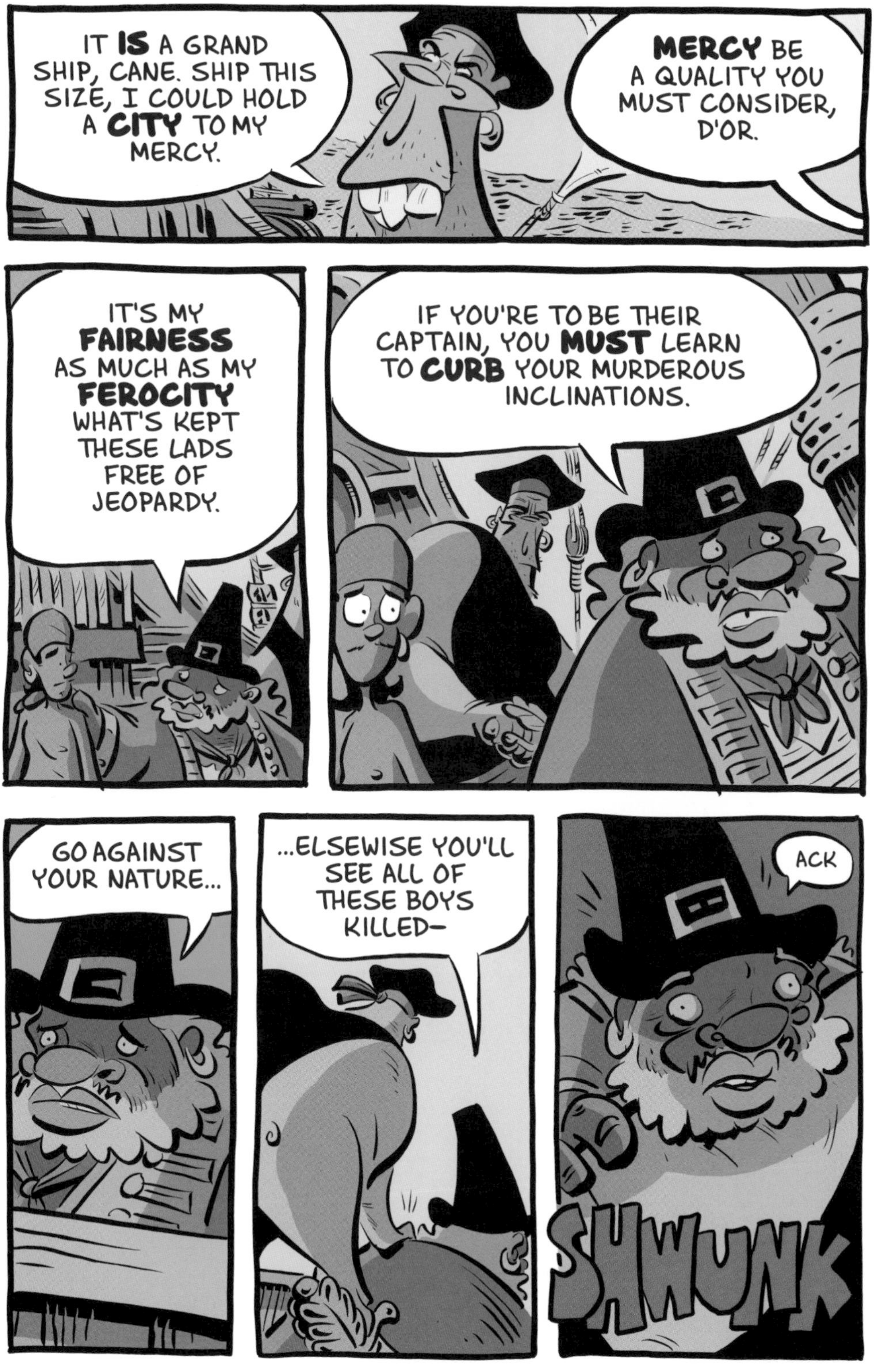
IT IS A GRAND SHIP, CANE. SHIP THIS SIZE, I COULD HOLD A CITY TO MY MERCY.
MERCY BE A QUALITY YOU MUST CONSIDER, D'OR.
IT'S MY FAIRNESS AS MUCH AS MY FEROCITY WHAT'S KEPT THESE LADS FREE OF JEOPARDY.
IF YOU'RE TO BE THEIR CAPTAIN, YOU MUST LEARN TO CURB YOUR MURDEROUS INCLINATIONS.
GO AGAINST YOUR NATURE...
...ELSEWISE YOU'LL SEE ALL OF THESE BOYS KILLED—
ACK
SHWUNK

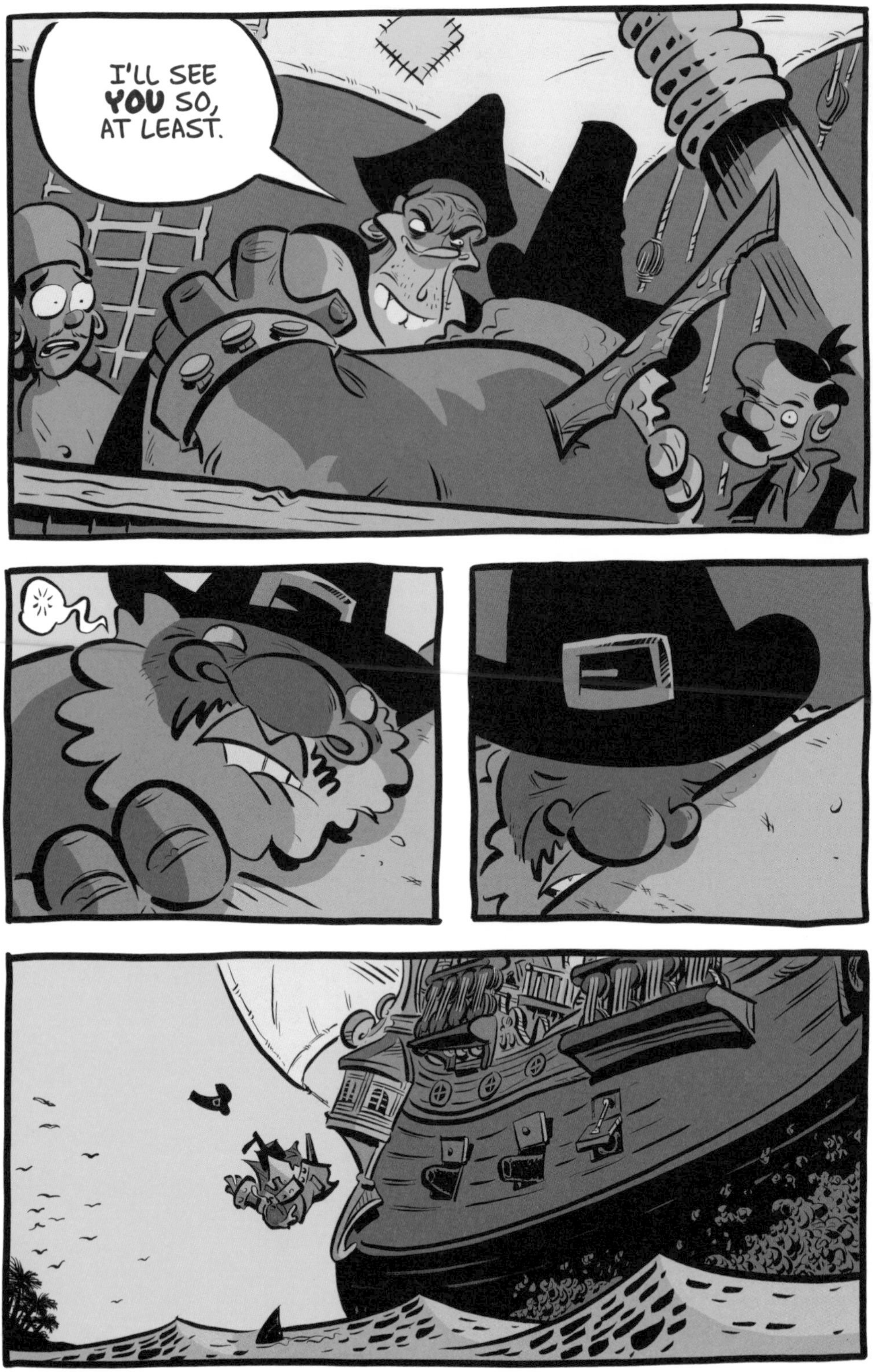
I'LL SEE YOU SO, AT LEAST.

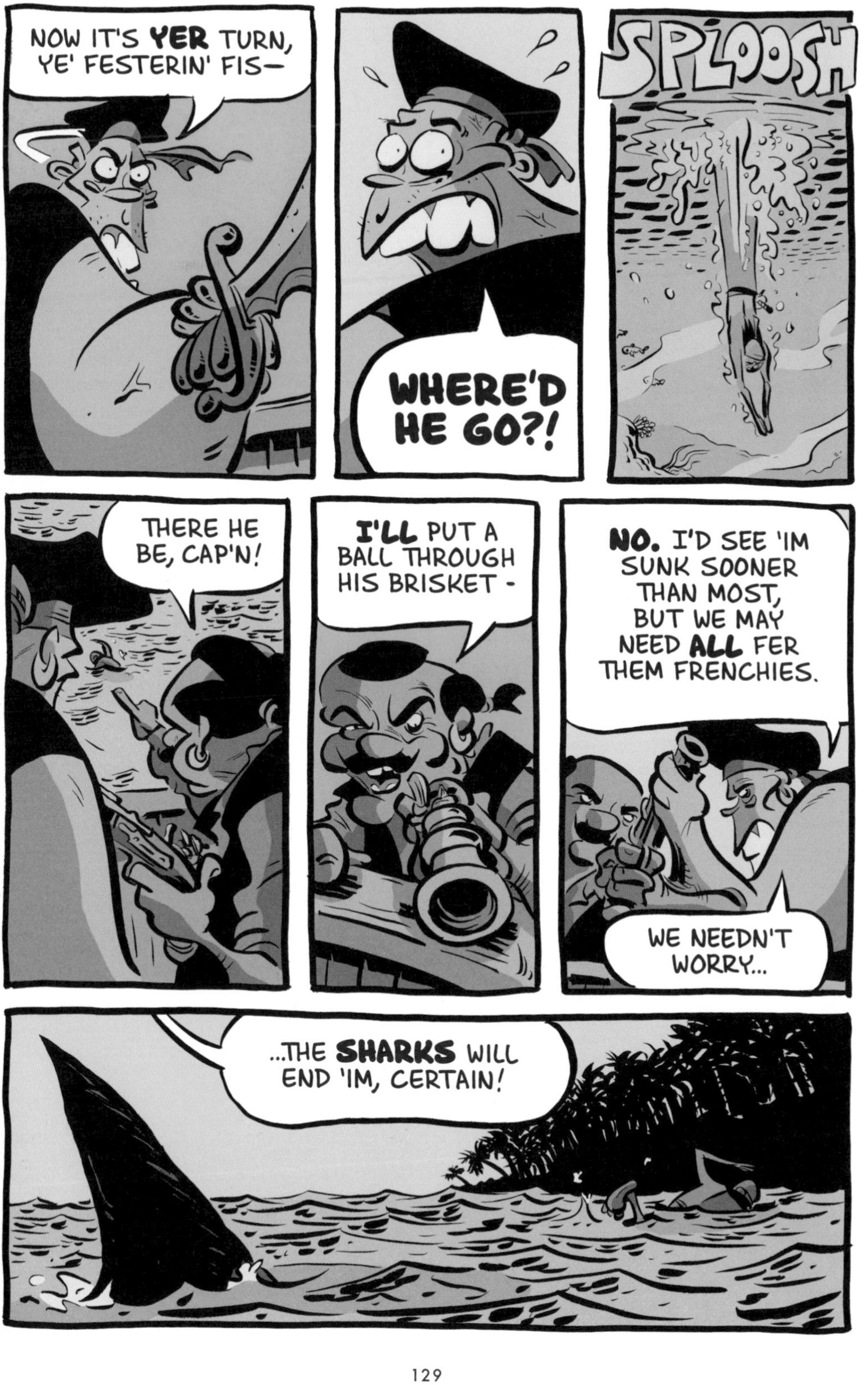
NOW IT'S YER TURN, YE' FESTERIN' FIS—
WHERE'D HE GO?!
SPLOOSH
THERE HE BE, CAP'N!
I'LL PUT A BALL THROUGH HIS BRISKET -
NO. I'D SEE 'IM SUNK SOONER THAN MOST, BUT WE MAY NEED ALL FER THEM FRENCHIES.
WE NEEDN'T WORRY...
...THE SHARKS WILL END 'IM, CERTAIN!

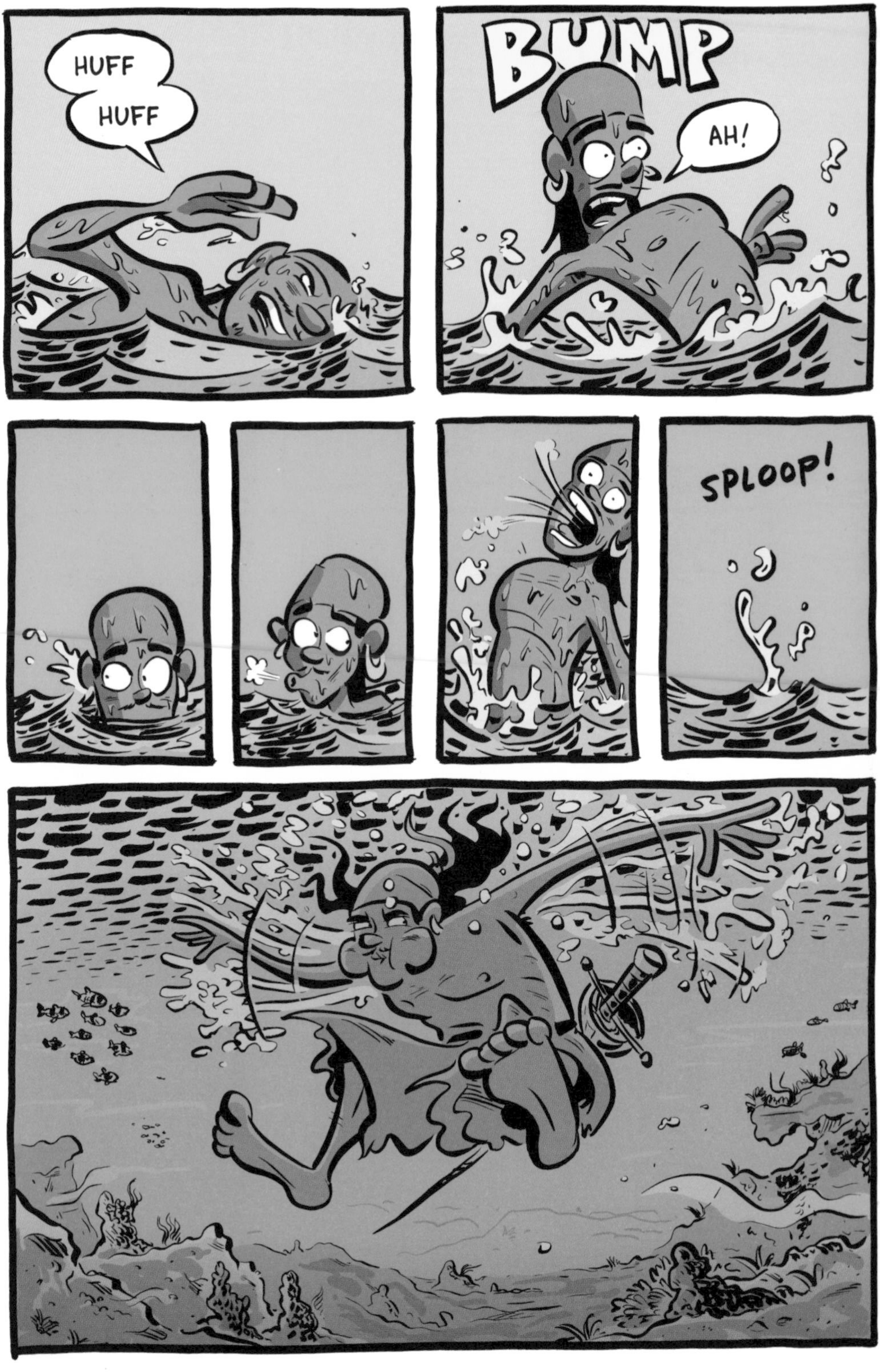
HUFF
HUFF
BUMP
AH!
SPLOOP!

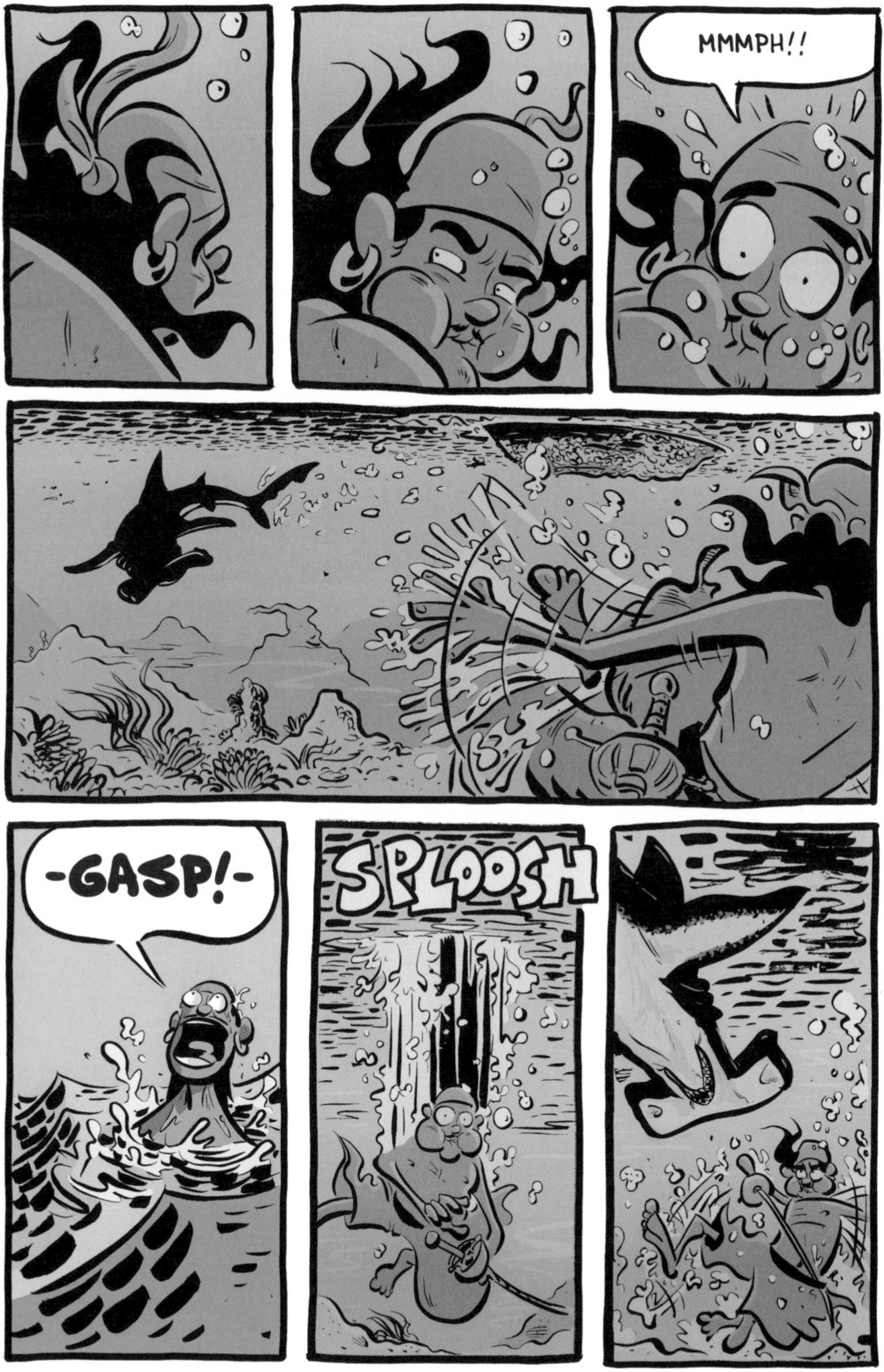
MMMPH!!
-GASP!-
SPLOOSH

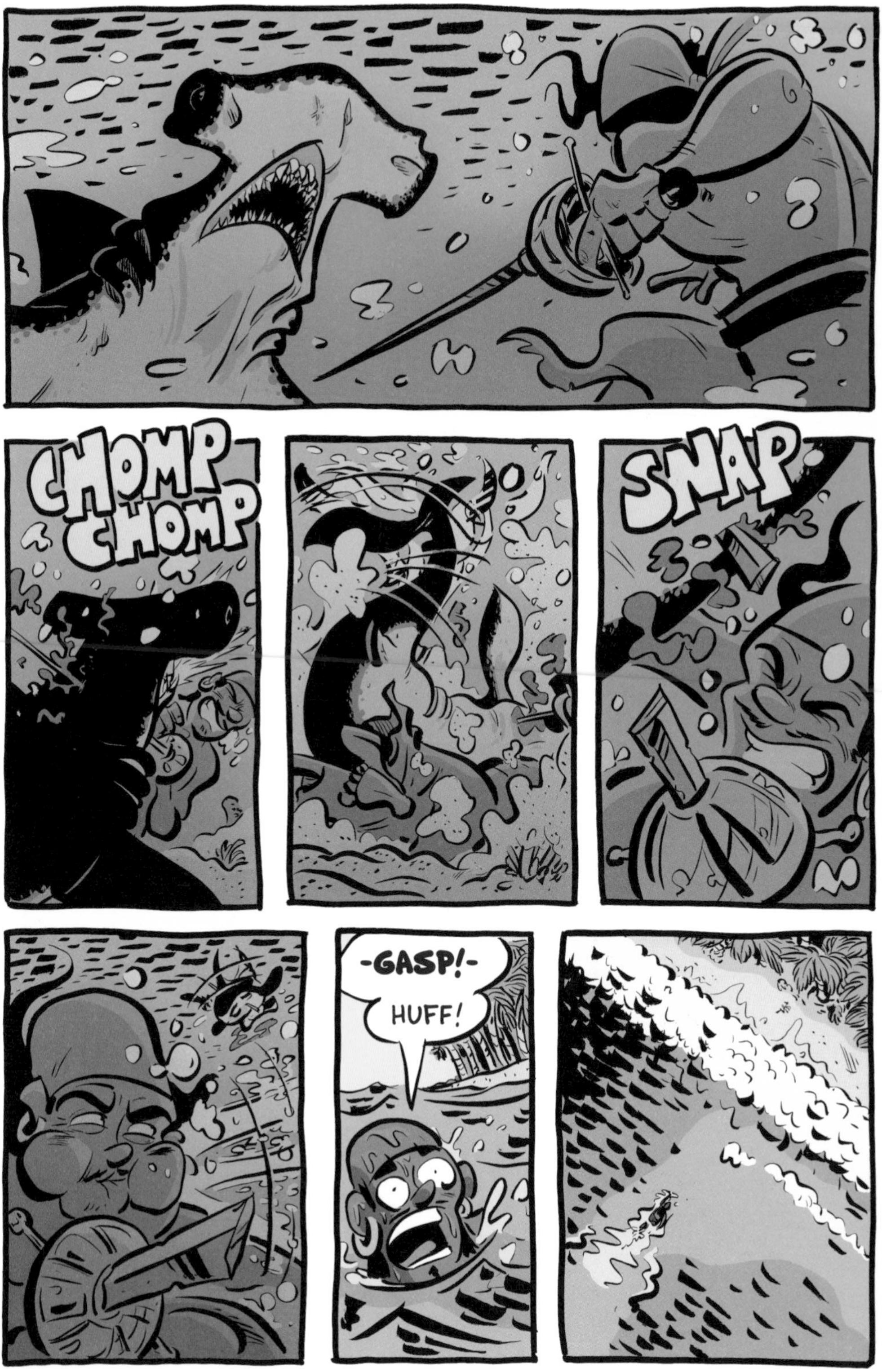
CHOMP CHOMP
SNAP
-GASP!-
HUFF!

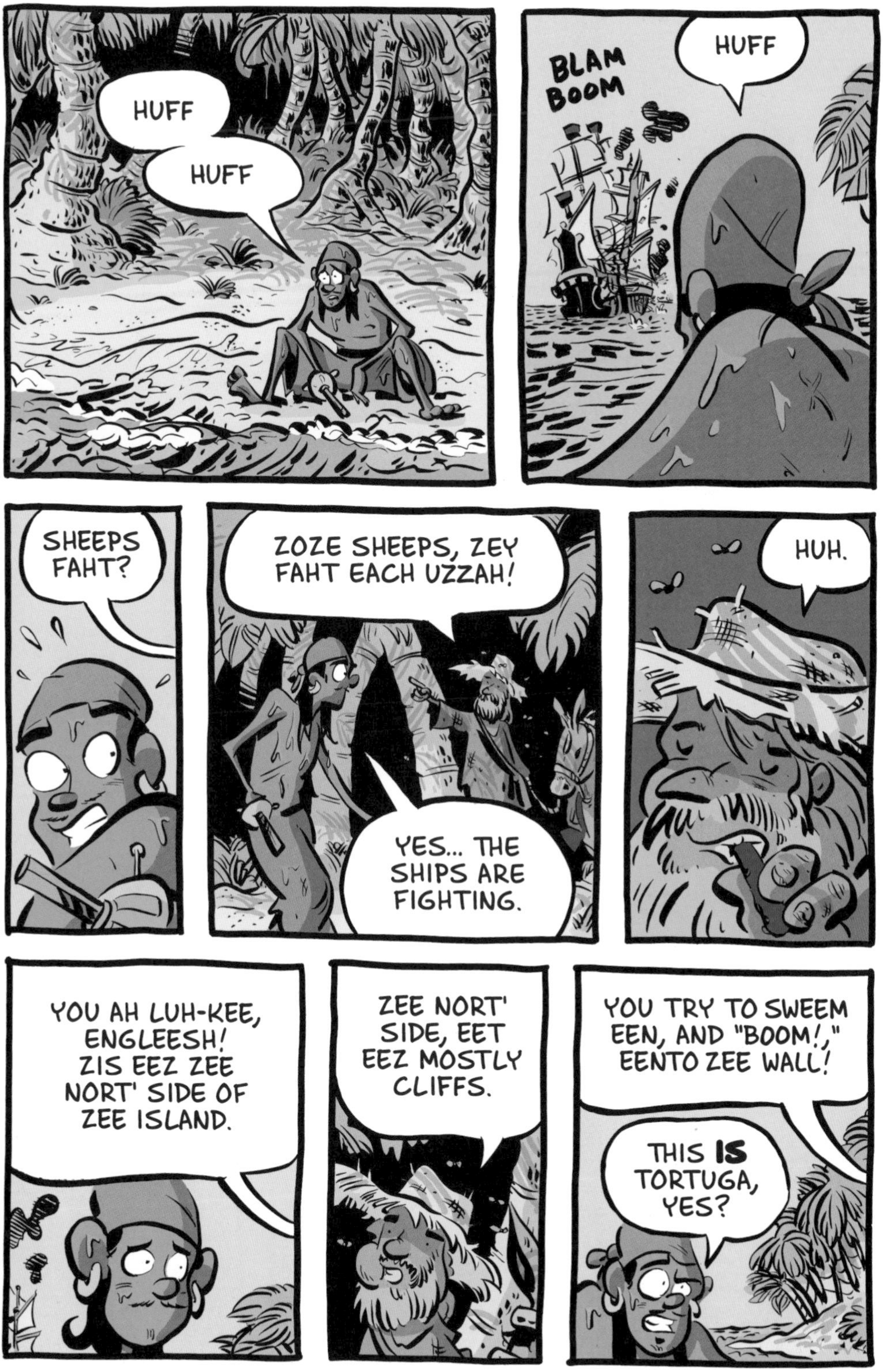

HUFF
HUFF
BLAM BOOM
HUFF
SHEEPS FAHT?
ZOZE SHEEPS, ZEY FAHT EACH UZZAH!
YES... THE SHIPS ARE FIGHTING.
HUH.
YOU AH LUH-KEE, ENGLEESH! ZIS EEZ ZEE NORT' SIDE OF ZEE ISLAND.
ZEE NORT' SIDE, EET EEZ MOSTLY CLIFFS.
YOU TRY TO SWEEM EEN, AND "BOOM!," EENTO ZEE WALL!
THIS **IS** TORTUGA, YES?

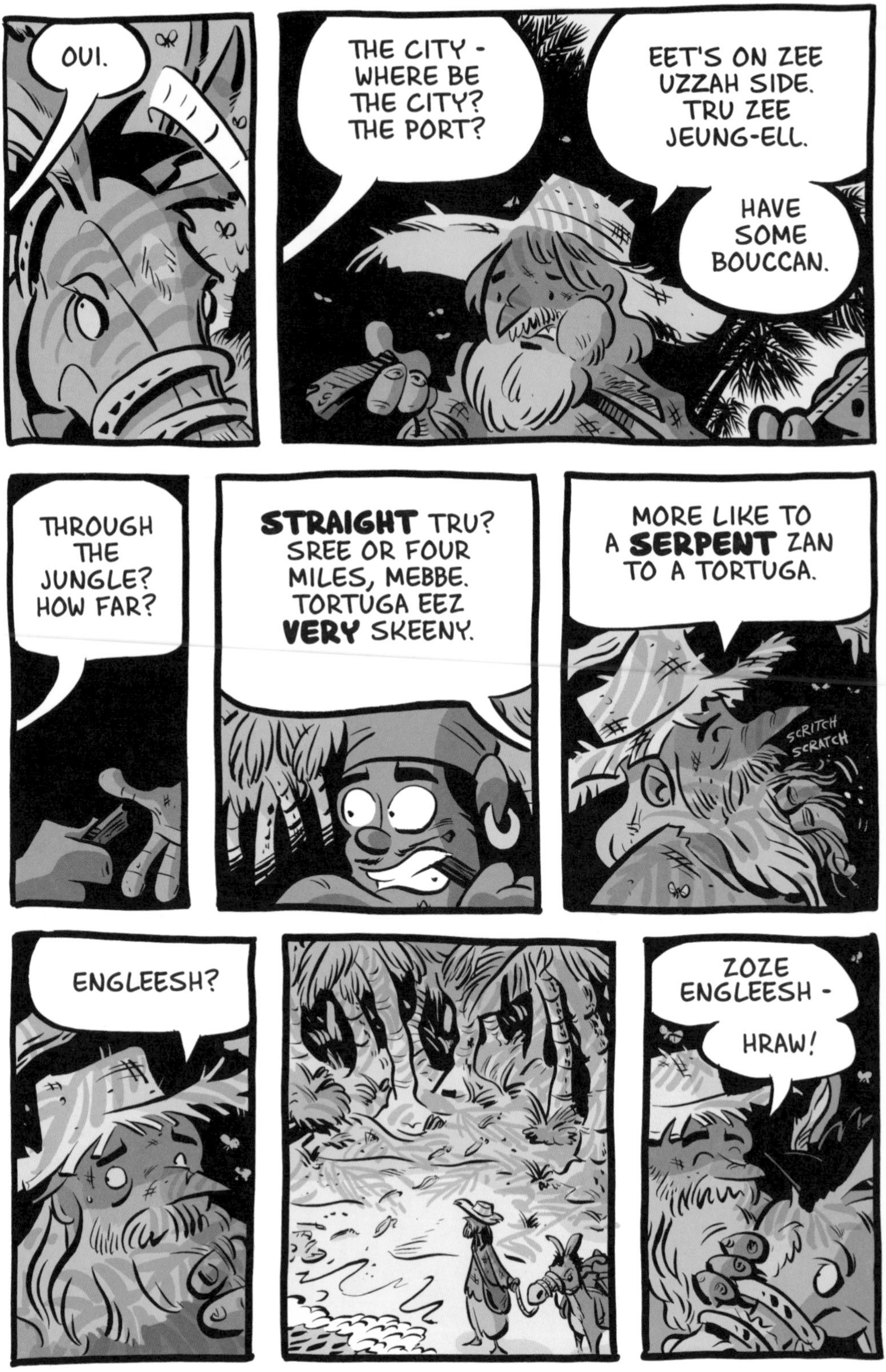
OUI.
THE CITY - WHERE BE THE CITY? THE PORT?
EET'S ON ZEE UZZAH SIDE. TRU ZEE JEUNG-ELL.
HAVE SOME BOUCCAN.
THROUGH THE JUNGLE? HOW FAR?
STRAIGHT TRU? SREE OR FOUR MILES, MEBBE. TORTUGA EEZ VERY SKEENY.
MORE LIKE TO A SERPENT ZAN TO A TORTUGA.
SCRITCH SCRATCH
ENGLEESH?
ZOZE ENGLEESH -
HRAW!

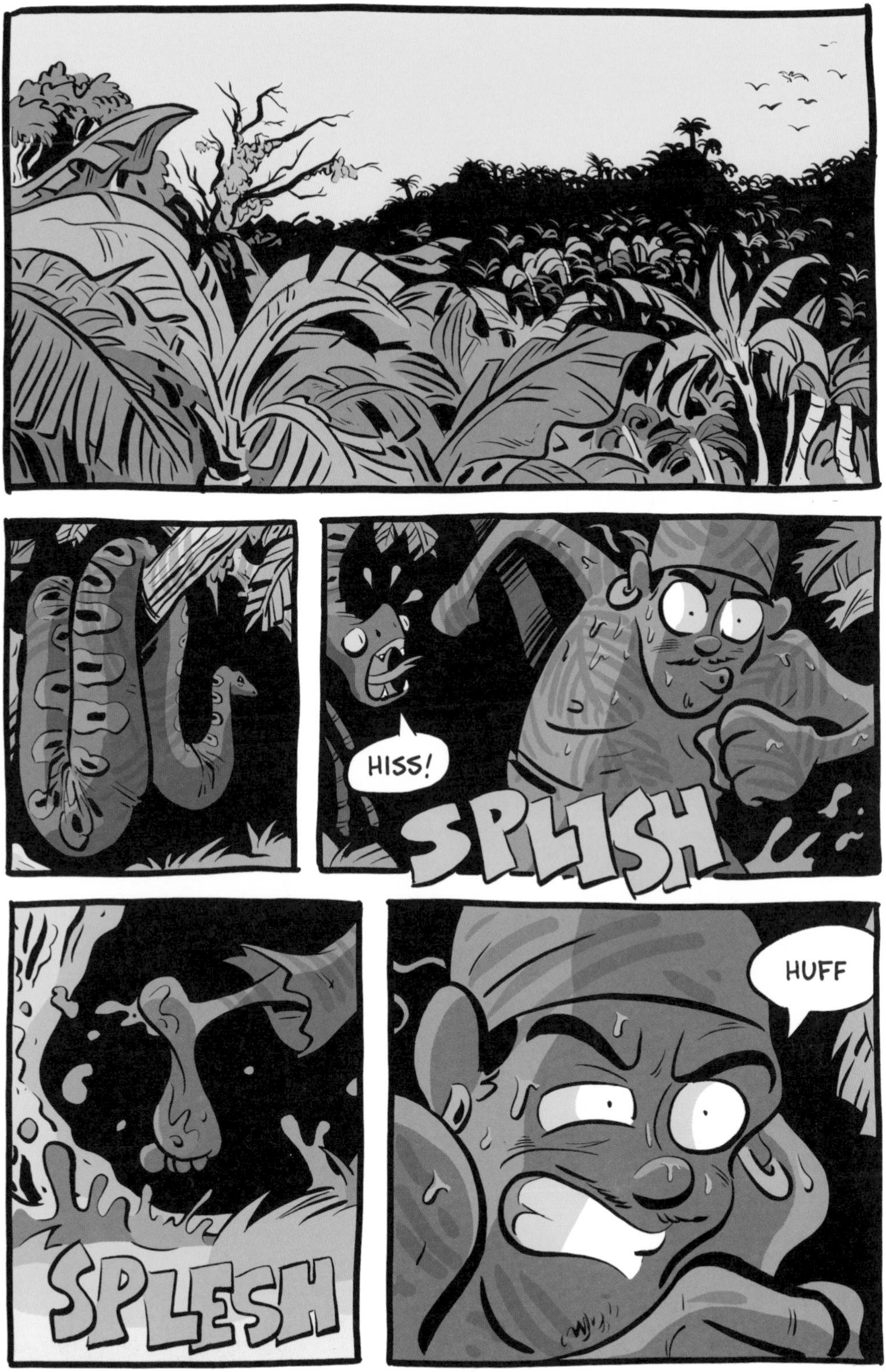
HISS!
SPLISH
SPLESH
HUFF

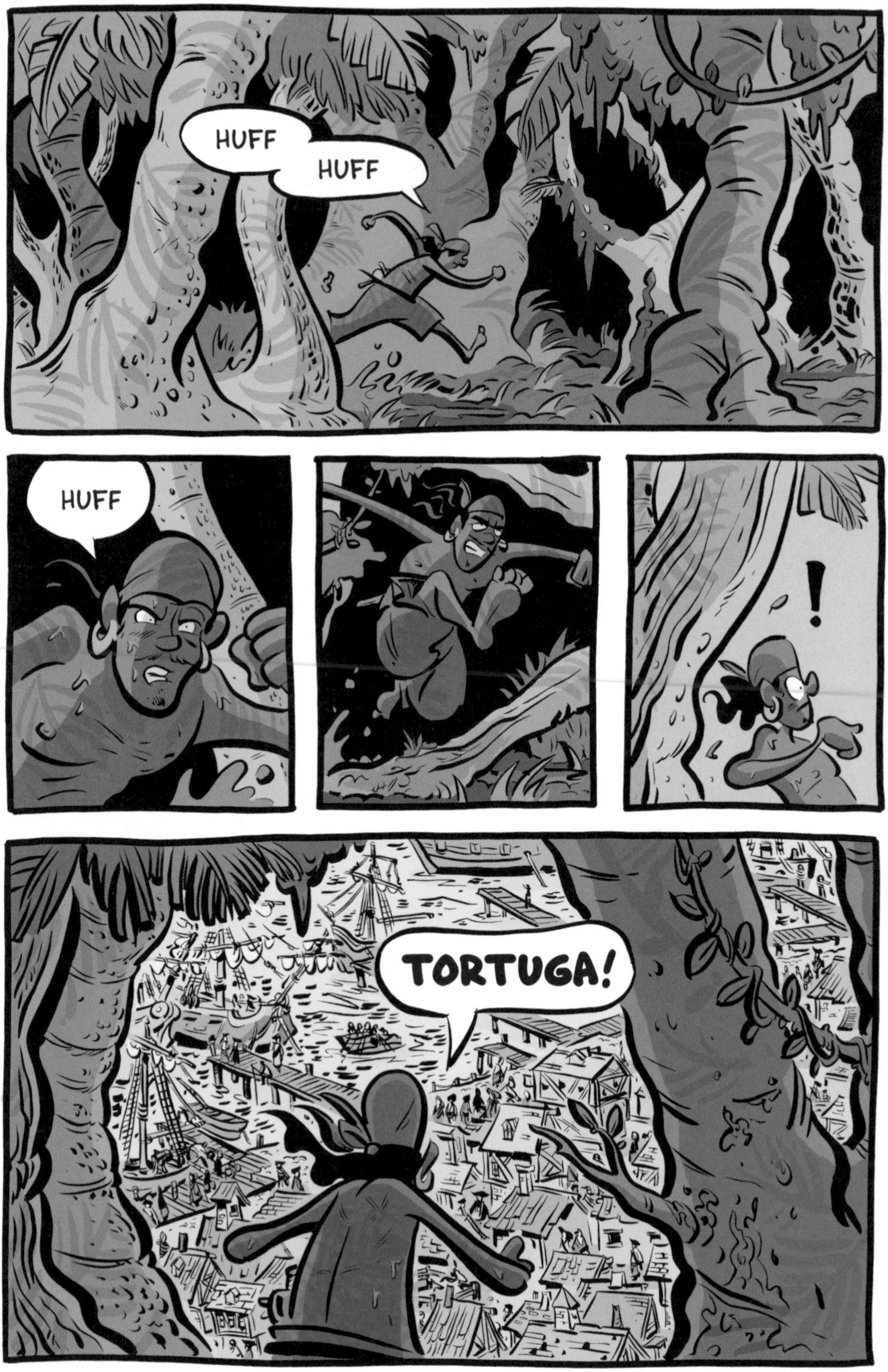
HUFF
HUFF
HUFF
!
TORTUGA!

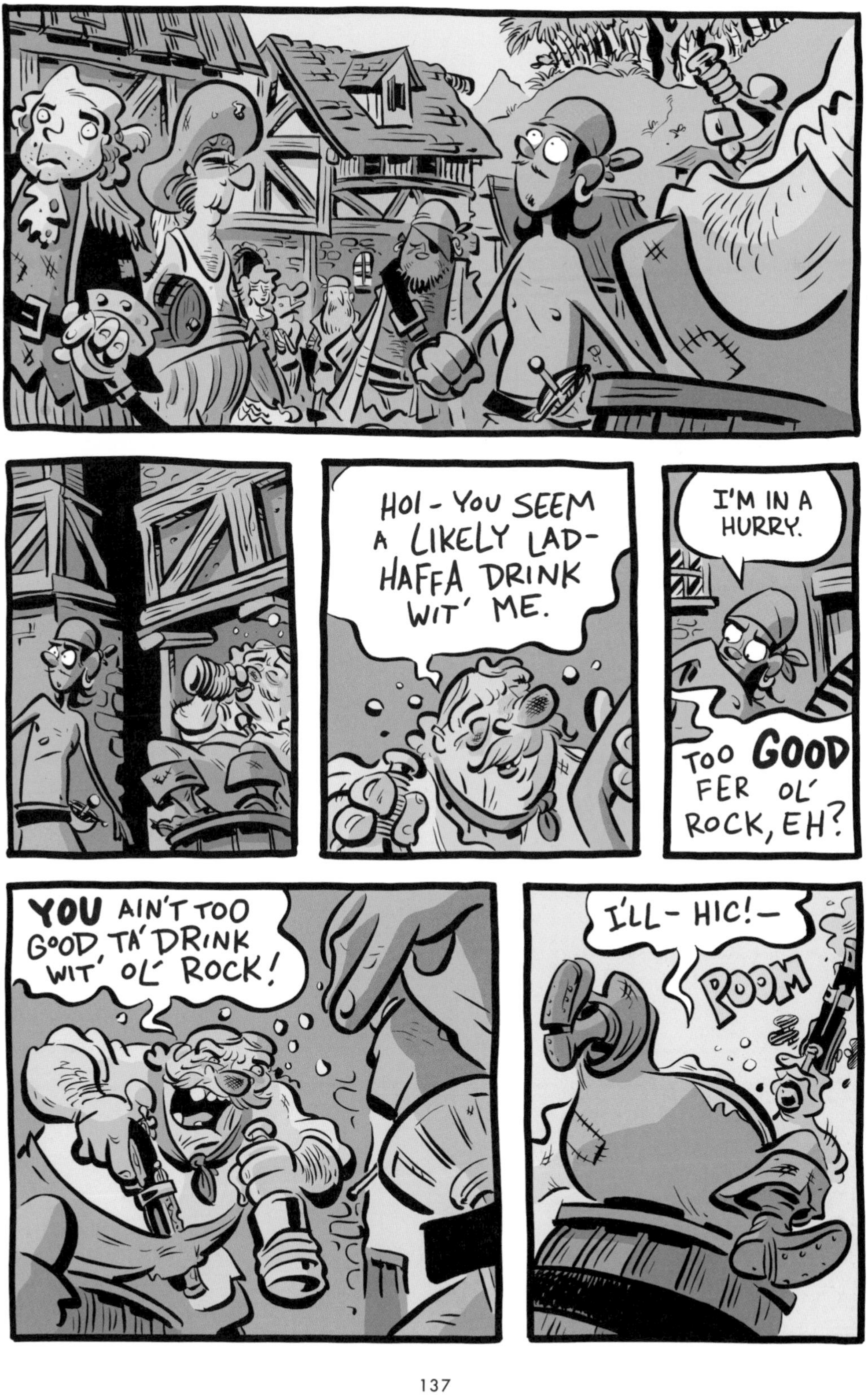
HOI - YOU SEEM A LIKELY LAD- HAFFA DRINK WIT' ME.
I'M IN A HURRY.
TOO GOOD FER OL' ROCK, EH?
YOU AIN'T TOO GOOD TA' DRINK WIT' OL' ROCK!
I'LL- HIC!-
POOM

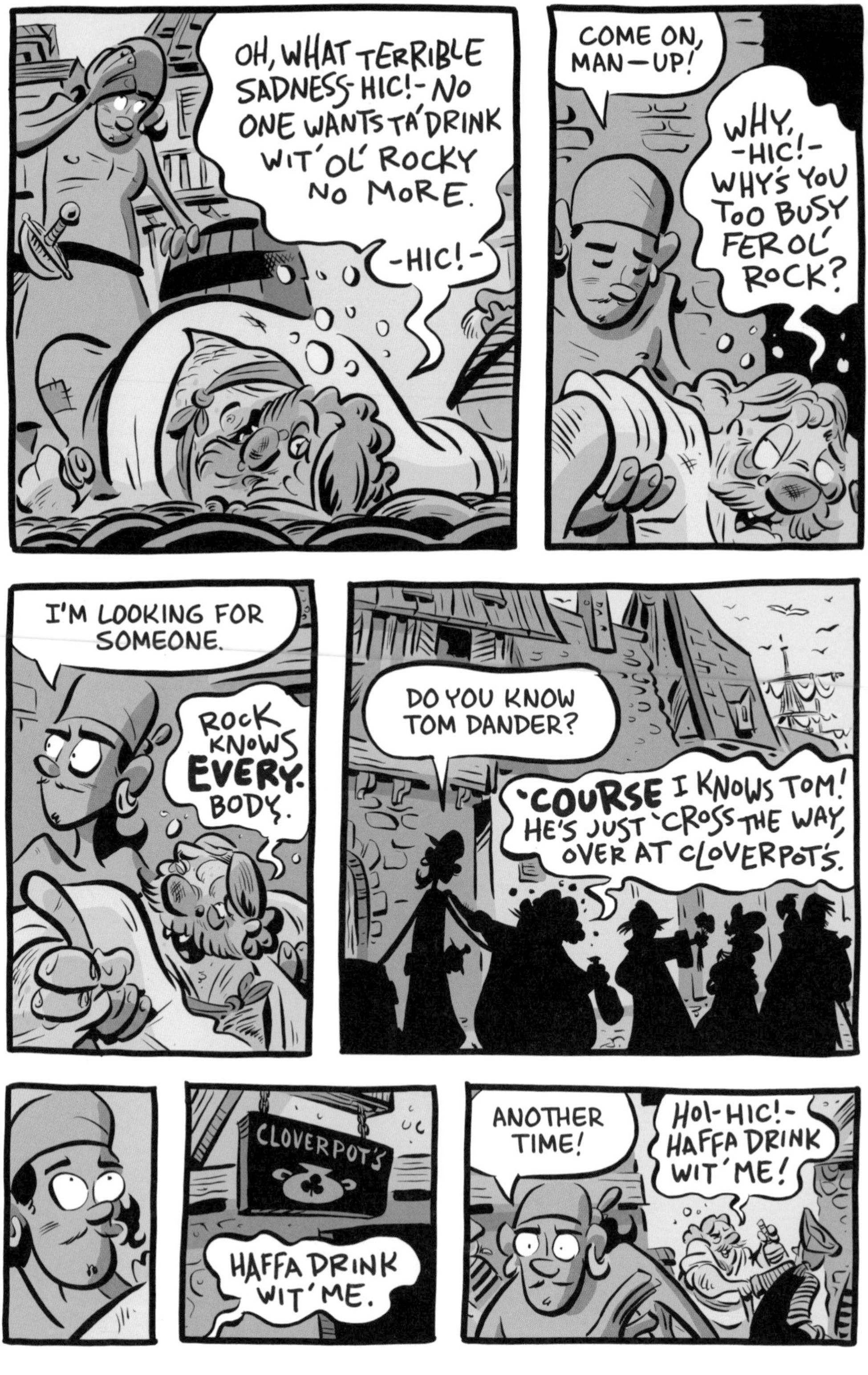
OH, WHAT TERRIBLE SADNESS-HIC!- NO ONE WANTS TA' DRINK WIT' OL' ROCKY NO MORE.
-HIC!-
COME ON, MAN—UP!
WHY, -HIC!- WHY'S YOU TOO BUSY FER OL' ROCK?
I'M LOOKING FOR SOMEONE.
ROCK KNOWS EVERY-BODY.
DO YOU KNOW TOM DANDER?
'COURSE I KNOWS TOM! HE'S JUST 'CROSS THE WAY, OVER AT CLOVERPOT'S.
CLOVERPOT'S
HAFFA DRINK WIT' ME.
ANOTHER TIME!
HOI-HIC!- HAFFA DRINK WIT' ME!

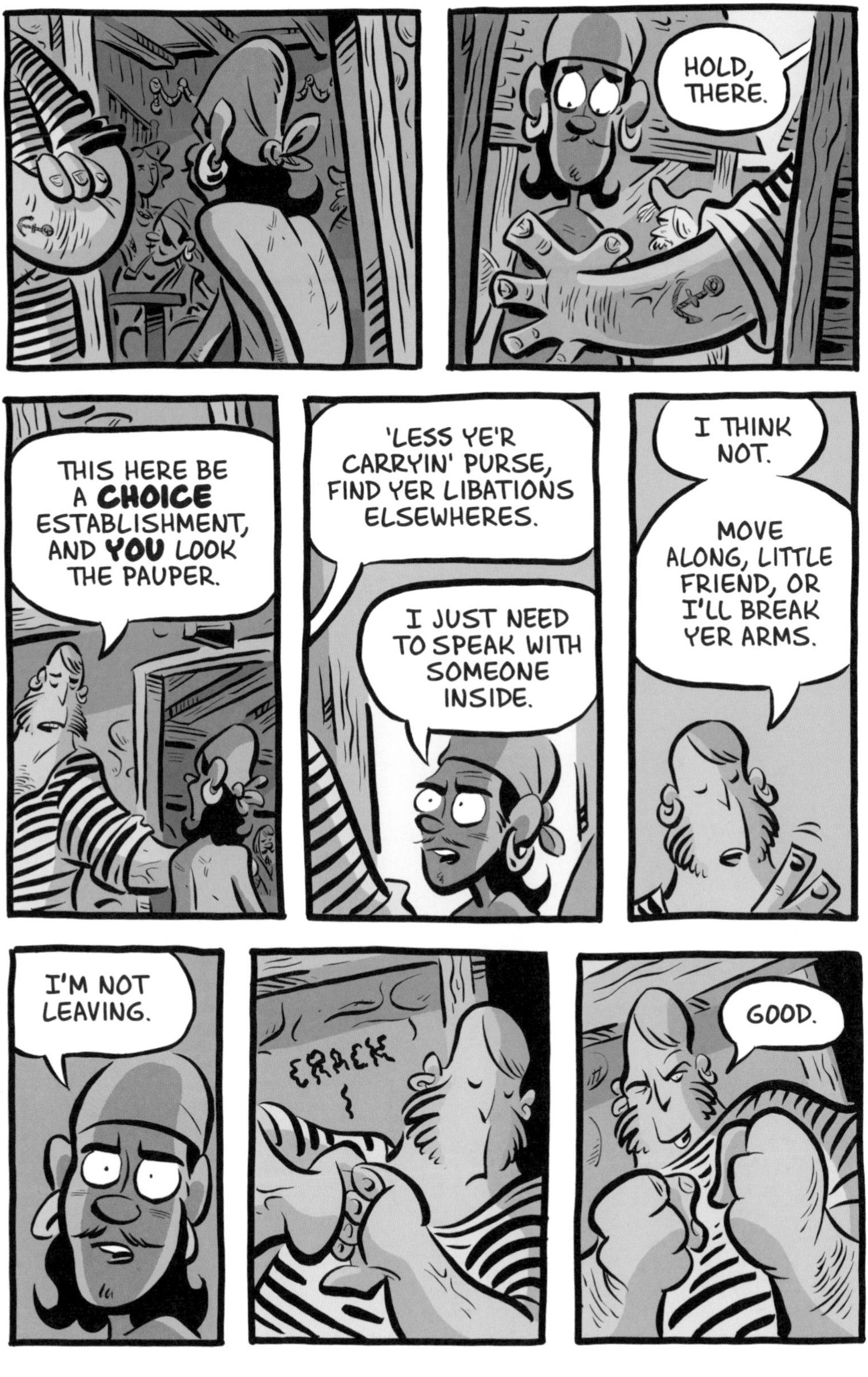
HOLD, THERE.
THIS HERE BE A **CHOICE** ESTABLISHMENT, AND **YOU** LOOK THE PAUPER.
'LESS YE'R CARRYIN' PURSE, FIND YER LIBATIONS ELSEWHERES.
I JUST NEED TO SPEAK WITH SOMEONE INSIDE.
I THINK NOT.
MOVE ALONG, LITTLE FRIEND, OR I'LL BREAK YER ARMS.
I'M NOT LEAVING.
CRACK
GOOD.

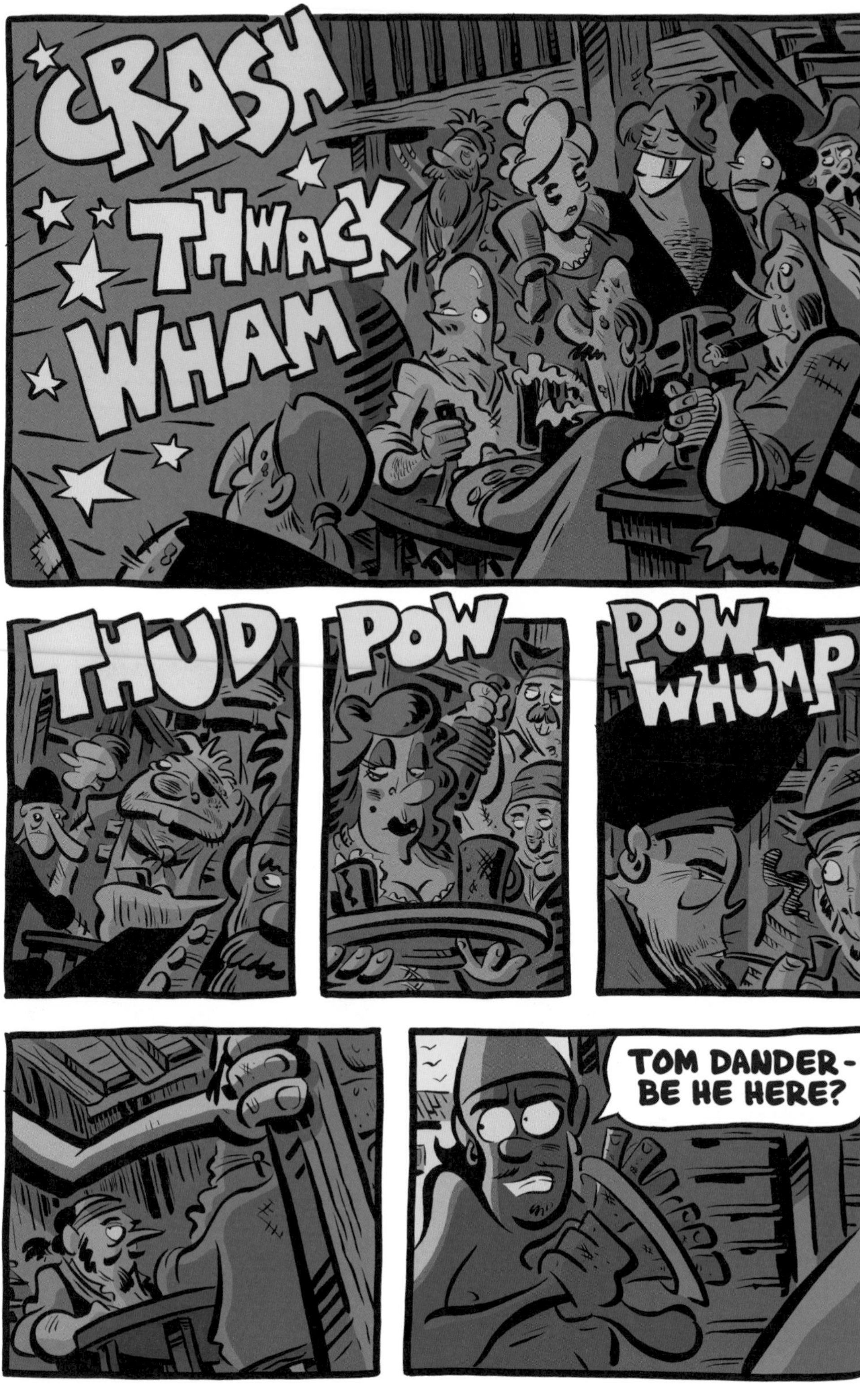
CRASH
THWACK
WHAM
THUD
POW
POW
WHUMP
TOM DANDER-
BE HE HERE?

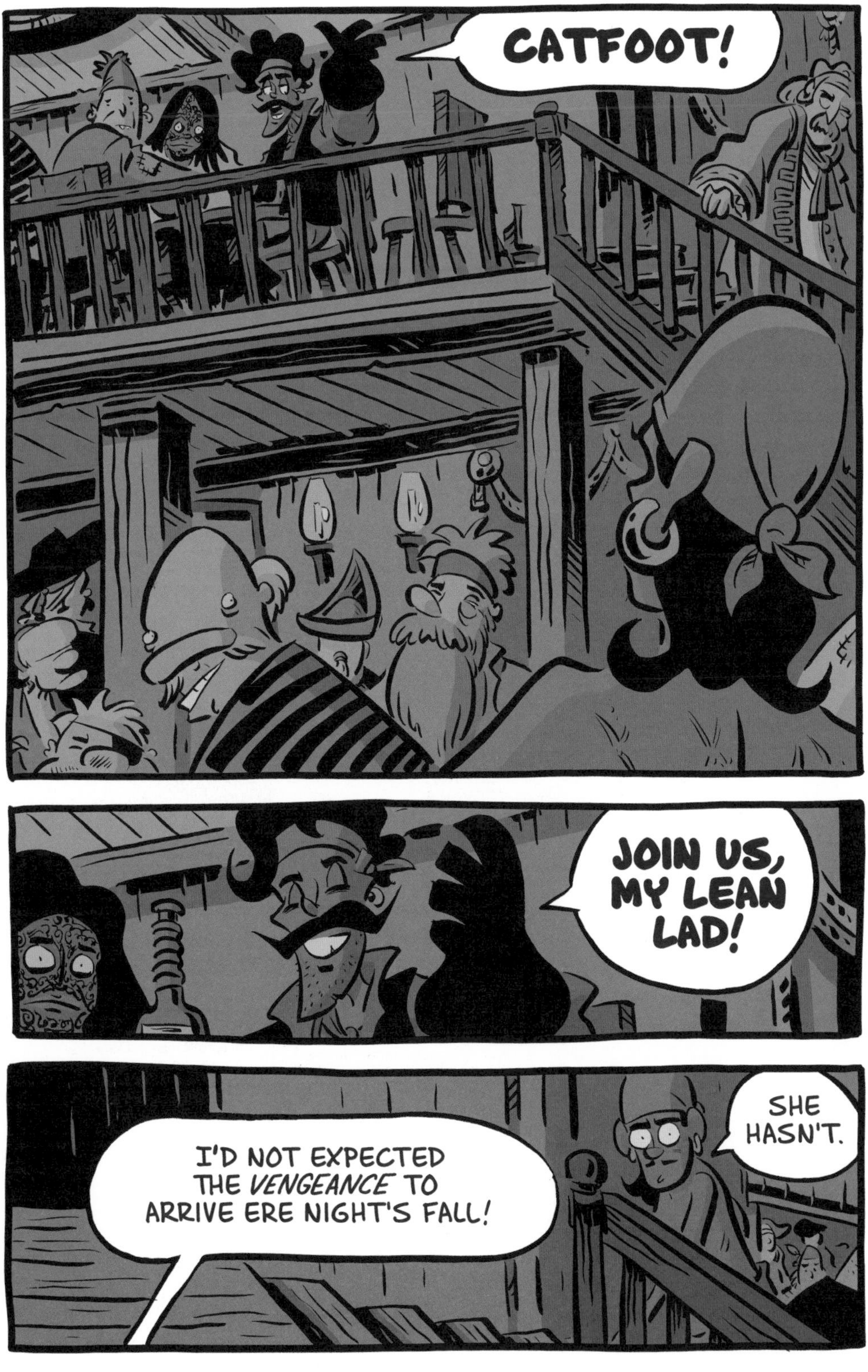
CATFOOT!
JOIN US, MY LEAN LAD!
I'D NOT EXPECTED THE *VENGEANCE* TO ARRIVE ERE NIGHT'S FALL!
SHE HASN'T.

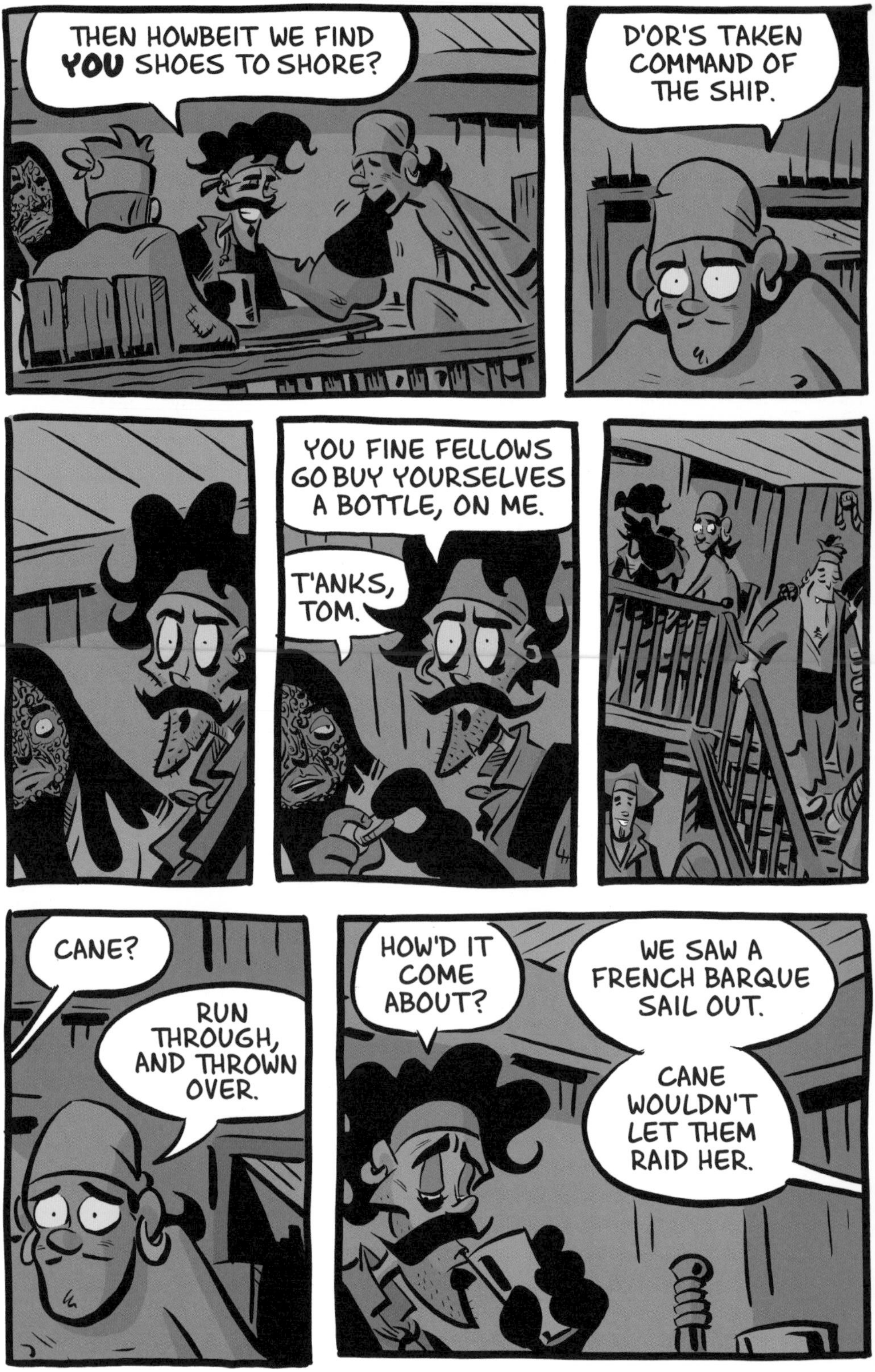
THEN HOWBEIT WE FIND YOU SHOES TO SHORE?
D'OR'S TAKEN COMMAND OF THE SHIP.
YOU FINE FELLOWS GO BUY YOURSELVES A BOTTLE, ON ME.
T'ANKS, TOM.
CANE?
RUN THROUGH, AND THROWN OVER.
HOW'D IT COME ABOUT?
WE SAW A FRENCH BARQUE SAIL OUT.
CANE WOULDN'T LET THEM RAID HER.

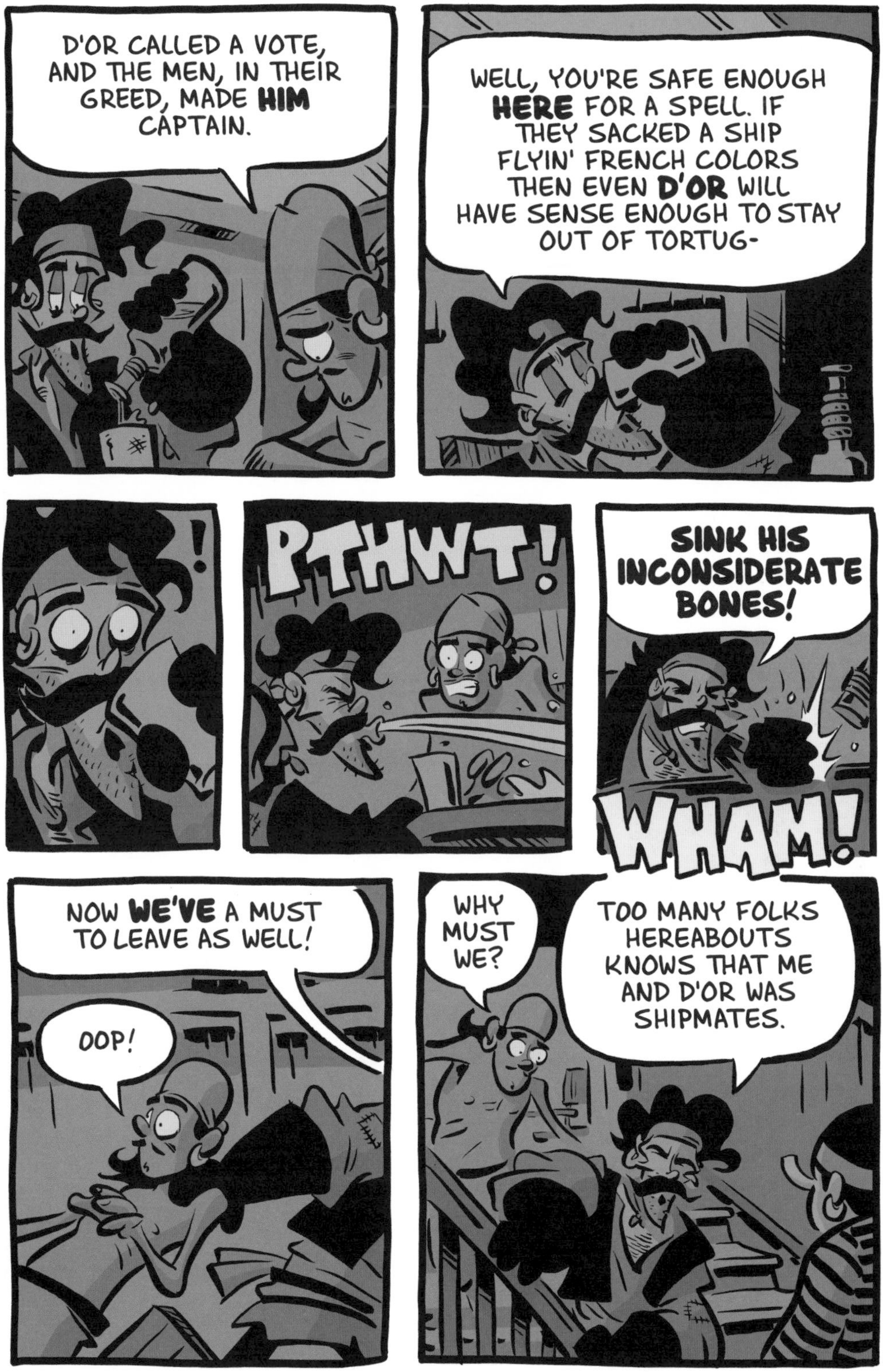
D'OR CALLED A VOTE, AND THE MEN, IN THEIR GREED, MADE **HIM** CAPTAIN.
WELL, YOU'RE SAFE ENOUGH **HERE** FOR A SPELL. IF THEY SACKED A SHIP FLYIN' FRENCH COLORS THEN EVEN **D'OR** WILL HAVE SENSE ENOUGH TO STAY OUT OF TORTUG-
!
PTHWT!
SINK HIS INCONSIDERATE BONES!
WHAM!
NOW **WE'VE** A MUST TO LEAVE AS WELL!
OOP!
WHY MUST WE?
TOO MANY FOLKS HEREABOUTS KNOWS THAT ME AND D'OR WAS SHIPMATES.

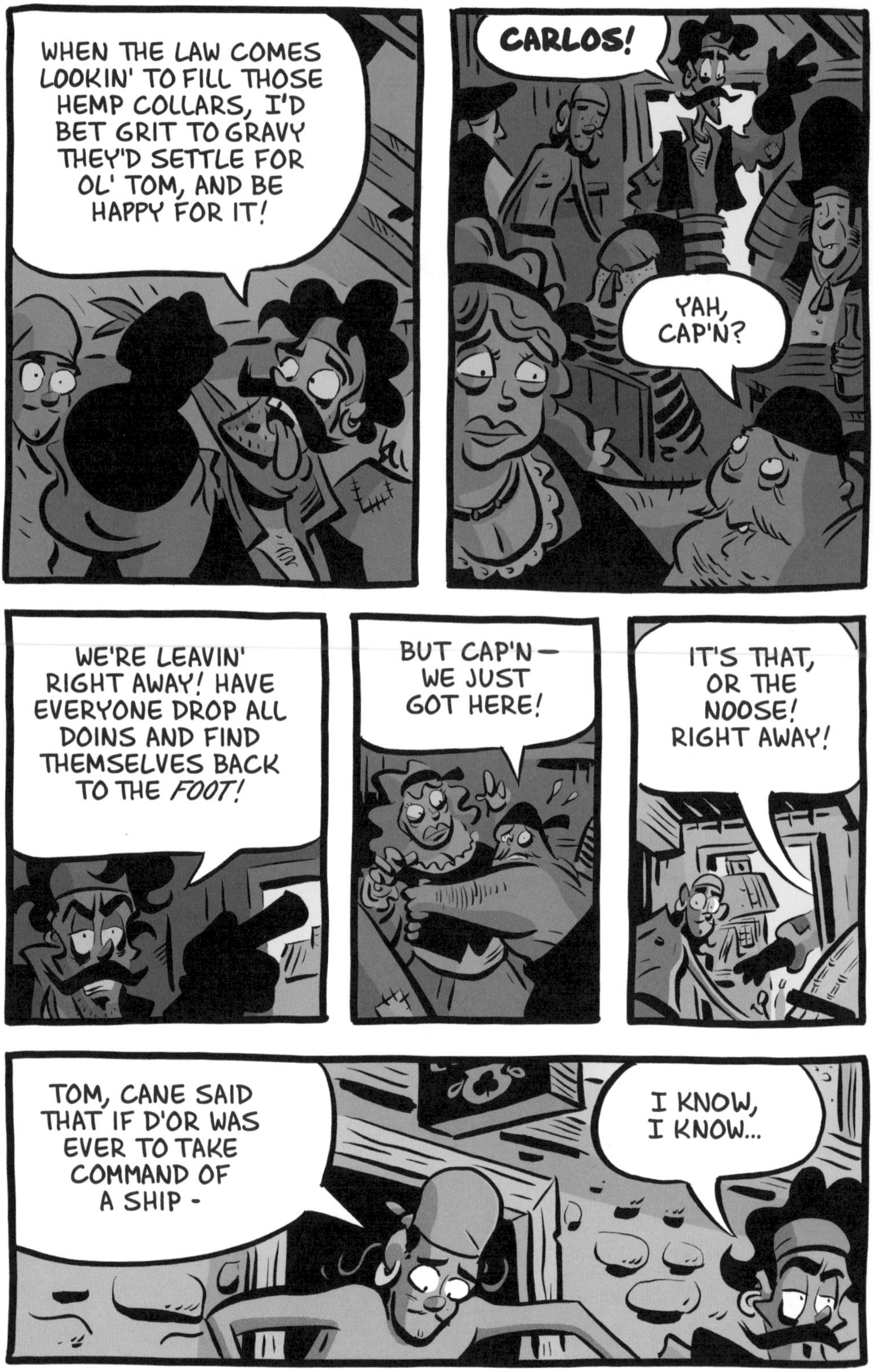
WHEN THE LAW COMES LOOKIN' TO FILL THOSE HEMP COLLARS, I'D BET GRIT TO GRAVY THEY'D SETTLE FOR OL' TOM, AND BE HAPPY FOR IT!
CARLOS!
YAH, CAP'N?
WE'RE LEAVIN' RIGHT AWAY! HAVE EVERYONE DROP ALL DOINS AND FIND THEMSELVES BACK TO THE *FOOT*!
BUT CAP'N— WE JUST GOT HERE!
IT'S THAT, OR THE NOOSE! RIGHT AWAY!
TOM, CANE SAID THAT IF D'OR WAS EVER TO TAKE COMMAND OF A SHIP -
I KNOW, I KNOW...

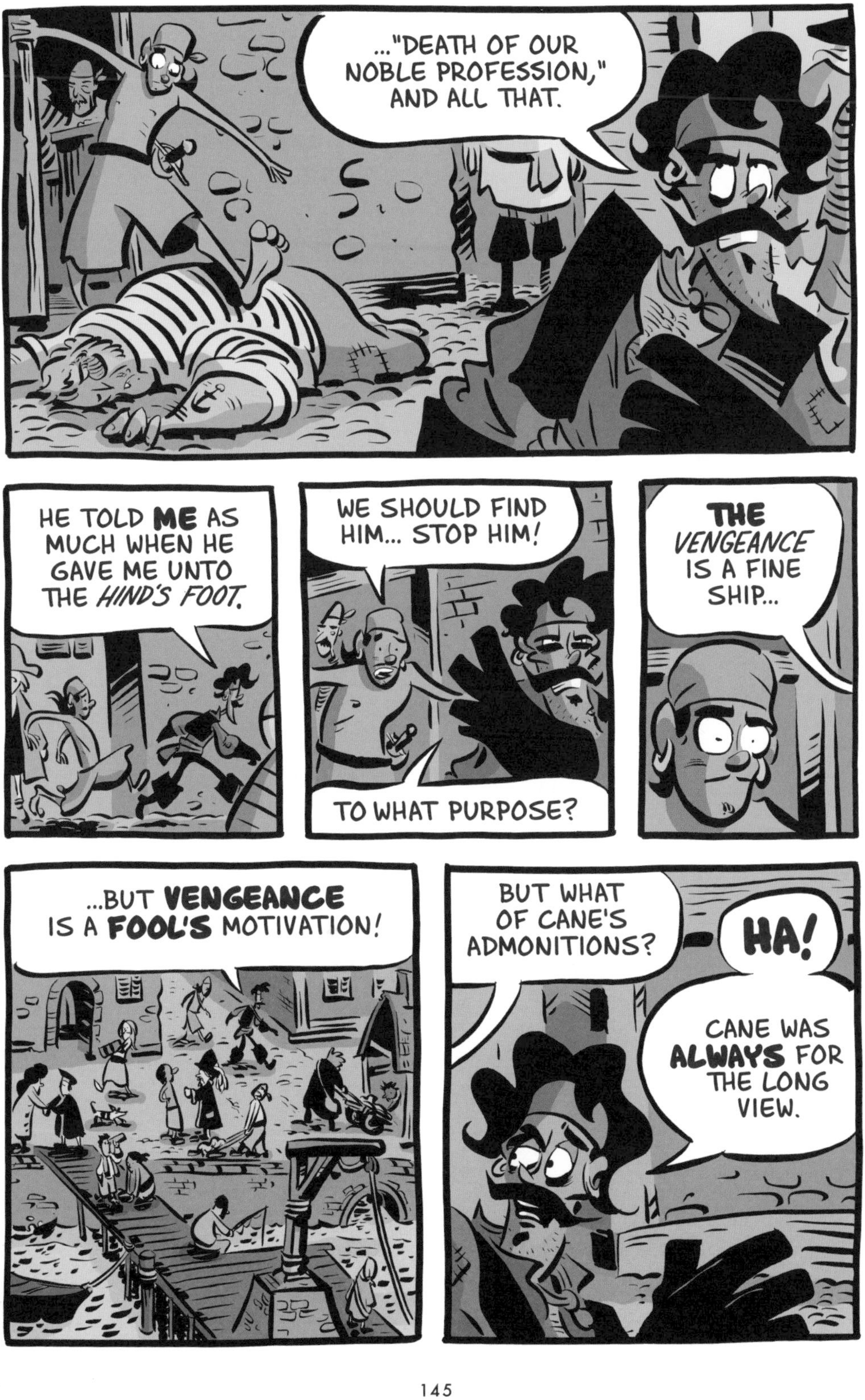
..."DEATH OF OUR NOBLE PROFESSION," AND ALL THAT.
HE TOLD **ME** AS MUCH WHEN HE GAVE ME UNTO THE *HIND'S FOOT*.
WE SHOULD FIND HIM... STOP HIM!
TO WHAT PURPOSE?
THE *VENGEANCE* IS A FINE SHIP...
...BUT **VENGEANCE** IS A **FOOL'S** MOTIVATION!
BUT WHAT OF CANE'S ADMONITIONS?
HA!
CANE WAS **ALWAYS** FOR THE LONG VIEW.

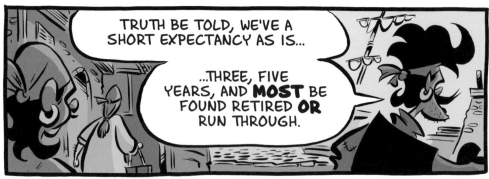

TRUTH BE TOLD, WE'VE A SHORT EXPECTANCY AS IS...

...THREE, FIVE YEARS, AND **MOST** BE FOUND RETIRED **OR** RUN THROUGH.

BUT D'OR **MURDERED** CAPTAIN CANE –

YOU JUST WANT AN EXCUSE!

CANE WAS **HARDLY** A FRIEND TO **YOU**.

HE ONLY TOOK YOUR SIDE 'CAUSE IT FELL TO HIS SORDID PRAGMATISM.

YOU **HATE** D'OR FOR BEING A MURDEROUS BEAST, AND **MORE** FOR BEING A MURDEROUS BEAST WHAT GAVE **YOU** INSULT!

LIKE I SAID, VENGEANCE BE A FOOL'S GAME, AND I'LL HAVE **NO** PART IN IT.

LEST YOU FORGIVE HIS VILLAINY ENTIRE, YOU SHOULD REMEMBER THAT HE'S OFF WITH **YOUR** SHARE OF THE *THAMES* LOOT!

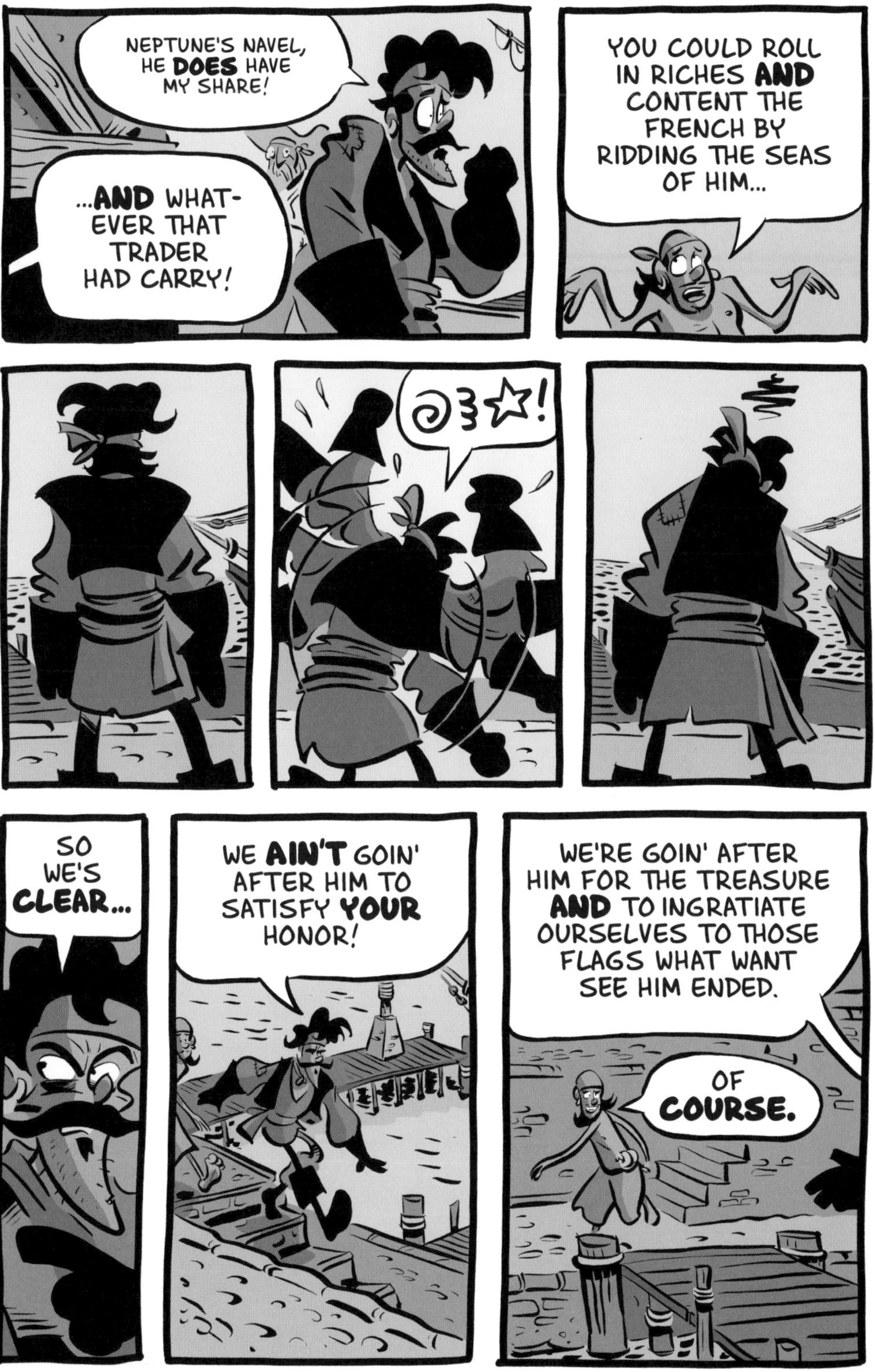
NEPTUNE'S NAVEL, HE DOES HAVE MY SHARE!
...AND WHAT-EVER THAT TRADER HAD CARRY!
YOU COULD ROLL IN RICHES AND CONTENT THE FRENCH BY RIDDING THE SEAS OF HIM...
SO WE'S CLEAR...
WE AIN'T GOIN' AFTER HIM TO SATISFY YOUR HONOR!
WE'RE GOIN' AFTER HIM FOR THE TREASURE AND TO INGRATIATE OURSELVES TO THOSE FLAGS WHAT WANT SEE HIM ENDED.
OF COURSE.

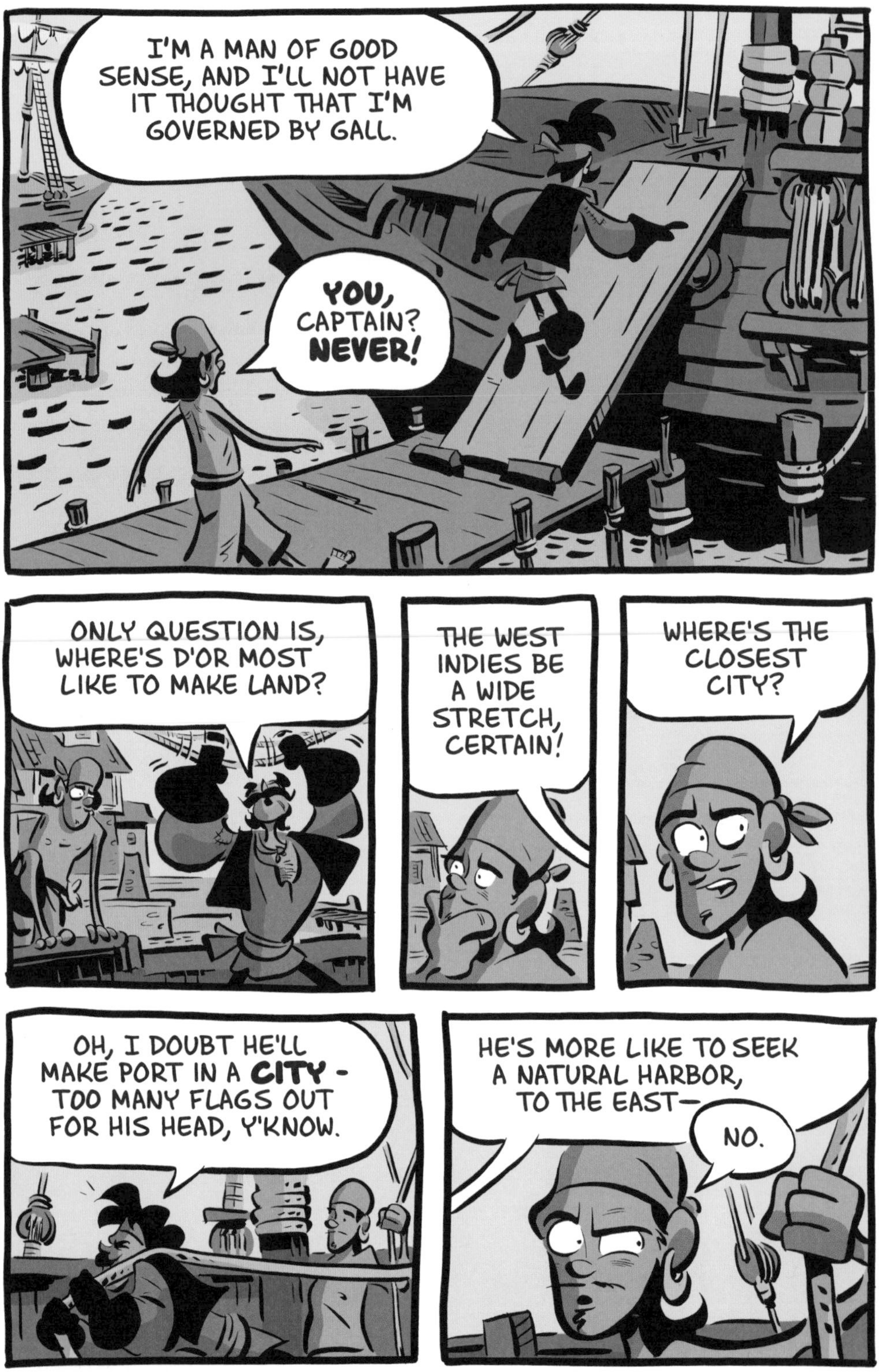
I'M A MAN OF GOOD SENSE, AND I'LL NOT HAVE IT THOUGHT THAT I'M GOVERNED BY GALL.
YOU, CAPTAIN? NEVER!
ONLY QUESTION IS, WHERE'S D'OR MOST LIKE TO MAKE LAND?
THE WEST INDIES BE A WIDE STRETCH, CERTAIN!
WHERE'S THE CLOSEST CITY?
OH, I DOUBT HE'LL MAKE PORT IN A CITY - TOO MANY FLAGS OUT FOR HIS HEAD, Y'KNOW.
HE'S MORE LIKE TO SEEK A NATURAL HARBOR, TO THE EAST—
NO.

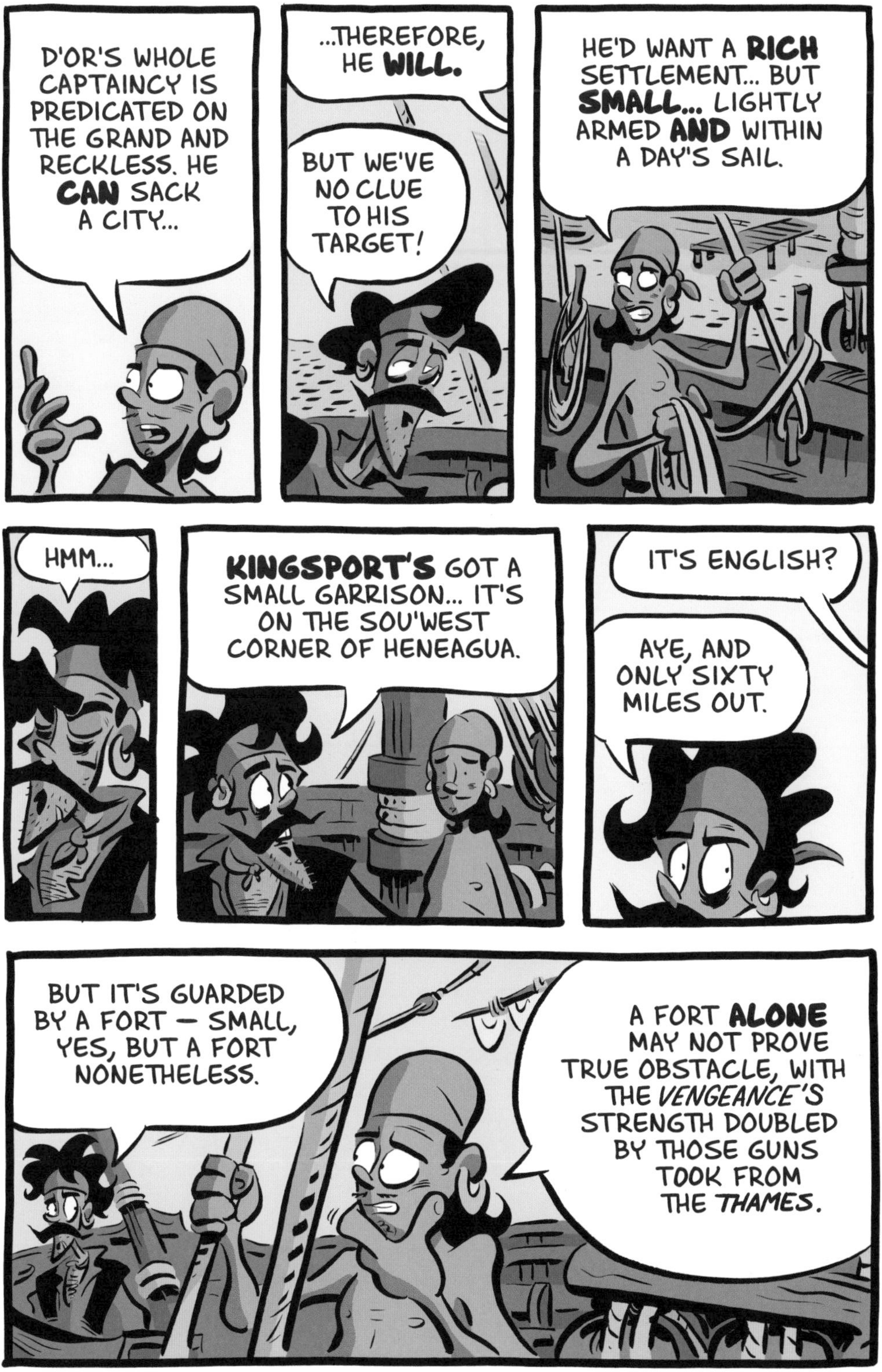
D'OR'S WHOLE CAPTAINCY IS PREDICATED ON THE GRAND AND RECKLESS. HE **CAN** SACK A CITY...
...THEREFORE, HE **WILL.**
BUT WE'VE NO CLUE TO HIS TARGET!
HE'D WANT A **RICH** SETTLEMENT... BUT **SMALL...** LIGHTLY ARMED **AND** WITHIN A DAY'S SAIL.
HMM...
KINGSPORT'S GOT A SMALL GARRISON... IT'S ON THE SOU'WEST CORNER OF HENEAGUA.
IT'S ENGLISH?
AYE, AND ONLY SIXTY MILES OUT.
BUT IT'S GUARDED BY A FORT — SMALL, YES, BUT A FORT NONETHELESS.
A FORT **ALONE** MAY NOT PROVE TRUE OBSTACLE, WITH THE *VENGEANCE'S* STRENGTH DOUBLED BY THOSE GUNS TOOK FROM THE *THAMES*.

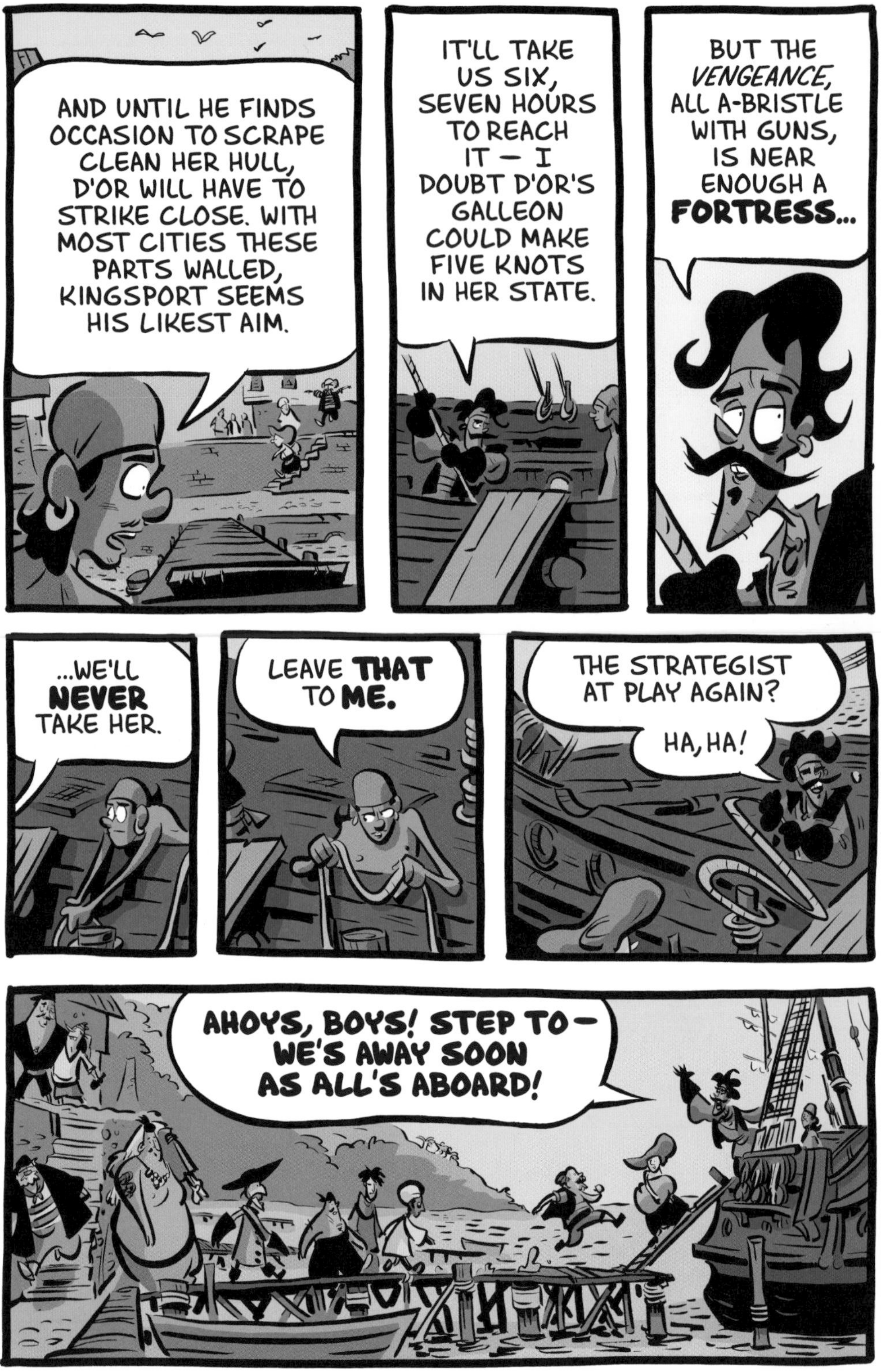
AND UNTIL HE FINDS OCCASION TO SCRAPE CLEAN HER HULL, D'OR WILL HAVE TO STRIKE CLOSE. WITH MOST CITIES THESE PARTS WALLED, KINGSPORT SEEMS HIS LIKEST AIM.
IT'LL TAKE US SIX, SEVEN HOURS TO REACH IT — I DOUBT D'OR'S GALLEON COULD MAKE FIVE KNOTS IN HER STATE.
BUT THE *VENGEANCE*, ALL A-BRISTLE WITH GUNS, IS NEAR ENOUGH A **FORTRESS**...
...WE'LL **NEVER** TAKE HER.
LEAVE **THAT** TO **ME.**
THE STRATEGIST AT PLAY AGAIN?
HA, HA!
AHOYS, BOYS! STEP TO— WE'S AWAY SOON AS ALL'S ABOARD!

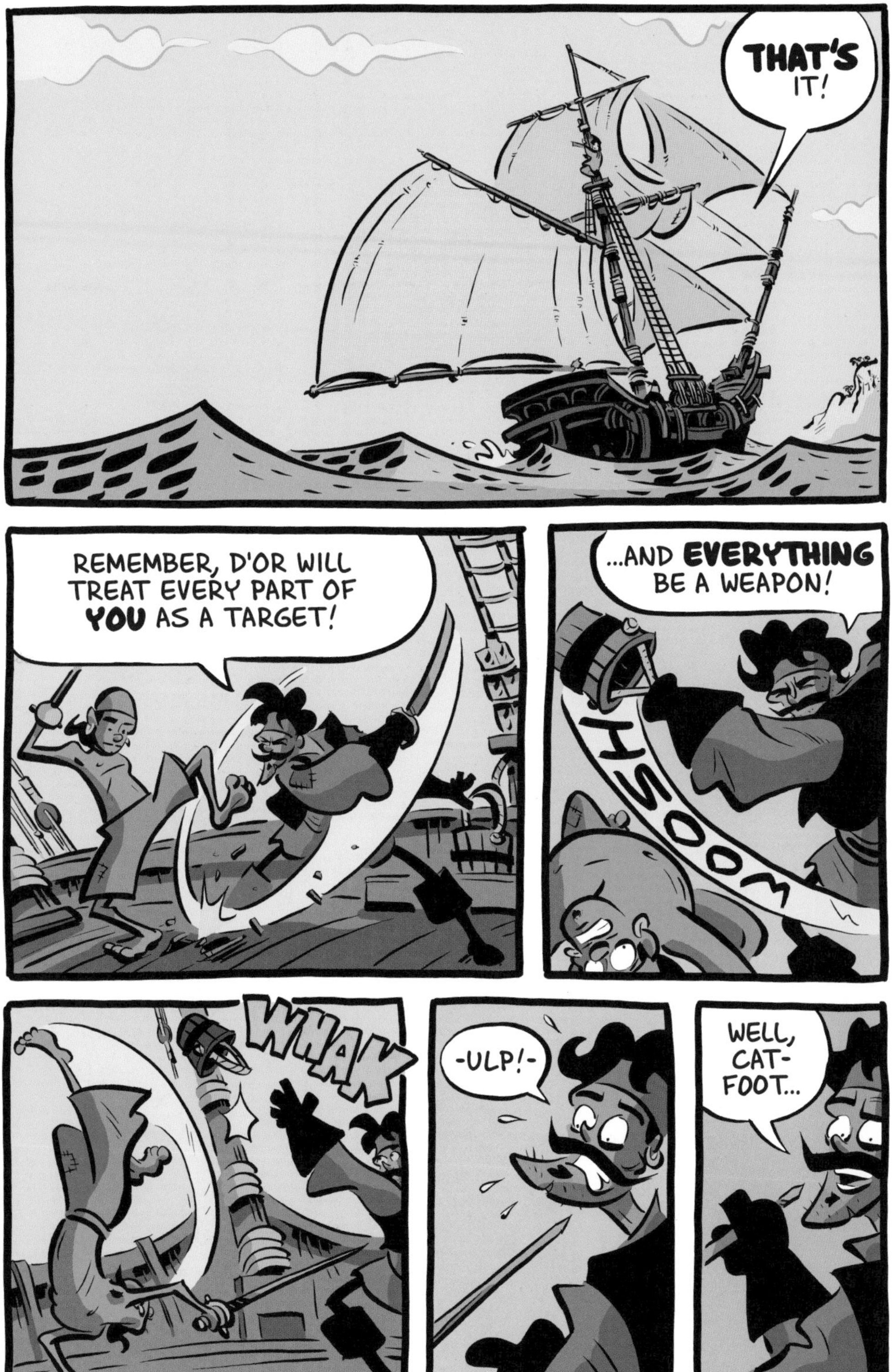
THAT'S IT!
REMEMBER, D'OR WILL TREAT EVERY PART OF YOU AS A TARGET!
...AND EVERYTHING BE A WEAPON!
WHOOSH
WHAK
-ULP!-
WELL, CAT-FOOT...

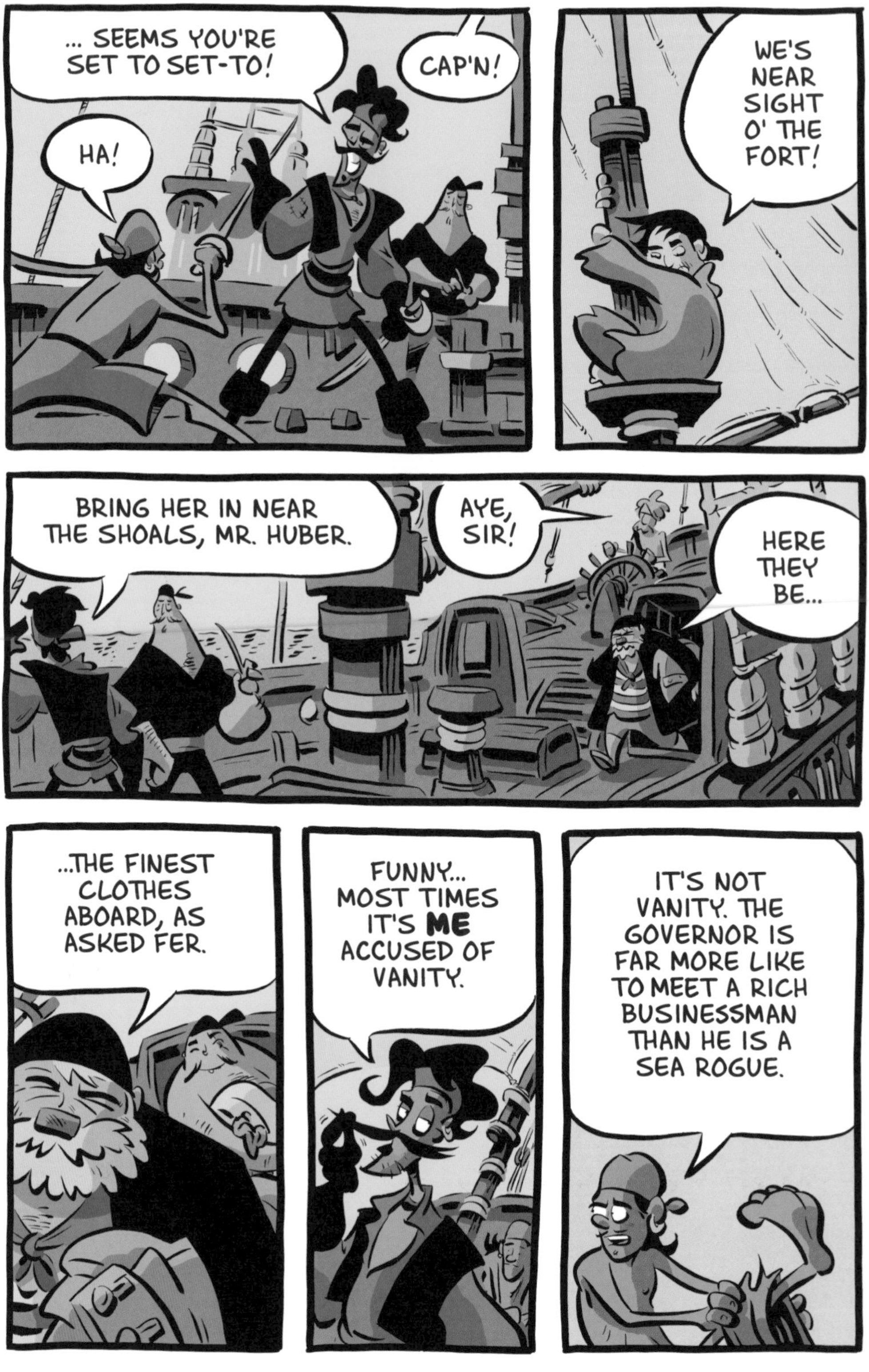
... SEEMS YOU'RE SET TO SET-TO!
CAP'N!
HA!
WE'S NEAR SIGHT O' THE FORT!
BRING HER IN NEAR THE SHOALS, MR. HUBER.
AYE, SIR!
HERE THEY BE...
...THE FINEST CLOTHES ABOARD, AS ASKED FER.
FUNNY... MOST TIMES IT'S ME ACCUSED OF VANITY.
IT'S NOT VANITY. THE GOVERNOR IS FAR MORE LIKE TO MEET A RICH BUSINESSMAN THAN HE IS A SEA ROGUE.

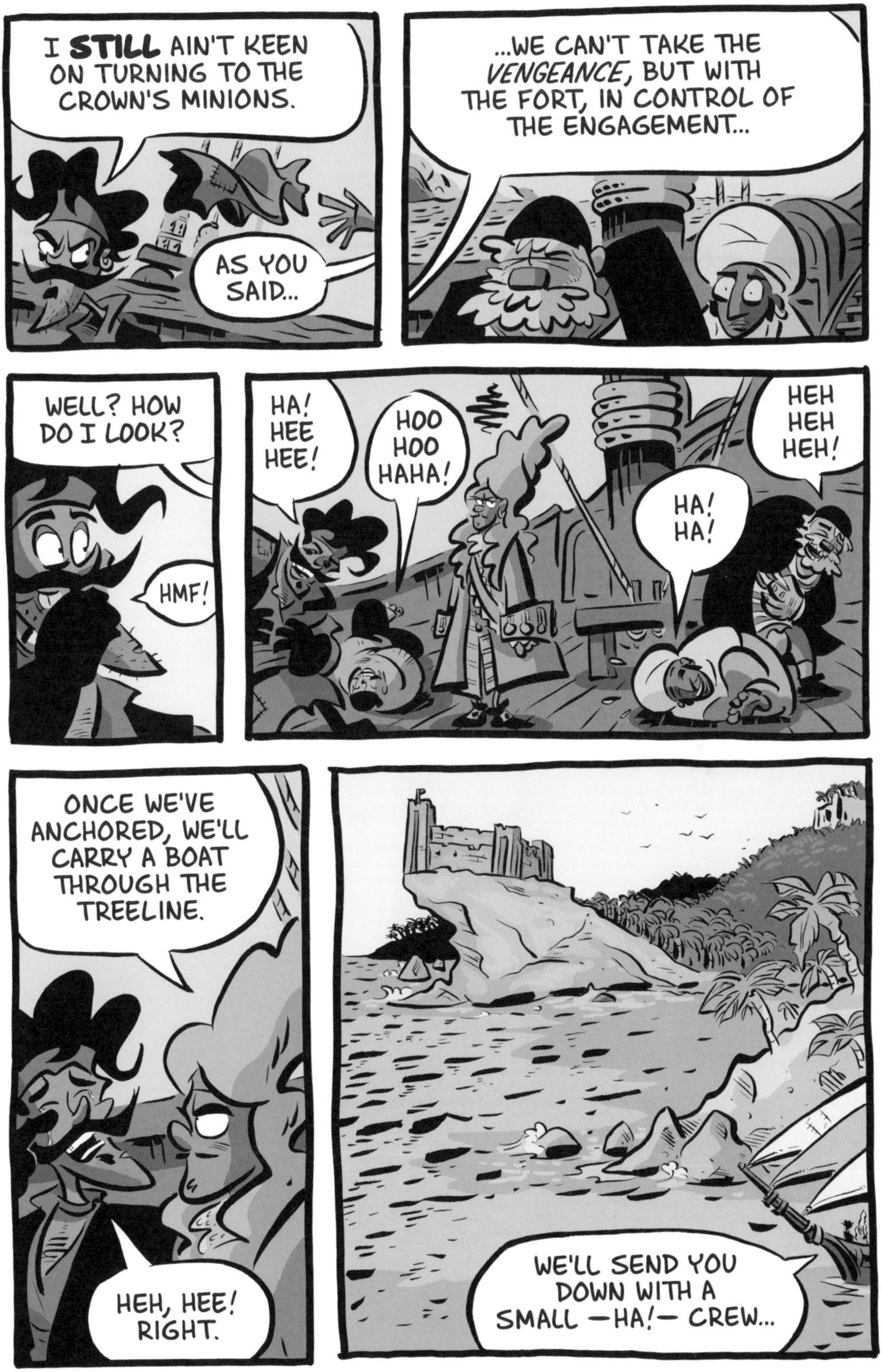
I STILL AIN'T KEEN ON TURNING TO THE CROWN'S MINIONS.
AS YOU SAID...
...WE CAN'T TAKE THE VENGEANCE, BUT WITH THE FORT, IN CONTROL OF THE ENGAGEMENT...
WELL? HOW DO I LOOK?
HMF!
HA! HEE HEE!
HOO HOO HAHA!
HEH HEH HEH!
HA! HA!
ONCE WE'VE ANCHORED, WE'LL CARRY A BOAT THROUGH THE TREELINE.
HEH, HEE! RIGHT.
WE'LL SEND YOU DOWN WITH A SMALL —HA!— CREW...

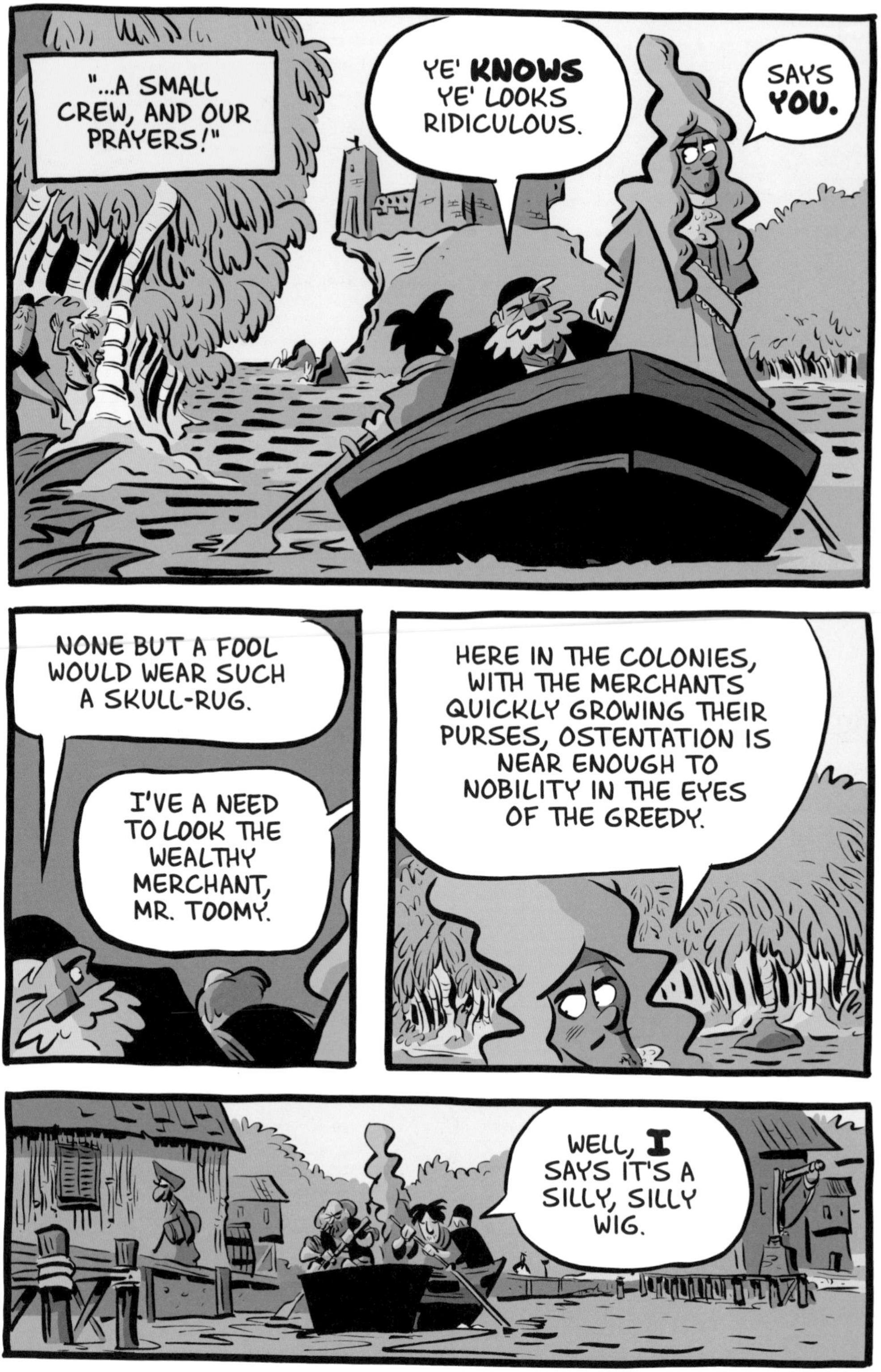
"...A SMALL CREW, AND OUR PRAYERS!"
YE' KNOWS YE' LOOKS RIDICULOUS.
SAYS YOU.
NONE BUT A FOOL WOULD WEAR SUCH A SKULL-RUG.
I'VE A NEED TO LOOK THE WEALTHY MERCHANT, MR. TOOMY.
HERE IN THE COLONIES, WITH THE MERCHANTS QUICKLY GROWING THEIR PURSES, OSTENTATION IS NEAR ENOUGH TO NOBILITY IN THE EYES OF THE GREEDY.
WELL, I SAYS IT'S A SILLY, SILLY WIG.

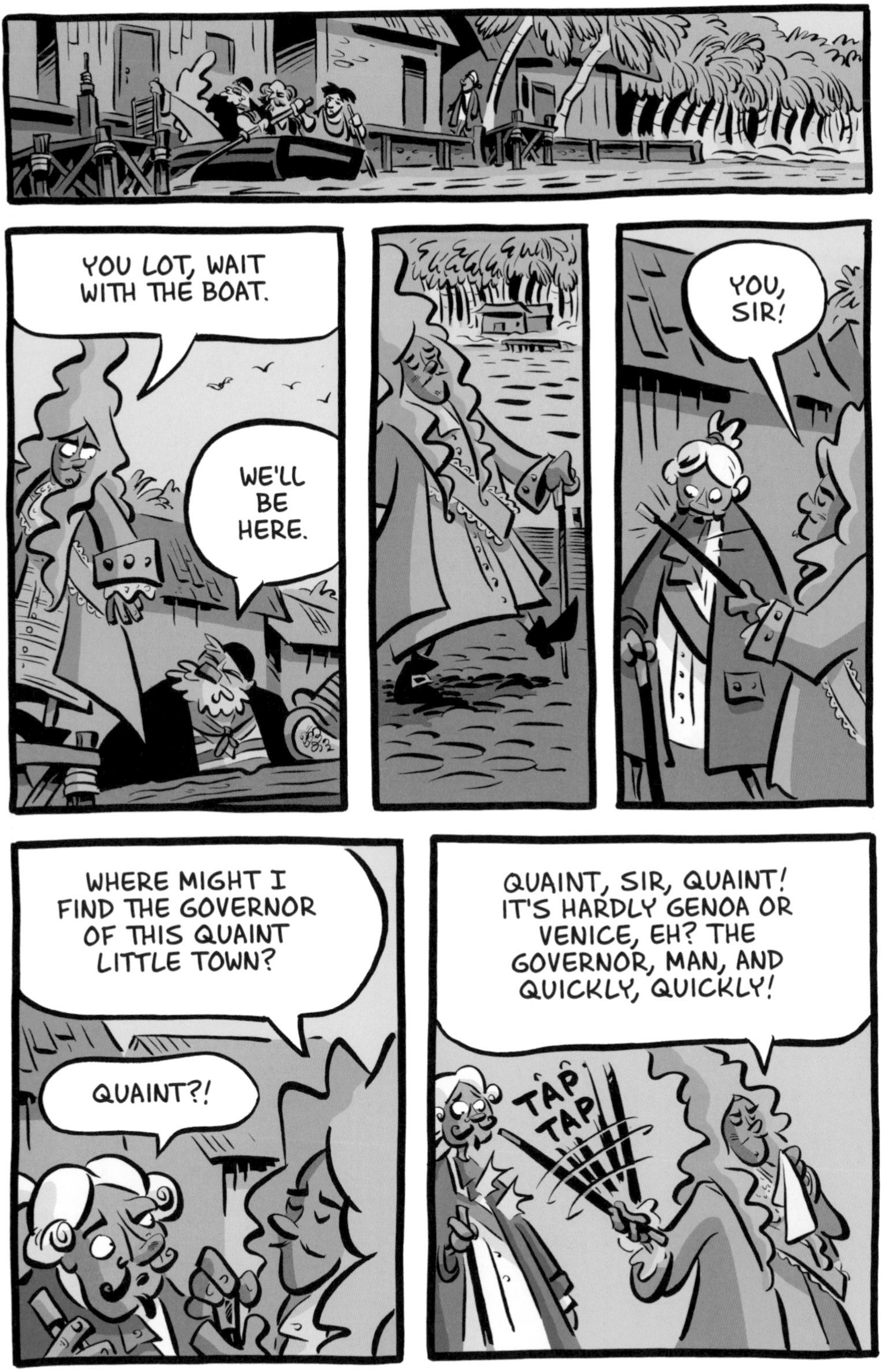

YOU LOT, WAIT WITH THE BOAT.
WE'LL BE HERE.
YOU, SIR!
WHERE MIGHT I FIND THE GOVERNOR OF THIS QUAINT LITTLE TOWN?
QUAINT?!
QUAINT, SIR, QUAINT! IT'S HARDLY GENOA OR VENICE, EH? THE GOVERNOR, MAN, AND QUICKLY, QUICKLY!
TAP TAP

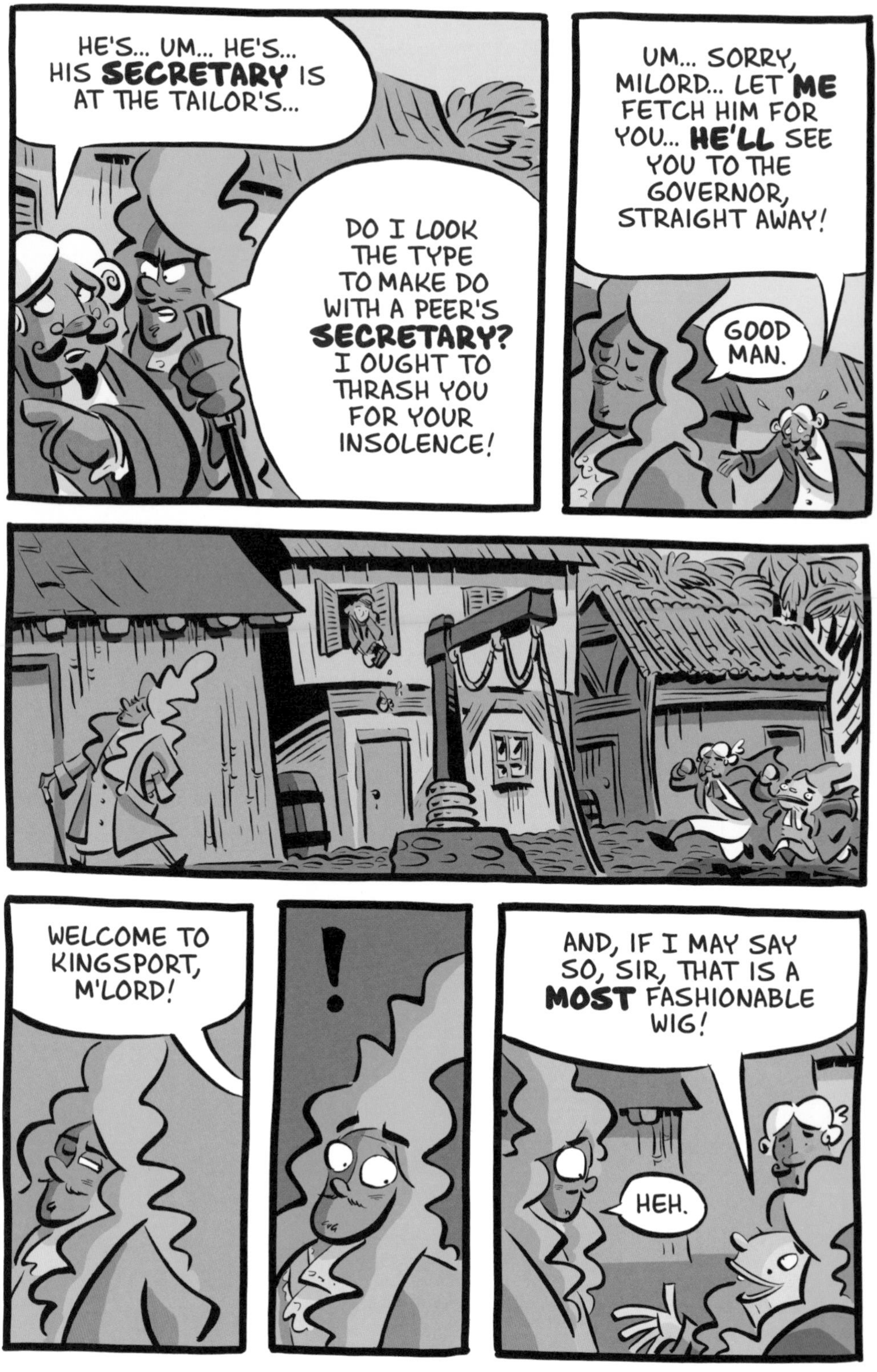
HE'S... UM... HE'S... HIS **SECRETARY** IS AT THE TAILOR'S...
DO I LOOK THE TYPE TO MAKE DO WITH A PEER'S **SECRETARY?** I OUGHT TO THRASH YOU FOR YOUR INSOLENCE!
UM... SORRY, MILORD... LET **ME** FETCH HIM FOR YOU... **HE'LL** SEE YOU TO THE GOVERNOR, STRAIGHT AWAY!
GOOD MAN.
WELCOME TO KINGSPORT, M'LORD!
!
AND, IF I MAY SAY SO, SIR, THAT IS A **MOST** FASHIONABLE WIG!
HEH.

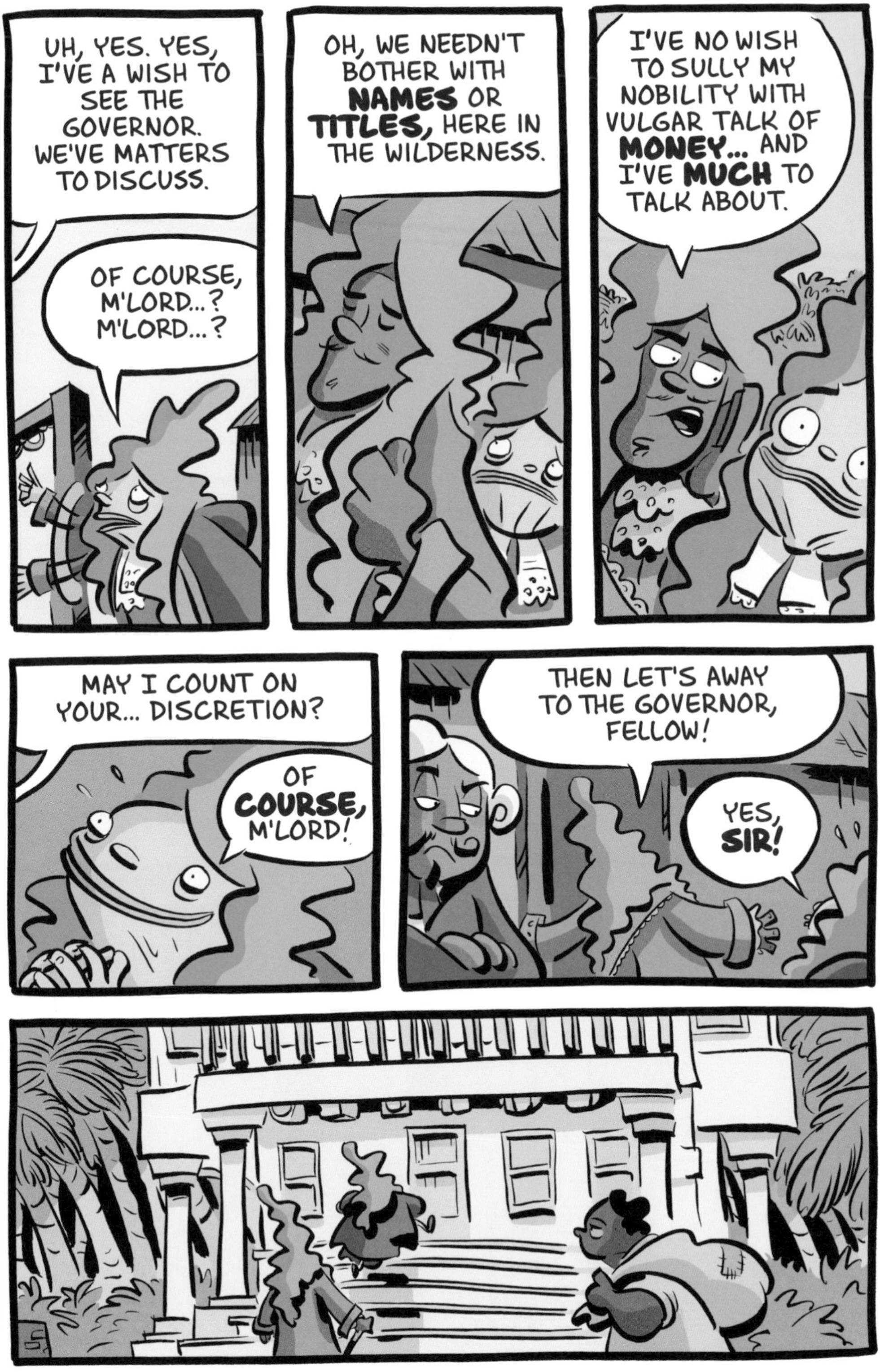
UH, YES. YES, I'VE A WISH TO SEE THE GOVERNOR. WE'VE MATTERS TO DISCUSS.
OF COURSE, M'LORD...? M'LORD...?
OH, WE NEEDN'T BOTHER WITH NAMES OR TITLES, HERE IN THE WILDERNESS.
I'VE NO WISH TO SULLY MY NOBILITY WITH VULGAR TALK OF MONEY... AND I'VE MUCH TO TALK ABOUT.
MAY I COUNT ON YOUR... DISCRETION?
OF COURSE, M'LORD!
THEN LET'S AWAY TO THE GOVERNOR, FELLOW!
YES, SIR!

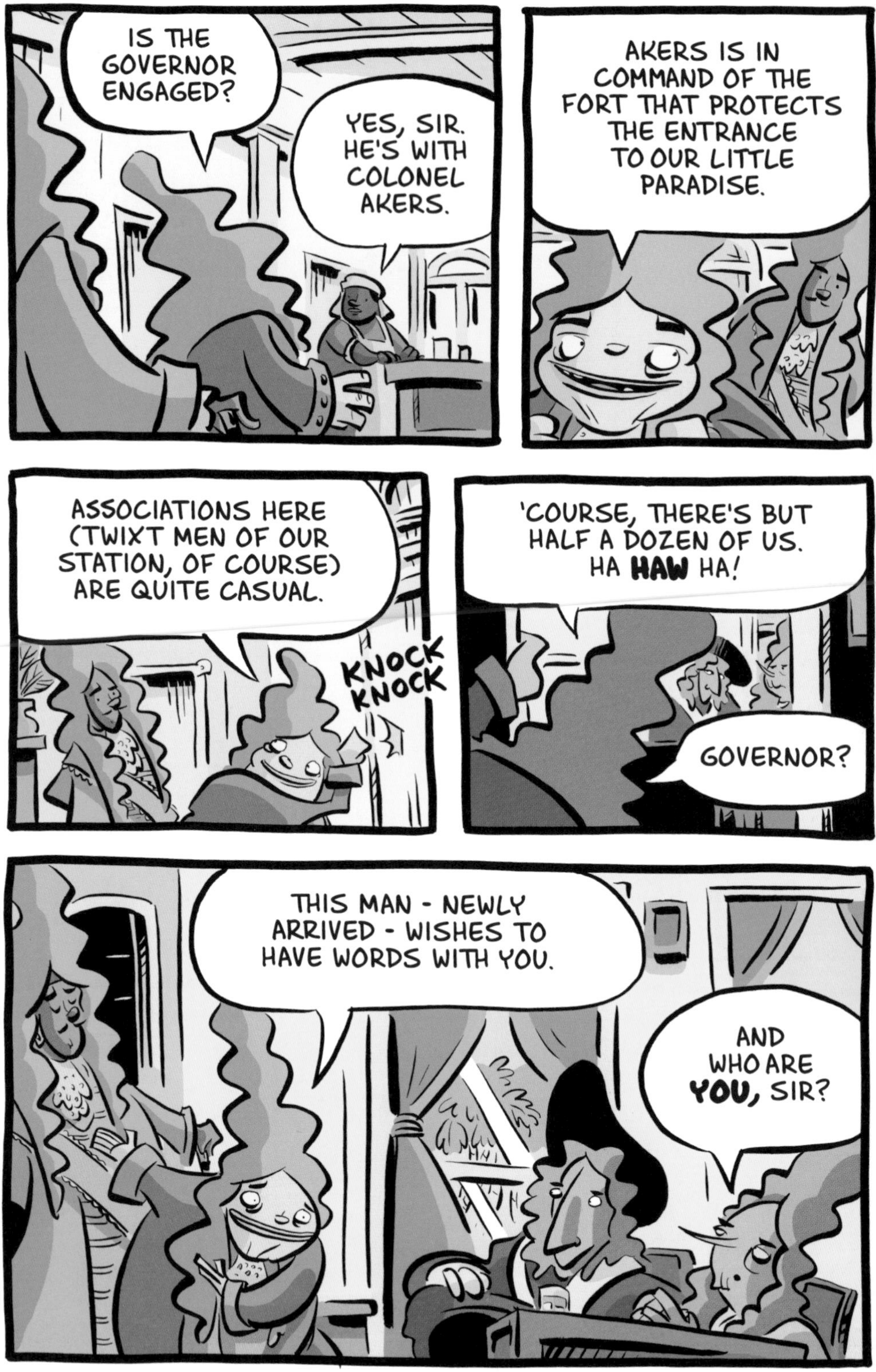
IS THE GOVERNOR ENGAGED?
YES, SIR. HE'S WITH COLONEL AKERS.
AKERS IS IN COMMAND OF THE FORT THAT PROTECTS THE ENTRANCE TO OUR LITTLE PARADISE.
ASSOCIATIONS HERE (TWIXT MEN OF OUR STATION, OF COURSE) ARE QUITE CASUAL.
KNOCK KNOCK
'COURSE, THERE'S BUT HALF A DOZEN OF US. HA **HAW** HA!
GOVERNOR?
THIS MAN - NEWLY ARRIVED - WISHES TO HAVE WORDS WITH YOU.
AND WHO ARE **YOU**, SIR?

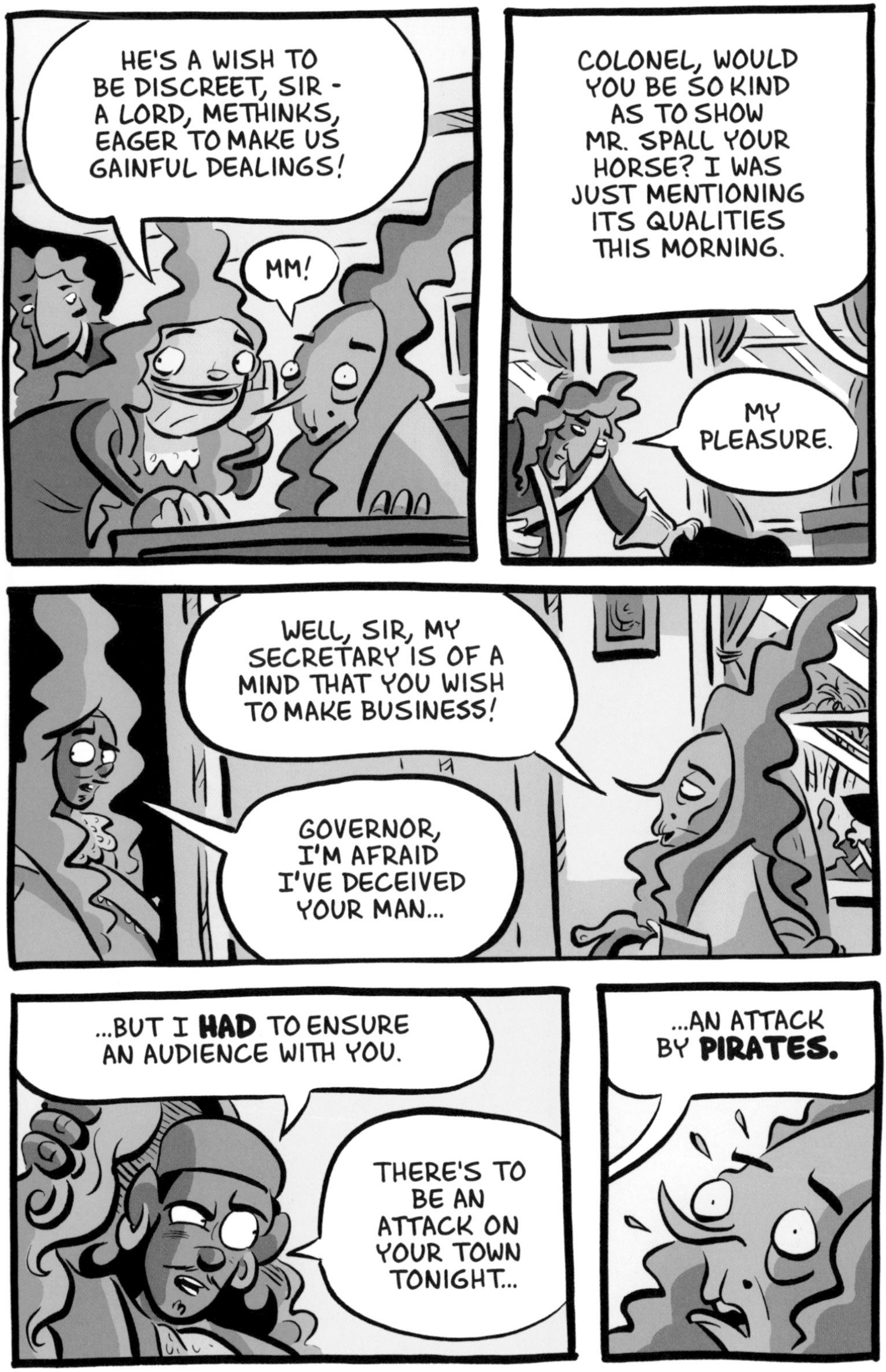
HE'S A WISH TO BE DISCREET, SIR - A LORD, METHINKS, EAGER TO MAKE US GAINFUL DEALINGS!
MM!
COLONEL, WOULD YOU BE SO KIND AS TO SHOW MR. SPALL YOUR HORSE? I WAS JUST MENTIONING ITS QUALITIES THIS MORNING.
MY PLEASURE.
WELL, SIR, MY SECRETARY IS OF A MIND THAT YOU WISH TO MAKE BUSINESS!
GOVERNOR, I'M AFRAID I'VE DECEIVED YOUR MAN...
...BUT I **HAD** TO ENSURE AN AUDIENCE WITH YOU.
THERE'S TO BE AN ATTACK ON YOUR TOWN TONIGHT...
...AN ATTACK BY **PIRATES.**

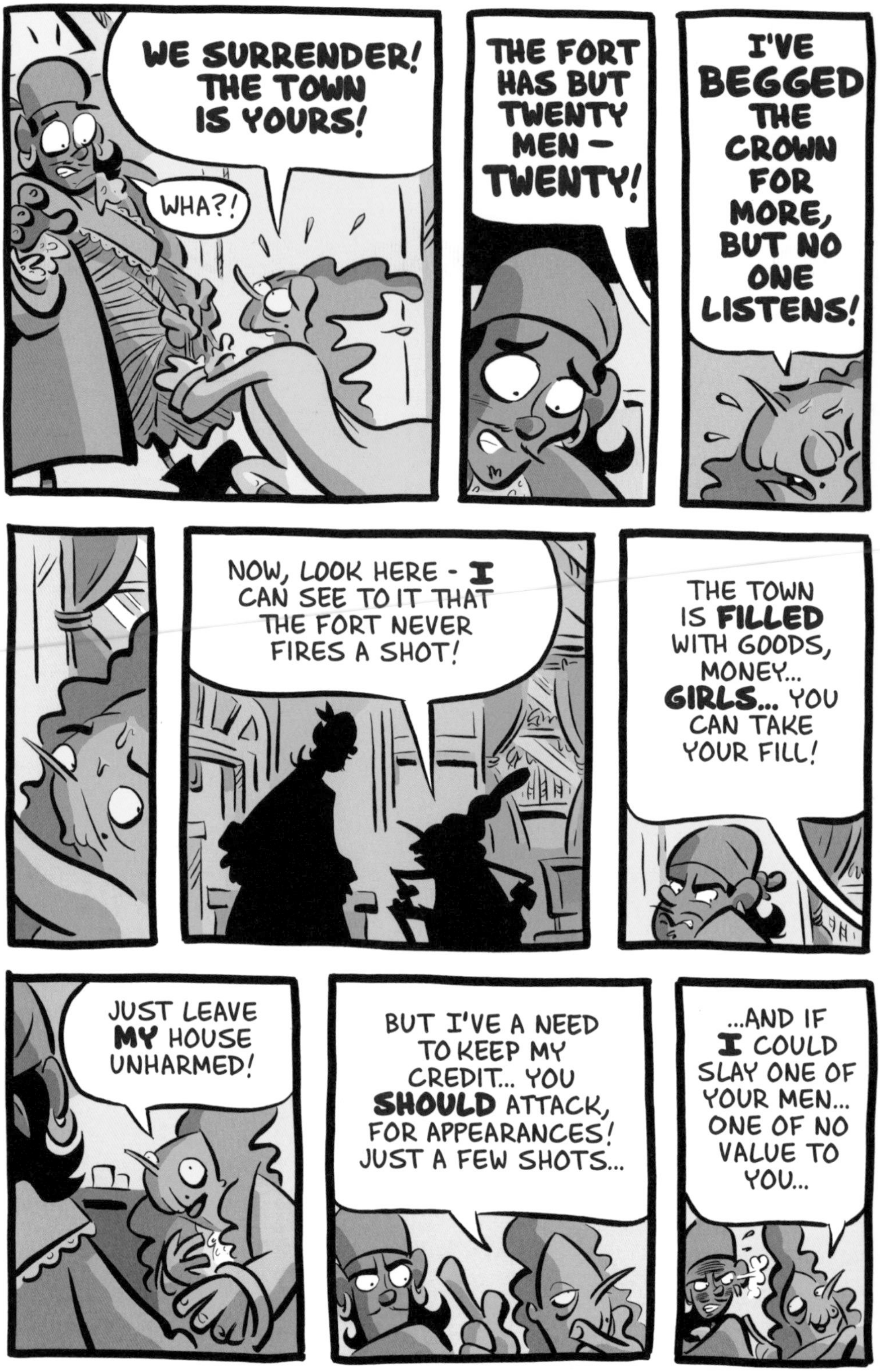
WE SURRENDER! THE TOWN IS YOURS!
WHA?!
THE FORT HAS BUT TWENTY MEN — TWENTY!
I'VE BEGGED THE CROWN FOR MORE, BUT NO ONE LISTENS!
NOW, LOOK HERE - I CAN SEE TO IT THAT THE FORT NEVER FIRES A SHOT!
THE TOWN IS FILLED WITH GOODS, MONEY... GIRLS... YOU CAN TAKE YOUR FILL!
JUST LEAVE MY HOUSE UNHARMED!
BUT I'VE A NEED TO KEEP MY CREDIT... YOU SHOULD ATTACK, FOR APPEARANCES! JUST A FEW SHOTS...
...AND IF I COULD SLAY ONE OF YOUR MEN... ONE OF NO VALUE TO YOU...

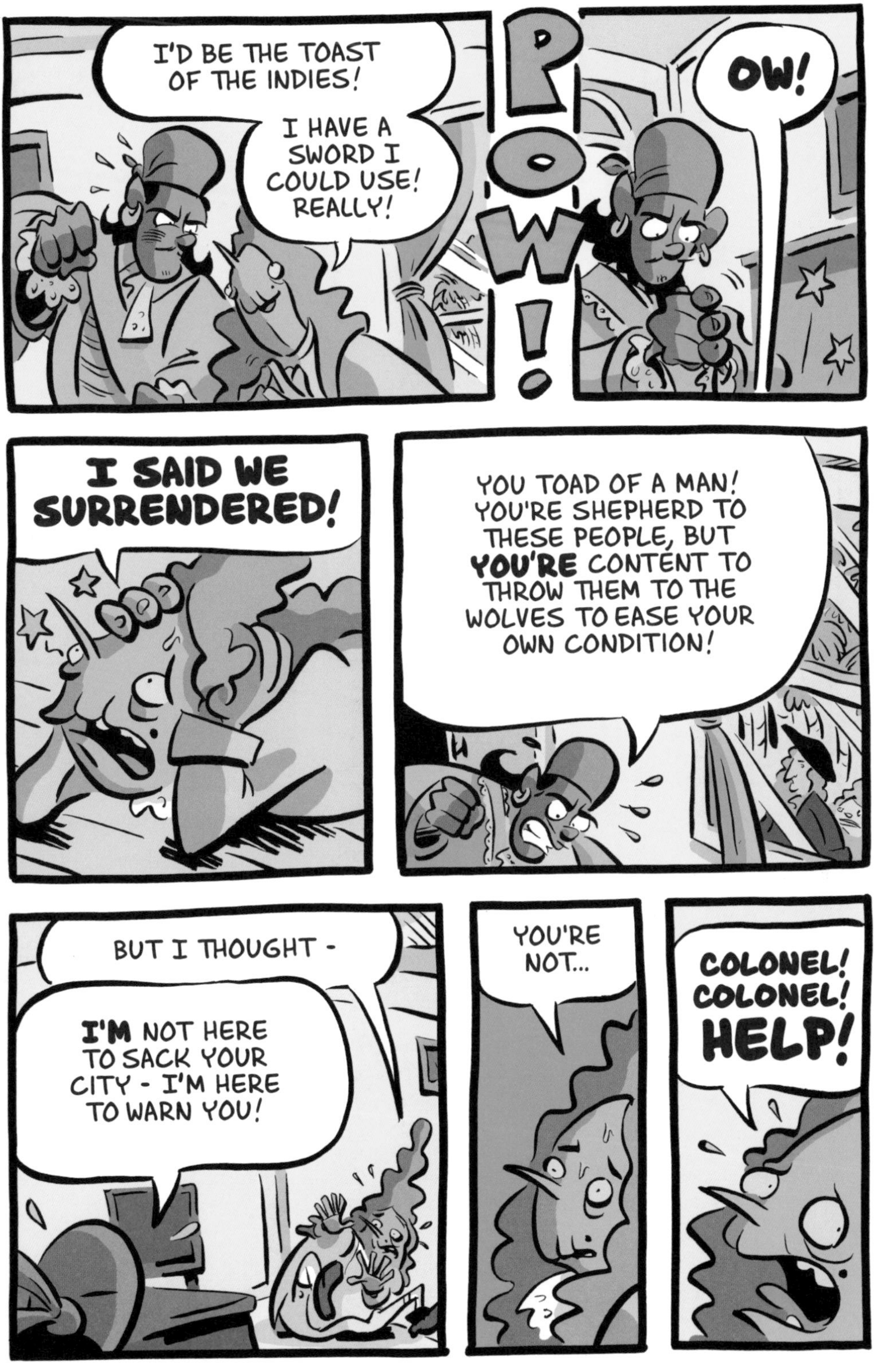
I'D BE THE TOAST OF THE INDIES!
I HAVE A SWORD I COULD USE! REALLY!
POW!
OW!
I SAID WE SURRENDERED!
YOU TOAD OF A MAN! YOU'RE SHEPHERD TO THESE PEOPLE, BUT **YOU'RE** CONTENT TO THROW THEM TO THE WOLVES TO EASE YOUR OWN CONDITION!
BUT I THOUGHT -
I'M NOT HERE TO SACK YOUR CITY - I'M HERE TO WARN YOU!
YOU'RE NOT...
COLONEL! COLONEL! HELP!

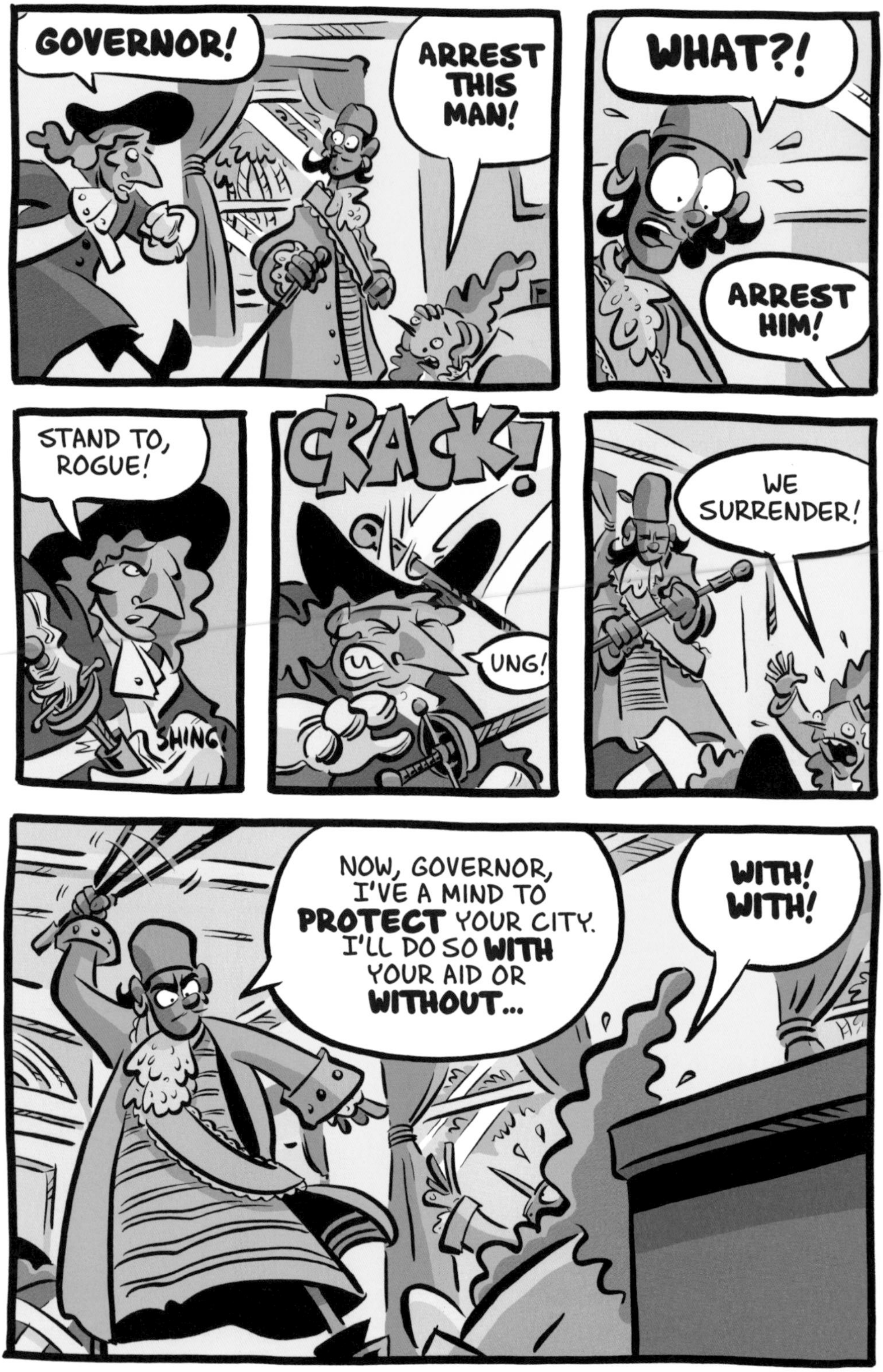
GOVERNOR!
ARREST THIS MAN!
WHAT?!
ARREST HIM!
STAND TO, ROGUE!
SHING!
CRACK!
UNG!
WE SURRENDER!
NOW, GOVERNOR, I'VE A MIND TO PROTECT YOUR CITY. I'LL DO SO WITH YOUR AID OR WITHOUT...
WITH! WITH!

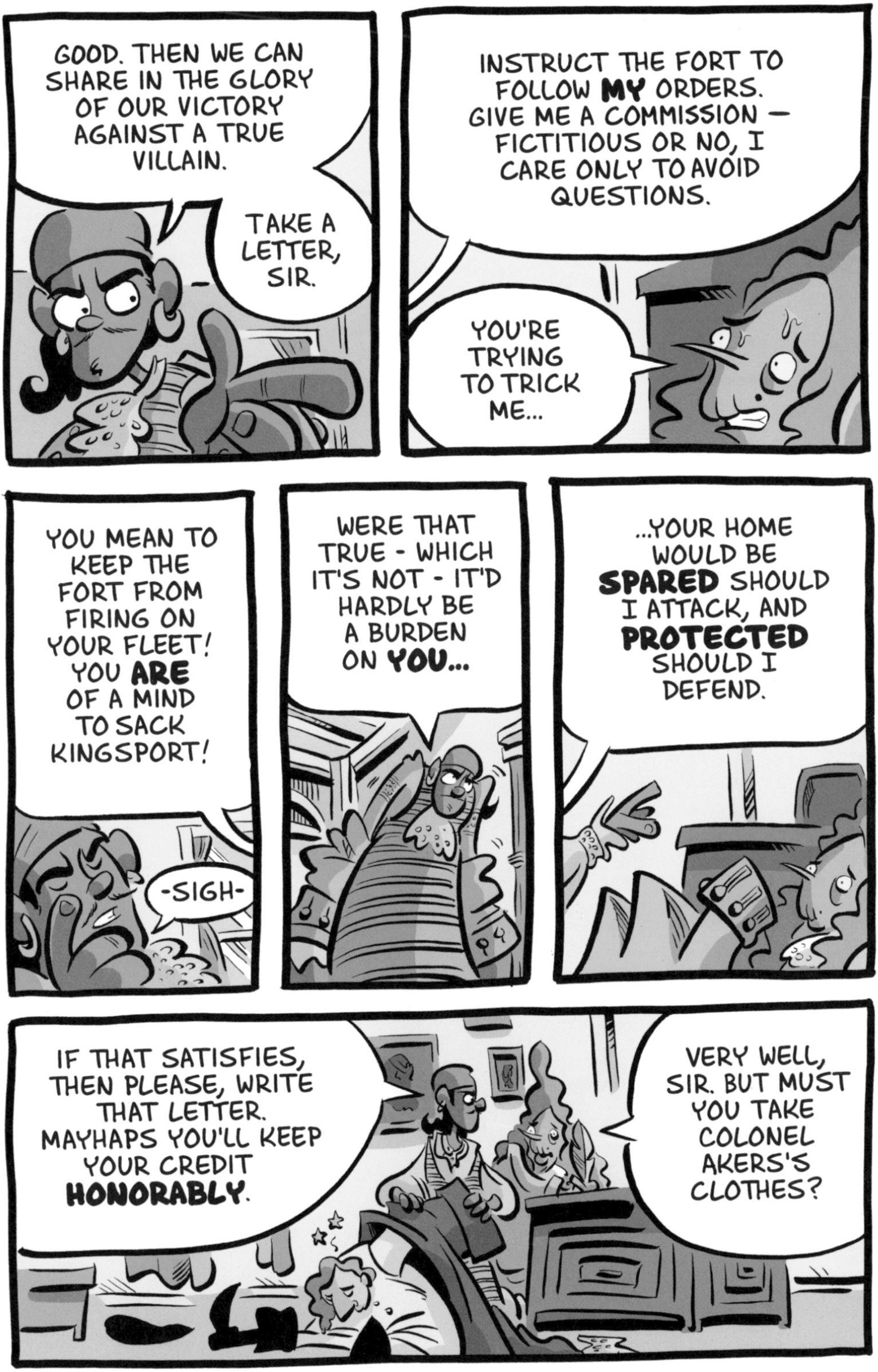
GOOD. THEN WE CAN SHARE IN THE GLORY OF OUR VICTORY AGAINST A TRUE VILLAIN.
TAKE A LETTER, SIR.
INSTRUCT THE FORT TO FOLLOW **MY** ORDERS. GIVE ME A COMMISSION — FICTITIOUS OR NO, I CARE ONLY TO AVOID QUESTIONS.
YOU'RE TRYING TO TRICK ME...
YOU MEAN TO KEEP THE FORT FROM FIRING ON YOUR FLEET! YOU **ARE** OF A MIND TO SACK KINGSPORT!
-SIGH-
WERE THAT TRUE - WHICH IT'S NOT - IT'D HARDLY BE A BURDEN ON **YOU**...
...YOUR HOME WOULD BE **SPARED** SHOULD I ATTACK, AND **PROTECTED** SHOULD I DEFEND.
IF THAT SATISFIES, THEN PLEASE, WRITE THAT LETTER. MAYHAPS YOU'LL KEEP YOUR CREDIT **HONORABLY**.
VERY WELL, SIR. BUT MUST YOU TAKE COLONEL AKERS'S CLOTHES?

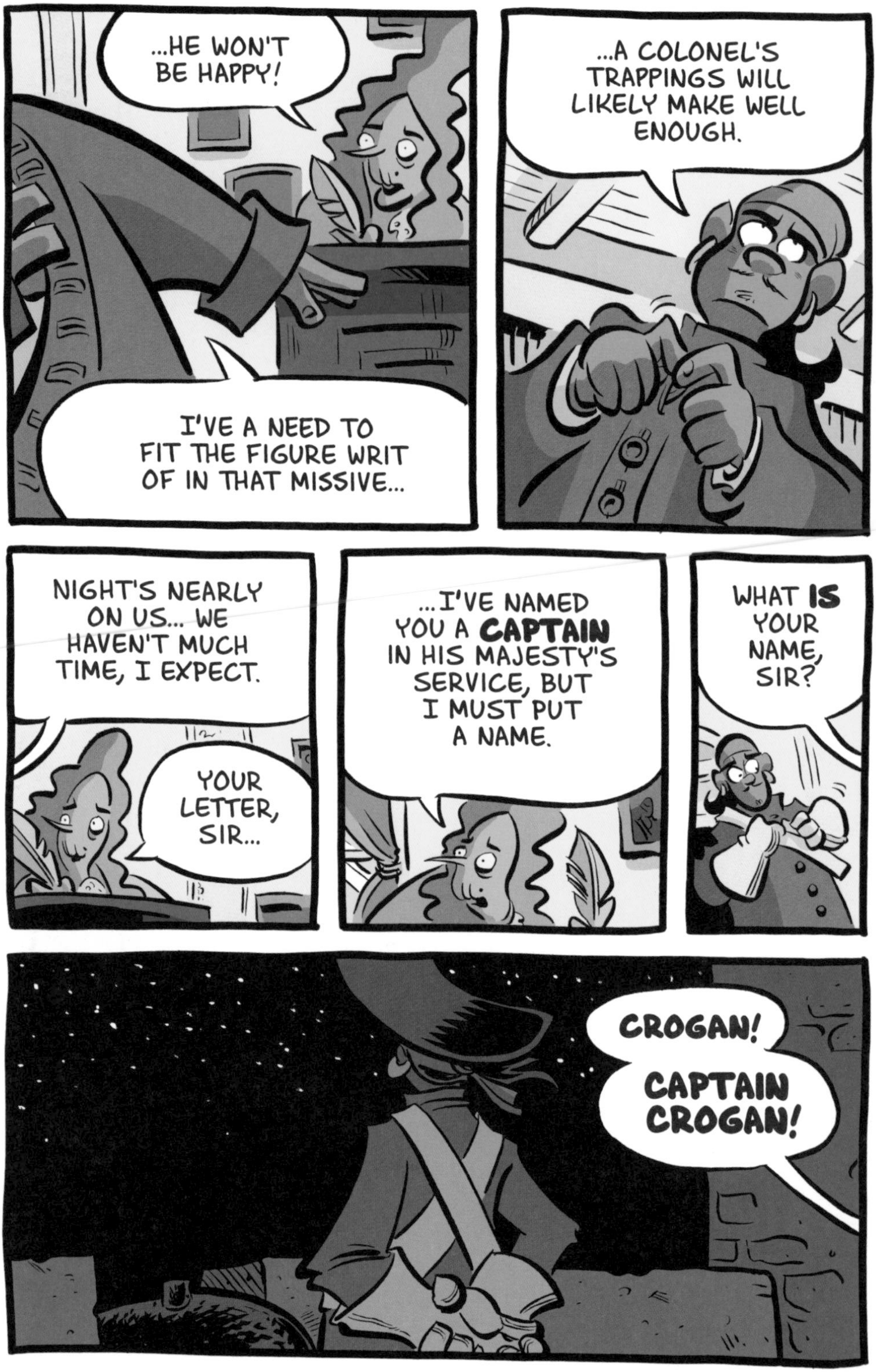
...HE WON'T BE HAPPY!
I'VE A NEED TO FIT THE FIGURE WRIT OF IN THAT MISSIVE...
...A COLONEL'S TRAPPINGS WILL LIKELY MAKE WELL ENOUGH.
NIGHT'S NEARLY ON US... WE HAVEN'T MUCH TIME, I EXPECT.
YOUR LETTER, SIR...
...I'VE NAMED YOU A **CAPTAIN** IN HIS MAJESTY'S SERVICE, BUT I MUST PUT A NAME.
WHAT **IS** YOUR NAME, SIR?
CROGAN!
CAPTAIN CROGAN!

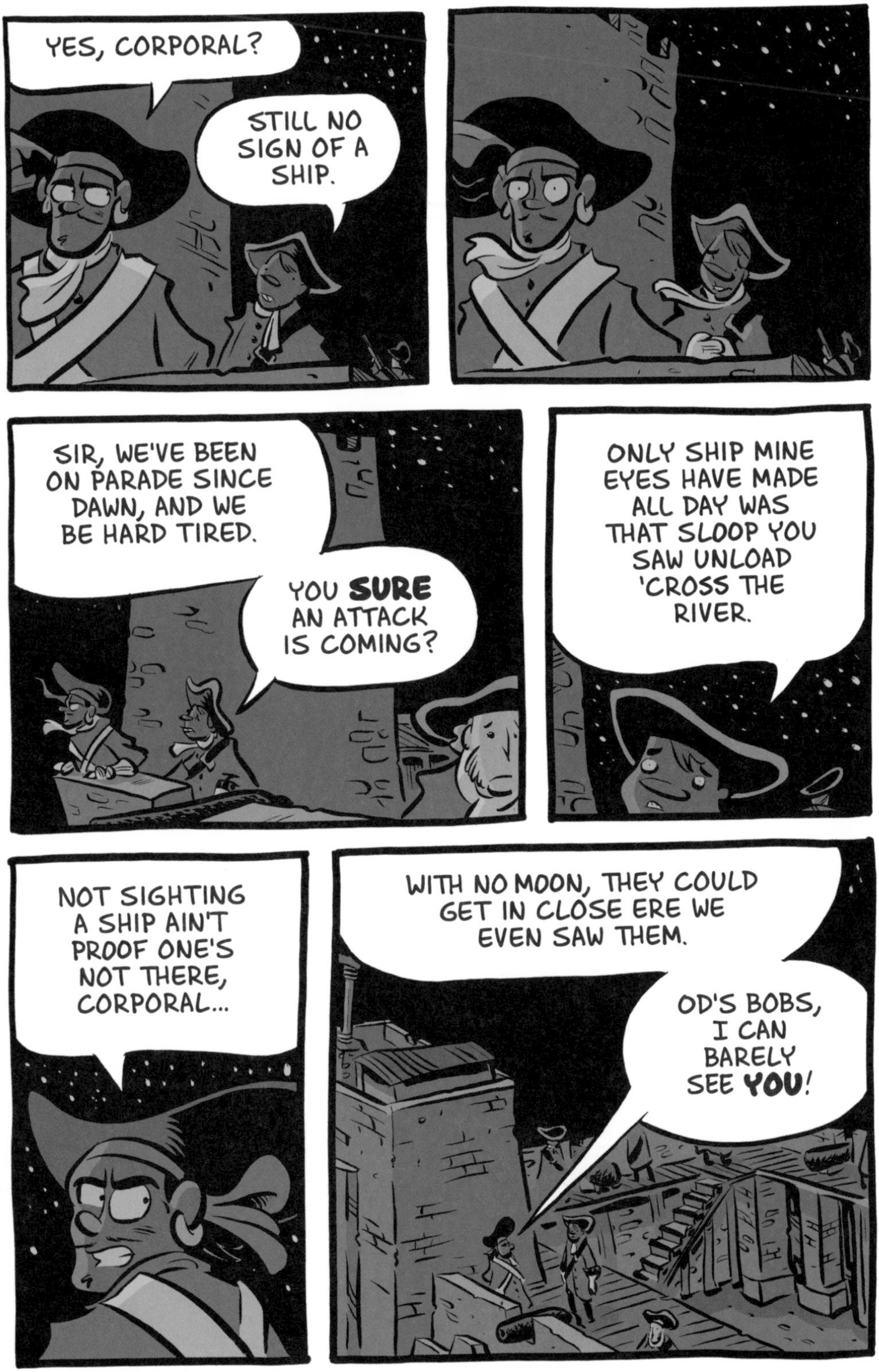
YES, CORPORAL?
STILL NO SIGN OF A SHIP.
SIR, WE'VE BEEN ON PARADE SINCE DAWN, AND WE BE HARD TIRED.
YOU **SURE** AN ATTACK IS COMING?
ONLY SHIP MINE EYES HAVE MADE ALL DAY WAS THAT SLOOP YOU SAW UNLOAD 'CROSS THE RIVER.
NOT SIGHTING A SHIP AIN'T PROOF ONE'S NOT THERE, CORPORAL...
WITH NO MOON, THEY COULD GET IN CLOSE ERE WE EVEN SAW THEM.
OD'S BOBS, I CAN BARELY SEE **YOU**!

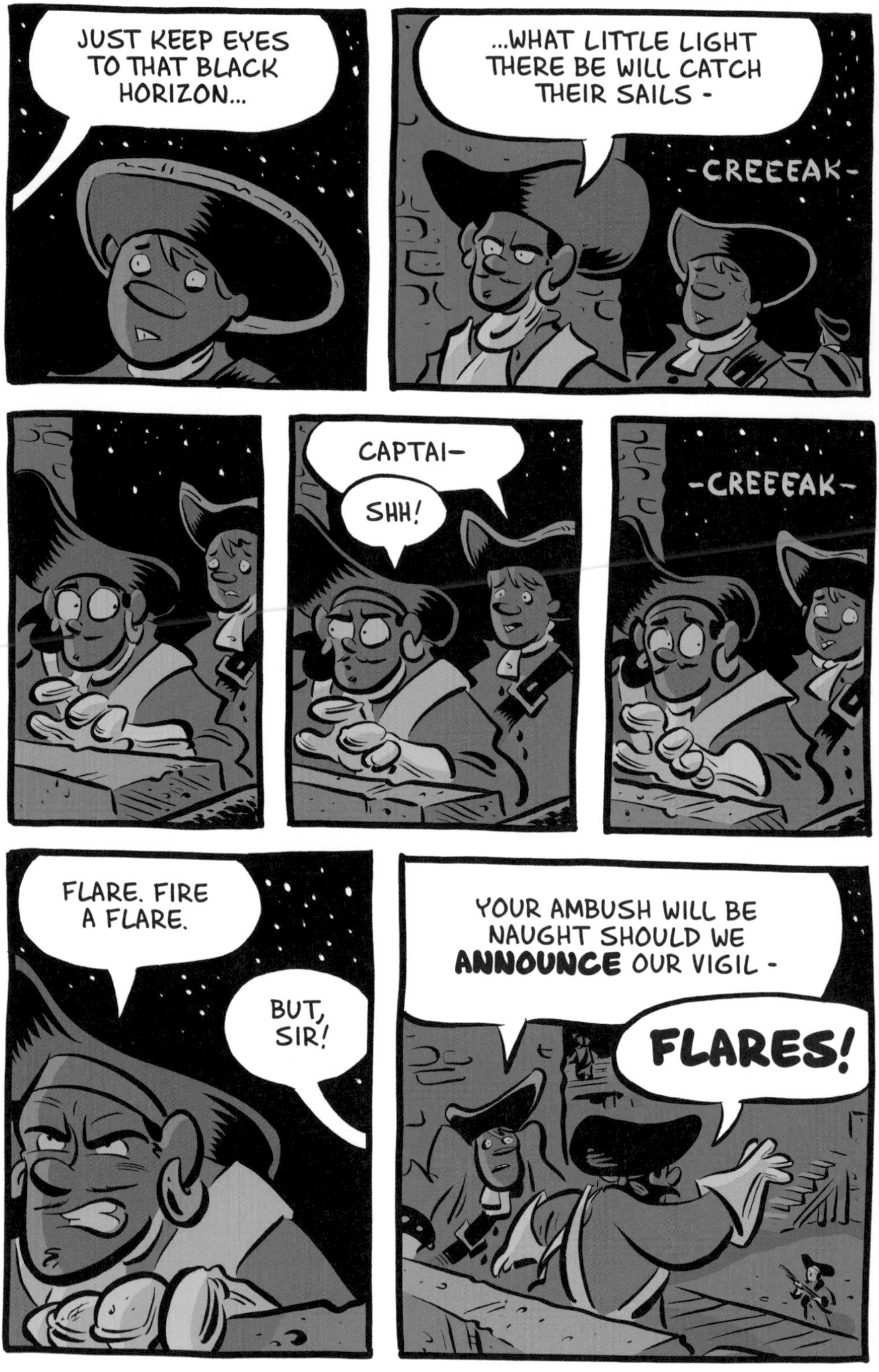
JUST KEEP EYES TO THAT BLACK HORIZON...
...WHAT LITTLE LIGHT THERE BE WILL CATCH THEIR SAILS -
-CREEEAK-
CAPTAI—
SHH!
-CREEEAK-
FLARE. FIRE A FLARE.
BUT, SIR!
YOUR AMBUSH WILL BE NAUGHT SHOULD WE **ANNOUNCE** OUR VIGIL -
FLARES!

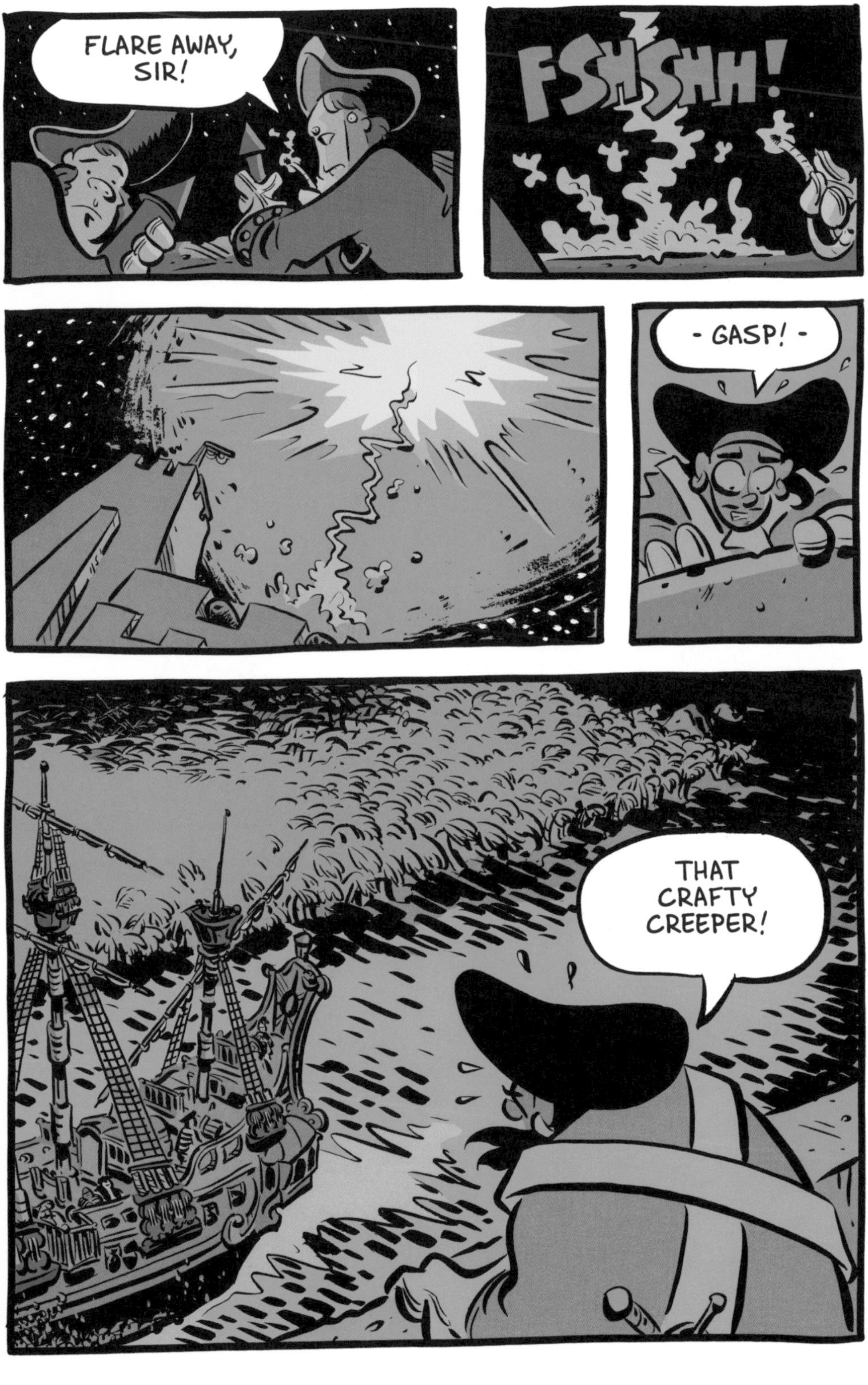
FLARE AWAY, SIR!
FSHSHH!
- GASP! -
THAT CRAFTY CREEPER!

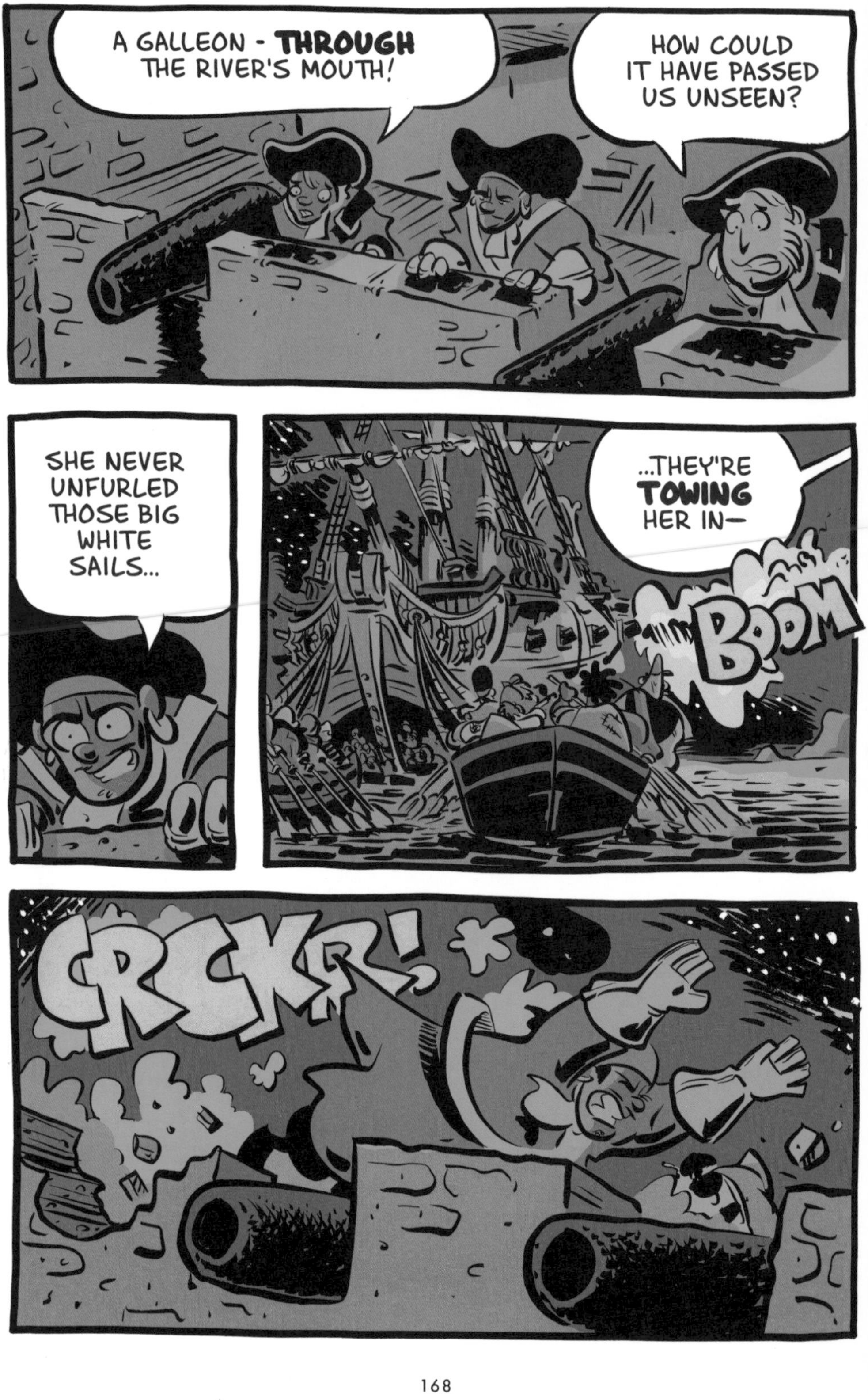
A GALLEON - **THROUGH** THE RIVER'S MOUTH!
HOW COULD IT HAVE PASSED US UNSEEN?
SHE NEVER UNFURLED THOSE BIG WHITE SAILS...
...THEY'RE **TOWING** HER IN—
BOOM
CRCKR!

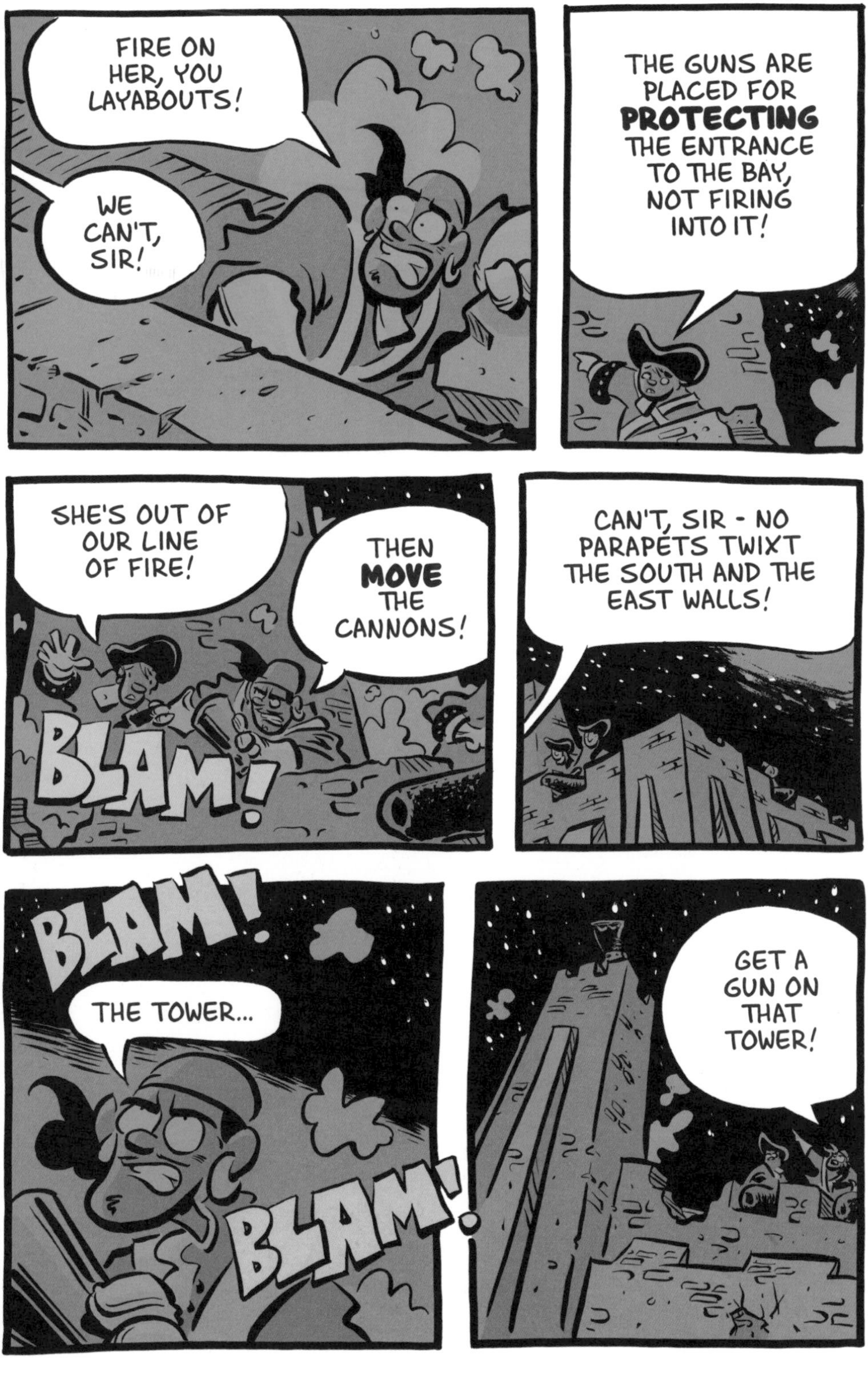
FIRE ON HER, YOU LAYABOUTS!
WE CAN'T, SIR!
THE GUNS ARE PLACED FOR **PROTECTING** THE ENTRANCE TO THE BAY, NOT FIRING INTO IT!
SHE'S OUT OF OUR LINE OF FIRE!
THEN **MOVE** THE CANNONS!
BLAM!
CAN'T, SIR - NO PARAPETS TWIXT THE SOUTH AND THE EAST WALLS!
BLAM!
THE TOWER...
BLAM!
GET A GUN ON THAT TOWER!

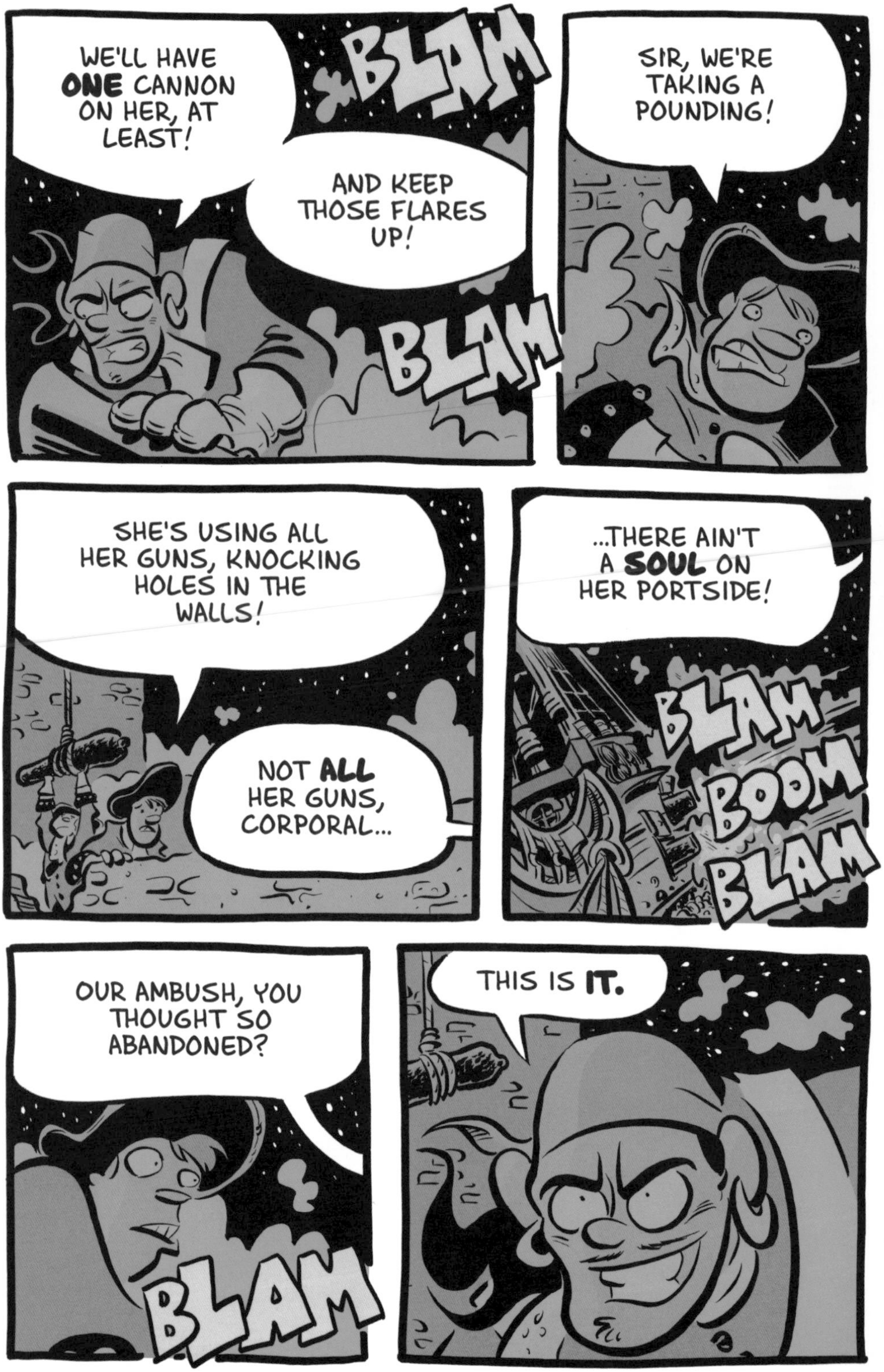
WE'LL HAVE ONE CANNON ON HER, AT LEAST!
AND KEEP THOSE FLARES UP!
BLAM
BLAM
SIR, WE'RE TAKING A POUNDING!
SHE'S USING ALL HER GUNS, KNOCKING HOLES IN THE WALLS!
NOT ALL HER GUNS, CORPORAL...
...THERE AIN'T A SOUL ON HER PORTSIDE!
BLAM
BOOM
BLAM
OUR AMBUSH, YOU THOUGHT SO ABANDONED?
BLAM
THIS IS IT.

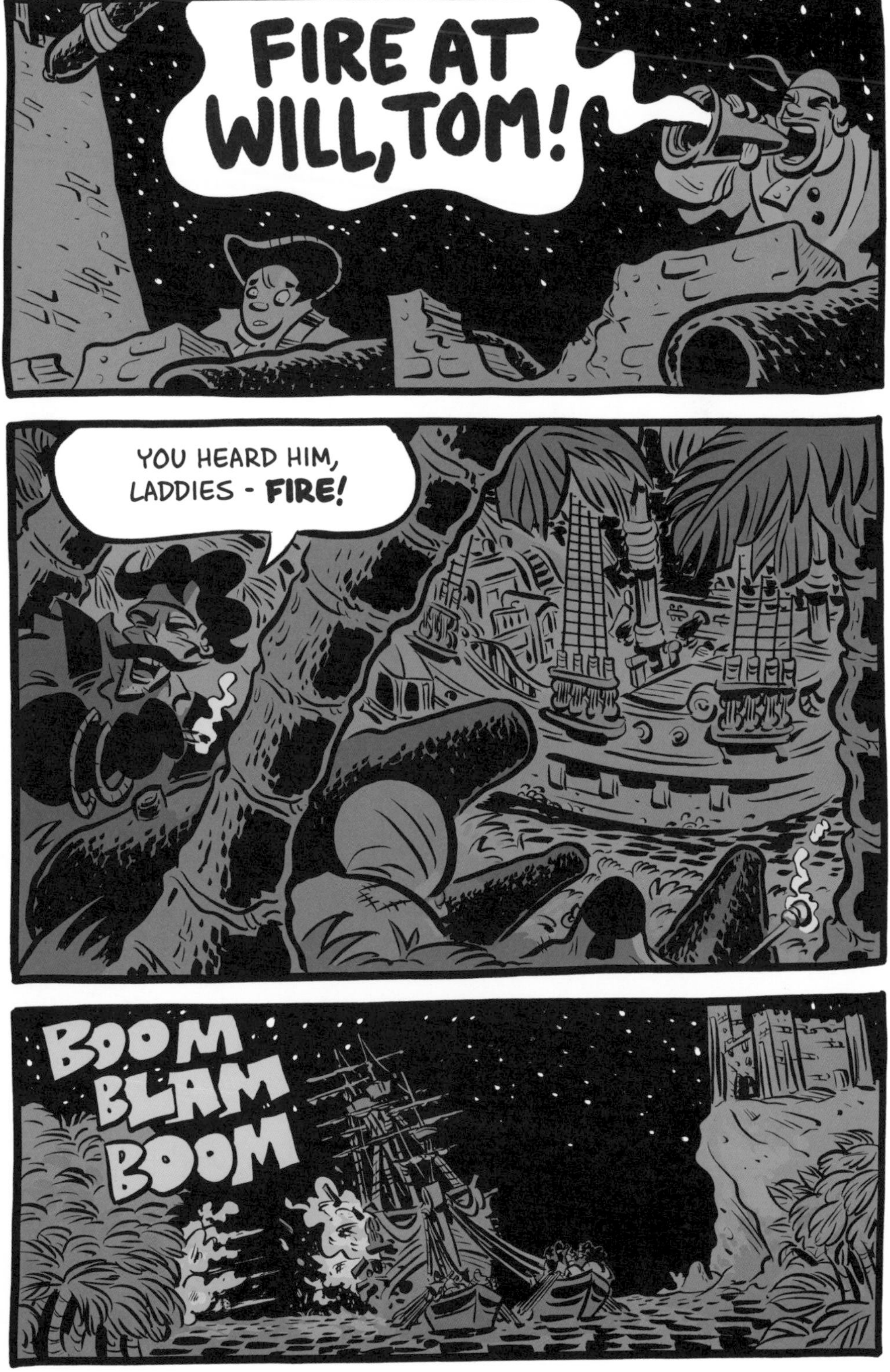
FIRE AT WILL, TOM!
YOU HEARD HIM, LADDIES - FIRE!
BOOM BLAM BOOM

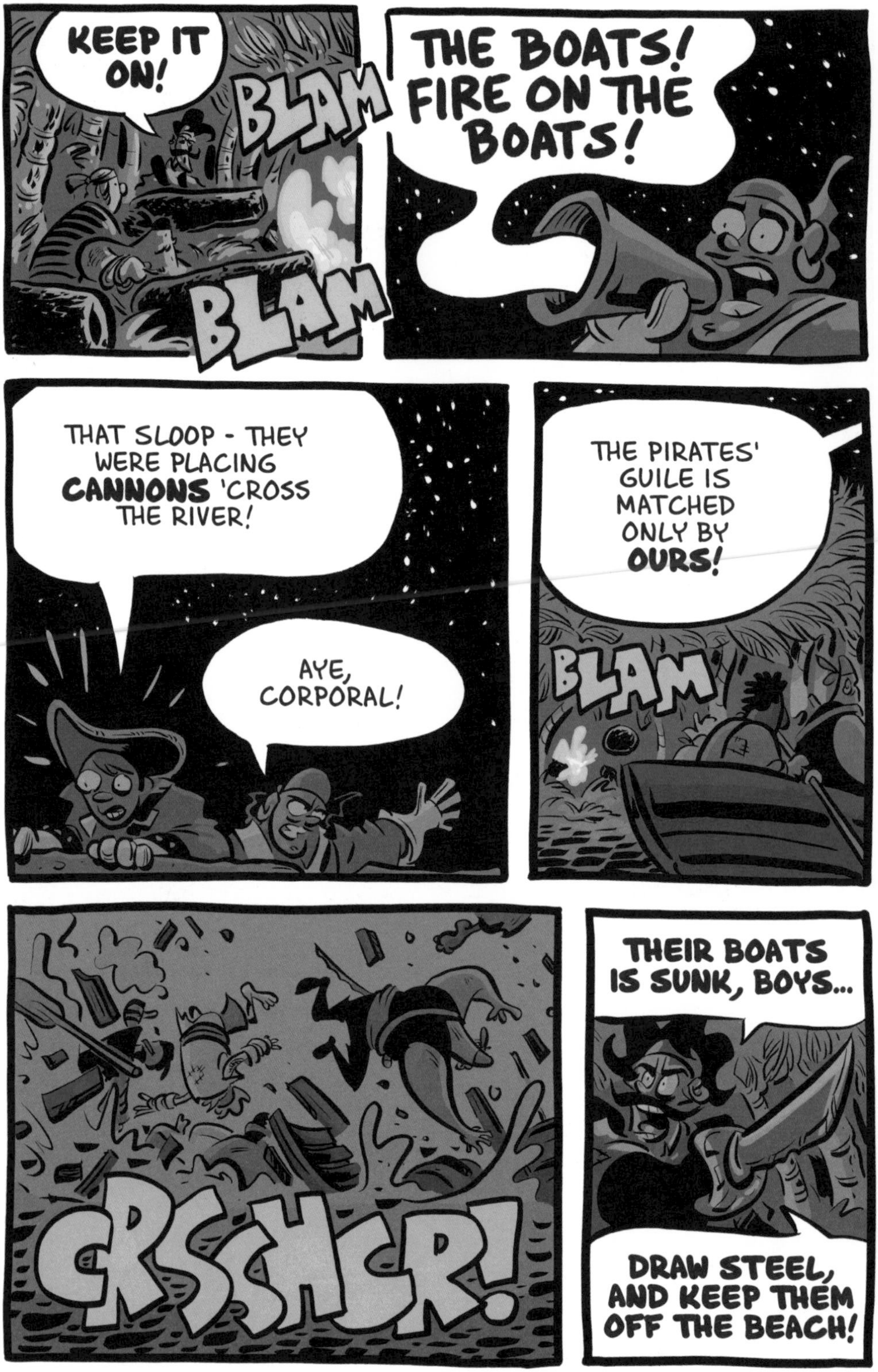
KEEP IT ON!
BLAM
BLAM
THE BOATS! FIRE ON THE BOATS!
THAT SLOOP - THEY WERE PLACING CANNONS 'CROSS THE RIVER!
AYE, CORPORAL!
THE PIRATES' GUILE IS MATCHED ONLY BY OURS!
BLAM
CRSCHCR!
THEIR BOATS IS SUNK, BOYS...
DRAW STEEL, AND KEEP THEM OFF THE BEACH!

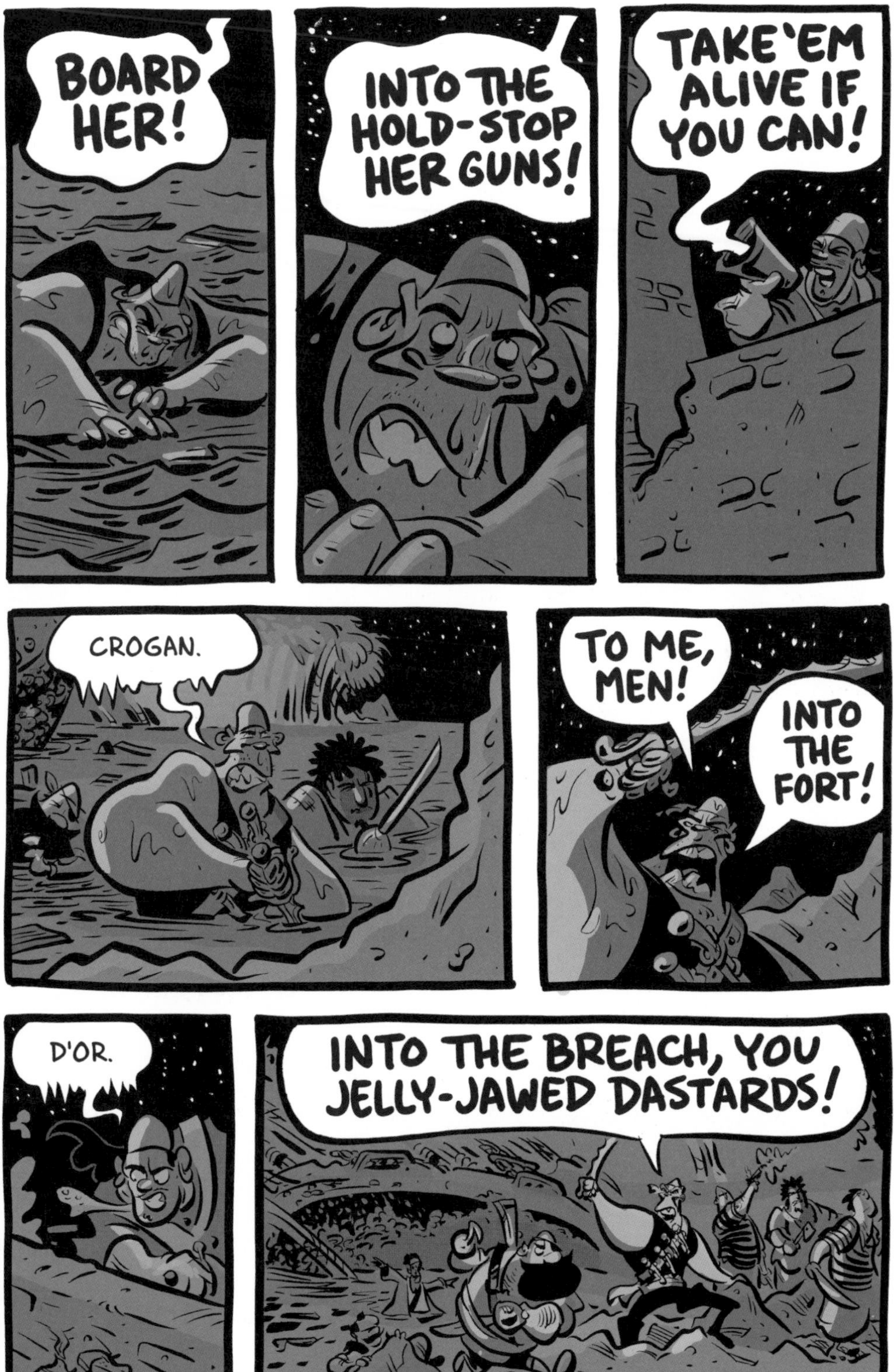
BOARD HER!
INTO THE HOLD-STOP HER GUNS!
TAKE 'EM ALIVE IF YOU CAN!
CROGAN.
TO ME, MEN!
INTO THE FORT!
D'OR.
INTO THE BREACH, YOU JELLY-JAWED DASTARDS!

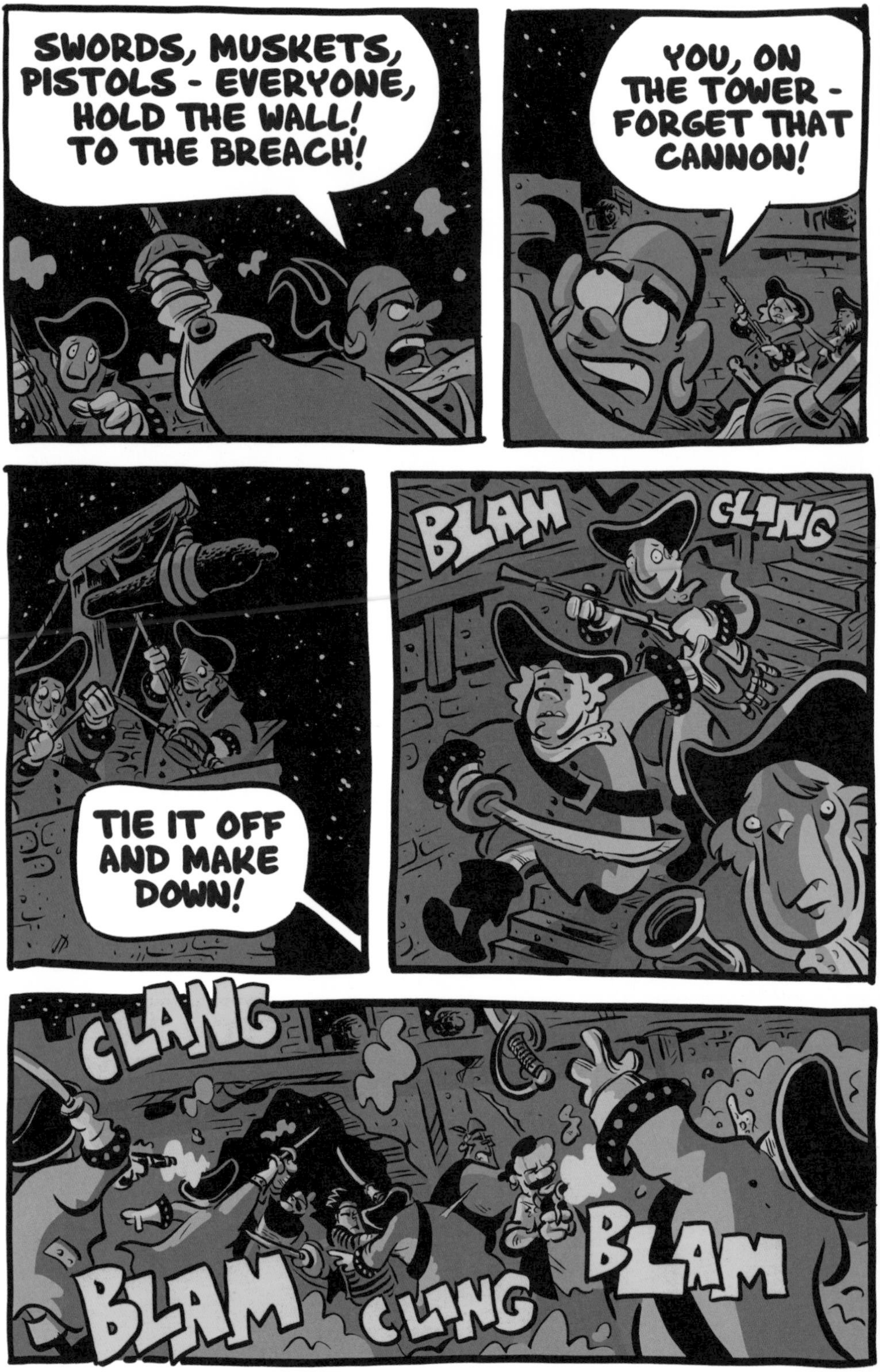
SWORDS, MUSKETS, PISTOLS - EVERYONE, HOLD THE WALL! TO THE BREACH!
YOU, ON THE TOWER - FORGET THAT CANNON!
TIE IT OFF AND MAKE DOWN!
BLAM
CLING
CLANG
BLAM
CLING
BLAM

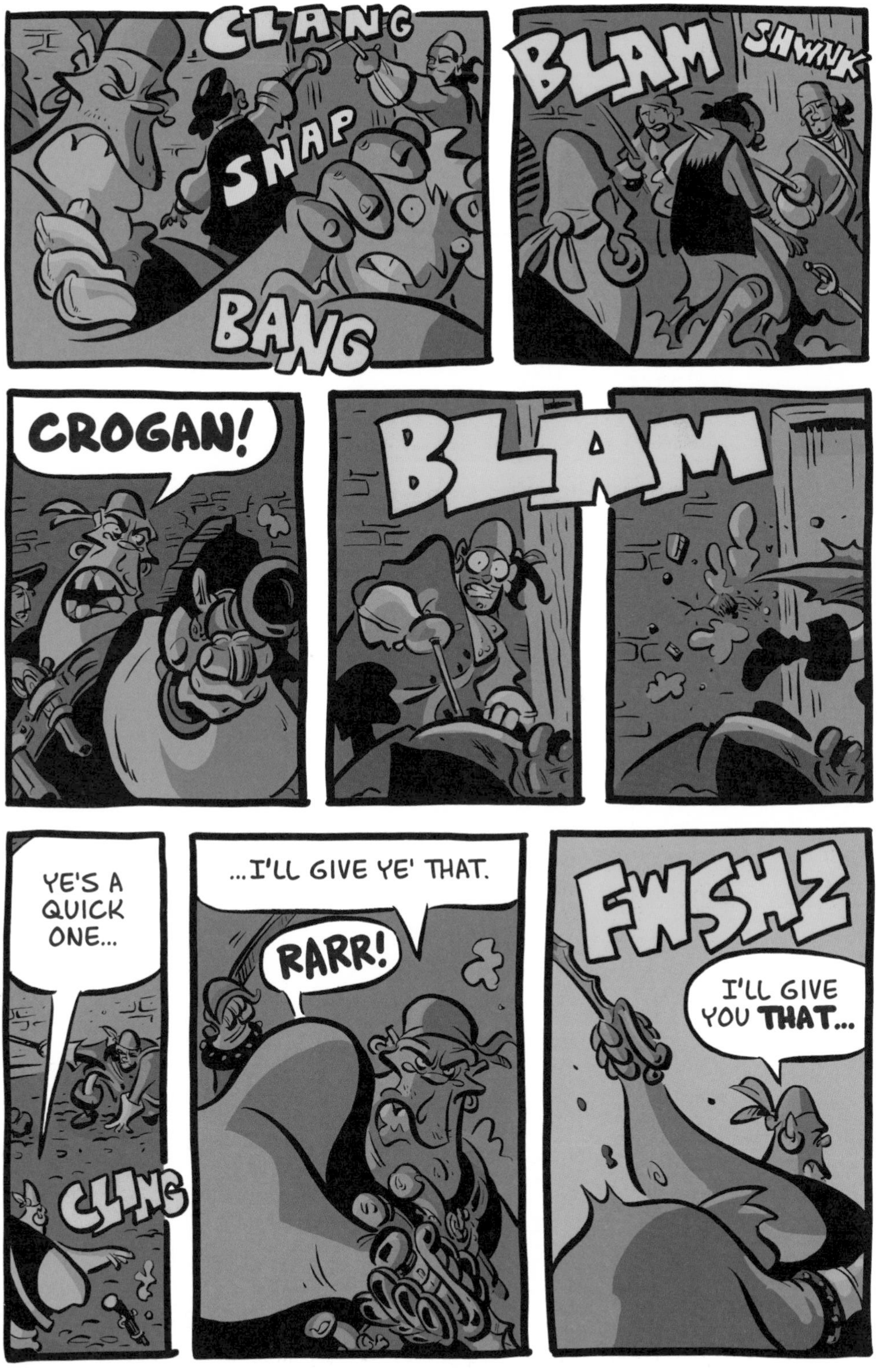
CLANG
SNAP
BANG
BLAM
SHWNK
CROGAN!
BLAM
YE'S A QUICK ONE...
CLING
...I'LL GIVE YE' THAT.
RARR!
FWSHZ
I'LL GIVE YOU **THAT...**

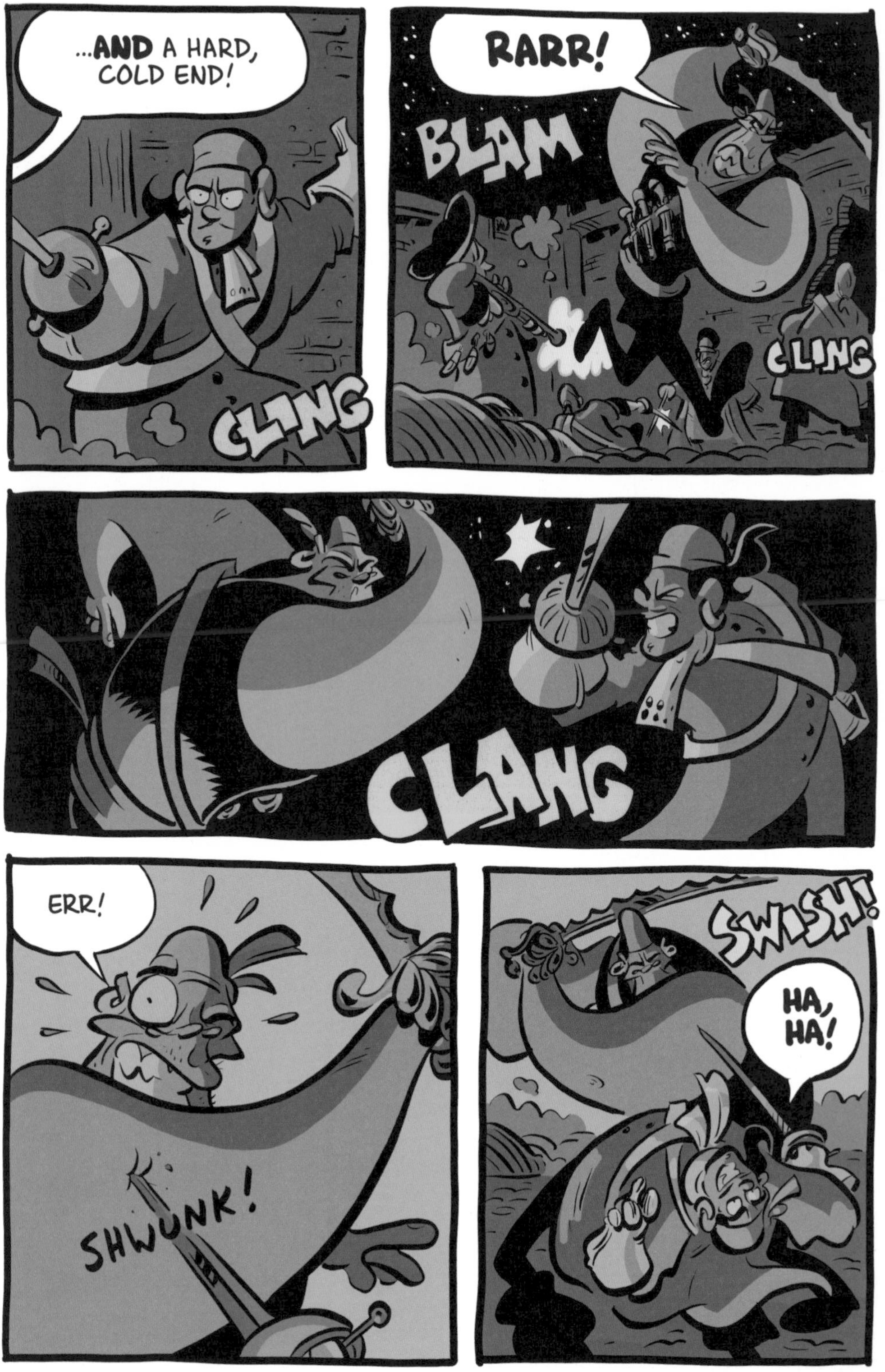
...AND A HARD, COLD END!
CLING
RARR!
BLAM
CLING
CLANG
ERR!
SHWUNK!
SWISH!
HA, HA!

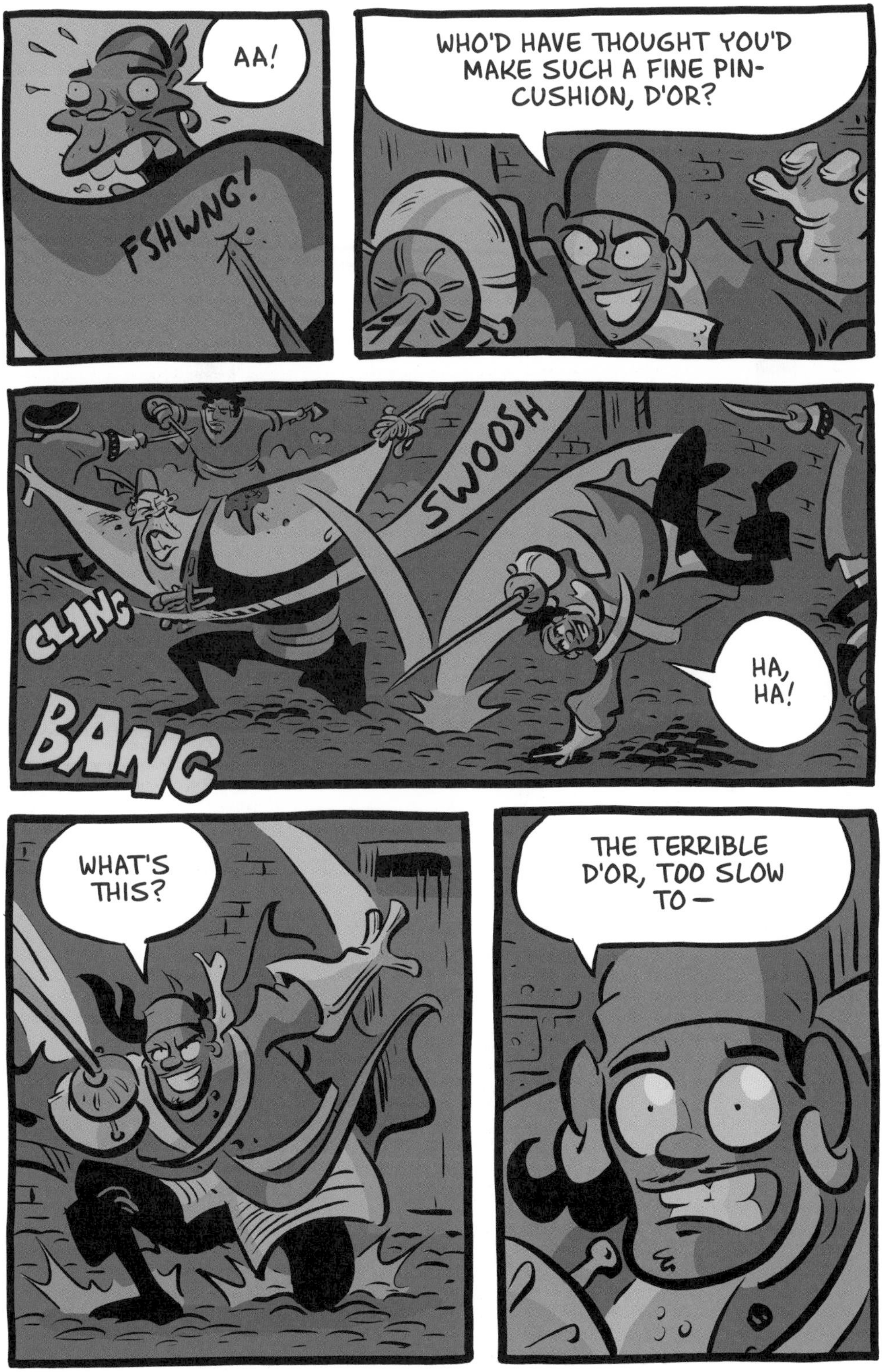
AA!
FSHWNG!
WHO'D HAVE THOUGHT YOU'D MAKE SUCH A FINE PIN-CUSHION, D'OR?
SWOOSH
CLING
BANG
HA, HA!
WHAT'S THIS?
THE TERRIBLE D'OR, TOO SLOW TO—

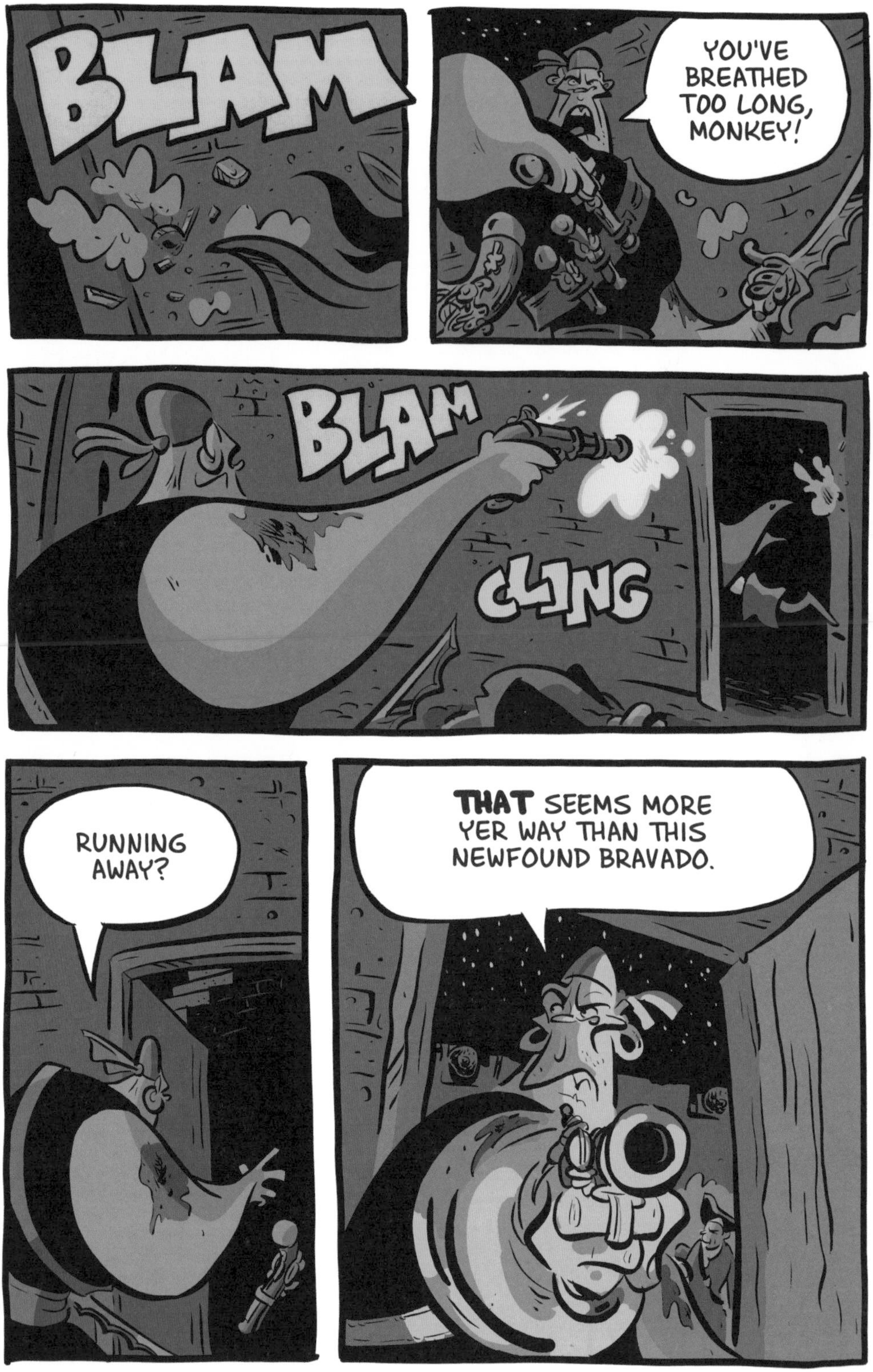
BLAM
YOU'VE BREATHED TOO LONG, MONKEY!
BLAM
CLING
RUNNING AWAY?
THAT SEEMS MORE YER WAY THAN THIS NEWFOUND BRAVADO.

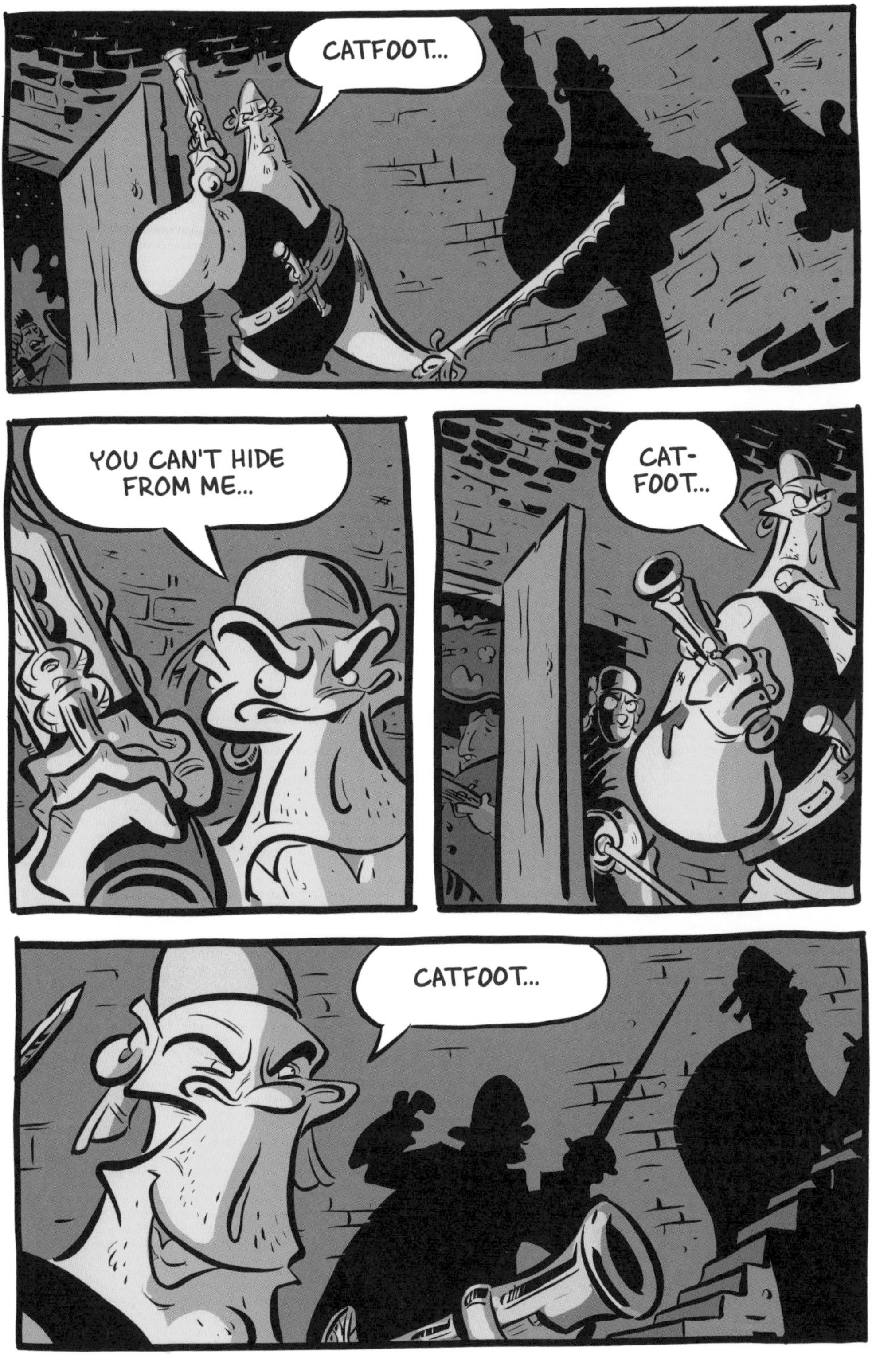
CATFOOT...
YOU CAN'T HIDE FROM ME...
CAT-FOOT...
CATFOOT...

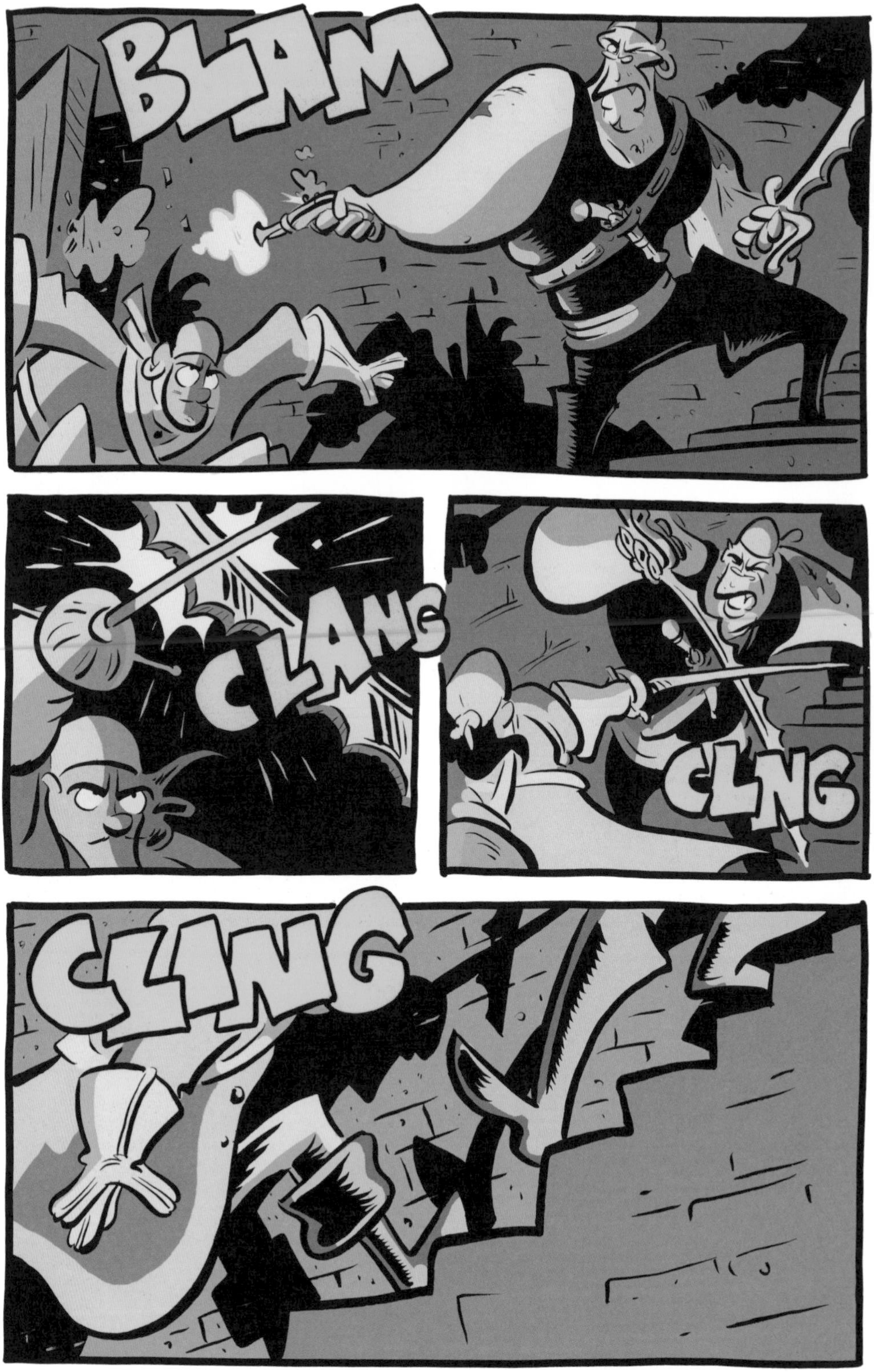
BLAM
CLANG
CLNG
CLING

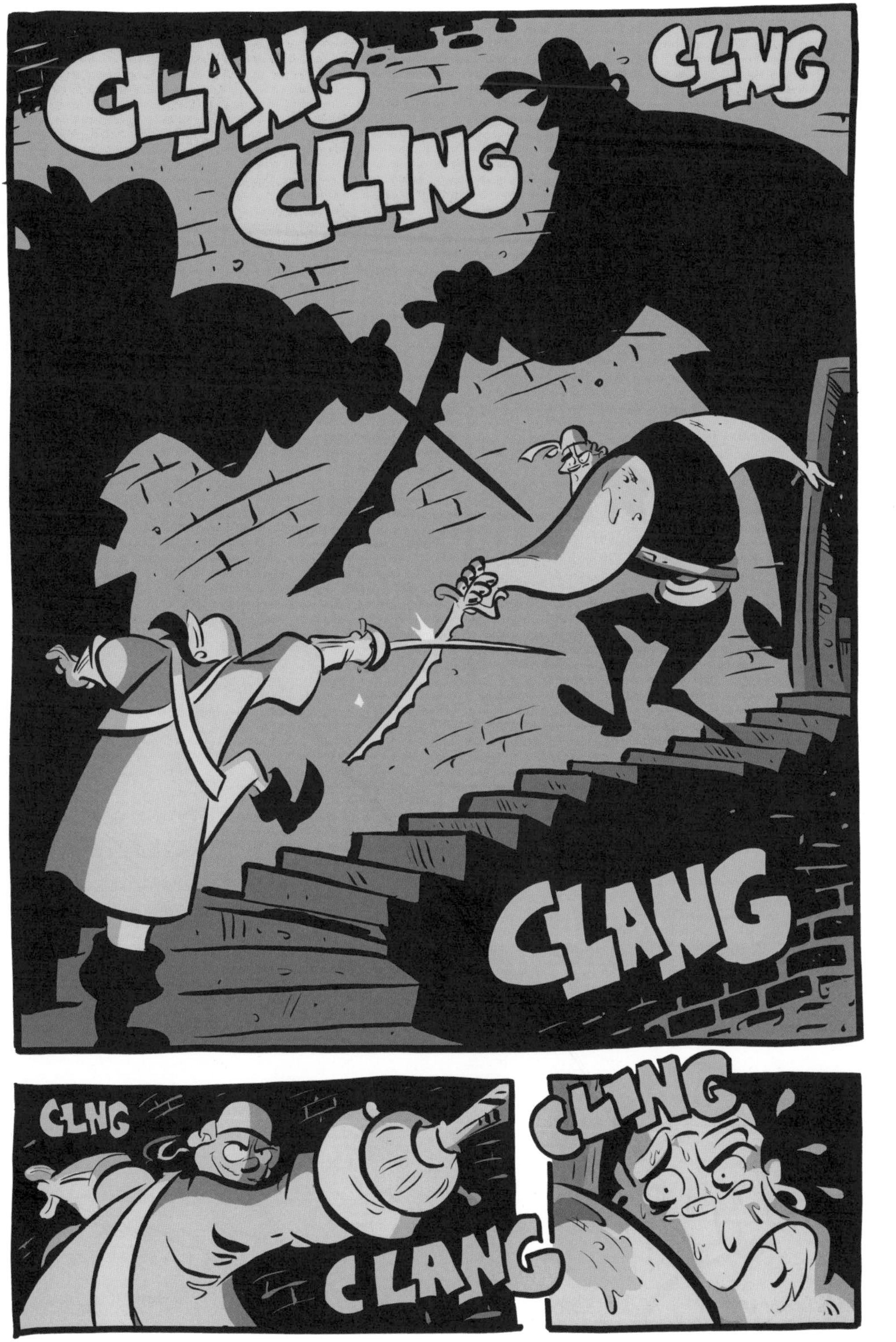
CLANG
CLING
CLNG
CLANG
CLNG
CLANG
CLING

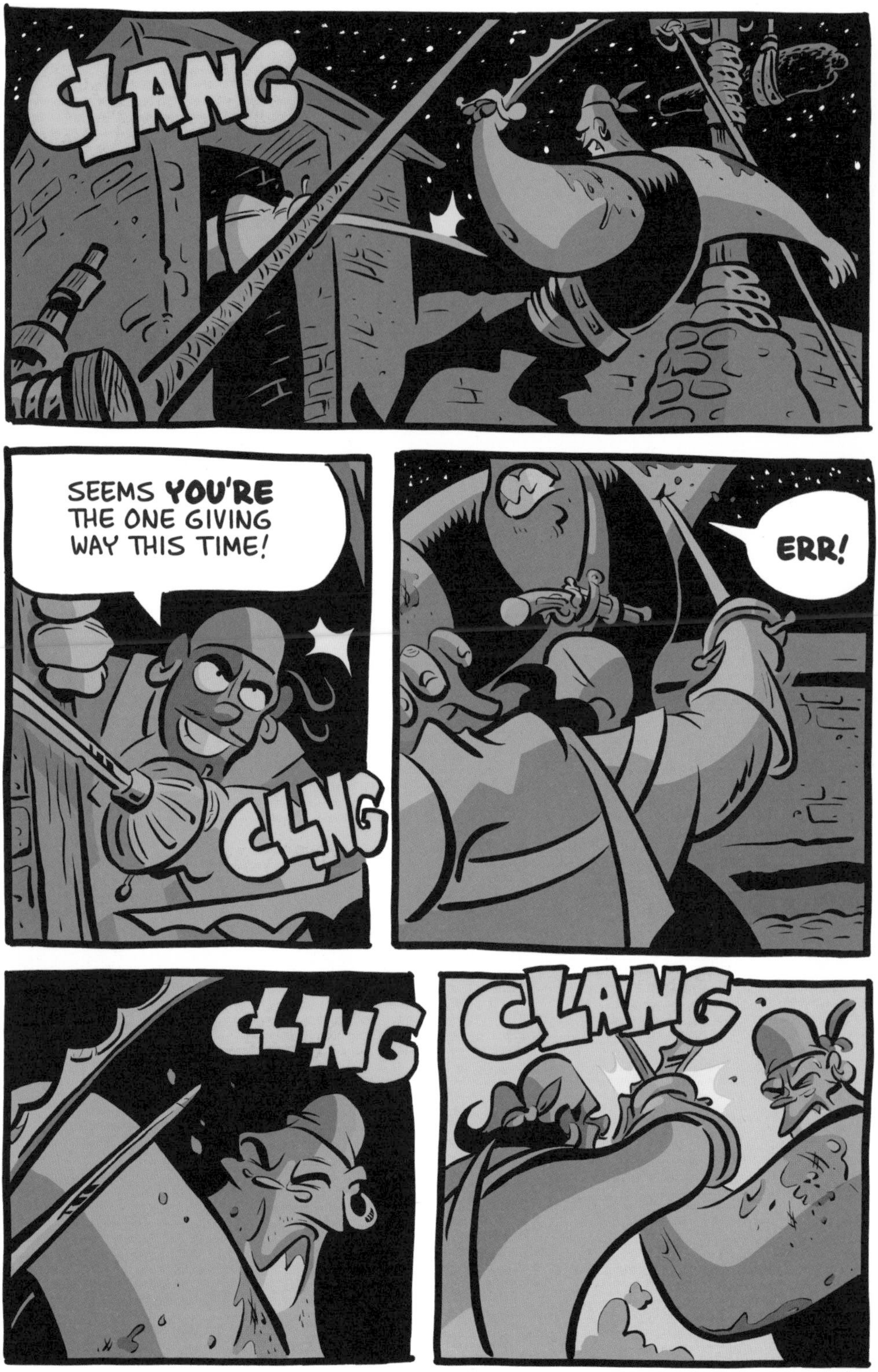
CLANG
SEEMS **YOU'RE** THE ONE GIVING WAY THIS TIME!
CLNG
ERR!
CLING
CLANG

SHWWWWWNK

BLAM

AAA!

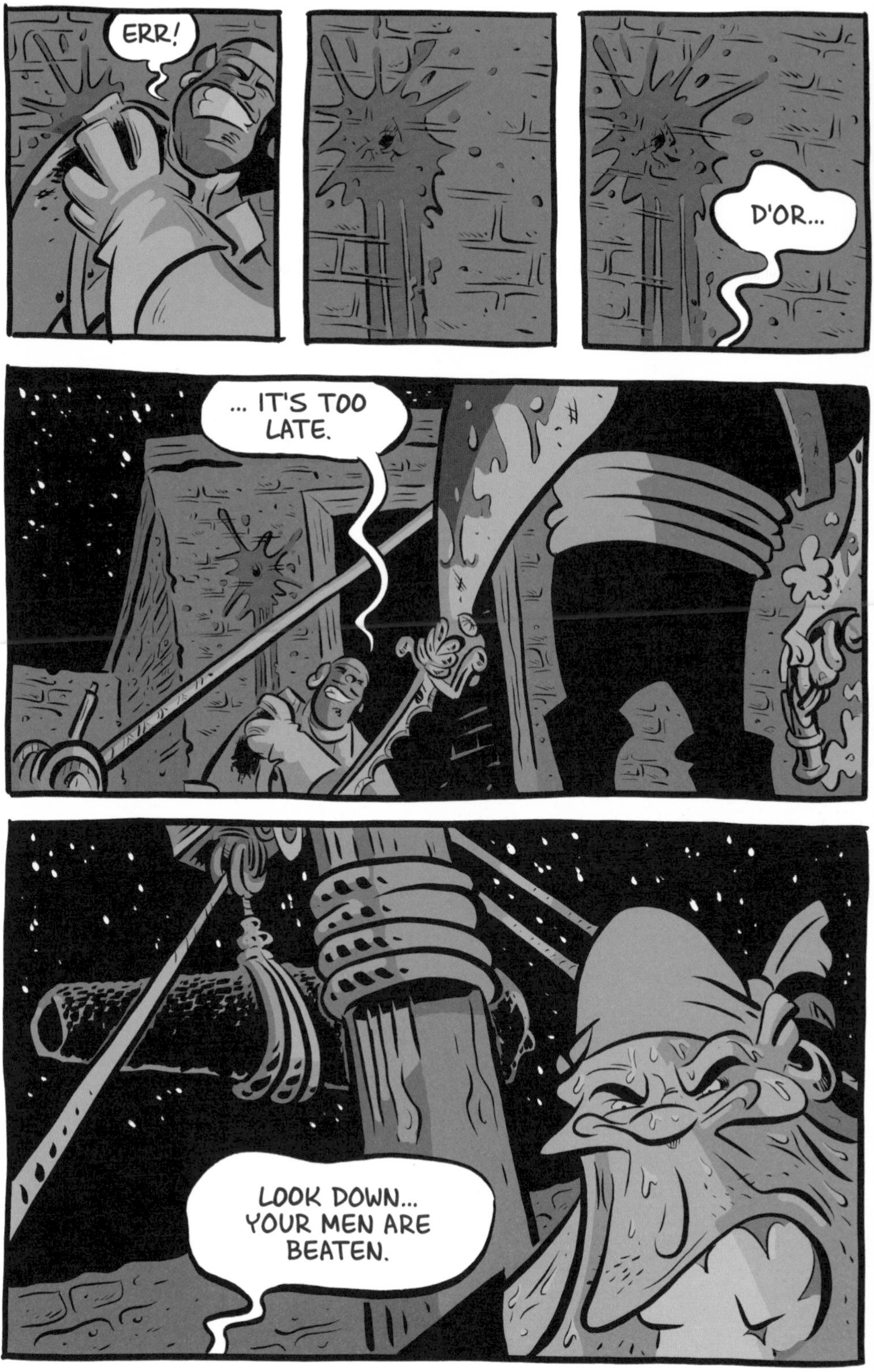
ERR!
D'OR...
... IT'S TOO LATE.
LOOK DOWN... YOUR MEN ARE BEATEN.

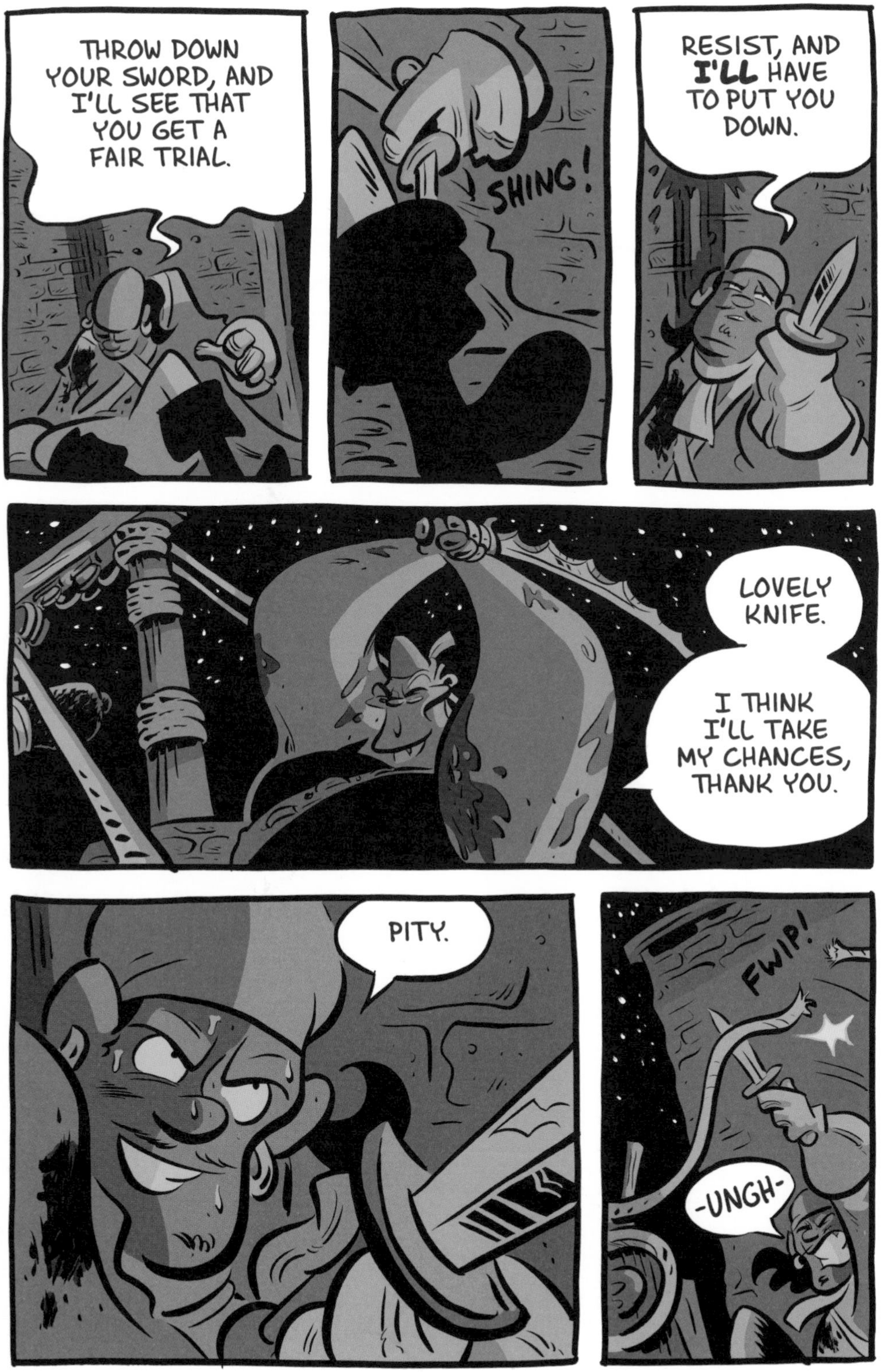
THROW DOWN YOUR SWORD, AND I'LL SEE THAT YOU GET A FAIR TRIAL.
SHING!
RESIST, AND **I'LL** HAVE TO PUT YOU DOWN.
LOVELY KNIFE.
I THINK I'LL TAKE MY CHANCES, THANK YOU.
PITY.
FWIP!
-UNGH-

WHIRRRRRRR

?

RRRRRR

OH, NO.

CRACK

SPLOOSH

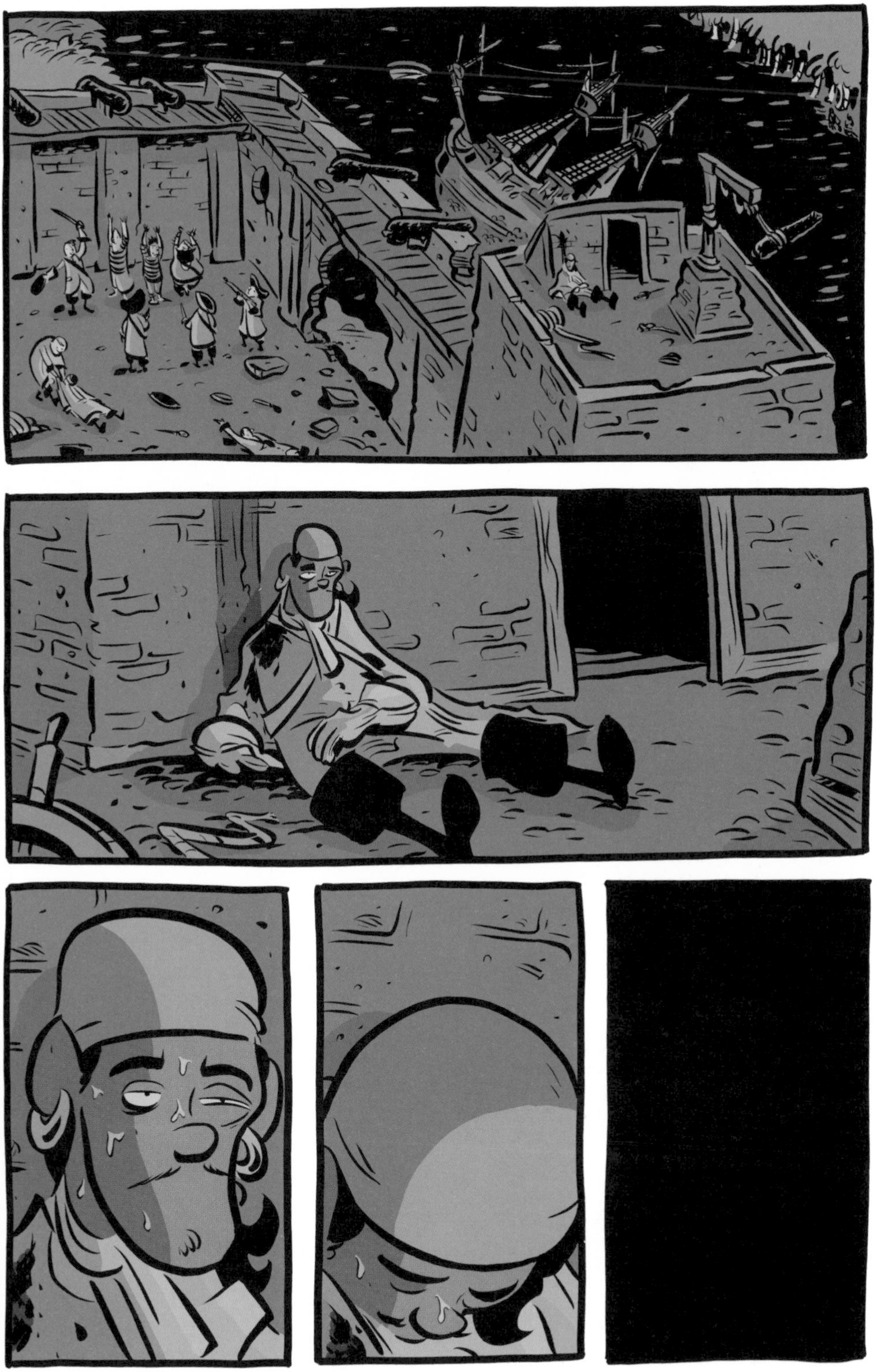

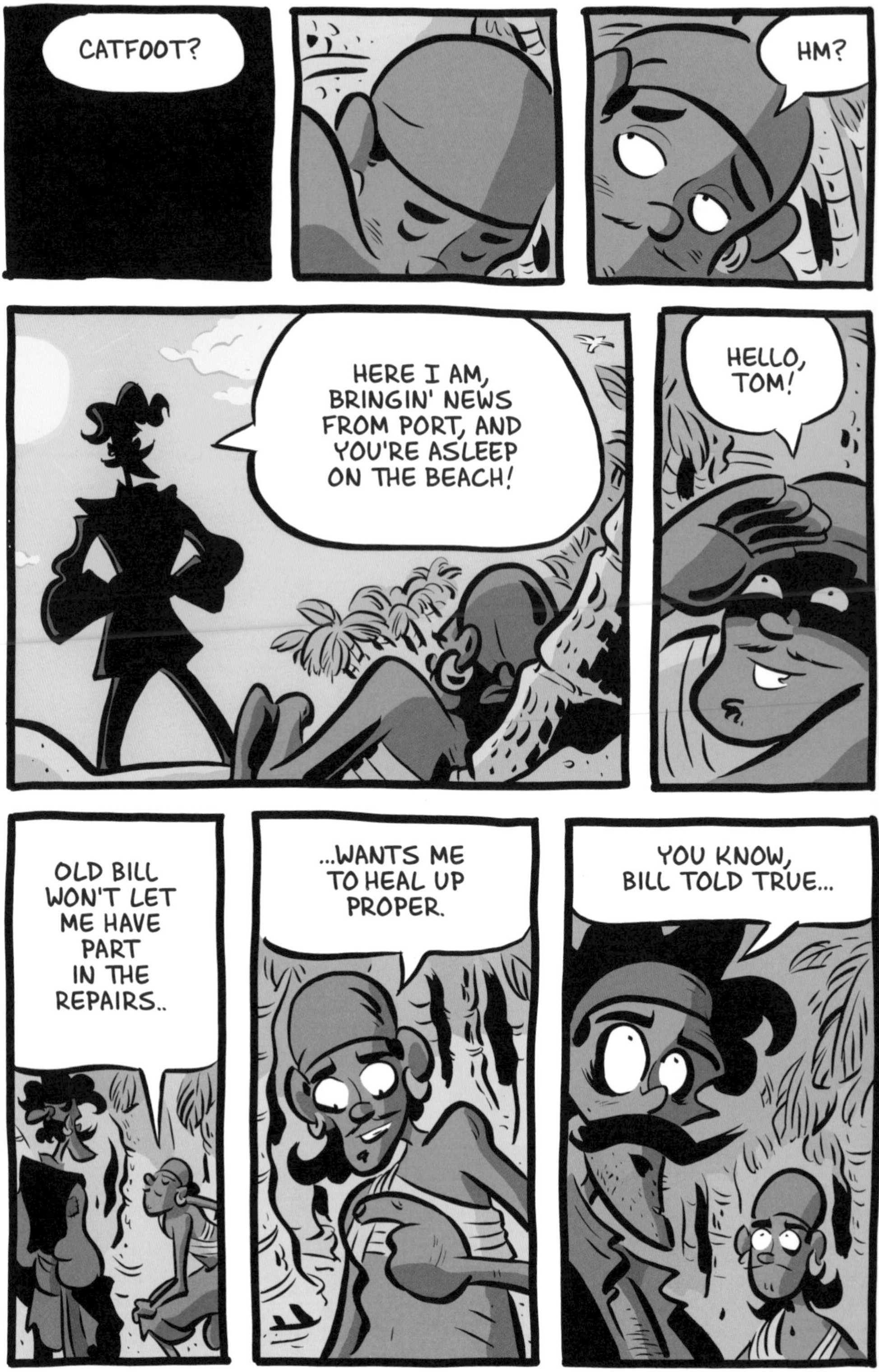
CATFOOT?
HM?
HERE I AM, BRINGIN' NEWS FROM PORT, AND YOU'RE ASLEEP ON THE BEACH!
HELLO, TOM!
OLD BILL WON'T LET ME HAVE PART IN THE REPAIRS..
...WANTS ME TO HEAL UP PROPER.
YOU KNOW, BILL TOLD TRUE...

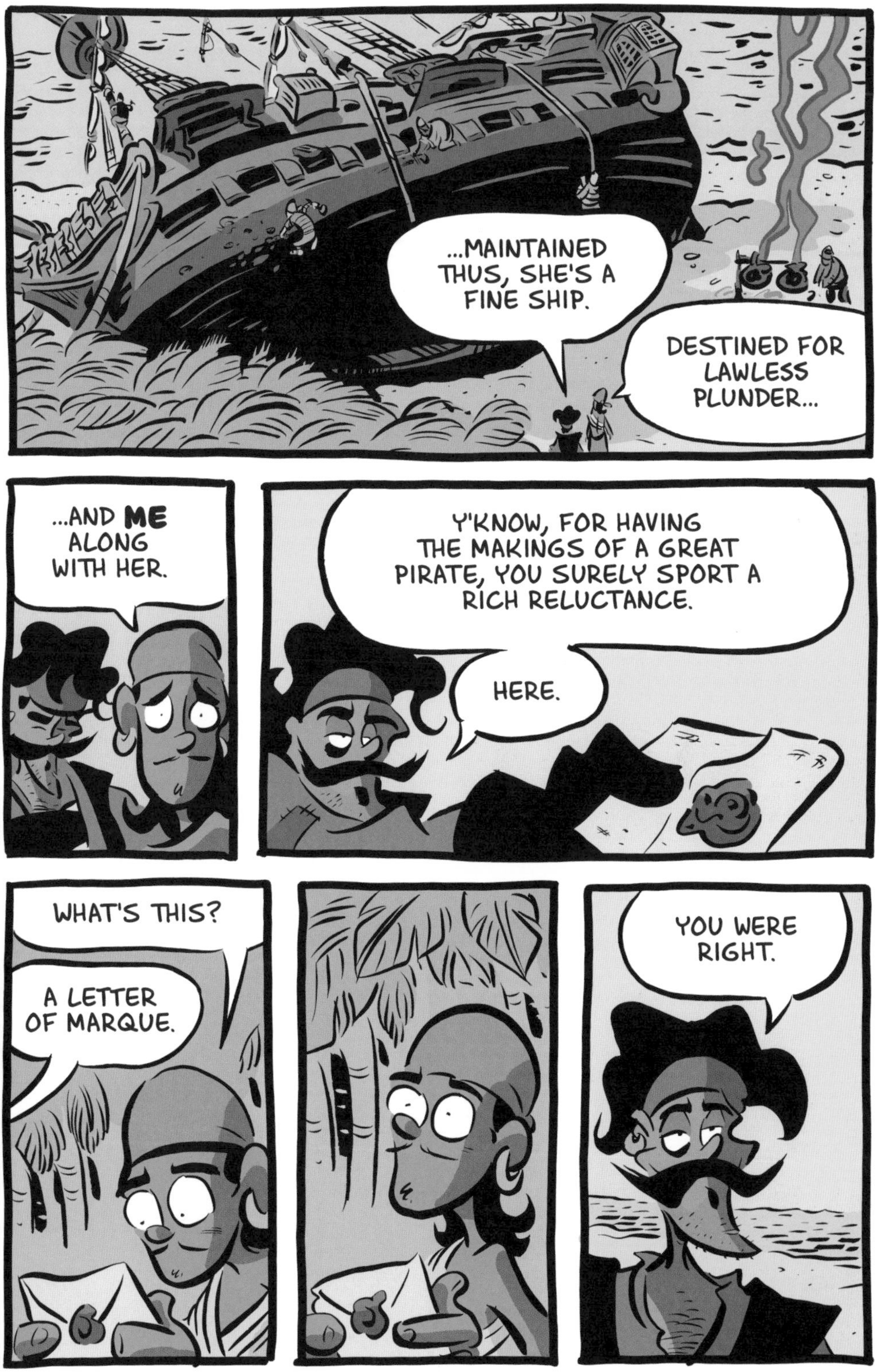
...MAINTAINED THUS, SHE'S A FINE SHIP.
DESTINED FOR LAWLESS PLUNDER...
...AND **ME** ALONG WITH HER.
Y'KNOW, FOR HAVING THE MAKINGS OF A GREAT PIRATE, YOU SURELY SPORT A RICH RELUCTANCE.
HERE.
WHAT'S THIS?
A LETTER OF MARQUE.
YOU WERE RIGHT.

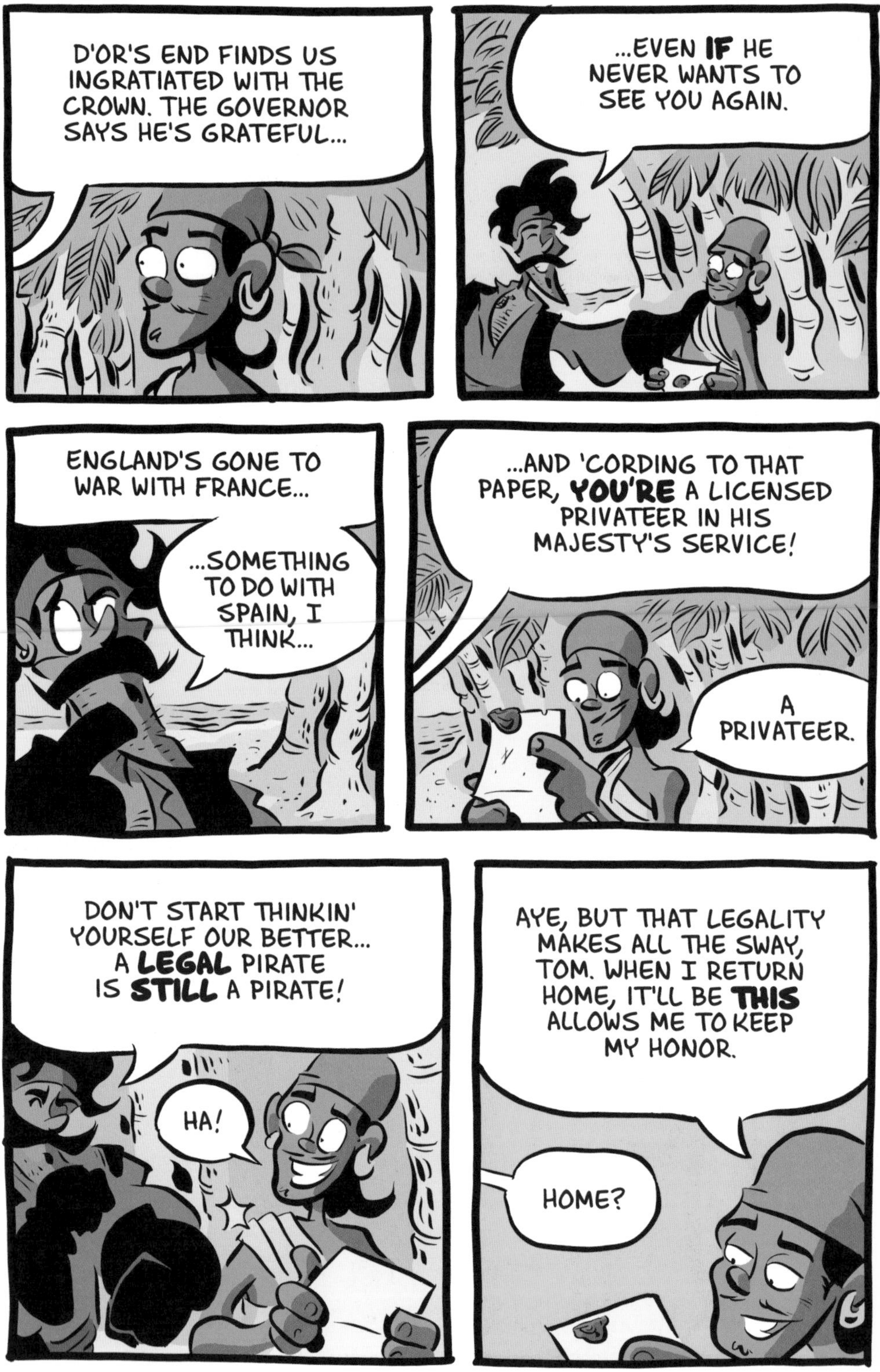
D'OR'S END FINDS US INGRATIATED WITH THE CROWN. THE GOVERNOR SAYS HE'S GRATEFUL...
...EVEN IF HE NEVER WANTS TO SEE YOU AGAIN.
ENGLAND'S GONE TO WAR WITH FRANCE...
...SOMETHING TO DO WITH SPAIN, I THINK...
...AND 'CORDING TO THAT PAPER, YOU'RE A LICENSED PRIVATEER IN HIS MAJESTY'S SERVICE!
A PRIVATEER.
DON'T START THINKIN' YOURSELF OUR BETTER... A LEGAL PIRATE IS STILL A PIRATE!
HA!
AYE, BUT THAT LEGALITY MAKES ALL THE SWAY, TOM. WHEN I RETURN HOME, IT'LL BE THIS ALLOWS ME TO KEEP MY HONOR.
HOME?

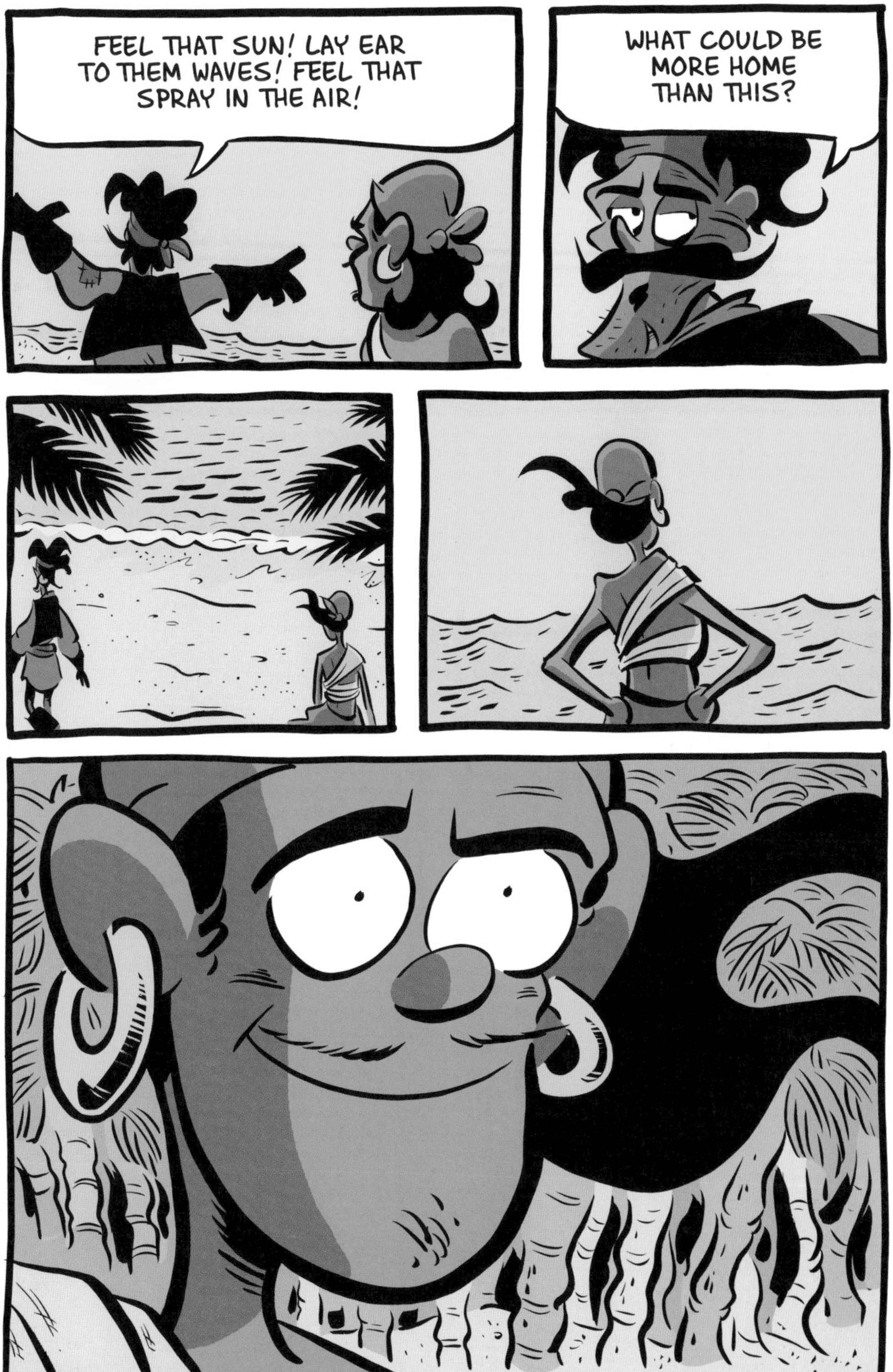
FEEL THAT SUN! LAY EAR TO THEM WAVES! FEEL THAT SPRAY IN THE AIR!
WHAT COULD BE MORE HOME THAN THIS?

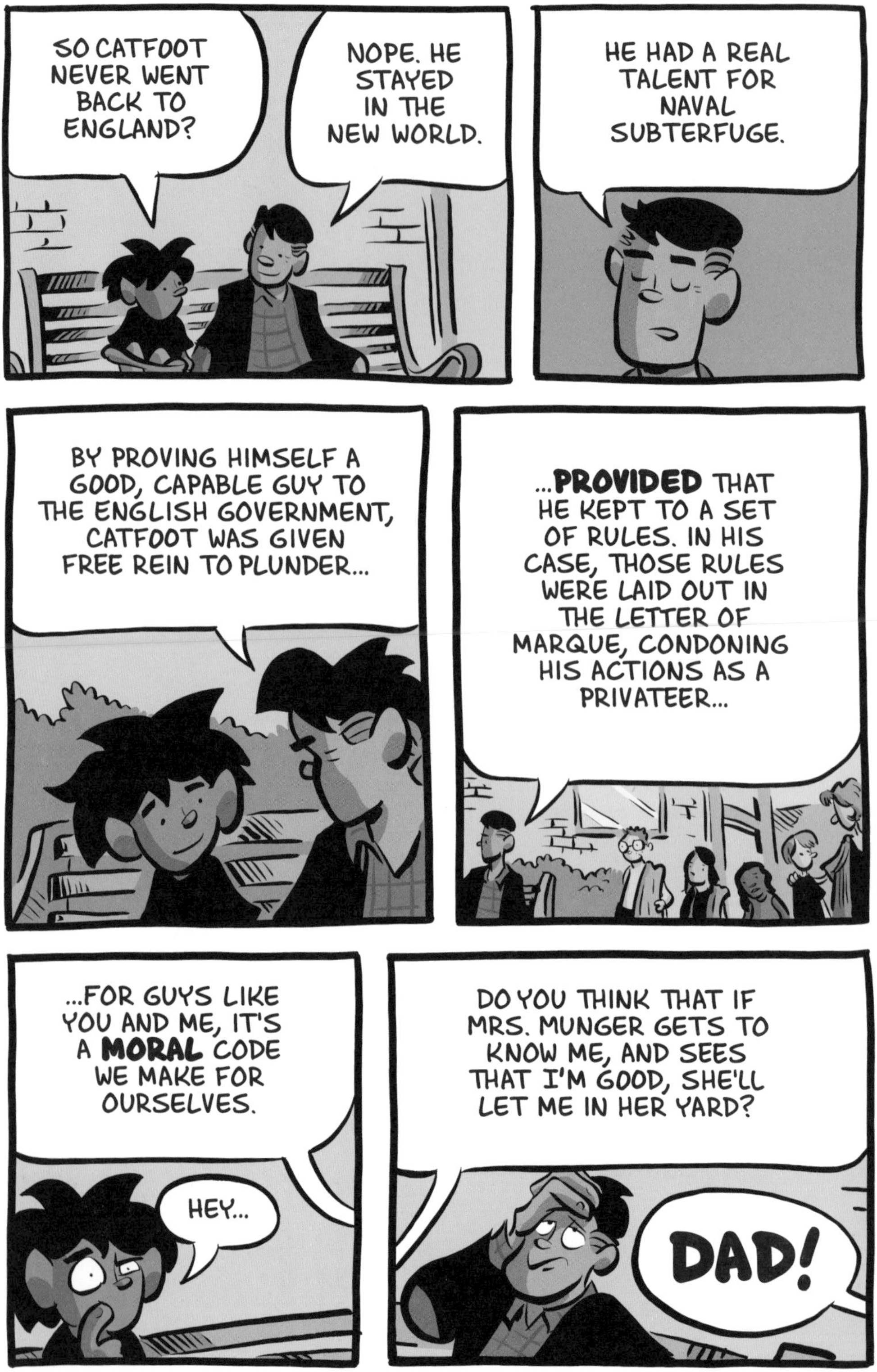
SO CATFOOT NEVER WENT BACK TO ENGLAND?
NOPE. HE STAYED IN THE NEW WORLD.
HE HAD A REAL TALENT FOR NAVAL SUBTERFUGE.
BY PROVING HIMSELF A GOOD, CAPABLE GUY TO THE ENGLISH GOVERNMENT, CATFOOT WAS GIVEN FREE REIN TO PLUNDER...
...**PROVIDED** THAT HE KEPT TO A SET OF RULES. IN HIS CASE, THOSE RULES WERE LAID OUT IN THE LETTER OF MARQUE, CONDONING HIS ACTIONS AS A PRIVATEER...
...FOR GUYS LIKE YOU AND ME, IT'S A **MORAL** CODE WE MAKE FOR OURSELVES.
HEY...
DO YOU THINK THAT IF MRS. MUNGER GETS TO KNOW ME, AND SEES THAT I'M GOOD, SHE'LL LET ME IN HER YARD?
DAD!

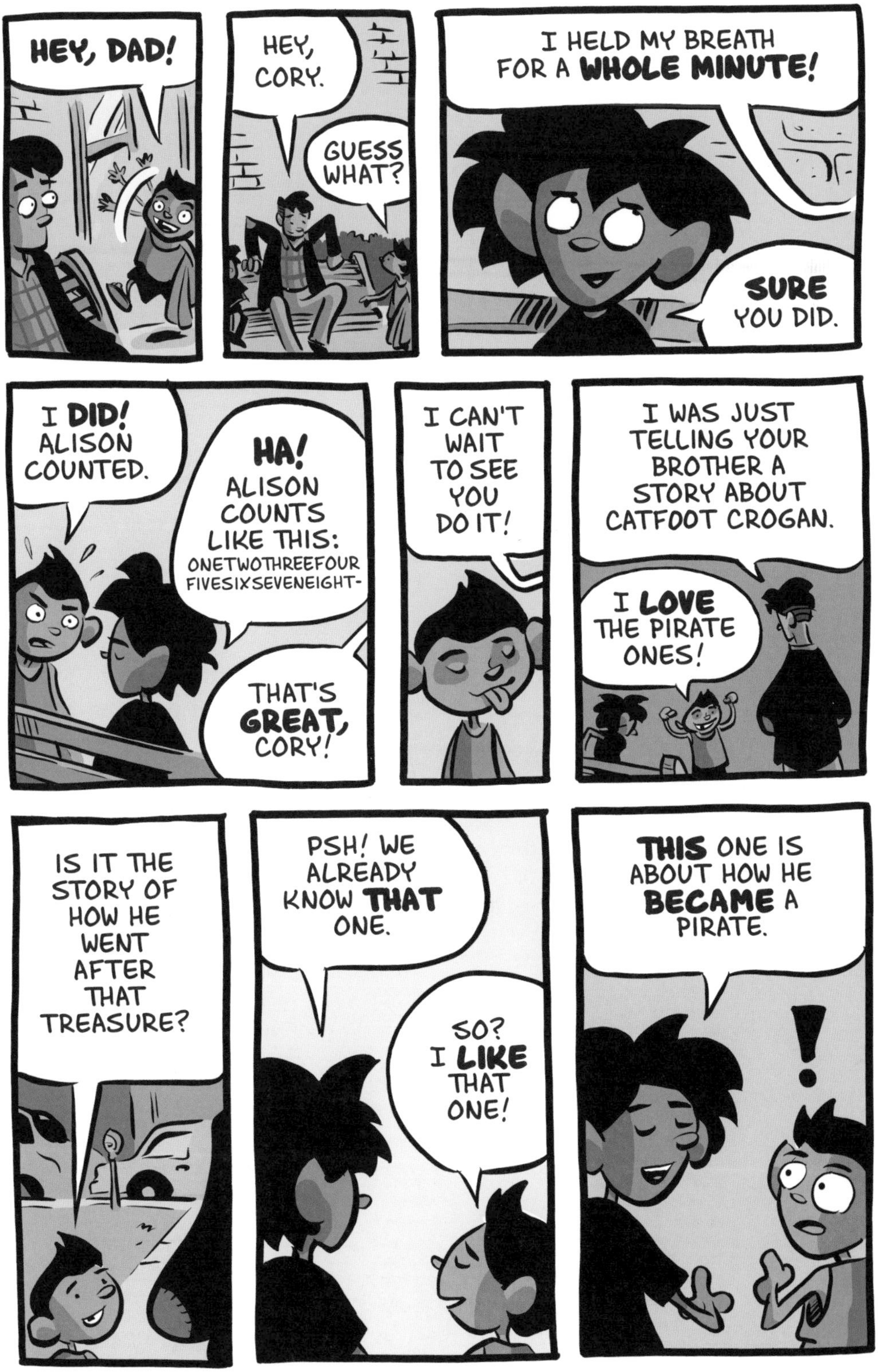
HEY, DAD!
HEY, CORY.
GUESS WHAT?
I HELD MY BREATH FOR A WHOLE MINUTE!
SURE YOU DID.
I DID! ALISON COUNTED.
HA! ALISON COUNTS LIKE THIS: ONETWOTHREEFOUR FIVESIXSEVENEIGHT-
THAT'S GREAT, CORY!
I CAN'T WAIT TO SEE YOU DO IT!
I WAS JUST TELLING YOUR BROTHER A STORY ABOUT CATFOOT CROGAN.
I LOVE THE PIRATE ONES!
IS IT THE STORY OF HOW HE WENT AFTER THAT TREASURE?
PSH! WE ALREADY KNOW THAT ONE.
SO? I LIKE THAT ONE!
THIS ONE IS ABOUT HOW HE BECAME A PIRATE.
!

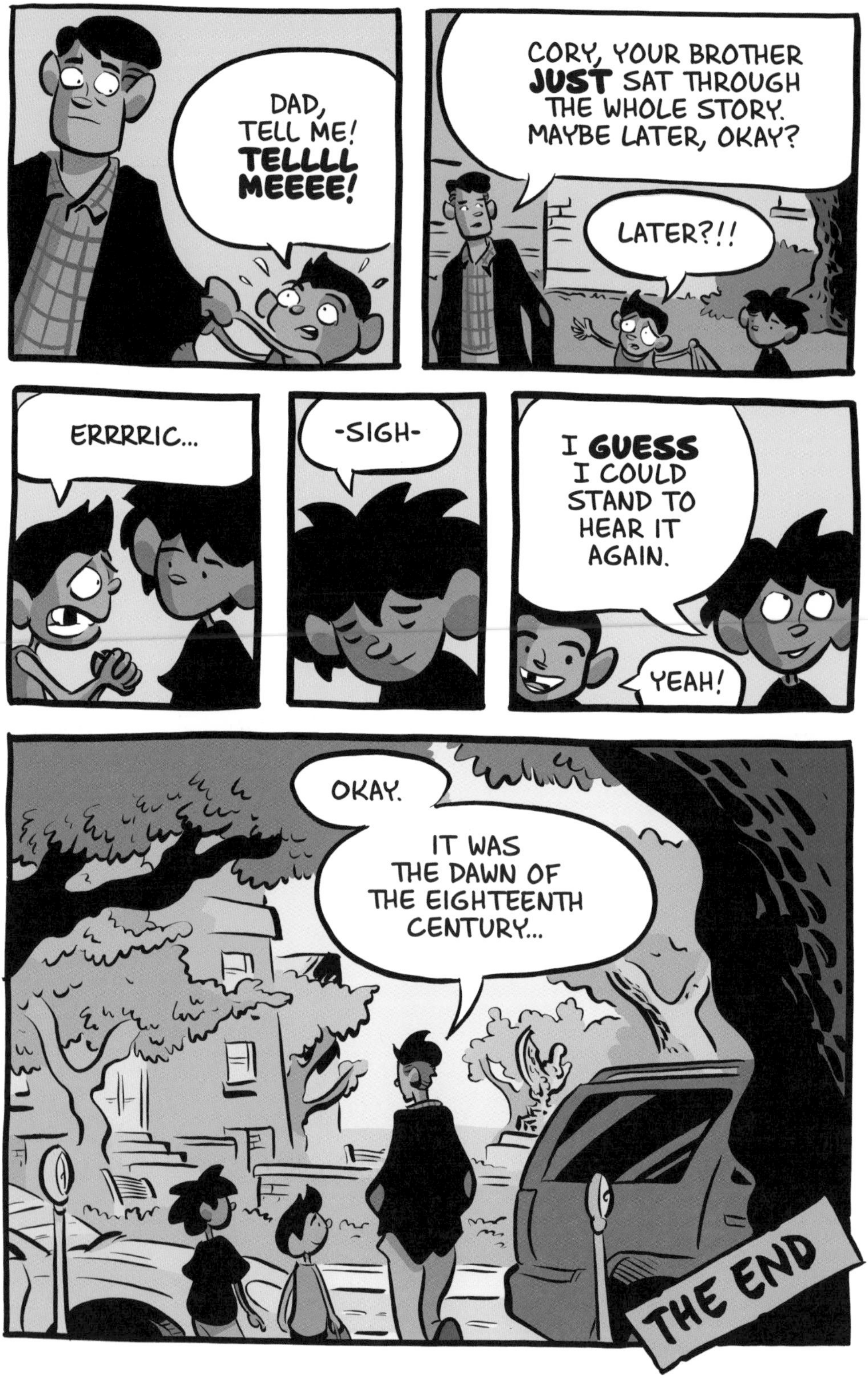
DAD, TELL ME! TELLLL MEEEE!
CORY, YOUR BROTHER JUST SAT THROUGH THE WHOLE STORY. MAYBE LATER, OKAY?
LATER?!!
ERRRRIC...
-SIGH-
I GUESS I COULD STAND TO HEAR IT AGAIN.
YEAH!
OKAY.
IT WAS THE DAWN OF THE EIGHTEENTH CENTURY...
THE END

THANKS TO:

My wife Liz, without whom this book would not exist. She has inspired me and supported me, emotionally and financially, throughout the course of its execution, and it is due to her unfailing patience, enthusiasm, and love that I am able to make comics.

Shawn Crystal, my mentor at SCAD-Atlanta, for serving as both my promoter to anyone who will listen and as a sounding board for many of the scenes depicted herein, as well as for teaching me a lot of invaluable lessons about making comics.

Everyone at Oni Press, especially James, for taking the chance on a huge project based on nothing more than a drawing of a family tree and my word that I could follow through, and Cory, who has tirelessly championed the book to everyone he comes in contact with.

My parents, for providing a household in which imagination was a key virtue, and for showing by example that one can follow their passions and make a life of it, provided that they're willing to work very hard. They have always supported me, and it is this support that gave me the confidence to pursue this field.

My grandfather, for instilling in my father a love and admiration of comic strips, a love and admiration which my father then passed down to me.

My friend Nick Croghan, an extremely talented artist with a timeless-sounding surname that he was kind enough to let me steal and misspell for this series.

Those teachers who, by virtue of their passion for teaching, instilled in me a love of reading, writing, and history; notably Kathy Munger, Louise Crane, Jane Connerly, Eileen White, Penny Blane, Robert Akers, Dr. Warren Edminster, Dr. James Galt-Brown, and Dr. Winfield Rose.

Dr. Richard Shephard and Scott Sontag, whose hospitality in the respective cities of York and Paris put me on my present track.

The students and faculty at SCAD-Atlanta for creating an environment in which everyone has a desire to better themselves and each other.

And I owe an inestimable debt of gratitude to those whose work has inspired and influenced mine; notably George MacDonald Fraser, Jeff Smith, Bill Watterson, Rafael Sabatini, Seth, Stan Sakai, Seth, Raina Telgemeier, and Larry Gonick.

Chris Schweizer
Atlanta, Georgia
July 2008

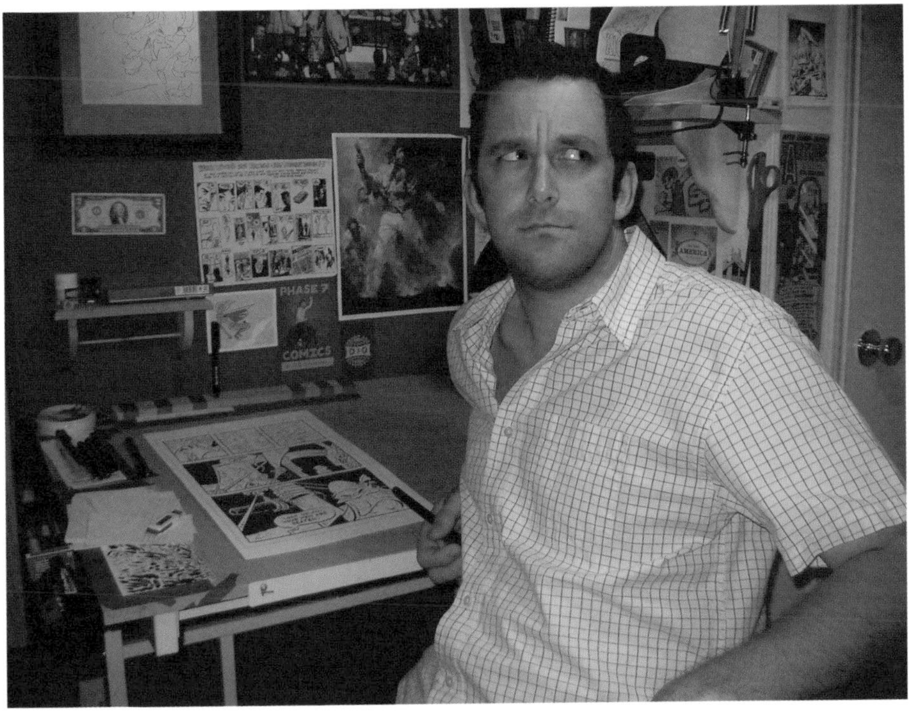

Photo by Liz Schweizer, circa this book's execution in 2008

CHRIS SCHWEIZER was born in Tucson, AZ at the tail end of 1980 to parents who are both classical musicians. He received his BFA in Graphic Design from Murray State University in 2004, and his MFA in Sequential Art from the Savannah College of Art and Design in Atlanta, where he went on to teach for five years. He now spends all of his time making comics, and lives in Kentucky with his wife Liz and daughter Penny.

Before becoming a cartoonist Chris was, at various times, a hotel manager, a movie theater projectionist, a guard at a mental institution, a martial arts instructor, a set builder, a church music leader, a process server, a life-drawing model, a bartender, a car wash attendant, a bagboy, a delivery boy, a choirboy, a lawn boy, a sixth-grade social studies teacher, a janitor, a speakeasy proprietor, a video store clerk, a puppeteer for a children's television show, a muralist, and a line worker at a pancake mix factory.

CASPAR CROGAN

ARQUEBUSIER, PORTUGESE EXPEDITIONARY FORCE, 1543

URSULA BERMUDES

BODYGUARD TO THE QUEEN OF ETHIOPIA, 1543

KUROGHAN JUNICHI

NINJA, 1768

CHARLES CROGAN

LOYALIST RANGER, 1778

MARTIN CROGAN

RAMONA DIAZ

MERCENARY, 1560   GUNSMITH, 1560

TAKAHARA YUKO

DAVID CROGAN

NINJA, 1750   SMUGGLER, 1745

JONATHAN CRO

TRAILBLAZER ARMY SCOUT,

TOM CROGAN

JOAN CLARK

SEA RAIDER, 1593   CARTOGRAPHER, 1593

CATFOOT CROGAN

BIG MARY DANDER

PIRATE, 1701   INNKEEPER, 1704

SUZANNE LAFLECHE

SAM CROGAN

MOONRAKER AND CONTRABANDIST, 1628

TAVERNIST AND FORMER MUSKETEER, 1628

GEORGE CROGAN

EMILY COBB

LAWYER, 1685   GUNNER, 1685

JWALA YATRI

BOOTLEGGER, 19

HENRY CROGAN

CHARLOTTE DUNWELL

IRONSIDE CAVALRY, 1650   NATURAL PHILOSOPHER, 1650

OTHER BOOKS BY CHRIS SCHWEIZER AND ONI PRESS

"THE ARTWORK IS EXCITING AND THE PACE NEVER LETS UP. CROGAN AND HIS FRENCH LEGIONNAIRES BRING HISTORY ALIVE!"
-JEFF SMITH, BONE
FRENCH NORTH AFRICA, 1912
THE CROGAN ADVENTURES
"FIVE YEARS' SERVICE"
BY CHRIS SCHWEIZER

"IT'S NO EASY FEAT TO COMBINE A HIGH-ENERGY HISTORICAL ADVENTURE WITH A SMART AND NUANCED LOOK AT THE MANY SHADES OF GREY THAT TINT NOTIONS OF PATRIOTISM, LOYALTY, AND FAMILY TIES, BUT SCHWEIZER DOES JUST THAT."
-BOOKLIST, STARRED REVIEW
THE AMERICAN FRONTIER, 1778
THE CROGAN ADVENTURES
"LOYALTY"
BY CHRIS SCHWEIZER

FIVE YEARS' SERVICE

Nearing the end of his five years' service with the French Foreign Legion, Peter Crogan finds himself on the front lines in a series of battles between a dashing French officer and a charismatic rebel leader.

Previously published as *Crogan's March*.

ercely
en up
When
, find
e the
must
their

For more information on these and other fine Oni Press comic books and graphic novels, visit our website at www.onipress.com.

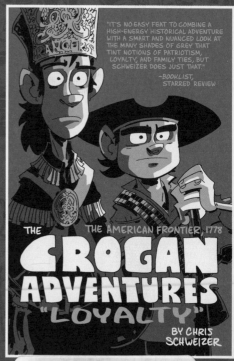

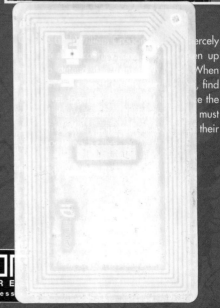